PRAISE FOR ALYSSA RICHARDS

THE HAUNTING OF ALCOTT MANOR is a fascinating tale of tragedy, ghosts, and soulmates. Mystery fans will enjoy this heroine's efforts to track down clues — both tangible and ghostly — while trying to find the truth about a woman's death. Romance fans will adore this match-up of a strong heroine and an enigmatic yet endearingly charming and earnest hero. I look forward to reading the next book in this tantalizing ALCOTT MANOR series." Fresh Fiction Review, THE HAUNTING OF ALCOTT MANOR

"Having read Alyssa Richards other books, I knew I was in for a treat, even though this was a slightly different genre. And gothic suspense being one of my absolute favorites, I was extremely psyched to read this book. Fortunately, everything that I anticipated about how good this book would be, and how much I would enjoy it, came true.

At first glance, this might appear to be your average haunted house story. But in the hands of this very capable, and highly readable author, it becomes so much more. The haunting was unique and the story revolving around the haunting was very intriguing. I totally did not anticipate the way the story was going or how it was going to end up. This was a great first entry in a new genre that I hope the author will continue. This book, as well as everything else this author has written, comes highly recommended." — DT

Chantel, book reviewer, THE HAUNTING OF ALCOTT MANOR

"Man oh man! Alyssa Richards has seriously outdone herself with this trilogy. It encompasses love, passion, deception, heartache, reality and alternate reality. Just stunning from start to finish. This trilogy is awesome. If you're looking for a paranormal romance that's focused around psychics and time travel, definitely grab this trilogy. It's simply amazing!" —*Nay's Pink Bookshelf, THE FINE ART OF DECEPTION SERIES*

5.0 out of 5 stars "Now this is what I'm talking about...absofreakingamazing!
"It's authors like Ms. Richards that really opened up the portals to my world, and instilled/nurtured within me a love for reading. Hook, line and sinker you are pulled fast and hard into her storylines and are wrecked when you've reached the end...you just don't want it to be over. The Haunting of Alcott Manor is no different and has a wonderful mix of gothic suspense/mystery with a titter of romance that will captivate you..and the end...omg I so didn't see that coming. What a stunning conclusion!"
—*Amazon Reviewer, THE HAUNTING OF ALCOTT MANOR*

5.0 out of 5 stars That ending...!? Are you kidding me?!
"Like others, I'm sure, I've read hundred(s) of these types of books. This was a great read, great twists and turns. ...and the end...? WOW! What's really getting me right now though? Henry and Gemma at still with me....days after I've finished the book! I cried with them, I loved with them, and they touched me deeply! Great job! (This is the first time I

have been inspired enough to write a review, too!)" *Amazon Book Reviewer, THE HAUNTING OF ALCOTT MANOR*

"A MURDER AT ALCOTT MANOR is very definitely a thrill-a-minute tale of evil trying to keep a stranglehold on the living. This is a perfect book for readers who enjoy non-stop action and suspense with a dash of sexy. ...This story will appeal to readers who love suspense, the paranormal, and everyday people who become unexpected heroes. Hope to read more gothic tales of love and paranormal peril by Alyssa Richards in the future." Fresh Fiction Review, A MURDER AT ALCOTT MANOR

Be the first to know about Alyssa Richards' next novel, sign up here: www.AlyssaRichards.com.

FORCED PERSPECTIVE

ALYSSA RICHARDS

Cover design by Shasti O'Leary Soudant
Editing by Peter Senftleben
Proofread by Charity Chimni
Contact Alyssa at:
authoralyssarichards@protonmail.com

PROLOGUE

osquitoes buzzed close to our ears, fed on our thin arms and legs. The wide duct tape around our wrists prevented us from slapping the bugs. We still wore the same pajama shorts and tanks that we put on six nights ago. The horrible man with the black front tooth stared at us, the one who took us from our bunk beds in the middle of the night, the one who stank like rotting meat.

I knew there was something wrong with him from the first time I saw him at the house. I spoke up about it, several times. But Dad said I was jumping to conclusions again, being overreactive, being judgmental. He said the man was harmless, that he needed some work to get back on his feet, that we should help.

But the way he looked at Catherine and me when no one was around, like we were thickly-iced cupcakes prepared just for him, made us think differently. That's the way it was with us. We were connected. Not all twins were that way, but I felt what she felt and vice versa. We were two sides of the same coin. Two versions of the same person. And we were afraid.

We'd spent the last few days in the basement of the big house, cameras mounted in the upper corners. Other girls came in, but when they left we never saw them again. When we left, three other girls remained. The space was divided by bars like a jail. Like cages. Each small cage had one dirty mattress on the floor and a metal bucket in the corner. No one heard our screams. Or if they did, they didn't care.

The man with the black tooth visited our cell twice a day. Each time he brought a small meal. Sometimes he emptied the buckets. Because of Catherine's and my food allergies we hadn't eaten much and we were weak.

He said the same thing each time we saw him, his words heavily flavored with his Spanish accent. "Your father pay ransom. You go home."

On this particular night they moved us to the outside patio area. Just us. The other girls were still down there. Trapped. I was not encouraged when they didn't replace our blindfolds. It was a bad sign.

The house was enormous, and busy. When they led us through the upstairs, we saw men chopping and weighing mounds of white powder and putting it into small plastic bags.

No one gave us more than a passing glance. Like it wasn't unusual to see two skinny, twelve-year-old girls in dirty paja-mas. Like kidnapping was part of the family business.

Maybe it was.

The black-toothed man tipped my chin, then looked at my sister, my identical twin. "Harper?" he asked, not sure who was who. No one from their family got our names right, and the only name they seemed to remember was mine. We never corrected them. He called Catherine his "special treat" and he rubbed her arm. He didn't think we understood him because he spoke in Spanish. He didn't know that our school taught Spanish to every student, beginning in kindergarten. Six years of studying one language went a long way.

He dragged his finger down Catherine's neck and along her collar bone, then he unbuckled his belt with his other hand, almost unconsciously. His smile was greasy and hungry and we knew he wanted to do something awful.

In broken English he said the ransom had been paid and that we were going home as soon as the boat came back. But neither Catherine nor I believed him because we'd seen it all—the drugs, their faces. We could see the distant city lights of Miami so we could reasonably figure out where on the coast this compound was located. Why would they let us leave now?

Several women, wives and mothers we guessed, stood nearby, watching children play on the dock and in the nearby yard. Boys and girls laughed and jumped and ran around in the grass, catching fireflies in mason jars, playing tag. Like we weren't even there. Like it was just another summer night. Like two young girls tied up wasn't uncommon at their house.

Maybe it wasn't.

A white boat pulled up to the dock, and the driver cut the motor.

The man with the black tooth watched while the driver lassoed the rope around a wooden post. Then he walked toward the edge of the marsh, fiddled with his trousers like he was unbuttoning and unzipping.

The driver of the white boat walked toward us carrying three blue duffel bags that were stuffed full. We assumed they were full of cash. The driver was short, round, and wore a black button-down shirt. His black jeans were so tight he nearly waddled. In Spanish he yelled to the black-toothed man that the alligators would take revenge on him for peeing in their water. Then he held up the duffels and said, still in Spanish, to wait until it was completely dark, then put us in the boat and drive to a nearby mangrove swamp—where the alligators would devour our bodies.

The black-toothed man responded that he would. Right after he got his fair share.

"Do it on the boat!" the man with the duffels barked and went inside the house. He didn't look at us when he passed by. He didn't think we understood what he said.

The solemn expression that fell over Catherine's face told me she knew what I was thinking. Twins just knew.

"Boat," I whispered. "As fast as you can. Take care of the rope and start the engine. I'll be right there." I was the impulsive one, the one who leaped first and asked questions later. I'd always thought it was a sign of bravery.

"What about a key?" Catherine was the one who thought everything through ahead of time. I'd always thought she played it too safe.

"He wasn't carrying one. It's probably still in the ignition." This was only a guess. But our parents owned a boat, and the only time they could find the key was when they left it in the ignition. So they usually did.

"What if they catch us?" Catherine's eyes filled with tears, her bottom lip quivered. Normally I deferred to her because my act-first-think-later approach often landed me in trouble. And she was the oldest. Only by three minutes, but she was accustomed to leading the way, being in charge, having the final say.

The joke in our family was that I resented being second. That I was always coming up from behind, fighting my way forward like a half-crazed bull. Too feisty for my own good. But tonight we had to do things my way, because there was no time to sit around and weigh rational options.

"Then we'll go down fighting. This is our only chance," I whispered.

Her worry lines told me she had lots of unanswered questions. Finally she nodded, once and quick. She ran to the empty boat, wrists still bound together in front of her. At the last second the little boys playing on the dock heard her footsteps and they moved out of the way.

The fast, spinning sensation in my chest, the feeling I always had before I sprang into action, told me it was now or never. I ran across the grass, toward the black-toothed man with my taped wrists and arms stretched in front. I shoved him hard from behind and he fell face-first into the salt-water marsh. I didn't wait to see what happened next, but the violent splashing told me that the alligators didn't give him time enough to scream.

When I reached the dock there was a boy running toward the boat, ahead of me and behind Catherine. He was tall, probably the same age as us. Maybe older. I couldn't let him get to her. I couldn't let him stop us.

She started the engine and I picked up speed.

The tall boy waved his arms, yelled for her to stop. I heard the women screaming behind me. "Matthew!"

I caught up to him, kicked one of his feet behind the other and he fell onto the dock with a thud. I leaped over him, took two steps and sprang toward the untethered and drifting boat, screaming when I was mid-air.

I slammed into the side of the boat and clung tight. "Go!"

Several children gathered on the deck, screaming, pointing, waving.

I threw one leg over the side and scrambled into the boat.

"Matthew!" I heard a woman scream, louder this time.

I stood, unsteady, and watched the tall boy stand upright. He ran to the end of the dock. Blood poured from his nose and mouth and he screamed, "Stop!"

Several men ran out of the house, waving guns.

I grabbed the wheel and the silver handle, opened the throttle. The boat engine roared, the front end tipped up. We held on and crouched low while I made a U-turn and steered the boat toward the distant glow of Miami's city lights.

Gunshots fired and we ducked.

Most of the men ran around to the other side of the house and I knew they were coming after us.

More gunshots fired.

"Did they get you?" I yelled over the noise of the engine.

"I'm okay," Catherine said weakly.

I kept my hands tight on the silver wheel, my wrists still taped together. We bounced over the waves and the door to the cabin swung open and shut again.

I silently thanked my father for all the times he let us drive his boat. We'd never driven at high speed before, but we both knew the basics.

"Can you find some scissors?" I nodded to the compartments below the steering wheel. "Something to cut the tape?"

"Yeah." Her voice was thin. It took her a minute to move.

I was scared to take my eyes off of the water ahead of us. I needed to get us all the way into the city where there were onlookers, witnesses, anyone who could help.

I turned for a quick glance behind us, and I couldn't see the compound. But I did see one round light on the water. A boat light. I knew it was them; I knew they were following us.

I also knew that at the edge of the city there were restaurants with docks over the water. Neither of us had ever parked a boat before. But I thought if I could get us close, and if we made a commotion, someone would see us. Someone would help.

The last of the sun's light faded, and speeding through the dark kept my heart in my throat. But the idea of being caught and fed to alligators kept me driving fast.

"Do you see a radio anywhere?" I asked and did a quick search around me. The boat tipped and slammed over waves and we fought hard to keep our balance. The cabin door opened with the boat's motion.

"There's a boy!" she said.

"A what?"

"There's a boy in the cabin! He's like, five or something!"

She took the wheel and slowed the speed.

"Not so slow!" I yelled and pointed to the light behind us that looked like an oncoming train.

I ducked my head inside the cabin and saw a small boy sitting on a narrow striped couch attached to the wall. He had dark hair, brown skin and eyes, and he looked like a miniature version of nearly every man we'd seen on the compound. He wore a red T-shirt, blue shorts and a frightened expression.

I returned to the wheel, shutting the cabin door behind me. My gut tightened, like a bucket of ice hit my insides. I pushed the silver handle forward.

"It's too fast!" she yelled over the noise of the engine and the wind.

"They're coming after *him*!" I increased the speed again and we fell to the floor of the boat.

She stood and screamed, "Slow down!"

Adrenaline sped through my veins, my heart slammed against my ribs. I grabbed the wheel again. My feet left the boat floor each time we hit the top of a wave. A violent jolt nearly pitched us into the ocean.

Suddenly I realized all the things I didn't know about driving a boat.

Catherine shoved me out of the way and slowed the speed. She didn't say anything but she pointed a finger close to my face, telling me not to cross her.

After a moment the light that was following us got so close I could make out the boat. It was white with no roof or shade and there were several men pointing in our direction. The Miami city lights were also bigger, closer and brighter, and I was looking for something familiar. Some place to pull over.

Our Dad loved taking us out on his boat for evening rides, then docking at a seaside restaurant for dinner. Surely one of those restaurants was coming up soon.

If it were daytime, if the sun were high in the sky, the ocean would be flooded with sailboats, yachts, motorboats of all kinds. But at night there were none.

I looked at the closed cabin door and my mind galloped like a wild horse. I thought about how frightened that poor boy must be. Certainly every bit as frightened as we were when we were taken.

"We're going to make it!" Catherine gripped my arm, pointed straight ahead. A neon blue pelican came into view like a beacon. "It's Rusty! Rusty the pelican! Go left! Go left!"

The giant bird was a sign that sat on top of Rusty's Oceanfront Restaurant. We'd docked and eaten there at least twenty times with our parents. She jumped up and down in tiny hops. I wanted to be just as happy but something bothered me. Something I couldn't quite figure out.

I looked behind us. The singular light was so close I recognized the four men in the boat. They veered to the left. It looked like they were trying to pull alongside us.

Gunfire popped like loud fireworks and we ducked. I steered to the right, away from the restaurant.

Catherine grabbed my arm, tugging it away from the wheel. "What are you doing?! Go that way!"

I shoved her away, pointing to the boat that followed us. "Too close!"

She turned the wheel toward the neon bird. Toward the floodlights outside the restaurant that shone on the dark water.

"Just get close! I'll blow the horn, scream and wave! Someone will see us! Someone will send help!" Catherine yelled over the engine.

With everything about to work for us I couldn't figure why something awful still nagged at me.

I glanced at the cabin door that was shut, and realized that even after we'd reached safety, those men would continue to come for us. They would want to punish us for taking this boy. This would never be over. I elbowed her out of the way, grabbed the wheel and accelerated.

She stumbled back and fell to the floor. After a moment Catherine rushed toward me, then she wrestled my hands off the wheel. She was a force when she wanted to be, overtaking me and anyone else on a whim. "Slow down!"

For the first time in our shared existence I fought her with all I had and we wrestled for control.

The impact was abrupt, jarring and loud. There was no holding on and we flew through the air. My screams mixed with hers and it was in that split second, a moment that stretched and slowed to minutes, that it came back to me. That nagging thing I couldn't place sooner.

We were in our father's boat, pulling up to the restaurant with the neon pelican. I stared at the dark blue water in the distance while our father eased the boat into the slip.

"What's that?" I asked, pointing to a long line of huge black rocks and concrete jutting far into the water.

"A jetty," my father answered. "It protects the coastline."

I landed on what felt like cement, and it was only when I inhaled salty water into my lungs that I realized I was in the ocean. Searing pain shot through every inch of my body. I swam as hard as I could with my wrists still taped together, fighting for air. I finally got above water and there was an explosion. Intense heat and pain slashed my body.

Flames raged and grabbed at me and all I could do was scream, "Catherine!"

1

———

TWENTY YEARS LATER

The shape of a man glided across the security monitor, his shadowy form dark and shifting. I threw my book aside and quickly turned off the light on the bedside table.

2:53 a.m.

No one should have been outside my house at this hour.

That camera view was from the upper left-hand corner of my small front porch. I watched him pull and push the handle of the locked front door.

I scrambled from the cool comfort of my bed and grabbed the air pistol from the top of the white fireplace mantel. I felt my way along the walls of the dark hallway. The renovation was ongoing and sconces hadn't yet been hung. The painting cloths were soft beneath my bare feet and I did a careful climb along the narrow half-spiral staircase to the top level. I pressed myself against the wall since the workers hadn't installed the railing.

Quietly, I opened the door to the rooftop, stepped quickly to the south side, and peered over the edge that faced East York Street.

He blended into the night with his dark pants, dark T-shirt, and dark shoes. Straight dark hair poked out from beyond his black baseball cap.

It had been twenty years since the Muñoz crime family kidnapped us, since they kept us in cages, since they tried to kill us. So what I should have seen in this wannabe intruder was a local criminal. Someone who wanted something for nothing. But what I saw was someone from the Muñoz family, someone who would never forget what I'd done.

He pulled hard on each set of bars that covered my first-floor windows.

I silently thanked God that I'd finally finished that install two days ago. A lawyer from the firm next door tried to dissuade me from putting them in, said the bars detracted from the original beauty of the house. While I was a fan of form over function—any historical preservation project made you that way—I was a bigger fan of being safe.

The guy stood back, stared at my house, like there must've been a way for him to get inside. He crept around the side, his movements sleek and catlike.

I followed him until I stood at the very far corner of my roof and aimed the air pistol at him, but my angle didn't give me a good shot. So I waited. Followed him with my gun while he worked his way around to every first-floor window of my four-story home.

I'd been shooting at targets since I was thirteen. The owner of the first range I visited said he preferred their customers to be at least fourteen. But they made an exception for me because they knew what I'd been through.

The man who searched for easy access into my house had a half-inch waistband of white underwear sticking out at the back of his dark pants. That's where I aimed. I waited for him to make a move.

The all-too-familiar pressure built in my chest. Panic tightened every muscle, convincing me to act first, think later. Memories flashed like disco lights: the man who told Diego, the black-toothed man, to kill Catherine and me. The boat crash, the death threats and the attempts on my life that followed the trial.

I tried to blink the memories away. But twenty years after the kidnapping, my every reaction to a new threat was still a raw and primal fear that the Muñoz family had found me. I tightened my grip on the trigger.

The therapists had said to simply let the memories flow, not to fight them. That one day they would run their course, that time would tame them. That was easier said than done. Because the emotion in those memories ran strong enough to drown me. No amount of tears, no amount of feeling could alleviate the pain or the anger over what I'd lost.

I rubbed my eyes, squinted, flexed my hand several times.

The man checked under flower pots, ran his hand above the shutters and window frames like he searched for a hidden key.

"Come on in." I adjusted my bead on him. "Please."

As if he heard me, he pulled a short metal bar from under his pant leg, smashed the window glass through the bars. My house alarm blared, but he didn't move. The noise didn't even startle him. Like he expected it. He stepped close to the broken window, looked inside, then backed away.

I raised my head from my pistol aim and watched him.

He turned. Slowly, like he moved through deep water. Until he faced me. Like he knew where I was, like he knew I was watching.

Icy dread hit my chest.

Then I saw it, the faint glimmer of white teeth. A smile.

We each stood there, facing one another.

His knowing smile taunting me.

Sudden fury burned away the icy dread and I aimed for center mass.

Without a flinch in his greedy smile, he spun around and ran toward Columbia Square. Fast from the start.

I pulled the trigger.

He dodged to the right and the pellets hit the street sign with a loud metallic ding. He turned the corner. I dashed to the other side of the roof and looked over the side.

He wasn't down below.

He must have cut down E. President Street, half a block over.

My cell phone buzzed. It was the alarm company. I told them I was fine, that it looked like someone broke one of my windows. I reminded them I had bars on all my first-floor windows, I told them I didn't need any assistance.

I sat down, leaned against the half wall that surrounded the rooftop and tried to catch my breath. Adrenaline surged and prickled my skin like I'd swallowed a beehive.

I turned off the alarm from my phone, my hands shaking. The desire to run, pack everything and leave was overwhelming, stronger than a bad drug.

As an adult, I'd never lived in one place for more than a few months. I'd only worked consulting jobs that required lots of travel. I'd never owned a permanent residence.

Until now.

I pressed my palms against my eyes, and I saw the man's smile broaden in my mind.

He'd looked right at me. Knew where I was, knew where I'd be.

I looked up at the stars, drew in a deep inhale.

I should have shot him.

I put the gun next to me. Exhaled short and quick. It was impossible that they could have found me. I'd been too good, too careful. I'd changed my name, my hair and my eye color. I'd moved too many times to count.

I made a plan to review the security camera feed, to see if there were any clear shots of his face. If there were, I would study them, memorize his features. I would send the photo to Agent Hernandez, who could determine if the image matched anyone in his files.

I raised up to a half crouch and searched for signs of movement. Somewhere out there were the men who still wanted me dead.

I examined the softly moving shadows and wondered if anyone could see me.

With my vision at 20/15, I saw all things more clearly than most. As an antique jewelry restorer and authenticator, my eyes were trained to notice tiny details that others missed. What was subtle or invisible to someone else was glaring and obvious to me.

I remained still, only my eyes shifting, combing the area. On the west side of the house, gas lamps flickered, casting a weak yellow glow into the green space of Columbia Square. Every house on the square was dark, except Bunny's, my neighbor across the green.

She paced in her lamplit front room, wearing a long, white nightgown. Her gray-blond hair that was normally tied up in a twist was loose and long and almost reached her waist.

The bells of St. John the Baptist Cathedral struck three, their full, rich tones lingering in the night air. 3 a.m. was the cusp of the Witching Hour. "That hour between 3 and 4 a.m. is when the veil between the living and dead is at its weakest," Bunny had told me once.

I wasn't surprised to see her awake at this hour. Bunny was a wealthy widow whose husband's absence surrounded her like a black shawl, like a cloud, like the invisible man who never left her side. She'd been to many a seance at 3 a.m. trying to contact her dead husband. Once I went with her. But all I saw was a fair amount of money given in exchange for an infusion of hope porn.

The past was dead.

So was her husband.

At the sound of the bells she stopped pacing, went to the bay window, looked out into the night. She took her dead husband's gold wedding band that she kept on a chain around her neck, held it to her mouth and kissed it. She struck a long match and lit ten ivory-colored candles, five to her left, five to her right. Then turned out the singular lamp. She faced her front windows and kneeled and pressed her husband's ring between her palms. She rocked back and forth, her lips moving nonstop like she recited a chant.

I didn't think she would get what she was looking for.

I pushed away from the ledge.

With the wannabe intruder nowhere in sight, I decided to go downstairs and look at the security feed. I headed toward the door. A movement on the other side of the park caught my attention. I crouched again quickly, this time to all fours.

I crawled back to the short wall and stood halfway. I kept one hand tight on my pistol. If the intruder was back, I'd shoot him. I wouldn't hesitate.

But it wasn't him. I squinted. Chills scattered up my back and down my arms. Because the movement I'd seen wasn't a person. It wasn't an animal. But it looked alive. A low, rolling fog that crept and clawed its way between the Davenport and Kehoe houses.

Opaque and gray, it snaked onto the grassy park, moving with darkness and purpose until it overtook all four corners of the square. A shiver built inside of me and I tightened every muscle to hold it down.

There was no breeze in the square, but a coolness brushed against my face. A young woman emerged from the fog.

A spirit.

A ghost.

She wore a red spaghetti strap dress that flared at the hem, giving the illusion that she wore a light crinoline. Halfway across the grass she stopped. She peered into the fountain like she saw her own reflection. Her light brown hair fell over her shoulders in loose ringlets. She stood upright, turned and looked directly at me.

I caught my breath. I leaned forward. I clutched the wide cement edge in front of me. My heart drummed and I heard pounding in my ears.

I was so taken by her beauty I couldn't take my eyes off of her. Even if I didn't have my scars she would still have been the prettier one. I'd always known that, but tonight I couldn't stop staring. It wasn't envy, not anymore, anyway. She was just stop-and-stare stunning.

As a child she had been incredibly beautiful. In public, when onlookers compared us, they had a hard time concealing their reaction. The differences were minor, but obvious. I was a slightly watered-down version of her startling good looks.

She was older now. As twins, of course, we were the same age when she died. Only twelve. Now, twenty years later, we were still the same age. Apparently you grew up in Heaven, too.

She was as tall as I was. If we stood next to one

another our heights could have been exact. Her hair was the same length as mine, probably also exact. We still looked remarkably alike. Except she didn't have my scars. And I'd darkened my hair considerably, while her hair remained its natural light brown. Her eyes were our God-given crystal blue mine were covered with dark brown contacts.

There was my life before the kidnapping. There was my life now. The only thing that connected the two were my conversations with Catherine. They were quiet, existed only in my mind, and they were continual. Because even after I'd killed her, I still needed to tell her everything.

"Is it really you?" I whispered.

Her eyes held my gaze for a long moment.

"Are you angry with me?" I was certain she would be, for taking her life.

She smiled, and I wondered if she understood.

Her hand swept low into the fog and brought up a dandelion. Grasping it tightly between both hands, she closed her eyes. Her lips flattened into a wince. Like she was poised to make a wish, and she needed it to come true more than she needed life.

She pursed her lips and blew the downy tufts into the air. When she opened her eyes again, she watched the seeds travel, then land.

"What did you wish for?" I asked, breathless from my out-of-control heart.

She stared at me but didn't give an answer. She just walked back to the fountain, like she couldn't say or that the answer was mine to discover.

I worried for her, as I had since the night she left my life. Was she safe, was she hurting, did she hate me for what I'd done?

You are still my best friend, my confidant, my twin. You have always been, and will forever be, a part of me.

She blew me a kiss.

Her love flooded my insides like warm sunshine, and that Wonder Woman kind of confidence I'd only ever felt with her filled me, strengthened me, made me invincible.

I've forgotten things about us since you died. But not our connection, not the completeness, not the way you made me feel. Never that. Maybe because we shared one womb. Maybe because we were together at the beginning of our time. Maybe because the mind, the body, and the soul can't forget that kind of deep connection.

Whatever the reason, even death didn't stop the sense of home and belonging we always had with one another.

She took two steps toward me and stopped.

Stared hard.

Last time I saw that intense concern on her face I was racing her toward certain death.

She was worried. Not at peace. A dull ache pulled at my heart.

Was she really here?

Savannah was a city that lent itself to afterlife magic. All the locals said the veil between this world and the next was thinner here than anywhere else. Not just during the Witching Hour, but always. Spirits came and went all the time here, perhaps for no particular reason other than they could.

That was possible. Even probable. But Catherine's presence felt intentional. Deliberate. Like there was a reason for her visit.

Wait.

Was this even real?

I looked across the green, where Bunny stood in the

front room of her antebellum home, seemingly in conversation with someone I couldn't see. I was tempted to think she was nuts.

But there stood Catherine, clear as day. I knew what it was like to love someone so deeply, so perfectly, so completely, that you couldn't let go. No matter what.

I reached for my sister. My knuckles ached, stiff from gripping the edge.

She turned away. The low fog rolled up slowly from the north end of the square and curled in her direction.

Old guilt, black and shifting, as poisonous as any water moccasin, slithered up from dark places within. It was born when I crashed the boat. Tonight it crept around my heart and squeezed, crushing with a strength I didn't like, and a strength I couldn't calm.

The fierce inner combat between the loss I carried in my heart—that insistent part of me that wanted to make everything right—and the other equally insistent side of me—the part that knew I could never make it right—brought angry tears to my eyes.

She returned her haunted gaze to me, pointed three times to a silver watch on her left wrist, like she was saying, "It's time."

"Time?" I asked. "What time? Time for what?"

The moving fog ushered her away and to the south, my left, and out of Columbia Square. It parted where she stepped, her bare feet pale in the muted light of the street-lamps. Her long brown hair trailed behind her in the gentle, imaginary breeze.

When she reached the end of the green, she stopped, turned toward me. She gave me a sad smile, a worried smile, a too-many-burdens-on-her-heart smile. The fog caught up to her and she disappeared into the fading mist.

Columbia Square was empty.

My heart ached in my sister's absence. The fierceness I'd been armed with earlier melted under the weight of my grief.

I fell to my knees and sobbed.

AFTER A LONG TIME I finally dragged myself from the roof. I went down to the main level and brewed a pot of coffee. Magnolia, the neighborhood cat who claimed me when I moved in, swished her fluffy-soft tail against my legs, looked up and meowed. I opened the glass jar of treats on the counter, took out two and put them on the floor for her.

I reached for a mug from the small cabinet, my hand paused at the multitude of prescription bottles. The nurse would come by in the morning to dole out a few of each: Anti-impulsivity meds, anti-anxiety meds, anti-depressants, anti-everything meds. My parents, mostly my father, had pushed these prescriptions on me since the accident.

I hadn't expected them. Although I took them. Because in the beginning, I hadn't had a choice. Also because they worked. They lifted the depression, lowered the anxiety, dulled the other pain my father had caused. Made it easier to cope. But over the years, I took them off and on. More off than on because I hated the way they numbed me out.

Taken as prescribed they did banish the past. And they quieted that paranoiac voice to a far back corner, the one that said the Muñoz family was still out to get me.

But they didn't rid it entirely. And in exchange for that partial relief, the meds took something sacred away from me —my ability to feel. Really feel.

With each pill, a thick, wool sweater covered my brain

and heart, muting my thoughts and melting my feelings into lukewarm nothingness. I could no longer feel the ups and downs of life. I became a mushy middle ground—neither here nor there. Certainly no longer angry. Which meant I was no longer a problem to my father.

I never knew just how much I needed to feel my way through life until I couldn't. Those silent nudges, those internal checks that helped me feel which choices would work and what ones wouldn't, who was on my side and who wasn't—I needed those feelings.

I told my father and the doctors that I didn't need the meds anymore. But they insisted that I continue to take them, arguing that my feelings couldn't be trusted, that they were faulty indicators. They said that if I was left unmed-icated, I was at risk of making bad decisions. Really bad decisions. They said my bad decisions could hurt someone.

What they didn't know was that they were wrong. Many of those meds I never needed. There were a few I benefitted from, and I took those. But I didn't need them anymore. I was better now.

I pulled my hand away from the bottles and doubled down on my recent decision not to take any of them anymore. When the nurse came in the morning I would do as I'd learned I could when I was much younger. I would pretend to take the pills so that she would give my father a good report. Then, after she left I would pull them from the back of my cheek and spit them down the drain.

I'd had my wisdom teeth taken out at thirteen, and that procedure left two gaps behind my upper molars. Those gaps in the back of my mouth came in handy for hiding tiny pills.

I grabbed my favorite mug, poured the coffee, added a

splash of cold milk. Stirred and sipped. I walked to the front bay window and stared into Columbia Square.

Bunny's house was now dark like all the others. Live oak branches and Spanish moss hung still in the damp summer heat. The nostalgic flame of the gas lamps and the bubbling fountain were the only signs of life.

I thought about the doctors' insistent warnings that going off the meds would cause hallucinations. But I'd done my research and I knew that staying on those meds carried a risk of hallucinations, too. As well as psychosis. Neither prospective scenario gave me comfort, so I had to be my own best advocate when it came to my health.

The park was empty.

Haunted.

Catherine's expression was burned into my mind and it wasn't soothing. If she'd visited me at all, and I wasn't certain that she had, she wasn't here to comfort me.

She was worried.

I wondered what she knew that I didn't.

2

———

Jenny Martinsen turned left onto her pebbled driveway and saw a man standing on her front porch. A jolt of adrenaline caused her heart to sprint. She and Kent only rarely had a visitor, and even then it was just the postman.

This man looked like he'd just knocked or rung the bell. Why hadn't her husband answered the door?

The man turned when she put the car into park and he smiled and waved. He was tall, dark-haired and handsome with a neatly manicured mustache. He wore black-rimmed glasses, khaki shorts and a muted orange T-shirt that looked freshly ironed.

Something about his smile made her insides want to curl in on themselves. She grabbed the pepper spray from her purse and held it ready but out of sight as she walked toward him. "Can I help you?"

He offered her an ivory-colored pamphlet with a pen and ink drawing of a small church on the front. "My name is Reverend Matt Franklin. I've started the New Revelation Church in town and I'm introducing myself to as many members of the community as possible. I hope you and your family will join us on Sunday."

She accepted the pamphlet but kept her eyes steady on him. "Sure." She knew neither she nor her husband would attend. Kent had never been a church-goer and she didn't go out in public. Except for necessary doctor appointments and grocery trips.

She studied his face carefully. She wasn't sure what a man of the cloth was supposed to look like, but this guy had a polished complexion and uber-white teeth. Like those teeth might just glow in the dark. Somehow she thought higher-ups in a church would be too busy serving their congregation to think about vanity.

"We'll see you soon, then?"

"Yeah. We'll see you soon."

"Wonderful!" His smile was broad and it was clear that he meant it to appear friendly and approachable. But the corners of his lips curled up too much at the edges. Like there was appetite behind that smile.

When he left without any trouble, she exhaled. Because it was odd that he'd found his way to their hidden house on the top of the mountain. They didn't have any neighbors and no one would even know they were there unless they already had the address.

She remained out front for several minutes to make sure he was truly gone. He'd arrived on foot and left the same way, walking along the main road. She glanced at the muddy footprints he'd left on their sidewalk and front porch.

When he didn't return she decided he could have been exploring the local hiking trails and stumbled upon the road that led to their house. Still, she walked back to the car, her eyes scanning the front area for any movement. She pulled the car into the garage, closed and locked the door. She carried the first two bags of groceries into the kitchen. Kent, her husband, danced at the stove while stirring a pot of red sauce. His earbuds were stuffed into his ears and she heard the tinny music from across the room.

So that was why he hadn't heard their visitor knocking.

"Kent!" she called.

He stopped dancing, removed an earbud and turned. "Hey!" He rushed over, took the groceries. Then he hugged and kissed her and said what she knew he would say, "You should let me do that."

He pulled out a chair at the breakfast table and placed a ready cup of chamomile tea in front of her. She'd never been all that patient at letting others wait on her. But since the pregnancy test had come back positive, she knew her body wasn't completely her own anymore.

So she allowed Kent to fuss over her, and boy did he enjoy the process. Which was good, because she wasn't sure she had any maternal instincts.

She'd never played with baby dolls or Barbies, she'd never had a pet. She and Kent didn't even have houseplants.

"Those instincts will kick in when you least expect it," her doctor told her. "Trust me."

Kent ran back and forth between the car and the kitchen, unloading groceries, and she told him about their visitor, the pamphlet and how uncomfortable she felt.

He sat in front of her and took her hand. "When the baby's born you're going to have to get more comfortable with strangers. He or she will need friends. We'll have to get out more and meet people."

She felt the blood leave her head, and he must have noticed because he asked, "Did something happen? Do you want me to call the police?"

She wanted to say yes but she shook her head. "No."

She knew what he was thinking.

He'd said it all before when she'd worried about noises in the night, or strangers who paid too much attention to her. That the event wasn't police-worthy. That he didn't want them to be known as the paranoid couple who cried wolf. And, of course, the most frequent comment, that she should consider therapy to resolve her fear of strangers.

She'd never told Kent about the kidnapping, she never would. She didn't want to leave that breadcrumb out there.

After Ricardo Muñoz was sentenced, a car sideswiped her and her father, tried to run them off a cliff. Not long after that she'd received a death threat that Agent Hernandez nicknamed the We Will letter.

Short, but to the point.

The note said the Muñoz family would never forget that she had testified against their patriarch, Ricardo Muñoz. One day they would pay her back in kind: They would kill her.

She and her father moved out of state and changed their last names. She cut her hair short and wore glasses and a baseball cap in public.

A child would put her back in circulation and she didn't know how to handle that. She wanted this baby with Kent, desperately. But she needed to stay anonymous.

Agent Hernandez had told her a long time ago that she needed to live her life. But he hadn't seen what that family was capable of. Not firsthand. Not like she had. That family was a special kind of evil.

Kent patted her hand. "Finish your tea. You'll feel better by the time you get to the bottom of the cup. I'm going to get the rest of the groceries out of the car and put them away."

She took off the baseball cap and put it on the table.

Jenny knew the tea wasn't going to cut it. The minister's smile with its wolfish curve had caused the memories to percolate again.

One by one, flashbacks from the kidnapping hit her brain like rapid-fire bullets. She was twelve again, taken and trapped. She could feel the cold steel bars in her hand where she'd clung to the sides of the cage, she could smell the stink of vomit and feces and hear the screams of the girls who were dragged away and never came back.

She drew in a deep breath.

The walls continued to close in.

"Actually, I think I'm going to go for a run." She stood, flexed and fisted her palms.

Kent stopped in the doorway, turned to face her. "You sure that's a good idea?"

"Dr. Thompson said it's fine. I'm young, in great health, and I was running long before I was pregnant. My body is used to it. I'd feel weird if I couldn't run." She forced a smile.

They stared at one another for a moment.

"Then I'll finish cooking the pasta and come with you," he said.

"I need alone time to think," she said, knowing he could see how agitated she'd become. "I just—I need to run. It'll calm me down."

He nodded reluctantly and like he held onto a breath. She knew he tried to understand when she got like this and he couldn't. She knew she couldn't explain.

"I'll run my usual back path away from the main road where the supposed minister came up." She cringed inwardly. She was trying to give Kent assurance by sharing that she would take a more careful route, but she realized she sounded paranoid about their visitor.

"Is that trail safe? I thought they closed it down?"

"They did. A long time ago, which makes me feel all the more comfortable using it, to be honest. I know no one will be back there, and it is safe as long as you stay away from the edge. Which I obviously will."

Kent nodded again though she knew he didn't agree.

She changed into black sweats and for the millionth time she entertained the idea of telling Kent about the kidnapping. How she'd changed her name and even twenty years later, she still basically lived in hiding. That this was the reason she stayed hidden and was so skittish.

But she knew that Kent would tell her that she needed to start living now—to put the past behind her. Or he might tell someone else about the kidnapping. Both possibilities meant exposure.

She stayed alive by keeping quiet.

She clipped the runner's light to the back of her sweats, not because she wanted to, but because Kent insisted. If it were up to her, she would have stuck with all black to stay nearly invisible.

She walked into the kitchen.

Kent was seated at the breakfast table with the church pamphlet in front of him. A torn piece of paper was laid to the side with numbers on it that matched the numbers on the inside cover of the saddle-stitched flyer:

24: 19-22

1/12 1/13 1/16 1/20 1/10 2/17 1/6

HE NODDED to the ripped piece of notebook paper. "That flew out when I tossed the flyer on the table. All those same numbers are on the back of the flyer, too. I was just trying to figure out what it all meant. I think I figured out part of it..."

He kept talking but she could no longer hear what he was saying. A slow tremor rose up from within and she wrapped her arms around her waist to hold herself together. 24: 19-22 was the same Bible verse painted on the cinderblock wall of the Muñoz compound.

Right in front of her cage.

The painted curves of the twos and the nine, and sharp angles of the four and the one loomed over her like a threat.

Like a promise.

Kent turned to her, his bright blue eyes so clear and trusting. He was the epitome of innocence and she'd taken advantage of that. Everything she'd told him about herself was a lie.

Now she'd have to tell him the truth. Because if they'd found her, and it looked like they had, he was at risk, too. When they broke in to kill her, they'd kill him. She'd have to move. They'd have to move. They'd have to leave tonight.

"Ready?" he asked.

She opened her mouth and tried to speak but couldn't. Dizziness hit her in waves and she stumbled and fell to the floor.

Kent called to her but his voice sounded like it came from the far end of a tunnel. From all fours she looked up and saw him hovering over her, blackness around the edges of his face. In a blink her world went completely dark, like someone yanked her power source.

Kent called her name again, yet she couldn't find the strength to answer. What she'd long feared was upon her: Her life was over.

3

———————

Fluorescent lights hummed above Agent Manny Hernandez's head in the near-empty FBI offices. He checked the clock for the fifth time in as many minutes, knew that if he wasn't on his way out the door soon, he would get a call from his wife, Blair.

Manny sucked at quitting. And although Blair continued to do her level best to keep him from working too much, she rarely succeeded.

He was one of only three agents in the Charlotte office on this Friday afternoon. None of them under the age of forty. All of them hunched over their desks, clinging to the idea that each solved case could make the world a better place. That they could defeat evil, at least for a while. That they could be the heroes they'd all once believed they could be.

Tommy from the mailroom tapped on the side glass window of Manny's office and waved a small manila envelope. He munched on the last bit of a cellophane-wrapped pastry that looked like a Twinkie. The nineteen-year-old kid with the buzz cut was as skinny as a twig and ate twice his weight every day.

Manny waved Tommy in. "Boy, I wish I had your metabolism."

Tommy gave him a crooked smile, shoved the last bite of the Twinkie into his mouth and crumpled the wrapper loudly. He handed Manny the envelope that was hand-addressed to Agent Hernandez in black ink, block letters. "This came for you," Tommy said with his mouth half-full. "It's been scanned, no traces of anything, no matching fingerprints. It's been logged into the system."

Manny had received his first anthrax letter in the early 2000s, the result of jailing the heads of the Provenzano crime family. Since then most of his mail, especially anything hand-addressed from the outside, was scanned and logged into the system before it reached him.

"Tanya in Evidence wants it back by Monday. You know how she is," Tommy said.

Manny did know how Tanya was. He appreciated her meticulous record-keeping. No one knew when some seemingly irrelevant piece of information could become useful.

"G'night," Tommy said and walked out the door.

Manny tipped the 4x9 envelope and a small piece of notebook paper slid into his open palm. "Night, Tommy," Manny said distractedly.

The rough-edged paper was hand torn with two lines of carefully written numbers. The handwriting matched the style of print on the envelope. The first line was a set of three numbers with a colon after the first. The second line looked like a list of fractions.

24: 19-22

1/12 1/13 1/16 1/20 1/10 2/17 1/6

The colon after the 24 gave the impression it referenced a chapter and several verses from the Bible. But there was no mention of any book of the Bible to reference.

The note, of course, was unsigned.

He opened a new private browser and typed in 24: 19-22.

Number one on the search results page was Deuteronomy 24: 19-22 which said: "When you reap your harvest in your field and forget a sheaf in the field, you shall not go back to get it. It shall be for the sojourner, the fatherless, and the widow, that the Lord your God may bless you in all the work of your hands."

He studied the note and compared it to the verse on the screen.

Something old and buried stirred, rumbled, like an ancient dragon waking from its long slumber.

He'd worked hard over the years to discern between the gut-level pull of worthwhile suspicion and the worthless scent of a rabbit trail. Detectives, FBI agents such as himself, didn't like to admit it because it wasn't scientific, but instinct was a real thing. Instinct was a divine clue, it was guidance that connected obscure dots and solved cases.

Emotion, on the other hand, specifically guilt, was a meaningless rabbit hole that resolved absolutely nothing. Least of all, the past.

That verse, though...wasn't it the same one—?

His memories were blurry. Intentionally so, from years of trying to block them out. He shook his head, tried to get it clear.

It had been twenty years since he'd worked on the Muñoz kidnapping case. But this seemed like the verse they'd used to justify almost everything they did. He was almost certain.

Manny should have handed this note over to his partner,

because he was prohibited from having anything to do with the Muñoz cases.

That dragon, an old hunger for justice, rumbled in the pit of his soul. Along with it was his old hunger for Jack and Coke, an appetite that soared whenever justice wasn't met.

He allowed his eyes to comb the surrounding glass-enclosed offices, he wavered between going home to Blair and their daughter like he'd promised, or delving into the old case that he'd been kicked off of for a good reason.

His palms pricked with sweat.

He could lose his way, like he had the last time.

Looking into it wouldn't be easy. His permissions for accessing the FBI's files on the Muñoz family had been revoked.

His heart rate sped. The idea of someone from that family getting the better of him again churned his gut. He opened a private browser and typed in: Muñoz Family Miami compound. The internet was like karma, it had a long memory.

Manny clicked through the crime scene photos that the newspapers had printed. At the same time, images from his own investigation of the crime scenes burst through his head like flashbacks from a war.

He rubbed at his forehead. He tried to keep his breath even.

Manny clicked until he found a photo of the chapel. Ricardo Muñoz ran an international drug cartel and kidnapping ring, but he built a chapel on the premises because he liked to say that he was devoutly religious. In that chapel he instructed his many wives to teach their children a very twisted truth that fit his perverse logic.

Manny zoomed in on one photo until he could read the

framed verse that Ricardo had nailed to the chapel door. His heart rate sped even faster.

When you reap your harvest in your field and forget a sheaf in the field, you shall not go back to get it. It shall be for the sojourner, the fatherless, and the widow, that the Lord your God may bless you in all the work of your hands.

He leaned into the back of his chair, feeling both satisfied that he had remembered the verse correctly and dissatisfied since he knew this verification wasn't solid proof of anything.

"We take from those who keep what they should share," Ricardo Muñoz had said from his jail cell when Manny asked him why. "And we give to those who need the most. We redistribute wealth as God intended. The wealthy should not keep so much for themselves."

Ricardo omitted the fact that once they collected ransom from the girls' wealthy, Christian parents, they typically killed the girls anyway. Ricardo bragged how he gave thousands upon thousands of dollars to the impoverished people in his hometown in Mexico. But he glossed over the fact that his family kept so much ransom and drug money for themselves that they ended up with far more wealth than the girls' families ever had. Neither did he mention the hundreds of thousands of lives and families he destroyed by pumping drugs into the country.

The tug of the rabbit hole beckoned and Manny clicked through more images. Most were photos that had been taken on the day they raided the compound. The day several more girls died. Because of him.

"What are you lookin' at, Hoss?"

Manny startled at his partner's unexpected presence, more so by the fact that Stanford could see Manny's computer screen.

Stanford Ames was Manny's past and, for as long as he continued to work with the FBI, a probable part of his future. They'd worked together in Miami as fledgling detectives, then on the Child Abduction Response Deployment team, now on a task force that worked to dismantle entire organizations through investigations and prosecutions.

Stanford stood tall at 6'3" and had always been fit and trim. But these days his shirt buttons strained across his gut, a new development since Alice filed for divorce several months ago.

Manny handed him the envelope and the note and calmly said, "Got this today."

Stanford read the note, re-examined Manny's screen and said, "Family's been quiet for what—two decades? It's a false flag. A copycat."

Stanford's flat expression said he expected his partner to be smart and strong and beyond the sticky emotional traps of the past. He expected Manny to let this go.

Manny clenched his teeth. "Could be."

"Want me to look into it for you?"

"Envelope was addressed to me," Manny said.

"I don't think higher-ups would let you take it." Stanford gestured to Manny's screen.

"I'm not looking to take anything on. Besides, I've done my penance, I've been clean for a long time." He nodded toward the note.

Stanford dropped his considerable weight into a chair. His eyes, green and penetrating, stayed on Manny with a particular ferocity that said he didn't want Manny doing this.

Then he turned the paper upside down and examined the depth of the indentations from the bottom side up.

Manny frowned. He leaned across the desk and pointed.

"Whoever wrote that pressed hard enough with the pen that they nearly broke through the paper. The author was angry, had a purpose and an intent. The verse matches the one the Muñoz family had posted next to the front doors of their chapel."

"Author might just be nuts or looking for attention or both." Stanford shrugged. "What do these fractions mean?"

"I don't know," Manny said.

"Fingerprints?"

"According to Tommy, no matches in the system."

"Meaning it wasn't handled by a Muñoz." Stanford studied the note. After a moment he put the paper on Manny's desk and pushed it toward him.

Manny picked up the note and studied it again. "Could have been written by one of the Muñoz kids who still has an axe to grind. They're all grown up now, doubtful we have fingerprints on all of them. What's the status of the family?"

Stanford sighed. "Given what went down, I understand your temptation to pick this up again, but it's not a good idea. I check our online files eight or nine times a year. For the last twenty years there's been no movement. The family fell apart when you arrested Ricardo and his brothers. Now that he's dead they're never coming back."

Anger churned the acid in his gut and Manny pointed to the cryptic note. "Not looking into it could be another mistake."

Stanford flattened his lips and stared at the floor like he was weighing something.

After a few long minutes he took Manny into his office, closed the door, and left his hand on the knob. "People say there's always one case that finishes you." He raised his eyebrows.

Manny held up the note. "This could be some sort of a

warning that they're active again. I don't want anybody else getting hurt because of me. Because of something I didn't do."

Stanford's features fell slowly. He walked to the other side of his desk and gestured that Manny should follow him. "I could get into a lot of trouble for doing this, but you could get into a lot more trouble if you get caught up in this again."

Manny steeled his stomach to control his anger. "I'm not getting caught up in anything."

Stanford opened a file that showed the Muñoz family tree. Ricardo Muñoz's photo was at the top with a red X drawn through it, since Manny and the team had locked him up. Below him were photos of Ricardo's five brothers, red X's drawn through those images as well.

Thin black lines were drawn from Ricardo to each of his eight wives, blue lines connected the women and their appropriate seventeen children. Manny hadn't seen these people in almost twenty years, but the familiar details of every person's face came rushing back in an instant—the shape of the eyes, the texture of the hair, depth of the skin color. He hadn't forgotten anything. Neither had he forgotten the faces of the six girls who died because of him.

Stanford pointed with the cursor. "The red circles around these five wives and twelve children indicate that we located them. Details of their locations are here." He clicked a link that redirected them to another page. "Six of the adult children are deadbeats—trafficking opioids mostly, out of Honduras and Mexico. We found these five wives in various U.S. cities with their six children, all under assumed names, all using the last name Smith.

"They came back to the U.S. to educate their kids, and they never left. We've interviewed them, watched them, they aren't involved in anything illicit. Kids have respectable jobs."

Manny tried to memorize their adult faces. "That means we're still missing six adult children and two of the wives," Manny said.

"True." Stanford shrugged again. "But the family's not active. The remaining wives and children, wherever they are, are quiet. So it doesn't matter." His phone buzzed and he glanced at the screen, declined the call. "If that note were genuinely from a Muñoz, there would have been activity in the family network at some point in the last twenty years. Right? At least something."

Manny didn't want to agree with his partner but he was right in that it would have been unusual for any crime family, much less a long-defunct one, to settle a vendetta twenty years after the fact.

Stanford grabbed his phone. "I owe my divorce attorney a call. Wait on me." He pointed at Manny, then disappeared down the hallway.

Manny waited. But one minute turned into several. When Stanford didn't return, Manny wondered if his partner left him access deliberately.

He clicked through the photos. Partly as a test to prove to himself that he could handle this material without being swallowed by the waves of fury that had nearly drowned him once before. Partly to satiate his hunger for information.

All went fine until he saw photos of the kidnapped girls who didn't make it. Long-buried memories shot across his brain like rapid fire from an assault rifle: Family graveside ceremonies—young siblings telling their dead sisters how much they still loved them. How much they missed them.

The rage in Manny's chest ballooned until he thought it

would burst. He pushed away from the computer. He could hear Stanford from around the corner, arguing with his attorney about the proposed divorce settlement. Manny stared at the monitor, then grabbed the note he'd received and headed toward his office.

Not a day went by that he didn't think of each girl they'd rescued from the compound, and he hoped that they were safe and happy. He'd offered each family the WITSEC program in exchange for the girls' testimonies. But before he could get them signed up, the D.A. insisted that every surviving girl be deposed, so they would know what they had. So they would know if each girl would be able to tell her story in court.

When the district attorney went to the defense with the depositions in hand, Ricardo Muñoz decided life in prison was better than the electric chair. After that the government no longer needed the girls' testimonies, so the WITSEC program was off the table.

A week later, the girls' homes were ransacked. Personal files and jewelry were stolen, and a death threat was left behind for each of them. Manny remembered those notes that came to be known as the We Will letters—simple notebook paper with different sized letters haphazardly torn from magazines and glued on white paper:

WE WILL NEVER FORGET.

Six months later, on Harper Silveria's birthday and thirty minutes before a few party guests were due to arrive, she found a package wrapped in balloon-themed paper on the front doorstep. There was tiny handwriting on the top of the box she couldn't make out. It wasn't until she'd picked up the box and read the word "boom" that she realized what she'd done.

Hundreds of four-inch nails exploded from the box and shot into Harper's thighs and stomach. Emergency surgery was required to save her life.

Similar close calls plagued each surviving girl and her family.

Afterward, every family changed their last names and left town.

His phone rang. He glanced at the phone screen, quickly unplugged his laptop from the monitor and slipped the computer into his briefcase. "Hey, babe," he said casually.

A blender abruptly stopped in the background. "It's margarita night. You're on your way, right?" his wife asked.

"Yep, just packing up."

An email alert dinged loud on his phone.

"I heard that," Blair said.

"I didn't. I'm on my way."

"You'd better be." The softness in her tone brought him back to the present, reminded him what was most important.

There had been a day when he wouldn't have left the office before midnight, when he would have argued and fought any suggestion that he ought to come home at a reasonable hour. That he ought to stop drinking. That he ought to quit the case.

That was his first marriage, a union that crumbled under the weight of all his if onlys from the Muñoz case.

Today he was smarter and more humble. He didn't know what he'd done in this life to deserve Blair, or their daughter, Reagan, or any other second chance he'd been given. But he would keep doing everything in his power to show God he was grateful. That he was sorry for past mistakes.

He took a photo of the note with the numbers on it, then folded the paper and reinserted it into the envelope. He entertained the possibility that someone was just messing with him, as Stanford had suggested. Twenty years ago the papers had covered the Muñoz case in nauseating detail. So today, anyone could find that verse with a simple internet search on crime families.

Halfway out the door, he stopped. It could have been a Muñoz son who'd sent the note; that would explain why he cited Deuteronomy. He would have wanted Manny to know it was him. The fractions he couldn't figure out.

As much as he wanted to go back to the FBI portal and dig through the Muñoz case files, Blair was waiting.

Manny knew that even if he spent the next fifteen hours at his desk poring over details, he still might not have the answers he needed.

He stepped into the evening heat and pressed the button on the key fob. In the distance he heard the ka-thunk of his car locks popping up. He took one final glance at the photo of the paper with the numbers.

Over the years he had received, he reminded himself, far more random, meaningless mail than he did death threats or anthrax letters. The truth was that people who wrote threatening letters rarely did anything to follow through on them.

He tossed his laptop bag into the passenger seat, hung his suit jacket on the hook in the back seat, and rolled up his sleeves.

He hoped that tonight he would feel he had done enough, that he hadn't missed anything, that it was okay to relax and be happy. He hoped he could let the mysterious notepaper go for the weekend.

Despite the amount of therapy he'd had over the years,

this balanced, healthier perspective was still unfamiliar to him. Truth be told, he didn't entirely trust this way of living. It just didn't feel wise to let things go. Like he could miss something.

He noted the worry that rocked in the back of his mind, that itch to obsess. Obsession had a serious downside. Though he came by it naturally.

He had been raised in a difficult home by a dedicated but unassertive and unhappy mother, and a narc cop dad who believed that any amount of nurturing caused a boy to grow up weak.

It seemed only natural that when Manny joined the force, he chose the most dangerous assignments. When asked by his superiors where he got his zeal for hunting down the most vile criminals, he could only answer that this way of life was in his blood. He never shared the real answer with anyone, that some part of him was endlessly desperate to measure up to a secret standard, set by someone he didn't even particularly like.

Once behind the wheel, Manny did a quick search of the parking lot. Seeing no one, he took the pen and small notepad from his shirt pocket.

Even though his partner's fingers had moved quickly over the keys, Manny caught the password combination: Moneybags11! It was a word Stanford had used unconsciously for years when referring to suspects. Mr. Moneybags. Mrs. Moneybags. Eleven was his jersey number when he'd played basketball in high school.

Manny closed the notepad and slipped it back into his pocket.

He drove out of the parking lot and caught sight of the sun that was still fairly high in the sky. There would be plenty of time tonight for the things that mattered: a lengthy swim with his young daughter in their new pool, pizza and margarita night with his wife. Lots of I Love Yous.

When the sun had fully set, and the moon took its place, he hoped he could hold his wife in his arms and be thankful and proud of all that they had. Of how far he had come.

At the moment, all he could think of was Harper and the other girls. How he had failed them and how his past mistakes were chasing him down.

4

———————

Officer Patterson took one final look at the broken window, but didn't get too close to the jagged glass. He handed me the top copy of the report. "Your incident number is in the right hand corner. Your insurance company will want that."

Officer Patterson was older, short, round. He had come out once before to investigate one of the previous break-in attempts. Firm voice, kind eyes.

"I'm not filing for insurance. I just wanted y'all to be aware. Would you consider increasing your patrol presence through here for a while?"

"Actually, I've been asked to do just that. Third attempted break-in this month. Good thing you have the bars on." He tapped the bars with his blue pen, then returned it to his uniform shirt pocket. "We recommend those to everyone in the historic district. Crime rates in downtown Savannah are up again this year."

"Third one? In this neighborhood?"

"Oglethorpe Square. Same thing, though, broken

window on the first floor. Only they didn't have bars on." He sucked air in through his teeth and winced, like the story didn't end well. "Get that window fixed before you go to bed tonight." He flicked one of the steel bars and it dinged. "No sense tempting trouble."

He frowned at the window, reached between the steel bars and the broken glass and retrieved a folded piece of paper. "This yours?" he asked.

I shook my head and shrugged.

He opened it, studied whatever was on the paper, then handed it to me. "Maybe it's a blessing to protect the house. We see that in a lot of older homes around here. Salt in the window sills to keep out evil spirits, or blessings or prayers written out and tucked into windows or taped on door jambs."

"Maybe the previous owner put it there." Although I knew that wasn't the case. Otherwise I would have seen it when I installed the bars.

Halfway to his squad car he stopped short at the No Parking street sign, and examined a few dents left by the pellets I shot the night before. He turned, gave me a hard stare. "You didn't shoot at him, did you?"

"No," I lied.

His warning glance said he didn't believe me. He got in his car and left.

I raised my hand to block the sun's blinding summer insistence and called Tim, one of my contractors who helped me with the restoration. I'd told him about the broken window earlier in the day and he said he would stop by to fix it. I confirmed with him that I'd brought the replacement window home, that it was ready for him. Then I gave him the new code for the basement level back door, because I changed the code daily.

I could have fixed the window myself. But it had to be installed from the inside out, and I wasn't going to stand inside that cramped basement and look out barred windows. I had enough vivid flashbacks that assaulted me when I tried to fall asleep at night, or when I stared out at the sea or when I did just about anything.

Once inside the breakfast nook I gazed at all the antique place settings I'd displayed inside the glass-front cabinetry. A gorgeous collection whose history read like a storybook to me, but today their symbols of strength and tradition didn't give me any peace.

Long night of no sleep. Long day of interviewing. I tossed the incident report on the table and rested my head in my hand. My twin was stuck at the forefront of my mind —red sundress, tapping her wrist, staring at me with that worried expression.

Could her spirit have actually visited? Did I bring her to me? Called her in, the way Bunny did to her deceased husband? Because I'd never stopped talking to her. Never stopped wishing that she hadn't been killed.

In Savannah, a city whose past and present blurred so beautifully, that type of intense focus could have acted like traction. It could have unwittingly pulled the dead to the living.

I lifted my head, stared through the arched doorway, straight through the living room window and into Columbia Square. The bells, the fog and the way her blue eyes locked with mine. For a moment I allowed myself to entertain the idea that she'd actually come to me, and that she'd brought a message.

My beautiful sister, what did you mean by tapping your wrist like that?

A universal gesture. Time.

Could have meant any number of things.

The time is now. The time has come. High-time. My time. Your time. Watch your time. Time's up.

It's time.

Time to go. Time to move on.

Fear grabbed every muscle in my chest so hard I felt like I was having a heart attack.

Are you warning me?

I gave the idea more thought, then shook my head.

No.

There was no way anyone from the Muñoz family could have found me. I'd been extremely careful. Plus, I couldn't. I just couldn't go back to running. It was a soul-stealing way of life. Paranoia lead to loneliness. And loneliness was a heavy load, a sad load, a destructive load. The sheer force of it wore me down, took its toll, left me flat and thin.

I stood and realized that I still held the strange note in my hand. The crisp paper cracked when I unfolded it. I read the handwritten message and I released the note. It floated to the floor and I backed away from it, staring at what was written on the page:

24:19-22

1/12 1/13 1/16 1/20 1/10 2/17 1/6

THE NUMBERS on the first line were the same as the Bible verse that Ricardo Muñoz used, and the second line was a list of strange fractions.

Terror struck deep inside like lightning, then spread rapidly until my entire body shook. I wrapped my arms around myself. An image of the man in the black cap pulling on the bars flashed across my mind. Only now I knew he wasn't trying to figure a way inside. He was buying time. He must have known I'd come outside and he wanted to make sure I saw him when he smashed the window. He wanted to make sure I'd find the note he left for me.

I could still see him turning toward me, and his smile made sense now.

They'd found me, and he wanted me to know.

I ran to the bathroom, retched and vomited.

SOMETIME LATER, my phone rang, its trill echoed off the tiled walls.

I stared at the screen: Levi Wright. My neighbor.

He'd lived in Savannah for several years and knew all the best places to go. He'd made me instantly feel at home here and was always genuinely interested to know how I was. So rare. Had I known from the beginning what a caring person he was, I would have gone out with him when he asked.

The crumpled paper that I'd dropped on the way to the bathroom caught my eye. I turned away and silenced the call. As much as I adored Levi, I was in no mood to chat.

I desperately wanted to call Nick and tell him about the note and what I thought it meant. I wanted his advice and his comfort. But he was out of the country, and there was no way of getting in touch with him.

I wanted to call him because I knew he'd be there for me. Not because we'd dated all that long, we really hadn't. And not just because he didn't see my scars. (It was like they weren't even there to him.) It was more than that. It sounded trite to say, but we had a connection.

From the first moment we met, the spark between us was brilliant. Intense. Like he saw *me*, the real *me*. The side of me I didn't share with anyone else. He woke up something inside of me. Something I didn't think could exist again, a better—no, the *best*—version of me.

Still, I couldn't tell him about the note, let alone my past. I couldn't tell anyone.

My phone rang again. It was Doctor Levi, as his young patients referred to him. I pressed my hand against my damp forehead.

"Levi, hey." I made my voice sound upbeat, in a great-to-hear-from-you-neighborly sort of way. I was surprised at how well that came out.

There was no response on Levi's end, only nondescript chatter in the background.

"Levi?"

"Hey, Harper." His tone was friendly and upbeat, but he gave a long exhale like he was frustrated or tired. "You on your way?"

I suddenly had a vague recollection of agreeing to meet him for a glass of wine. I hit the speaker icon and checked the calendar on my phone.

"You forgot me, didn't you?" he asked.

"No, I didn't forget."

There were four things I'd put on my calendar for the day. Two interviews in an attempt to get work. Nick's travel schedule in the Middle East this week. And drinks with Levi. I completely forgot about drinks. The attempted break-in, seeing my dead sister (did I?) and the note had me side-tracked.

"Normally you're early, so I'm just checking," Levi's voice was smooth, calm, friendly.

I stared at the paper on the floor and the bits of the

handwritten Bible verse peeking out at me like a threat. The deep quiver started again, quickly building in strength. I decided it would be better if I weren't by myself.

"Yes," I said quickly. No, I did not need to be alone in this big empty house. Obsessing. "I'm running late. Sorry. I should have texted. Someone tried to break into my house last night." My voice cracked.

"Are you okay?" he asked tenderly.

I told Levi that I'd had my air pistol, that I'd fired but missed and that I filed a report with the police. "They just left so I'll be there in fifteen."

I stepped over the note on my way to the study, got my handgun from the upper right hand drawer of my desk, slipped it into my purse along with a copy of my concealed carry permit. This wasn't the air pistol I'd aimed at the guy last night. This was my Sig Sauer 9mm that was made for self-defense.

I paused for a moment and thought of what Officer Patterson had said. That the note might have been a blessing. Then I dropped my purse by the front door. I wasn't taking any chances.

I kicked off my heels, removed my jacket and button-down blouse while I climbed the spiral staircase. I dodged paint cans, toolboxes and rolled up drop cloths. Tim and his contractors should have already finished the railing installation. I took my life in my hands every time I went up these stairs.

They did get one railing to me last month, but the measurements were all wrong. The second story railing was supposed to be quite a bit lower than the bottom story. The illusion was called forced perspective—a little architectural trick that made something appear different than it actually was. In this case the lower railing at the top made the spiral staircase look longer and taller than it truly was.

Nick had suggested the elegant solution. Architecturally it was spot on.

The restaurant Levi had chosen was an utter pit, but he was a smart dresser in his off hours. So I opted for a tailored white button-down, slightly baggy boyfriend jeans and leopard print loafers. A bit slouchy, a lot comfortable and a touch of my own style.

I grabbed my purse, slung it over my shoulder, checked my appearance in the full-length mirror. I wrapped a silk scarf around my neck to cover the scars more thoroughly, and pushed my dark hair behind my ears. I wanted so badly to return to my original hair and eye color. If I could, then I would see Catherine looking back at me right now.

Before leaving I conducted my usual security routine—I checked each main level window to ensure that the locks were fastened. I checked the security system to make sure the cameras were recording, turned on the motion sensors for the main and upper levels. I changed the codes to the front and back door locks, as well as the lock on the door that separated the basement from the first floor. Once on the front porch I locked all three door locks and set the alarm from my phone.

With both hands tucked into my pant pockets I went down the front steps, then stopped. The water from the simple fountain in Columbia Square bubbled up and splashed into the pond below. In my mind's eye I saw the gray fog rolling across the green, I saw my twin in her red dress and I saw her pointing at the watch on her wrist.

I wanted to say that I hadn't seen her, for the sake of my sanity. But the memory of her presence hung with me like the remnants of a flavor. A scent.

You're losing it. The dark little voice inside of me scoffed. *Just like the psychiatrists warned: Going off the meds causes hallucinations.*

Shut up.

Shut up, shut up, shut up.

5

———

Kent closed and locked the door behind the EMTs, and Jenny heard the ambulance drive away and around the first curve of mountain road. It was all Jenny could do not to wrestle Kent into the car and leave right then.

But she had to be careful how she told him. He already thought she overreacted too much about her need for privacy and her concerns about exposure to strangers. She had to deliver the information in such a way that he wouldn't discount her.

He pushed his hand through his short blond hair and it stood up and away from his forehead. He picked up the bowl of pasta from the coffee table and handed it to her. "Eat some more. It's good."

"Thanks." She took another bite and wiped a bit of sauce from her lip.

"The pasta is lentil-based, because when you're pregnant you need more protein than usual. The sauce is organic, because organic is always a good idea. I added some fresh tomatoes from the garden. Also organic—"

"I'm sorry I scared you," she said.

"Not your fault. Just—eat more. Like the EMTs said: small meals, more frequently. To keep your blood sugar up."

"It's not that. I mean, maybe a little bit, but—Kent I have something to say and I need you to listen to me."

Kent lowered himself to the couch. His face was snow white with worry. She didn't want to burden him any further but there was no better time to tell him what he needed to know. Time was the one thing they didn't have.

She pointed to the breakfast table and the pamphlet. "That minister and the material he left behind—"

"Oh, that." He glanced at the breakfast table and waved his hand like the information was inconsequential. "I found the verse he referenced." He brought his phone over, tapped the screen a few times, and cleared his throat.

Jenny squeezed her eyes shut, bracing herself for the Bible verse she never wanted to hear again. She would wait until he was finished reading, or maybe she would recite along with him, from memory. Then she would tell him what the verse meant. How she had been kidnapped and how this Mexican drug cartel used that verse to frame their heinous crimes as justice. Sending it here was a threat and they would have to leave their home tonight.

"The earth is violently broken,
The earth is split open,
The earth is shaken exceedingly.

THE EARTH SHALL REEL to and fro like a drunkard,
And shall totter like a hut;
Its transgression shall be heavy upon it,
And it will fall, and not rise again.

. . .

IT SHALL COME to pass in that day

That the Lord will punish on high the host of exalted ones,

And on the earth the kings of the earth.

THEY WILL BE GATHERED TOGETHER,

As prisoners are gathered in the pit,

And will be shut up in the prison;

After many days they will be punished."

"WHAT?" She opened her eyes, took Kent's phone and examined the passage.

"It's from the book of Isaiah," he said. "And inside this flyer it says Reverend Matt's sermons are particularly relatable to Californians. Sounds like he's saying this verse is about punishing corrupt politicians. We have a lot of those in this state. That first paragraph seems to reference earthquakes. Hey, are you okay?"

Her body shook with relief and she cried and Kent drew her into a tight hug. He rocked her gently, shushing her sweetly until she calmed.

She pulled away and he studied her. His eyebrows rose in question.

"I'm okay, I'm fine. Good grief, it's all the hormones!"

He took her hands in his and gave them a squeeze. "I'm going to say something and I don't want you to take offense or get upset, okay?"

She drew in a deep and shaky breath. It hadn't occurred to her that there could be different places in the Bible that had the same numbers the Muñoz family used. But of course there was. And of course a church would use them. "Okay."

"I want you to see someone. A therapist."

Something inside of Jenny soured and she looked at the floor.

"Just hear me out. Okay?"

She nodded.

"Since you found out you were pregnant, twice you thought someone was following us in the grocery store. Then when the florist delivered those lilies to us by mistake, you thought it was a death threat." Kent gave several more examples where she'd overreacted to nonthreatening situations, been too afraid to do simple things, and how she'd lived like a recluse. "I want you to be happy. You need the help."

She had thought they were being followed and the floral arrangement looked like something that went on a casket. She hadn't realized these situations had escalated since she'd learned she was pregnant. "Maybe it really is the hormones," she suggested.

"Maybe," he said. "But you can't live like this. It's not healthy. After the baby's born we'll have to be involved in the community. And...are you going to be able to do that?"

"I'll work on myself."

"We all need a little help sometimes," he said. "There's no shame in it."

The seriousness in his eyes told her he wasn't going to take no for an answer.

She knew she couldn't tell any therapist the real reasons why she was so damaged. But she thought maybe she could make up a similar story, one without any revealing details. Maybe she'd learn something that would help her. "Okay," she whispered.

Kent made suggestions for more tea, a foot rub and a good movie.

She accepted all three, then, at the prospect of relaxing fully, remembered how unnerved she felt about the visitor from earlier. She remembered how her father had told her to honor her gut, no matter how small the nudge. No matter how much it didn't make sense.

"I really didn't like that guy, the one who came by earlier. And I am wondering if he was a real minister."

Kent shrugged. "All kinds of creeps out there. I wish I'd heard the doorbell." He brought up a browser and typed in the web address listed on the flyer.

"I would like to go to the police. I realize there's no crime to report, but his being up here was odd. I don't know, I can't explain it. I want to put him on their radar."

"And if it turns out to be nothing?" He showed her a web page with a one page site and a photo of a church on the front. The same one that was on the front page of the pamphlet.

She looked at the site, bit the corner of her lip and shrugged. "Then I'll be grateful," she said, her heart still thumping harder than usual.

Worry lines appeared across Kent's forehead.

"What were the fractions about?" she said to change the subject.

"I'm not sure. I was going to look into that. Shall we figure it out now?"

Together they tried to find a message behind the numbers. She did internet searches, while Kent added, divided, searched for a pattern, mathematical and other-wise, but nothing made sense.

Finally Kent put his pencil and paper down and emptied the remaining pasta into a Tupperware container. "We could go to the church on Sunday and ask the minister directly if you want?"

"No thanks." She shook her head. "But I am going to take that run before the foot rub and the movie."

"No you're not." He stood in front of the open refrigerator and put his hand on his hip.

"Yeah, I need to. Too many emotions all pent up. I'll sleep better if I do.

"It's getting dark."

"Not so dark, and I'll keep it short."

His look was stern and full of disapproval. But she knew he wouldn't fight her. It wasn't his way. He was a gentle soul who gave her plenty of space to do what she needed to do.

After a moment he came to her, leaned down and kissed the tiny swell of her belly. "This is against my better judgment. But hurry back before it gets really dark."

When she opened the door she looked back at him and snickered.

"What's so funny?"

"You already look like a parent. Hands on your hips, cautioning me about being out after dark."

He shook his head. "Be careful. You and that little one are my whole world."

She kissed him, turned the flashing light on at the back of her waistband. Gave him the thumbs-up sign, and walked out the back door and into the night.

The cool Northern California breeze was damp and scented with salt from the nearby sea. The daylight hadn't completely disappeared but the full moon was already high in the sky, the path had more than enough light. Dusk was her favorite time to run since that was when most people finished their day and went inside.

Since the kidnapping almost twenty years ago she'd only

been truly comfortable when she was alone, which didn't make much sense. At least not to her. Seemed like she ought to have found comfort in numbers. But her endless suspicion forced her to question anyone and everyone, and it never let her relax.

Thankfully that didn't apply to Kent. He'd won her heart from almost the first time they'd met. Both computer science majors, he'd given her his chair when she'd walked in late to a full class with no available seating.

She started down the dirt path, the public hiking trail that very few people even knew about. Or if they did, they didn't want to risk hiking it. After a young man fell to his death because he strayed from the main area, the State of California posted numerous signs on a wide chain, warning visitors that the area wasn't safe.

She ducked under the chain.

She did a few spinal twists and caught sight of her beautiful cabin on the secluded hill. The interior lights gave off a cozy warm glow. Kent was visible in the kitchen window. As much as she looked forward to her run, she was doubly excited to return home and sleep with his warm body pressed against her back.

The home had been a gift from her father on her twenty-first birthday. He'd known she couldn't live in an apartment complex like other kids her age. And he, too, liked the idea that she would live hidden away. Out of sight.

She rounded the corner at the bottom of the hill and took a sharp right. Mud from the recent rain squished beneath her shoes. Ocean waves crashed far below. She and her father discussed how being too visible was how the Muñoz family had found her.

Her father had been a single parent and a very busy software company CEO. That left her with too much time on her hands, and she posted endless videos on social media. She didn't realize then, but she'd given away: where she hung out, which restaurants she liked best, which sporting events she frequented.

One week she'd posted every day, sometimes twice a day, about an upcoming concert she was attending with her best friend, Susan.

When her dad dropped them off at the local civic center, he'd told them all the things a good father should: stick together, don't wander off, keep your cell phone with you at all times.

But the concert ran long and Susan wanted to buy a T-shirt. Jenny had promised her father they would be on the front sidewalk exactly at 11 p.m., not a minute later. It was already 10:54.

Jenny made her way to the front of the civic center, and Susan stood at the T-shirt counter. There was a long line of cars stretching from the front doors to as far back as the eye could see. Plenty of other parents were picking up their kids. Her dad was somewhere in that line. He probably even saw her, she rationalized.

When a woman walked up to her with tears in her eyes, and said in broken English that she was searching for her little girl, Jenny didn't think anything was suspicious.

Jenny searched the line of cars, and thought she spotted her father's Lexus about 12 cars away. She waved. He waved back. She flashed him the just-one-minute finger. Then she looked around for a police officer or security guard.

The woman tugged at Jenny's arm and cried, "Please help me!"

Jenny followed, not that she had much choice, as the woman was short but strong. Jenny tried to explain that they needed to find a security guard. She also tried to pull away from the woman's grasp.

Throngs of concert-goers poured out the front doors and the woman pulled Jenny close. She jabbed something into Jenny's side.

Jenny looked down, a small silver gun pressed into her ribs. She resisted, tried to break free. The woman's grip was bone-crushing.

"Come with me now, and I won't kill your father." The woman's tone was no longer worried, and her English was no longer broken. Jenny's strength melted.

A white van near the front of the circular drive opened its side doors. The moment Jenny stepped foot inside that van, she knew she'd made a horrible mistake.

Jenny picked up the pace, her feet pounded on the soft, damp earth. The constant jolt to her body knocked the stress clean out of her. She reminded herself that she had survived the kidnapping, the starvation, the rape.

The incline became steep and she trudged uphill. She was nearly to the top, and the view of the moonlit Pacific would be worth all the effort.

A rustling noise startled her and she stopped, turned around. Something off to the left sounded like leaves crunching underfoot.

She searched the shadows, nothing moved. She reached to her waistband and turned off the stupid blinking light.

Suddenly a doe bolted from behind a large bush, ran across the forest.

Jenny gasped, grabbed her chest.

When the deer disappeared, she laughed at herself. "Good grief, you're fine. Let it go, Jen." She ran a hand over her face, then continued running.

She ran harder, faster, tried to outrun the memory of

Diego dragging Heather from one of the cages. Occasionally new girls came in. But when they left, they never came back.

Jenny watched helplessly while Heather screamed and hit at him. When she bit his hand, Diego grabbed her head and twisted it. A sickening crack, then she went limp.

Jenny pushed up the rest of the climb until she reached the partial clearing where the cliff jutted over the ocean. Half-Moon Point, they called it. She stood a good distance from the fence that the state had erected to keep the public away from the edge and admired the moon—high, round, bright. Its glow streaked across the ocean like a wide splash of luminescent paint.

A twig snapped.

She knew it was just another animal and she wasn't going to send her blood pressure sky-high over a raccoon or another deer. But then, in the silence, she felt a presence. Her throat went dry and she turned, slowly.

A man stood there, facing her, pointing a gun. He was tall and slender, with dark hair and dark eyes that blended into the night. He didn't wear glasses this time. But she recognized him. It was the minister.

"Hello, Jenny," he said.

Her name on his lips turned her heart to ice.

She'd been careful not to share her name with him.

"My name's Matthew. You visited my family's compound a long time ago. You gave a deposition against my father. It's taken me a long time to find you."

He stepped toward her and she backed up.

"You're not a minister," she said.

He smiled.

In the bright moonlight she saw the thing about his smile that she hadn't been able to pinpoint earlier. Happiness but no warmth. The kind of smile a person gives when they hold all the cards. The kind of smile that lacks even an ounce of generosity.

"How did you find me?" She stepped backward, her heart banging so hard against her chest that it hurt.

He shrugged. "Patience. Persistence."

"What do you want?" she asked. But she knew the answer to that question.

"Justice," he said.

"Kent!" she screamed.

He shook his head, clicked his tongue against the roof of his mouth three times. "That's what I've loved about these nighttime runs of yours. No one around. Except for me. And you, of course."

She tried to figure a way out. But she was on the southern tip of Half-Moon Point and surrounded by a cliff on three sides. The only safe way down was the way she had run up, and that path was behind him.

He walked toward her, gestured with his gun that she ought to move backward. "I've watched you for a few weeks now. Entertained several different options. Thought about killing your precious husband first. I wanted you to know what it was like to lose your family. Turnabout being fair play and all that."

He grinned wide and the moonlight glinted off his unnaturally white teeth.

Jenny bumped into the fence behind her and one of the boards fell with a clatter.

"Climb over," he said.

She shook her head. "No!"

"I can shoot you and toss you over, if you prefer."

It happened without notice. Like a lightning bolt rising up from her soul, the need to save what was hers. She pressed her hands protectively against her stomach.

He motioned to her midsection. "Yes, pregnant. I heard."

She climbed over the fence. Tried to remember how high the cliff was, if there was water below and if she might be able to survive the fall.

"That's what made me come after you, and you alone. Because when you jump off that cliff, you'll know what it feels like to lose family. Not a husband. They come and go. They can even be replaced.

"But, blood. Losing a blood relative is different. And knowing that it's your fault they died? That will haunt you all the way down. It will leave a mark on your soul."

He smiled again.

He was significantly bigger than she was, she couldn't fight him and win.

"I'll give you whatever you want," she said. "My father has money, lots of it. He'll pay you."

His smile flatlined. "I don't want your money. What I want is justice."

He ran toward her, his movements nimble and fast.

She looked left and right, but the land behind the fence ran out in just a few short yards. She could outrun him if she could just get past him. She dodged left and climbed through the open fence this time, but he caught her before she could gain any speed. He grabbed her around the waist and lifted her off the ground.

She kicked, elbowed, screamed. When she fell through the air, she reached and grabbed, tried to find a branch, a ledge, something, anything. When she knew she was going to hit the rocks below, when she knew that the impact would kill her and her child, she wrapped her arms around her midsection and loved her baby with all that she had.

6

———

Manny sat in his home office and powered up his laptop. Blair called this space the garaoffice, because they had taken the small one-bedroom, one-bath apartment over the garage and converted it into his personal office. Manny was unconcerned about its lack of sophistication, because what mattered most was the privacy. Since their daughter Reagan had come into their lives, their home was happy, but no longer quiet.

He brought up the FBI portal login page. His fingers hovered over the keys, ready to tap in Stanford's passcode. Internal warnings sounded loud and clear: That he would get fired if anyone discovered what he was doing. That Blair wouldn't understand why he dove into the case that once destroyed his sobriety, his job, his first marriage.

Considering everything he had done for his partner, Manny thought Stanford should have given him his login credentials outright. But maybe they were even.

In Miami, Manny had pulled his partner's head out from the bottom of a liquor bottle too many times to count. He let

Stanford sleep off his benders at his house, or any other time his wife Alice threw him out for the night.

But when the Muñoz case blew up, when innocent girls died and Manny fell apart, they switched roles. Stanford got his act together long enough to help Manny back on his feet, and for several years after that their friendship was solid.

Then last fall Alice filed for divorce, and something changed between Stanford and him.

Manny couldn't quite put his finger on it, but their relationship was different. Distant. Not on the surface, nothing he could point to. Just a feeling. He glanced at his wedding photo on the corner of his desk. Stanford had been his best man that day.

Manny sank deeper into his black chair and his black mood. The night before had been fitful and sleepless. Today was not the new day he'd hoped it would be.

He typed in Stanford's passcode. Manny couldn't help it. He was flawed in many ways, but at least he knew who he was. He was the sort of man who, when faced with the chance to make wrongs right, would not walk away. No matter the cost.

He navigated to the Muñoz files and noticed a small red exclamation point over the police report tab. He hovered over the icon and the words "New Activity" appeared in a small bubble. He clicked on a police report filed in Crescent City, California.

Jenny Martinsen had fallen over the side of a cliff. The coroner ruled her death an accident.

He expected to feel grief. This young, beautiful girl had survived so much only to have her life cut tragically short by such a stupid accident. But instead of grief, a cold chill sank into the pit of his gut.

The date of her death and the police report were a little over a week old, just after he received the Bible verse note at the office. Jenny had been running on a closed trail that ran cliffside, there was recent rainfall, wet mud, unstable and shifting ground, not the first person in the area to die in the same way. All the specifics stacked up to look like an accident, one of the hallmarks of a Muñoz killing. Manny glanced at the photo of the handwritten note he'd taped to his desk.

He searched through the details of Jenny's file and found her husband's name and number. Manny dialed, then hung up. If Jenny had followed his advice from years ago, her husband might not know anything about the kidnapping. It would be hard for Manny to explain, without completely overwhelming him, why an FBI agent was interested in her death. Now would not be the best time for her husband to discover that his wife had kept secrets.

Instead he called Jenny's father. He let the phone ring twice, then hung up and dialed again. It was the signal he'd set with the girls and their parents so if he ever needed to contact them, they would take his call.

Jenny's father answered on the first ring of the second call. "It was them, wasn't it?" His words were quick, his voice was panicked.

Manny felt Bruce's heart-stabbing loss like it was his own. "I don't know."

He told Bruce about the note he'd received in the mail. Which was one more thing he could have gotten into serious trouble for since the note hadn't yet been substantiated as a valid threat. But today, he told himself, he wasn't representing the federal government. He was nothing more than a concerned father, talking with another concerned father. He was a simple man trying to do what he could to make up for his past mistakes.

"Did Jenny receive anything similar? A piece of paper with numbers that look like a Bible verse or fractions or both?"

"Let me get Kent." Bruce lowered the phone, and the voices in the background were indistinguishable.

Manny paced. Whichever Muñoz family member had gotten to Jenny, it wasn't Ricardo. He was rotting in the ground. Neither was it any of Ricardo's brothers. They were rotting in jail.

This had to have been the work of one or more of Ricardo's children. The Muñoz compound was little more than a breeding ground, a training ground for Ricardo and his wives to raise up their next generation army.

"Manny, I have Kent on the line. I've explained to him that you're an FBI agent who's interested in helping on the case. So, go ahead, Kent."

"Yeah, uh. There was a guy, a minister who visited just a few hours before Jenny's fall. I didn't meet the man but he rattled Jenny. He'd handed her a pamphlet with a Bible verse on it and for some reason that Bible verse caused her so much distress she fainted. I-I— She didn't like strangers, she worked really hard to keep to herself. So I thought she was just overreacting and—I should have—" Kent's voice cracked with emotion. Manny heard him crying in the background.

"He's torn up," Bruce said. "Listen, Manny. The local police called the new church that was promoted on the pamphlet. But when they showed the church administration the still shot from Kent and Jenny's security camera, no one recognized him. They said their minister didn't have dark hair. They also didn't recognize the pamphlet he'd left behind. It was similar to their community leave-behinds, but different. Namely, theirs didn't have that Bible verse printed on the outside. No one knew what the fractions meant. I'm going to send you a text."

Bruce texted Manny a photo of the pamphlet, Kent's research on the verse, and the security footage of the man even though there wasn't a clear shot of his face. He also sent the police report saying they were investigating Jenny's death as an accidental fall.

"It's not an accident," Bruce said. "Jenny would never have gotten that close to the edge and she definitely wouldn't have climbed over that fence. I told the police about the Muñoz family and the kidnapping and they said they're referring the case to you guys.

"That verse proves there's a connection. They're at it again, and I need you out here, Manny. I need you to look into this."

A rock formed in Manny's gut. "Let me see what I can do."

7

———

There was never a rush hour in the old downtown area of Savannah. With the exception of the occasional packed-full trolley, tourists stuck mostly to River Street. Which was just the way the residents liked it. Peaceful.

But tonight, even with the warm, salty breeze blowing through the branches of the live oaks, stirring the long, ragged tendrils of Spanish moss, the vacant streets were not a comfort. In the quiet, I couldn't help but think that a Muñoz was hiding around each corner, waiting to murder me.

My cell phone rang and the caller ID said: Mom.

Guilt wormed through my insides as it always had since I'd killed her favorite daughter.

"Hi, Mom." I tried my best to sound upbeat, cheery.

"How are you, sweetheart?" She spoke her words slowly. When she wanted to draw out the length of any conversation, she set the pace from the beginning. She made it clear when she didn't want to hurry.

My father and I were the only ones who knew mom

before our relocation, and also knew her now. After we cut all ties with former friends and neighbors, we changed our last names. So anyone in her life now had no idea who she really was. It was the same for me.

As a result, our calls with one another were like a meeting of a secret club and they usually went on for an hour or more.

By the same token, my father and I never did more than exchange a few strained pleasantries. Especially since the crash because Catherine had died.

My mind drifted back twenty years, when I was in the ER, after they'd pulled me from the water. My mother held my hand, my father stood three steps behind her. His expression turned to disgust when the doctors peeled away my charred skin in sheets. His upper lip curled with revulsion when they picked shards of glass and steel from my flesh.

"Harper? Harper? Are you there?" My mother's voice brought me back to the thick heat of Savannah.

"I'm on my way to meet a friend, can I call you back later?"

"Oh, honey, I'm so glad you're getting out!" Her tone held obvious relief and I knew what she was really saying. *Oh, honey, I'm so glad you're not being paranoid. So glad you're taking those meds! So glad we don't have to act on the legal agreement we forced you to sign!*

Unlike my father, she never brought up the legal document. But satisfying the terms of our most recent agreement was always at the forefront of my mind. My father's attorneys drew it up at his direction, and it was designed to give him total control.

It worked, because that document dictated my every move.

There had been several agreements before this one. The terms differed, but all of them determined how much control I would have over my freedom, my inheritance, and ultimately, my identity.

My father, being the negotiator that he was, upped the stakes with every new version. The current document put everything on the line. We'd reached the point of all or nothing.

"She's had enough time to develop healthy, mature habits," he said to my mother when she objected to the latest agreement. "She can either do it, or she can't."

By signing the current document, I agreed to live and work in one locale, stay on my medication (as verified by a nurse), check in regularly (every week initially, then every other week when I was deemed trustworthy).

I voiced many objections over the requirement that I live and work in one town, since that eliminated my consulting practice. But his argument was that traveling didn't allow me the opportunity to build relationships. "Healthy relationships are the hallmark of healthy people," he said. "Being dedicated to one workplace every day reveals how well you can get along with people."

It wasn't necessarily an unreasonable test to demonstrate mental and emotional health. If we went to court over the guardianship and inheritance, most any judge would approve his request. So I accepted the terms and signed the agreement.

In return for demonstrating my accomplishment of his objectives, I would receive full control over my trust account, and my parents would agree to rescind their guardianship of me. Then I could begin living my own life.

Of course, if I failed to meet his criteria, he had enough

on me to legally remove my inheritance and my freedoms forever.

"Anyone I know?" she asked gently.

"Levi," I said.

"Oh, the doctor. I like him. I think he's still got a thing for you."

I couldn't see her but I knew she was pointing. She did that. Pointed when there was a point to be made.

"He's seeing someone. Besides, I'm with Nick." I'd told her all about Nick and how much I cared about him. I assumed she and my father did internet searches on him and I hoped they were impressed with what they'd found.

"You're out and about, living your life. That's what matters most." She exhaled and I felt the ease.

Since Catherine's death, making my mother happy was as necessary to me as breathing. For that reason alone I didn't tell her about the note, the almost-intruder—who I thought was a Muñoz family member—or that I carried a gun. And I definitely didn't tell her that I'd seen my long-dead twin, because none of that would have suited her perception that I was moving ahead and living my best life.

"I called because I was re-reading Genesis this morning and I got to the part where God changed Abram's and Sarai's names to Abraham and Sarah. And I couldn't stop thinking of you."

I remembered the story about Abraham and Sarah from the days when I did a daily Bible study. The name Abraham meant Father of Many Nations and the name Sarah meant Princess. God changed their names because He wanted them to remember the promises He'd made to them. But my stomach tightened because I knew the question that was coming.

"Why did that make you think of me?"

"I don't know. It just did. Maybe God's getting ready to do something in your life. Are you still reading your Bible, honey?"

There it was, the question I didn't want to answer. "Not as much as I'd like."

The truth was I didn't read my Bible at all. Not because I didn't feel nudged to; I felt nudged to all the time. But I didn't act on that nudge because each time I considered reading, a cloud of malaise descended over me. A spider's web of discouragement. I was too far gone for help.

I didn't bring that up because my mother would have told me it was better to trust God. She would say: Trust that He is bigger than your problems! Trust that He has the answers! Your strength is found in that trust!

But after all that I'd been through, I couldn't find the strength to trust anyone.

She asked that I call her back when I could.

Three blocks from the restaurant my phone rang again. Caller ID read: No ID. I startled. Then realized it could have been one of the companies I'd interviewed with recently. I took the call.

"Hey, Harper."

The sound of his voice shot me into an instant state of panic, like someone pumped adrenaline into my chest. I ducked left into an old alleyway, between two one-story red brick buildings. The faded white remains of the scripted word Coca-Cola looked down on me.

My heart banged against my ribs and I felt like I'd shrunk from my current 5'7" stature to my twelve-year-old height of four feet even. Without the meds it was very hard to maintain control. I grabbed the gun handle inside my purse.

"This is Agent Hernandez."

I squeezed my eyes against the pain in my chest. "Yes, I know." My voice was strained because Agent Hernandez said that I'd hear from him only if there were reasons to be concerned.

"Sorry to call you out of the blue like this. Your father gave me your number." Agent Hernandez's voice was smooth and calm and professional, as it always had been. He went on about how he'd decided to touch base with each surviving girl and their families, just to check-in.

I could barely hear him over the white noise that whooshed in my ears. It was the sound of blood flow. Or oxygen, since I finally decided to breathe again. I looked across the street and saw several people wandering among the headstones in Colonial Park Cemetery. They strolled, laughed, enjoyed the evening.

"I understand that you settled in Savannah recently? And that you've bought a fixer-upper?"

It was odd to talk with someone, a stranger basically, who knew me before Savannah, before I'd left Miami. I wanted to tell him to keep his voice down. I wanted to tell him about the note. I also wanted a cigarette. If I still smoked I'd be sucking a filterless Camel until it burned my fingers. Such a disgusting habit and I'd had to have my front teeth bonded to cover the stains the cigarettes left behind. They only ever calmed me down long enough to light up another one. But at the moment I would have done anything for those ten seconds of peace.

Have a real smoke, have a Camel. The old ad slogan slid through my mind. The memory of the strong, smooth flavor ran across my taste buds.

"Yes," I answered curtly, the irritation in my voice bristly and nearly three-dimensional.

After a long, quiet moment of perhaps not knowing what to say, he said, "Right. Good. That's good."

"Why are you calling?" I almost hoped he'd say they had proof that the Muñoz family was after me. Because then I could tell him about the note and I knew he'd take me seriously.

"I uh, well, as I said, I just wanted to check in," he said quietly. "I wanted to make sure you were okay."

That he should ever think I would ever be okay turned my panic to fury quicker than a flash of jagged lightning. All the old if onlys tumbled through my mind: If only Agent Hernandez had followed up on our neighbors' complaints and concerns about Diego, the black-toothed man. The odd-job handyman who gave candy and small gifts to their kids in unguarded moments. Who took photos of their homes.

If only Agent Hernandez hadn't been a drunk, and had done his job, he would have found his connection to the Muñoz family, an organization who ran well-known drug and kidnapping rings.

But he didn't.

One week later my sister and I were taken from our bedroom in the middle of the night.

Not long after that, my sister was dead.

"What makes you think that I will ever be okay?"

He made a noise, something between a grunt and a sigh, and I felt him deflate on the other end of the line.

Two odd-looking twenty-somethings stopped short at the entry to the alleyway and stared at me. The twiggy female with her spiky green hair looked like a coked-up elf. They took one look at me and ran.

It was then that I realized my gun was out of my purse and I gestured with it when I spoke.

My parents, therapists, and countless physicians had

begged me to drop my guard, drop the paranoia and for the sake of all things holy, drop that dangerous gun! Each time I refused, I'd been met with more meds, more counseling, and more book titles on trust and healing. And, of course, tighter reins from my father.

I shoved the gun back into its holder in my purse, but I kept my palm on the handle.

Agent Hernandez rattled on with a vague apology I'd heard before, and didn't want to hear again. If he was about to work in any sort of advice on relaxing and living life I'd hang up on him.

Because I'd seen the evil in my kidnappers' eyes firsthand. They had no rock bottom, no care when it came to human life. Their only rule was a strict and strange loyalty to family.

In the same way I'd seen ranchers heat iron and press their symbol to the side of their cattle, my body, mind and spirit were branded with the memory of that evil. A part of me was owned by that family.

I wiped the sweat from the back of my neck and turned toward Colonial Park Cemetery again. A gray-haired couple made their way around the headstones. They held hands, smiled, hugged. So in tune with one another, so comforted and familiar with one another, they moved like a well-rehearsed dance. It was obvious they'd been together for so long they no longer needed words.

I felt the flicker of old memories—feeling safe and happy when I woke up on sun-drenched Saturday mornings in my sister's and my bedroom, the heart-warming scent of pancakes and bacon wafting up from the kitchen, the sound of golden-era cartoons echoing up the stairs.

There were no stressors then. Nothing to fear, and we planned our lives like we thought we could. My sister said she would be a lawyer, fighting for justice, righting wrongs. She said she knew there was someone special for her, they would marry before she turned thirty, that they would have two children, girls. I said I would be a jeweler, that I wanted to know all about stones, I wanted two girls as well. We agreed to have a double wedding, to live on the same block, and to raise our children together.

Before I turned ten I was certain of true love and happily ever afters. Before the kidnapping I was certain of hope. After the kidnapping, I was certain of nothing.

But there was Nick, an unexpected gift. There was a fit and a flow to us. And I could see myself in him. My best self. Maybe the most revealing sign, the one that pointed toward something inevitable, was that when I was around him I tended to think only of the future. The past never reared its ugly head.

From the couple's location in the cemetery, I knew they'd found the burial site of Button Gwinnett, the most famous resident of the historical graveyard because he was a signer of the Declaration of Independence.

He'd lost his life to Lachlan McIntosh in a duel. Using the bullet to settle irreconcilable differences was how it was done back then. I squeezed the gun handle. It was how I would do it today if I had to.

"If you're certain there's no new information I need to be aware of, then I really don't get the point of your call. Unless you've changed your mind about doing those background checks I asked for," I said, referring to several requests I'd made of him a while back.

Before I moved to Savannah, when I began dating Nick, I'd emailed Agent Hernandez and asked him to please, please investigate. Do background checks, run his photos through the system, just do whatever he could do so I would know the truth.

He said that he couldn't. Wouldn't. That what I needed to do was to live my life. Carefully, cautiously, but unafraid. He'd suggested I try different meds to ease the anxiety and suspicion.

He sighed heavily, and I couldn't tell if he was frustrated or internally debating my request. Finally he said, "I wish I could, but at this point I can't. Remember, no matter what's happened, you can get through it. Call me if—if there are any new developments in your life that concern you. Do your research on whomever you associate with. I wish I could do more—"

I hung up.

8

———

Historic live oaks shaded the last three blocks to the restaurant. I walked at a fast clip, studying each person I saw for any resemblance to the Muñoz family. The crumpled notepaper was never far from my mind. The gun was never far from my hand.

Hernandez. Because he'd screwed up, I lost my sister.

I lost my life.

I lost myself.

I made a decision never to speak with him again. He wrote off my concerns as crazy anyway. Just like my parents.

So there was no point.

The cathedral bells of St. John the Baptist echoed across the city as they had for over 100 years. I looked above the trees, at the spires, toward the source of their melodic song. I thought of Bunny in her ghostly white gown, how she lived with loss as a lifelong burden, and she reminded me a great deal of my own mother.

I thought of the day I finally left home. I stood at the top of our long driveway with my mother. My heart aching from the deep emptiness of all things unsaid, all dreams unful-filled, all things unfinished.

Her eyes brimmed with tears, her breath was sour from booze. She said, "Make something beautiful of your life, Harper. If you won't do it for yourself, then do it for me. Do it for Catherine. Do all the things Catherine will never have the chance to: Fall in love. Get married. Have children. Travel the world. Live your dreams!"

She sobbed. She made me promise.

I'd never known it before the accident. In fact I really believed it was the exact opposite. Because it's an easy misunderstanding when so much care, concern and atten-tion goes to the child who needs it most.

But on that day, when the weight of my mother's lost dreams left me feeling sick to my stomach, I knew for certain. Catherine had been my mother's favorite, and my mother would never get over that loss.

My phone buzzed, a short text from Nick just to say hello. To let me know he's thinking of me, and missing me. Unexpected warmth spread through my chest.

In my mind's eye I saw my sister tapping the top of her wrist.

It's time.

I stopped walking.

If you did come to me, what did you mean?

That it's time to honor the promise I made to our mother, that it's time I lived? Before I miss out on life completely?

I peeled back the cuff on my sleeve and rubbed my thumb over the initials and surrounding angel wings I'd had tattooed on the inside of my wrist: C.S.

C.S. for Catherine Silveria.

I needed to live for her.

For Catherine.

Another text came in from Nick with an x and an o. This time love burst through my heart like a fireworks show on the Fourth of July.

I took a double breath.

I walked toward the restaurant again, thinking how Nick and I had only been together for a short while. And yet I'd thought more times than I could count of how perfect we were together, and how I wanted to share a life with him.

I felt the weight of the gun in my purse. My gut felt the weight of the note that had been left in my window.

Like a bullet to the forehead, I was struck by how quickly life could change, how quickly lifelong love and dreams could disappear.

And I decided.

I wouldn't let my dreams get stamped out again. If they'd found me, and I knew they had, I would figure out who and where they were. I would stop them.

It was time.

9

The deep-fried scent of oil hung thick inside the Mexican restaurant. It clung to my skin, the inside of my nose, my lungs. If I hadn't felt so unsafe on the streets I would have asked Levi if we could go to a different restaurant.

Levi sat in the corner booth, moving a straw around a nearly-empty margarita glass. A young waitress with too much makeup reached the table before I arrived. She set a new margarita in front of him. Her smile was wide and flirty, raising no doubt she'd found interest in Levi's tall handsomeness. His blue eyes, blond hair and tanned skin made him a heart-stopper, a head-turner. He barely brightened at her attention and even then only briefly, like a royal prince who could afford to be choosy.

I scanned the restaurant. No one paid me any attention. I made my way to Levi. He hugged me, gestured to the other side of the booth and ordered a margarita for me. I shook my head and before I could say no he said, "When I was here for lunch the other day, I researched all the ingredients for you, it's safe."

I didn't take anyone's word for it when it came to my food allergies. Which was why I typically stayed away from restaurants altogether. Even though Levi was a physician, even though he understood the seriousness of my condition and even though I knew he was a friend, I told the waitress I'd have a glass of wine.

Levi gave me a closed-lip half-smile tinged with disappointment. Maybe even some sadness, which I found annoying. I also found it familiar and I tried to remember where I'd seen that exact smile before.

"I thought you might want to try something new?" he asked, as if the margarita was still an option. "You know—branch out. Enjoy life."

I raised an eyebrow. "Drinking a life-threatening margarita from this hole-in-the-wall restaurant could accomplish that?"

"We have to start somewhere." He closed his lips, the weak half-smile returned, and it hit me.

His expression was remarkably similar to Catherine's worried smile from the night before. Nearly identical. I shifted in the booth and tried to avoid a wide crack in the red leather.

"You need this after the adventure you had last night."

I said nothing.

Levi took my silence as an opportunity and asked the waitress to bring the margarita as well as the ingredient lists.

When the margarita arrived I pushed my hand into my purse and traced the outline of my EpiPen. I didn't need reminding that one errant drop of peanut oil made my throat close like a boxer's fist.

Levi and I talked about work, schedules and requisite vacations that we wanted to take before the weather turned cold. I scanned the restaurant again. No one looked suspicious, no one seemed to notice me at all. I was a quiet sort and, because of the conservative way I dressed, invisible to most people.

I drew in a deep breath, feeling safe with Levi, being one in a crowd. Not at all looking forward to going back home and being alone. Being with that note.

Levi took a long sip and nodded at the lower left side of my face. "You've never told me what your scars are from."

My guard went up. So did my hand, and I readjusted my scarf. I made a face like he was nuts. "I did tell you. It was a car accident."

Levi adjusted the silverware in front of him to perfect alignment. "In med school they taught us how to spot signs when someone is lying. Because people will lie about their habits and their histories to hide things they aren't ready to face. You know, sometimes a woman will tell you she walked into a door, when really she's in an abusive relationship." He cut his eyes toward me.

He gave several more examples of how and when patients lie to their own detriment and my stomach tightened a little more with each story. Outwardly I chuckled. "Are you saying I'm covering for a former abuser?"

"I'm saying I don't think you've recovered emotionally from whatever happened. Otherwise you would be able to talk about it more openly." He raised his glass like he'd made his point and he took a long pull from the straw. "So, maybe not hiding from a former abuser. But you are hiding something."

I didn't say anything.

Levi responded to my quiet with a soft gaze filled with compassion, like it would have been okay with him if I wanted to open up. I appreciated his care. I appreciated his kindness. I appreciated his friendship. Truth be known I would have loved nothing more than to confide in him, to confess. I thought if I could, I might feel somewhat human again.

But the rules Agent Hernandez set for us were very specific. Once we'd changed our names, our appearance, and our locations, none of us—neither the girls nor their families—were allowed to discuss any details of the kidnapping, the escape, the crash, the rescue, the depositions— nothing. Any one slip could cause a crack in the facade of our assumed identities. One crack could lead to another, then another. Those exposed details could lead someone in the Muñoz family right to us.

"Whatever happened that caused those scars, I think it's holding you back from living a better life." Levi leaned in, didn't wait for me to respond. "I realize that I'm sticking my nose where it doesn't belong, but I care about you. We've been friends for a while now and— Well, you're in that big house all by yourself—I guess there's Magnolia, your cat. But who do you talk with—I mean really share things with?"

His comment about Magnolia hit me like a brick to the side of the head. I thought about mentioning Nick but Nick and I didn't have much of a history. "My career keeps me busy—"

"It's probably just me. But I think success isn't worth much if you come home to an empty house every night. I think it's the deep connection with another person that makes life worth living." He formed a fist and shook it in the air, like a life worth living was worth fighting for.

I felt some invisible force inside of me fall.

It must have shown on the outside, too, because he relaxed his fist, winced, looked down. "I'm sorry. I'm not phrasing this well at all."

He sighed hard, like he was going to try again. "It seems like you're dragging around a heavy burden of some kind and I hate to see that. You're such a good person, you deserve a good life. Look, whatever happened, you don't have to tell me about it. I just want you to know that you can get through it.

"I tell my patients this all the time—we can get beyond whatever life throws at us. But we have to go through it. The recovery, you know? There aren't any shortcuts."

Levi wore that smile again and I wanted to throw my margarita at it. His advice was similar to what Agent Hernandez had said repeatedly over the years.

"I'm sure you already know all that. My point is that I'm here for you. I don't want you to live life like a martyr."

Martyr.

How I hated that word.

He extended a hand across the table, palm up in an invitation. Slowly, cautiously, I put my hand in his.

He turned my hand over, pushed my cuff up and pointed to the edge of the tattoo of Catherine's initials and angel's wings. "You lost someone you loved?"

I'd known that putting Catherine's real initials on my skin was a potential crack that could shine a light on my true identity. I also knew it was obscure enough that no one could figure out who I was by that detail alone.

A pretty brunette—tall, slender, flirty, a friend of Levi's from the hospital—stopped by our table. "Levi! Hey!"

I pulled my hand from his.

Levi stood and hugged her. "Harper, this is Sheila Gabrick."

Sheila gave me a once over. Her eyes lingered on my scarf. She shook my hand. "Levi and I work together at the hospital."

"That's great," I said.

"I don't want to interrupt. Just wanted to let you know that it looks like North Dakota Children's Regional is joining DHS, systems are compatible."

Levi stepped closer to her. "Really?"

I excused myself and made my way to the ladies' room. I pressed my thumb against my tattoo. Once at the sink I ran cold water over the inside of both wrists, combatting the effects of Savannah's heat, fresh fear and old fear. I looked in the mirror, lowered my scarf and examined the ropey scars left by hot flames, jagged glass and mangled steel. If I'd left those exposed, they would have gotten more stares than the scarf.

I dried my hands and drew in a couple of deep breaths. I didn't like it when someone nosed too far in my past.

I'd done quite a bit of research on Levi. He went to the University of Tennessee for undergrad, Emory for med school, then the Children's Hospital of Atlanta for his internship. He moved to Savannah so he could work in a research hospital that focused on finding cures for pediatric diseases. He was a good guy all the way around.

But I still wasn't going to open up to him.

When I arrived at the table, Sheila was gone and Levi had placed a coaster beneath my margarita. Like a gentleman he half stood when he saw me. "Sorry about that. Sheila's our rep with Data Health Search. It's this big research thing, helps us diagnose patients more quickly and —anyway." He waved his hand like none of that was relevant. "Look, I'm sorry about sticking my nose in your business earlier. I made you feel uncomfortable and that was the exact opposite of what I was trying to do.

"You're smart, beautiful, kind." He put his hand on mine. "But you stay hidden away like something's weighing on you. Feel free to tell me to buzz off." He squeezed my hand. His laugh was friendly and lighthearted.

My instinct was to tell him to buzz off. But his smile reached the lonely places inside my heart and I offered him my well-practiced cover story. "I lost my sister in that accident, and I guess there is a part of me that will never get over that."

He studied my face. "I'm so sorry."

I inhaled and let that new information sit between us.

"Older? Younger?" he asked.

"Younger," I said. "She was younger."

"You were driving, I guess?"

All internal alarms rang at DEFCON one. I shook my head because Agent Hernandez had been insistent that we should never let anyone know I was the one driving that boat. I shrugged. "I don't really love talking about the accident. I've made as much peace with my past as anyone could."

I was lying, of course. I hadn't made any peace with what happened. I blamed Agent Hernandez and the Muñoz family. I also blamed myself.

He studied me for a moment. His gaze was intense. "I understand. It's never easy. I just wanted you to know that I'm here if you need a friend."

I looked at my margarita. As much as I didn't want to drink it, I was prepared to do it, then take a shot from the EpiPen and make a trip to the ER if it would bring the current conversation to a close.

"Thanks." I brought the straw to my lips. "Maybe I'll take you up on that sometime."

He put his hand over his stomach and stared at his drink. "I think something might be wrong with the margaritas."

10

We walked back to our neighborhood. Levi asked lots of questions about the progress I'd made on my home renovation. I kept a careful eye out and touched my gun several times to make sure I had it at the ready.

Then he said, "How about letting me take you out Friday night? I've heard good things about The Alligator Soul Restaurant."

I turned. There was something different in his tone, something soft and questioning. His blue eyes were searching, and I was so caught off guard I stopped walking.

"What?" I asked. Not because I didn't hear what he said.

He raised his eyebrows in response, and his smile turned sly.

"Oh," I heard myself say stupidly. "I'd love to. But I've been seeing someone."

Levi stepped back, put his hands on his hips. "You are not."

My laugh sounded nervous. This was the fourth or fifth time he'd asked me out and it was uncanny how bad our timing was. "Yes, it's been a few weeks now," I said like I was dealing with some sort of an illness.

He shook his head like he couldn't believe it. We began walking again.

"I thought you were seeing someone named Tina?" I asked.

"Eh—" Levi shrugged like he'd lost interest, or maybe never had any. He put his hands in his front pockets, nudged me with his elbow and flashed a half-grin.

We shared a friendly laugh together.

We walked the rest of the way home in awkward silence.

We reached Columbia Square and sat together on one of the green benches. I studied the area for some sign of the fog that had slithered through the night before, some sign of the dandelion that my sister had wished upon.

But there was nothing.

Nothing but the romance and mystery of Savannah's bygone era—the ancient brick streets, the graceful architecture and the elegant beauty of one of its many historic squares.

In all likelihood, I had imagined her.

A strange loneliness curled around me and squeezed.

Levi and I sat together on a park bench.

My house was on the far corner, a gray beauty from the 1700s that I'd bought to update and upgrade. The plan was to sell it once it was completely rehabbed. At least that's what I'd told my parents. But I'd fallen in love with the house, the square and the neighbors, and I didn't want to sell.

I looked at my living room windows and knew the crumpled note was just beyond it. Soon enough I would have to deal with that. Worry churned in my stomach.

Levi's apartment was on the opposite side of the street,

in a building on the far corner that was also from the 1700s. Sadly it had been divided into two spacious condos years ago.

"Are you feeling better?" I asked.

"Yeah." He pressed a hand against his stomach. "Normally I could digest steel. It was the mix, I think. Too sour. Next time we'll find a better place for you to try something new."

Bunny, the woman who lived directly opposite my house, walked toward us with her white chihuahua named Eudora. As in Eudora Welty, the Southern Pulitzer-winning author from the sixties and seventies. Eudora wore the tiniest pink tutu with silver sequins on the edges.

"How are y'all doin' tonight?" Bunny's ever-the-hostess smile accented her slow, Southern drawl. She looked like she'd just stepped out of a department store window. Her brightly colored and perfectly coordinated outfits were her standard, whether she was gardening or off to a hospital fundraiser. She wore her signature gold jewelry. Loads of it. Tasteful earrings and multiple strands of necklaces, one with her husband's wedding band.

She twirled her fingers around Eudora, and Bunny's gold rings clicked against one another. On cue, the small dog stood on her hind legs and turned in circles. Levi and I applauded Eudora, chatted with Bunny about the heat and how we hadn't had any rain in over two weeks.

"Oh, there's Walter." She smiled and waved to Mr. Miller. He weeded his front flower bed on the opposite side of the square. "Haven't seen him out of the house since Betty died two months ago. She was a real pill that one, but I know Walter's adjustment to being without her is hard just the same.

"She was close friends with Jim Williams, who restored

so many historic homes in the area. Of course he's not remembered for that. He's known for killing that boy in his home and that book."

"*Midnight in the Garden of Good and Evil*," I said.

"The one," Bunny pointed at me, and again she reminded me of my mother.

"How long have you lived in this neighborhood?" Levi asked with a friendly smile. "I'll bet you know everything about everyone."

"Well, let's see." She adjusted a gold cuff that she once told me she'd picked up at a bazaar in Egypt. She glanced toward the house like it might be listening. "We moved in when the boys were small. Tucker's writing career was still just an idea in the back of his head. So, I guess I'm coming up on forty years now. The house is really too big for just me and Eudora. But you know I raised my boys there and it holds so many good memories. When I finally leave this old house it'll be feet first."

She waved again to Mr. Miller, then patted my knee. "I hope you'll find time to stop by for that glass of tea. The offer is good anytime."

I smiled, enjoying the warmth of her friendship. "I'd love that."

Bunny patted Levi on the knee, too. "Always good to see you, sweetheart. Don't be a stranger now."

She headed toward Mr. Miller, and for a few minutes Levi stayed quiet. The splashing from the fountain and the birds were the only sounds. I watched Bunny with Mr. Miller. She touched his arm and smiled brightly. He stood a little taller in her company.

"How did you meet this guy?" Levi asked.

"Who?"

"The guy you're dating," he said.

"Oh, Nick," I said.

He nodded.

"Business," I said. "A Savannah client of his was renovating her home over on Calhoun Square and she found this black box hidden in one of the living room walls. Turns out it was filled with pearl necklaces, ruby earrings and several diamond rings from before the Civil War. Of course the box also held several stacks of Confederate money, which is as worthless today as it was in November 1865."

Levi cocked his head in question.

"The date of the final ceasefire of the Civil War."

"Ah," he said. "That era is your specialty, right?"

I nodded.

"So, you're working for him?"

"No," I said, stifling a wave of worry about needing to find work. "He retained me to provide a valuation on the jewelry. Things just sort of evolved from there."

I had often been asked by firms around the country to provide valuations for their clients and that specialty had allowed me to keep traveling. But it was also why I'd moved to Savannah after my father said he didn't want me traveling anymore.

The city's architecture had survived the war intact, and as such, many inheritances from the era were still local. I'd applied to several local appraisal firms and hoped for the best.

"Is he divorced? Kids?" Levi asked.

"Divorced. Short-lived marriage, apparently. No kids," I said.

"Huh. What's his last name?" he asked.

"Chamberlain."

He shook his head like the name wasn't familiar.

"Is it serious?"

I shrugged, not willing to place any bets. But I felt a brief smile pull at my lips.

He punched his heart with the top of his fist like I'd wounded him.

I gave him a gentle shove. "Oh, stop. You could have any woman you wanted."

He chuckled, but it was strained. "Well, if you ever change your mind..."

"Levi, your friendship, our friendship—I've really appreciated it and I hope this doesn't negatively affect—"

"It's all good." He waved his hand at me, like I didn't need to worry. "I feel the same way."

A gray pigeon landed on the sidewalk and gave us a side glance.

Levi stared at the bird, and his jaw muscles worked.

I decided it was probably time to bring our evening to an end. Even though I dreaded having to face the note alone. I also dreaded the anxiety that was going to unleash when I did face it.

"So, no go with Tina, huh?" I asked, buying more time.

He continued to stare at the bird. "I thought I liked her. She's smart, we had a lot in common. But the more I got to know her, I realized I only found her interesting."

As often happened, a fitting line from a book came to mind. Like guidance somehow, making things more clear. "I wasn't actually in love, but I felt a sort of tender curiosity."

He turned to me, his eyebrows drawing close together in question.

"It's a line from *The Great Gatsby*."

He nodded, like something had just clicked for him. "So those books in your front room aren't just for looks, huh?"

"Nothing better than a good book. Especially a classic." I

cringed inwardly, still painfully uncomfortable sharing any small truth about the real me.

"Now when do I get to see all these renovations you've been working on?" Levi checked his watch, and I knew the night was over.

"Next week?" I offered. "I'll give you a tour of the progress and then we can have a glass of wine next to the pool. It's nice out there at night. Always a good breeze."

"You let me know which day and I'll bring the wine."

We hugged and he held on a second longer than I did. Then we headed in opposite directions.

I reached my front steps and turned. As was typical, Levi was halfway inside his front door, waiting for our wave good-night to one another. It was a simple gesture, but I looked forward to it like a bite-sized, after-dinner chocolate.

I triple locked the front door behind me, set the security alarm and checked the outdoor security cameras to make sure they were recording. I moved the gun from my purse to the coffee table. Made sure the other guns around the house were loaded and ready, including the air pistol in my bedroom.

I stared at the notepaper on the floor, my heart pumping, my head spinning, my breath quickening.

Cautiously, I picked it up by a corner, like I'd lifted a rat by its tail. I laid it on the coffee table. Then I went to the study where I downed triple doses of every natural anti-anxiety supplement I could find.

I smoothed the notepaper open:

24: 19-22

1/12 1/13 1/16 1/20 1/10 2/17 1/6

I OPENED my Bible to Deuteronomy. The numbers on the note synced up with the same verse I'd seen painted on the walls at the Muñoz compound. It was the same verse they'd used to justify their kidnapping, rape, ransom and drug dealing.

The fractions didn't make sense, I'd never seen those before.

I felt the same old nudge to read my Bible and I wondered if my mother was praying for me. Still, I refused.

I realized Deuteronomy wasn't written on the paper.

"If I searched through the Bible I could probably find numerous passages that sync up with these numbers. Maybe that's why I feel a nudge to read the Bible?" I said aloud.

Magnolia leaped onto the far side of the square coffee table, sat and glared at me. Like she disagreed. Like she was the outer manifestation of the still, small voice within. Like she knew I should know better.

I threw the notepaper to the floor.

I went to the butler's pantry, made a tea of chamomile and skullcap and returned to the couch where I had a full view of Columbia Square. Magnolia remained on the coffee table, still wearing an unerring expression of disapproval.

I sat still in my armed isolation. It was loud in contrast to the camaraderie I'd enjoyed with Bunny and Levi.

I thought, as I often did, of Matthew. The boy who'd fallen on the dock when we were making our escape from the compound. At the time, I thought he was trying to stop us from leaving.

Since then, I realized he had probably been trying to save little Alejandro who had stowed away on the boat.

I picked up the notepaper, studied it again.

This didn't reference some other book or chapter in the Bible. This was about the verse in Deuteronomy.

Of course it was.

I didn't know what the fractions meant. But I knew the note was put in my window by a Muñoz. There was no other reasonable explanation.

My hand shook, the notepaper fell to the floor.

There wasn't anyone I could discuss this with. No one I could run it by.

Nerves knotted tightly in my chest and my gut. I felt sick. Dizzy. I sipped the tea.

The cicadas' song buzzed from the treetops. The bells from the Cathedral of St. John the Baptist rang in the distance. I curled into the far corner of the couch, tucked my gun at my side and was reminded, not so fondly, of a quote from a Faulkner novel. "The past is never dead. It's not even past."

The email alert dinged loud from my phone. With a start I realized I'd fallen asleep on the couch. I rubbed my eyes, and squinted at my phone screen: 3:01 a.m.

The email was from Max Crandall, owner of Tatnall Antique Appraisals, one of the businesses I'd sent my resume to a couple of weeks ago.

Dear Harper,

Thank you for sending your resume. The depth of your experience is, indeed, impressive. Two of my senior associates and I would love to know more about your past projects to see if they're a fit for our current needs. I'm out of town through Monday. But I've tentatively set up Tues 9 a.m. for an interview. Let us know if that works.

Sincerely,

Max

Truth be told, I felt that my life as a consultant, with its lack of routine, kept my identity more hidden and anonymous. But my father's terms had to be met, so I typed out a thank-you email and accepted.

I lay there considering my own bed, until I decided that even if I went upstairs, I wouldn't be able to go back to sleep. I sat upright, looked out the front window, searching for some sign of Catherine or the fog.

There was nothing.

You stopped the meds, the nasty voice in the back of my head whispered. *And now you've started seeing things.*

I pushed my hands through my hair, backed away from the window.

I went to the little butler's pantry tucked between the dining room and the spiral staircase. I pushed the button on the side wall to call the dumb waiter up from the spacious kitchen downstairs. Then loaded in yesterday's teacup, and sent the dumbwaiter back downstairs. The porcelain rattled and the wires and gears churned in the silence.

This tiny jewel of a room had been used centuries ago to help serve meals in the formal dining room. I used it to make coffee and tea. I inhaled the dark, spicy scent of tea leaves and coffee beans, then poured the water, started the hotpot, and dropped a teaspoon's worth of black tea into the strainer.

I flexed my toes against the original, slightly-warped hardwoods. They were cold beneath my bare feet. I watched the water in the clear pot. Levi's comments ran circles in my head.

Martyr.

How I hated that word.

I waited for the water to boil. I checked the coffee table, my handgun was in plain view. Like a security blanket, just knowing it was close-by and within reach made me feel better.

I opened a drawer in the tiny tea and coffee room and checked to make sure the pepper spray, several knives and a small handgun I'd hidden were still there. My father wouldn't like all the weapons I'd hidden throughout the house.

He didn't want problem-child-Harper firing bullets into her new, going-far-better-than-he-expected life. But I was going to keep doing whatever was necessary to protect myself.

I made the tea and dreaded my next step. Researching Max's background—or investigating anyone's background—for connections to the Muñoz family made me feel like I was fumbling in the dark for some light switch I desperately needed to flip but could never find.

Yet I knew it was there.

Halfway to the couch, I spotted the note. The timing of its arrival in the window coincided with Max's invitation to interview. Anxiety wriggled through my veins like a live wire. The teacup rattled against the saucer.

This wasn't a flashback. It was lingering terror—an endless nightmare that began over twenty years ago and wouldn't end.

I put the teacup down, wrapped my arms around myself and squeezed, like I could stop the tremor.

This was a bad one.

The worst I'd had in a long time.

If I missed something it wouldn't be death that awaited me, not immediately. Because not only had I given testimony that put Ricardo Muñoz away, but I had also driven the boat that killed little Alejandro.

We will never forget...

Before the darkness could swallow me whole, I crawled to my office where I kept a new bottle of Pharma GABA in my desk drawer. The Naturopathic doctor I'd seen recently said the regular dose was two tablets, so I flipped the cap and chewed four. Then I took two more.

They tasted like Sweetarts. They were supposed to function like anti-anxiety meds by raising my GABA levels, without any side effects.

I closed my eyes. Waited for the supplements to enter my bloodstream. Reminded myself that no one was going to do my due diligence for me. Not my parents, not Agent Hernandez. Nor was I going to run again.

And then, as I had literally millions of times before, I also reminded myself that I couldn't change the past. There were no redos. I'd made my choices, Catherine was dead. All I could do was move forward.

I swallowed a few more supplements. Then, after a few minutes, the shaking slowed. The panic dulled to a minor roar.

I went to the bathroom and splashed water on my face.

I looked pale. Drawn.

I went back to the main room and grabbed the pile of yearbooks I'd ordered. I returned to the couch. I felt hollow and tired, like I'd spent the last several years crawling through the dark toward a pinpoint of light.

On the About Us page of the Tatnall Antique Appraisals website, Max's biography said he'd lived in Savannah most of his life. It also listed his college and graduation year. So, after I'd sent Max my resume, I contacted the local public and private schools and ordered yearbooks from the timeframe when Max would have been there.

I sipped the tea. My hands still weren't steady and the tea sloshed over the edge. I searched the indexes of each yearbook and found him in the public elementary school and the private junior high and high schools. Tatnall, the name of his company, was also listed and belonged to a girl named Charlotte. The name Muñoz wasn't listed, no surprise there.

In the high school yearbook, Max had been in almost all of the group photos, including those from foreign trips. He usually had his arm around various petite, attractive, dark-haired girls. A real gadabout.

None of that surprised me, either.

Max and I initially met in a coffee shop in Beaufort, S.C., a nearby town. Next thing I knew Max came up to me and said, "Oh, it's you!"

When our eyes met, the attraction was strangely fierce, instant, devastating. The kind that made the wiser voice inside of me, the voiceless voice, nudge me to walk away. Because anything that intense probably wouldn't last. Probably shouldn't last. Probably wouldn't go well if it did last.

It was a strange attraction because physically he wasn't my type. He was polished, but not particularly handsome, so his looks weren't what drew me in. He was one of those men who met me where I was. He not only saw me, he wanted me to *know* that he saw me.

His eye contact made it clear that he was interested. Interested in making me happy, knew how to make me happy. If only I'd give him the chance.

I'd picked up on a glint of desperation in his expression that day. Like he was a prisoner on parole, and determined to make the most of his tethered freedom.

I often felt alone and lonely. If I were being honest, that kind of attention from a man was like finding an unexpected spring in the middle of a desert. But I knew that men who targeted a woman like that, who acted like a prescribed remedy to whatever ailed you, it was for their own gain.

I'd caught myself wringing my hands. I'd turned to leave without comment.

He stopped me and said, "I was shooting the local architecture and I think I accidentally caught you in two of my photos!"

He showed me the digital images on his camera screen and there I was, looking up at the home he'd been photographing.

The shots of me did look like an incidental inclusion. But I couldn't shake the feeling that he'd targeted me in some bizarre setup. Neither could I discount that that feeling was a part of my ever-increasing paranoia.

"Oh!" I said. "How about that."

We stood there waiting for our coffees, a bit of awkward silence between us, until he asked, "What do you do for a living?"

"I'm a consultant for various appraisal firms."

"Do you have a specialty?" he asked.

"Antiques. Civil War and pre-Civil War jewelry and antiques."

He seemed strangely unsurprised. Perhaps because of the historic area. He handed me his card. "Would you send me your resume and a list of clients or references? My firm often has a need for that type of appraiser."

I signed on to the three online investigative tools I'd purchased a couple of weeks ago, and typed in Max's full name as it was listed on the Tatnall website. There were no known lawsuits and only two addresses for him—his childhood home and his current home.

His childhood home, a very modest house in a low-income area, was less than fifteen miles from his current home. His dad was listed as unknown. His mom, Jane Crandall, still lived in town. I input her name and found that she lived in a much nicer neighborhood today. Maybe Max bought her a new house once he earned a good living.

I opened a private browser and typed in: Jane Crandall Savannah. A social media page was the top result. I hated social media and considered it a bizarre experiment in narcissistic posturing. But I didn't complain about the amount of information people stupidly shared. As a research tool it served my purpose.

Jane posted lots of pictures of her and Max through the years. In many of the early photos there was an amber bottle of beer in her hand, and several more sitting in the background on chunky plaid furniture. She looked quite different today than she did twenty years ago. Her once-beautiful features had been transformed by deep facial lines, puffy under-eye bags and the leathery complexion of a lifelong drinker who enjoyed the sun.

Her most recent post was a side-by-side photo of her working in a toll booth on Jekyll Island against a more recent photo of her floating in a small, in-ground pool while holding a cigarette and a green beer bottle. The caption read: "I've come a long way, baby!"

I did the mental math on the distance between the Jekyll toll booth and their Savannah home—hour and a half one way. Three hours of commute time and the long hours of shift work probably meant Max must have fended for himself quite often as a child. I doubted she could have afforded babysitters.

I scratched the dates onto my notepad and compared them to the dates when the police raided the Muñoz compound. Max's and Jane's life began in Savannah roughly twenty years ago. No mention anywhere of birthplaces or any history prior to that. They could have escaped the Miami compound and begun new, anonymous lives in

Savannah. As the FBI suspected the Muñoz wives and children did.

Jane had been attractive enough in her earlier days to be one of Ricardo Muñoz's wives. Max was dark-complected enough to have had a father of South American descent. I nervously tapped the edge of my laptop.

Under normal circumstances this was enough of a coincidence to make me back away from the opportunity. But I had to be gainfully employed by the end of the month or my father would act on the agreement I'd signed. He'd say that my inability to find steady employment was due to overactive paranoia or some other mental defect. Given my history, it would be hard to prove him wrong on that.

I searched the platform for any groups relating to their junior high or high school years. Up popped one dedicated to getting the word out for reunions.

I filled out the Why Do You Want to Join form with the generic name Susan Brown and Go Bulldogs! in the comments section. My membership was approved immediately.

The page was incredibly social and seemed to be what this high school crew used for staying in touch. People not only poured out sacred details from their own lives onto the page, but whatever they happened to know about others as well. Photos and newspaper clippings were included.

I pieced together various gossipy bits and discovered that Max married Charlotte Tatnall shortly after they graduated from high school. She was blond and well put together, but not pretty. In every photo she was conservatively dressed, like she'd just walked out of Talbot's. They had one daughter, Annabelle, born just shy of seven months after the wedding.

Charlotte often used the word preemie when describing

her. Like, "Look at my beautiful Belle at her coming-out party. Hard to believe she used to be that delicate preemie!" Or "My beautiful Belle is on her way to law school! Being born a preemie gave her a fighting spirit!"

Given my experience with Max, I figured shotgun wedding was the more likely scenario.

Charlotte was well-moneyed and old-moneyed. I clicked on a video of her standing next to the newel in her historic family home on Monterey Square. She said, "My ancestors had a beautiful ivory button inlaid right at the center top of the newel post when they paid off the mortgage. A common practice back in the day—referred to as the brag button or the mortgage button!" The camera closed in on the brag button. After a few seconds she flipped the camera around for a wide-smiling, selfie view and walked toward the home's front room.

"These bookshelves are original to the home, and the Haviland china displayed here is the exact pattern chosen by our nation's former first lady, Mary Todd Lincoln.

"When she arrived at The White House, she was expected to entertain, but there wasn't any official White House china! So, she worked closely with Haviland of France on this design and their dedicated team of artists hand-painted each piece."

Charlotte flipped the camera around again and zoomed in on the center of one of the dinner plates showing an eagle clutching arrows and olive branches. It was, indeed, elegant and extraordinary.

"My great-great-grandmother fell in love with the reddish-purple border and the patriotic design when she and my great-great-grandfather dined in the White House with the Lincolns, and she ordered a full set! The china arrived in our house in April of 1862 and has been here ever since."

On the other side of the room and over the fireplace was an oil painting of Max, Charlotte and Annabelle. Max wore a white suit, Charlotte, a simple white dress accented by her signature pearl choker, and Annabelle's white dress fashioned with a petal-pink sash.

With Max's image immortalized and surrounded by such splendor, I decided that he was the one who had come a long way, baby.

In fact I wondered why he and Charlotte were together. Or rather, still together. I could see his attraction to all that Charlotte had to offer—prominent family, money, societal standing. All the things he was probably desperate for while growing up on the poorer side of town. But I couldn't figure why she stayed married to him.

Charlotte kept the camera panning until she homed in on a collection of men's and women's rings from the mid-1800s. I paused the video and controlled the feed so I could examine them more carefully.

Several of Charlotte's family heirloom rings were made from gutta percha, a dark, leathery material that resembled rubber. Those rings would either have been worn by Civil War POW soldiers or they could have been mourning or sweetheart rings. It was hard for me to tell without a closer inspection. Regardless, soldiers' names were engraved in the center on silver, with filigree on either side.

There was also a gold snake ring, very popular in the 1860s, its coiled form symbolizing eternity. This particular ring had two snakes wrapped together with their heads decorated in old cut emeralds and diamonds. The remaining rings were definitively masculine—an onyx signet, a wide dendritic and a large, flat garnet with a claw cut diamond inside of an octagram, an eight-angled star polygon, and several old-European cut diamonds on the gold band. I recognized the garnet ring, Max had been wearing it on the day we met.

Charlotte curated three more rings, three sets of cufflinks and four necklaces, all from the Civil War era, all passed down from Charlotte's ancestors. Then she mentioned that her husband's firm was the largest appraiser of Civil War and pre-Civil War antiques in the country. I thought it interesting that she referred to the firm that bore her maiden name as her husband's firm.

My attention wandered when there was no more jewelry to discuss, and while Charlotte droned on about how her family had lived in Savannah since *before* the Civil War. When the video ended, I laughed at the jokes in the comment thread that Max had worked his way into wealth and Southern society the old-fashioned way: He'd married it.

Another member quipped: He's a member of the Lucky Sperm Club!

That comment had 72 laughs. One response said: No, he married into the Lucky Sperm Club.

That comment had 1012 likes.

I drank the remainder of the tea, which had become ice-cold. Then went to the Tatnall blog and watched footage from a regional TV show called Hidden Treasures. Residents brought in various antiques and Max appraised them on the spot.

His tone and demeanor exuded patient confidence. Like he was ahead of any game, like he had all the time in the world to accomplish his goals, like life had come easily. But he also micromanaged nearby assistants who ran lighting and coordinated guests. He had that need-to-know vibe for the tiniest of unimportant details.

His suits were expensive, custom-made. The classic cut and dark colors gave him the appearance of stature. But he was short. He was barely taller than me, and I was only five-foot-six-and-a-half.

He had a crazy good feel for spotting valuable antiques. In the videos he typically sized up a piece with just one touch, but his hands were short and grubby. Like they had been made for a far less elegant business.

When the last video ended, I sat in the dark, knowing I still didn't have enough answers to give me clear direction. What if Max was one of the Muñoz children? What if he had stalked me that day in Beaufort? What if he was drawing me in to work with him because he couldn't get close enough to kill me otherwise?

What if... I pressed my hands against my forehead and groaned.

My what-ifs were going to be the death of me.

I slumped into the couch. I was tired. So incredibly tired. Not from lack of sleep, although that wasn't helping. I was tired of worrying. Tired of being afraid. Tired of wondering...what if.

It was a masochistic question to ask, and it made everything worse. I stared out the window and thought for a long moment about what to do.

Then I realized I should pose a different question. One I hadn't dared to ask myself in an awfully long time.

What...do you want?

My mind settled obediently under its new directive, and went to work on solving the problem. I didn't have to search for long to find the answer, because beneath the layers of the many prescribed drugs I'd taken over the years, and beneath the layers of trauma I couldn't manage to fully escape, I knew I was still there. And I knew what I wanted.

It was the same thing I'd wanted as a child. I wanted *my* life, *my* future, as I'd designed it with *my* twin on those laconic Saturday mornings, the safety and perfection of which I thought would last a lifetime.

"Our lives are God-given," the minister had preached in our tiny midwestern church, in the town where we'd relocated under our assumed names. "And to be truly happy we must follow the path He's designed for us." I felt the sanctity of what the minister taught. Even though I'd often questioned if I had any path left at all. It had been destroyed by evil men and best intentions.

Regardless, I wanted my freedom as much as I wanted to breathe. Which meant I had to do the presentation-type interview, and if was offered, I'd have to take the job. I wouldn't have to stay there forever, just long enough to get my life back from my father.

I drew my legs in close, and stared into Columbia Square with its yellow cast and pre-Civil War homes. It appeared the same today as it had in the 1700s. Without a car in sight, it felt as though I'd drifted back in time. I wished I had.

In the far right corner I spied a few fingers of fog, reaching, grasping, inching their way forward.

The fog moved achingly slow, around the fountain, keeping to the grass, not a speck of it spreading beyond the interior green of the square.

I pinched the delicate skin on the top of my hand. Once, twice. Definitely awake.

Hallucinating?

I squeezed my eyes shut in a long blink then opened them. The fog was still there, creeping forward.

Not hallucinating.

I didn't think, anyway.

My beloved sister emerged slowly from the darkness, like a daughter of Poseidon rising from the sea. Her steps were graceful and deliberate.

I crawled into the window seat for a closer look.

12

Like a Gothic vision, Bunny stood on her front porch in her long white nightgown, watching the fog. Her hands clasped in front of her, she looked like a lonely housewife, waiting for her husband to disembark from the evening train. After a moment she smiled and gestured to her open front door like she offered someone the opportunity to precede her into the house. She shut the door behind her, then reappeared in her front living room, again surrounded by candles and in conversation with someone I couldn't see.

My sister didn't look at me. Her eyes were focused straight ahead. But she must have known I was here. I had the sense that nothing was a surprise to her. I had the sense that she had a mission, and that it related to me.

When she passed the fountain I stood and wondered if she was going to come inside my house. Like Bunny's guest went into hers.

I was ready to open the door for her, but she stopped directly across the street. She turned and faced me. This was the closest we'd been since she'd died, just a street's width away.

There was no smile this time, and I asked, "Are you mad?"

It was a reasonable question and I waited for her eyes to narrow or for her to scream. Because I was the one who had killed her, surely she would have something to say about that.

But she didn't respond. She just tapped the thin silver wristwatch three times, slowly, the one that used to be our grandmother's.

"Time. It's time?"

She nodded. Looked over her shoulder and pointed in the direction she'd just come from. As if on cue, the fog lifted and she backed away from me.

"But you just got here."

She didn't seem to hear me. She crossed to the other side of the square and disappeared into the mist. The fog rolled itself up behind her, and within a couple of seconds, disappeared.

The ache of guilt and sadness pulled deep and strong in my heart.

Magnolia jumped onto the cushion and faced me. Her majestic blue eyes unflinching, they missed nothing. I stroked her white fur and she arched beneath my hand.

"That watch," I said softly. "Can only mean one thing. That it's time. Time to start living. My life."

I heard my mother's voice in my head, words of wisdom she'd spoken just after I'd just graduated from the University of Iowa. That was where we relocated after the trial. I was struggling to find the courage to get my first job.

She'd said, "It's not your fear of consequence that's

making you so miserable. It's not moving ahead that causes your pain. Life is movement. Life is forward motion. You've got to learn how to take a chance. Face those fears head-on."

I made a second cup of tea and returned to the couch. Magnolia joined me.

Columbia Square was empty.

A creak sounded from somewhere in the house.

I was alone in a big empty house with just my cat.

My phone rang, startling me.

I splashed hot tea over the rim and onto my leg. Magnolia jumped down. I jumped up, and I stared at the name that shined on the caller id.

"Nick?"

"Hey, sweetheart." Nick's voice was smooth and comforting. Pure bliss spread from my chest and tingled down my back.

Just like that, I was no longer alone.

"I thought you were on a flight?"

"I was. I am. Somewhere over North Carolina right now, I think. But the flight attendants let you make a call over WiFi if you ask nicely."

I rubbed at the burn on my leg. Nick was nothing if not smooth. Charming. I imagined the flight attendants falling all over themselves to help him.

"Did I wake you?" His tone was gentle and caring and sensitive, wrapping around me like a warm hug, and I sank into it.

"No, it's been sort of a strange night so I was up. Why are you over North Carolina? I didn't think you were supposed to be on the East Coast today?"

"We had a little engine trouble and had to make an emergency landing in New York."

"An emergency landing?"

I did the flight math and still couldn't figure out why he was over North Carolina.

"We were over the Atlantic when one engine caught fire. Just exploded into flames. Frightening as—"

"Oh, my gosh—" My heart plummeted. I'd just found him and couldn't imagine losing him.

"Pilot made an emergency landing in upstate New York. No one was hurt, amazingly. It's all over the news."

"When? I mean, you're on another flight now?"

"Yeah. I didn't call sooner because I wanted to be sure. I wanted to think it through."

I put the call on speaker, opened a browser on my phone and started searching: plane emergency landing New York. Video footage showed several firetrucks spraying water onto a burned-out Airbus. Photos showed the entire plane engulfed in fire. "Think what through?" My hands shook.

"I know we've only known one another for a few weeks. I can't explain why my feelings are so strong, other than to say that I'm old enough to...I mean, I know myself and... Anyway, when I thought we were going down, my first thought was of you."

"Really?" My voice pitched high, like he had just told me he'd spent the afternoon on a spaceship. I didn't mean to sound surprised. I didn't want to sound doubtful that I could be someone's dying thought. The idea was supremely romantic.

I knew that I loved him.

I didn't realize he felt so strongly about me.

I suspected he was reeling from the near-death experience and he didn't mean what he was saying.

"Yes. Really. I thought of everything we wouldn't get to

share and I don't want to live another minute without you. I'll get down on bended knee when I see you face-to-face. But I had to call. I had to let you know how I feel. I have to ask—Harper, will you marry me?"

My eyes widened.

I loved Nick since I first laid eyes on him in his New York gallery. I'd never been in love with any man before. But with him it just happened. Just—*whammo.* All at once.

I thought the attraction would fade with time and distance. But everything had been so ideal, it was like I hadn't had the option to not fall in love.

I wanted to say yes right away. But I forced myself to draw in a deep breath, because I had to consider all of the consequences up front.

Problem number one: We didn't know one other as well as two people should when they were headed down the aisle. Heck, he didn't even actually know my real last name.

He didn't know that I came from money, so much money that my sister and I were kidnapped and held for ransom. Money caused all kinds of conflicts with couples, especially when the female had quite a bit more than the male. A sad truth, but it happened. Egos got in the way.

He didn't know that a crime family was, in all likelihood, searching for me, planning my death. I knew I should have argued that they were long gone. But the possibility remained that they were still on the hunt and that that could put him in harm's way. He didn't know that I was supposed to be on meds and that I refused to take them, that I'd quit cold turkey and I might have been hallucinating as of late.

"I love you," he said. "I've loved you from the start."

I looked out the window at the lamplit park, at the illuminated fountain. I remembered Catherine standing there, staring at me, pointing at that silver watch.

It's time.

"I'm sorry. I'm scaring you off by being too honest, aren't I?" he said.

"No," I whispered. Although I wasn't sure what scared me more. His proposal or the fact that I wanted this with him almost more than I'd ever wanted anything.

"Are you certain? Because I would never want to—"

"Yes," I said quickly. Adrenaline fueled my focus, making it seem like I was crystal clear for the first time in my life.

"Yes, as in you're certain I'm not scaring you off or yes, you'll—" His words were cut off.

"Nick?"

Nothing but dead space.

I paced. *Take a minute, take a breath, take your time.*

But my brain wouldn't calm. Visions of the married-to-Nick-life danced in my head and bounced in my heart—coming home after a long day, sharing work stories—stories he would understand because he worked in my industry. Sharing a glass of wine, perhaps he would rub my feet while we discussed our day. He traveled internationally a lot. We could take European vacations together. I could be myself again. I could live the life I'd always wanted. The thought of living life openly and free as me—no contacts, no hair dye, no fake name—filled me with joy, happiness, ecstasy.

Freedom.

I craved it like oxygen.

What was I thinking?

I pressed a hand to the top of my head.

I couldn't do that. For so many reasons I couldn't live in the open like that.

My father, for one would make Nick aware of my mental health challenges and that would be enough to...

"Harper?"

"Yes—"

I should have said, "Let's wait." I should have said, "Let's take our time and think this through!"

"You hardly know me," I brought myself to say. Because in all fairness, it needed to be said. It was the truth. He should be warned.

"I know you well enough to recognize that you're the one," he said.

I focused again on Columbia Square. What would I say to my sister the next time she looked at me with those brilliant blue eyes? That a handsome, intelligent, successful man fell in love with me, asked me to marry him and I said... I said what? That while I loved him, too, I preferred living in a big, empty house with a cat? That I preferred to enjoy my success at a table for one?

All I could do, as our mother made me promise, was make something beautiful of the life I'd been given.

For her.

For Catherine.

"I've said too much, haven't I? I sound like a lunatic. It's too soon!" he said.

I laughed, even though I felt like I was on the verge of another catastrophic mistake. My hand was on the proverbial silver accelerator bar and I wanted to push forward.

"No. You haven't said too much."

"If you need more time, it's okay. Take all the time you need. I won't change my mind."

I glanced at Magnolia. Her fixed stare was unnerving.

I looked away.

"Because I get it now," Nick said. "Life is short. So short.

None of us knows how long we have. I got a pass today, Harper. I started my day busy, distracted, running. Then a few hours ago I was a hair's breadth away from being a pile of ash." He exhaled hard and I imagined him shaking his head or staring out the window. He did that when he needed to buy time. To think.

"I'm on my way to Savannah right now. I'll be on your doorstep just after the sun comes up. If you're sure, we'll be married before nightfall."

The mug slipped from my hand, crashed on the floor and split into two pieces.

How? My heart screamed as it often did when faced with an opportunity. *How could you even think of doing something so impetuous again? You've completely lost your mind. What happened the last time you just raced ahead at top speed?*

I stepped away from the broken pieces and said, "Impetuous choices rarely work out well."

"I know what you're thinking, that I'm only proposing because of the crash. Or the almost-crash. But all that did was make me realize that I need to act on what I've wanted for some time now. I don't want to wake up one day and realize I've missed out on the best thing that's ever happened to me. Which is you."

At the sound of his assurance, love spread throughout my chest like a wide spill of warm golden honey. That feeling of love was as natural to me as breathing and yet the only time I'd felt it since the accident was with Nick.

I wanted to say yes, I wanted to believe that his feelings for me were real. I wanted to believe that our relationship could find happily ever after, the same way it did for thousands of couples around the world every day.

Nick was right. No one knew how long they had. If I wasn't careful I'd wake up one day and realize I'd missed it all. I would have spent too much time running, too much time hiding, and life would have passed me by.

My sister was also right.

It was time.

Because the years that had passed since her death could not, by anyone's definition, have been called a life. I'd not lived. Not fully. Not in the least.

"Yes, Nick. Yes. I'll marry you."

13

———

One-quarter mile from his house, Manny slowed to a stop to catch his breath. He'd run harder this morning than he usually did. His body was soaked in sweat, his lungs ached, and the muscles in his quads were knotting into a cramp.

Long ago he'd heard the rumors that the corruption in D.C. had filtered down to the local branches. Naively, he'd thought that his little office, his friends and team members were exempt. Today he realized how stupid he'd been to think that.

He gathered his strength and finished his run. When he reached the garage he grabbed his ankle, pulled it to his glute and stretched. He stared at the sky that was streaked with harsh pinks and blues. An hour ago the wind had been blowing so hard the trees nearly bowed.

Now they were still, like an amateur artist had painted them against a canvas of cheap, off-color pastels. Even the birds were quiet. The atmosphere was thick and pensive. Like all of nature was preparing for the other shoe to drop.

Manny knew from his drinking days that quiet without peace was a bad sign.

He'd learned the hard way that you could numb your pain and your problems however you chose, but that didn't make either go away.

The signs were there.

Something was tragically out of place. He felt like he was caught between moments, between breaths. The world was perfectly frozen, pausing between what was and what will be.

Manny wandered in that gap, not liking what his four unreturned calls to Stanford meant.

He lowered his leg, grabbed the other ankle and stretched again. He scanned the forest around his house.

He thought of the note he'd received at the office. He thought of Jenny's death and he felt it in his bones—there was a connection.

He called Stanford for the fifth time. As expected, the call went straight to voicemail. Since he'd already sent four texts and left as many voicemails, he didn't leave another. He curled his hand into a fist.

Stanford would know that he had to be the one to let the other women know about Jenny. He would know that if Manny did it he'd be fired.

When Stanford first discounted the note Manny had received, Manny thought it might have been genuine care and concern. Now he realized that his partner wasn't that obtuse.

"If you ever want to know why something doesn't make sense," his father always said, "just follow the money trail."

The pamphlet that was hand-delivered to Jenny was a notice that she had been found, a notice that her life was about to end, and a notice that no one could stop it.

The message that Manny received was also a notice, but he didn't think it was a personal threat. It was more of a promise—that what the Muñoz family had begun over twenty years ago, they would finish. And Manny wouldn't be able to stop them.

It hadn't hit him until three o'clock that morning—someone who sends advance notice like that, someone that cocky, that confident, they had information. They had insurance, they had an insider.

If Manny got called in for his activity on the Muñoz case, he could justify his actions to date. He could say that Bruce called him with the news about Jenny's death. Manny used to be the families' primary contact, and none of them knew that he had been forbidden to talk with them again.

He could also cover the general check-in call he'd made to Harper and the other women, considering he'd just received the cryptic note. He had all the parents' phone numbers from years ago. He had reason to be concerned about their welfare, so he wouldn't get much more than a slap on the wrist. Or a few appointments with the Bureau's psychiatrist to make sure he wasn't turning to the bottle again. But he wouldn't get away with another attempt at contacting them.

Manny ran up the stairs to his office over the garage, grabbed a water from the small fridge and fired up his laptop. He searched for a secure email service, one where the emails would self-destruct after a certain amount of time. That way he could discreetly alert the girls and their parents about the note he'd received and the details surrounding Jenny's death. But he couldn't find a service that he thought was truly secure and allowed him to stay anonymous.

Once he'd alerted them, the women's families would

flood the department with phone calls about this mysterious email they'd received. It wouldn't take much for the Bureau to figure out who had sent it. Plus, there were spam filters. The families might not even receive his email.

He thought about buying a burner phone and sending all the parents texts. That might work but it felt cowardly. And he wanted to warn the girls immediately. Not an hour from now when he would have the phone. He'd already wasted time doing this the right way, waiting for Stanford to call him back.

He stood, cracked his knuckles. Ricardo Muñoz's greasy smile flashed in his mind, his arrogant laugh echoed in his head. He squeezed his eyes shut and said a short prayer for help.

But all he felt in response was the old guilt, regret and self-loathing that began over twenty years ago when he didn't investigate soon enough. When little girls died because of him.

If he got fired, Blair wouldn't understand. When she gave birth to Reagan, she was clear that she wanted to stay home and enjoy the time with their daughter. "These are precious years with her that I don't want to miss, these are years I'll never get back," she'd said. When she resigned from the Bureau, he became their provider.

Still, he couldn't do nothing.

Manny picked up his personal mobile phone and dialed Harper's number. When her voicemail answered, he dialed again with the same result.

He realized she wouldn't know this number because he hadn't called from his personal phone last time he reached out to her.

He sent her a text: It's Agent Hernandez calling you from my personal phone. Call me back.

14

———

"Hi, Harper," Manny said.

She'd called him back within the minute, sounding as irritated and standoffish as she had before.

"I have some bad news about Jenny." He kept his tone gentle.

He waited.

He paced.

Harper didn't respond.

"She had a visit from a dark-haired man who pretended to be a local minister. He left a pamphlet behind. The Bible verse that the Muñoz family used was on the pamphlet. As well as a list of fractions. That night she went for a run and ended up at the bottom of a mountainside. Police are calling it an accident."

Vivid memories exploded in Manny's mind—Harper lying in her hospital bed, her sister's funeral, her mother's breakdown.

Guilt raged in his gut.

He'd learned the hard way not to deny it. Usually that went a long way to keeping him sober. But today the sheer force of it nearly stole his sobriety.

"I wish I could say that the man's visit and the pamphlet weren't related to Jenny's death. That they weren't related to the Muñoz family. But I think that would be foolish."

He waited again.

He listened closely.

Harper still didn't respond.

"I also received a note with the same Bible passage and fractions just before Jenny died. I can't discount the significance of this either. I want you to be on guard."

This time Manny heard Harper's rapid breathing. Like she was hyperventilating. Then there was a screeching sound, like a chair scraping against the floor.

"Are you okay? Harper?"

"I knew it was from them," she said finally. Her voice was breathless. "I knew it."

"You received a similar note?" he asked.

"Someone tried to break into my house. I mean—I don't think they were trying to break in." She quickly told him about a man in black who broke the bottom floor window, then smiled right at her, deliberately, and got away before she could land a pellet in his backside. "The next day a policeman found a piece of folded paper in the broken window. It had a Bible verse and fractions written on it.

"That smile, it was like he knew right where I'd be, like he was one step ahead of me. I have guns all over the house, I'm always armed, and I filed a police report, but—" Her voice caught with emotion. "Hang on. I can't breathe."

"Take your time." Manny winced at her comment about being well-armed. He worried about the rapid pace of her words and her breathlessness. She was having a panic attack. While he couldn't blame her, he also knew that she had some sort of a diagnosis, a disorder that caused her to lose control and hurt people. He worried that she might hurt someone again.

"She's just a kid!" Manny had blurted out after the accident while he stood in the hospital with Harper's doctor and her parents.

Dr. Silveria, Harper's father, stepped toward him. His fierce expression made it clear that Manny's comment was unwelcome.

"You don't know what Harper's like. She needs meds!" He lifted his shirt sleeve and revealed a number of ugly scars on his arm.

Harper's mother cautioned her husband. Wordlessly, he closed his eyes, balled his hands into fists. Like it was all he could do to get control of himself. When he opened them again he said, "We've worked extensively with private doctors to find the right blend for her. Without her meds she's—she's dangerous." He stepped away, put his hands on his hips and stared out the window.

Manny looked to Harper's mother and whispered, "I'm familiar with the drugs the doctors are talking about, but I've never heard of those being prescribed to a young person before. The dosages are high."

"Harper has a history," Lara said, her voice thick from crying. "She's not stable. She's been diagnosed with severe anxiety, although we think it's something more complex than that. She set several small fires. One got out of hand and she burned down our garage. Although we wonder if she did that intentionally.

"She thinks people are out to get her when they aren't. She took a knife to school once—or once that we know about. I found another knife hidden under her pillow."

Lara's chin quivered, tears ran down her face. After a moment she drew in a deep breath, then said, "One night she snuck into our bedroom while we were sleeping and stabbed her father. She got him seven times in the arms and hands before he stopped her."

Manny cocked his head. He couldn't believe that the soft-spoken girl in the hospital bed could have harmed anyone, much less her own father. The meds must have served their purpose.

Harper's mother looked at the floor, empty, defeated, like her soul was quietly slipping away. "Left untreated, she's at risk to hurt someone—" She lowered herself into a nearby plastic chair, and her body shook with quiet sobs.

At the time Manny had wanted to convince Lara that there had to be another way, but he knew that parents often understood their children best. When he'd called Lara recently to get Harper's phone number, Lara had bragged about how well Harper was doing. She credited the meds for Harper's stability.

Regardless, he knew that telling her about Jenny's death and the notes could be a problem. And the risk was two-fold.

First, since she was armed, she might think someone was after her when they weren't. She could hurt an innocent or even kill them.

Second, with that same bad lens, she could pick the wrong ally. She could think someone was trustworthy when they weren't. If the Muñoz family had found her—and it sounded like they had—Harper could get herself killed, too.

"How did they find Jenny?" Harper asked.

"I don't know. To be clear, I don't have specific proof that the Muñoz cartel was the one responsible. I just personally find it suspicious, so I wanted to make you aware. I want you to be on guard."

"Is the FBI going to investigate?" Her voice pitched high. She sounded almost hysterical.

"I don't know that either," he said with a calmness he didn't feel. "I think it should be investigated. But I'm not the one who determines which cases get attention."

"But she died!" Harper exclaimed. "And there was a note! Why is there even a question about investigating?"

"I feel the same way," he said, hoping she could read between the lines.

She didn't say a word for a few minutes and he wondered if she could.

"Who?" she asked finally. "Who from the family would this be?"

He shook his head. Answering this question was crossing yet another line, because he didn't have any proof to back up his suspicions. But he was in this deep, he wasn't stopping now. "I think it might be one of the sons. We didn't get a clear view of his face from Jenny's home security footage, he was good about avoiding the camera. Given his physique and the relatively taut skin along his neck and jawline, he could very well be within a couple of years of your age."

He knew he should say that his theory was all conjecture and unsupported theory. But he let his hypothesis stand. "Regardless of what the FBI decides to do, I'll help you however I can. In the meantime, don't allow any new people to get close."

"I'm interviewing," Harper said quickly. "If I get the job, I'll have to take it."

Lara had already told him that Harper was dating

someone as well as interviewing for work, that they were insisting she work in one location.

"As long as you've checked them out thoroughly, you're probably fine. Obviously stay away from blind offers for interviews and headhunting calls."

15

———

Sitting on the edge of my bed, staring at the blank white wall of my room, I imagined what the worst of Jenny's suffering might have been.

Fearing the pain of the rocks below wouldn't have been the worst, she had to have known that pain would be temporary. Neither would it have been her knowing all the way down that she was going to die.

Her worst suffering would have been knowing that her baby, that tiny expression of love, that perfect soul who was completely dependent on her for its life, was going to die.

And there was nothing she could do about it.

I knew what it was like to lose someone irreplaceable, to have played a role in their death, and to never get over it.

I thought of the fake minister and the pamphlet, and my heart picked up its pace. They could have been unrelated to her death as Agent Hernandez had suggested. But I didn't believe that. Neither did he or he wouldn't have called.

I'd read about the historical patterns and habits of the Muñoz family cartel. Their signature murder looked accidental, natural—a fall, an animal attack, a drug overdose, or even the appearance of suicide. That way their connections to the murders were hard, if not impossible, to prove.

They killed that way not just to keep themselves from being convicted, but also to intimidate and to control. It was one thing to fear being murdered. It was another to fear being murdered by someone you knew would never be caught. That sort of bone-chilling fear caused people to give up the fight, to stay quiet, to lose hope.

I moved to my desk and played the security footage of the man who broke my first-floor window. The same man who probably killed Jenny. I scrolled frame by frame until I found the exact moment when he slipped the note into the window. The man's hat was pulled low and the camera didn't catch much of his face.

That was the problem with security cameras. If they were anchored low, criminals just knocked them down. If they were mounted up high, criminals could obscure their faces intentionally. This guy knew where the camera was before he approached my house.

How had he found me?

I'd been careful.

Did I know him personally? Had he wormed his way into my life?

I fast-forwarded a few frames until he gave his can't-lose smile, his can't-catch-me smile, his man-with-a-plan smile. He was cocky. Self-assured.

Agent Hernandez had said that he didn't know if there would be an investigation into Jenny's death. The concern in his voice told me he didn't have any hope that there would be.

I stared out the window, into Columbia Square and remembered how Agent Hernandez had never been willing to do the background checks I'd asked him for.

And I wondered. Not willing? Or not able?

Had this man on the video feed gotten to someone inside the FBI?

Had Agent Hernandez's hands been tied?

And the bigger question—how had this Muñoz man found me?

There was always some public story about corruption in the three-letter agencies. Money made things happen and the Muñoz kids probably still had plenty of it. I could easily imagine Ricardo leaving them a secret stash. I could also imagine one of the sons using that stash to find those of us who testified against Ricardo.

Killing us. One by one.

I lowered my head into my hands, feeling beaten and victimized all over again. My arms and legs trembled. Anxiety bulldozed its way through my body, driving me toward hysteria.

That man on the screen was a Muñoz.

He would be back to get me.

There was no one I could turn to for help.

I FINALLY GOT off the floor.

I felt lost, empty, shaken.

Deeply alone.

Still weak, I made my way downstairs, swallowed two or three of every anti-anxiety, anti-depressive supplement in the house. I made sure every gun was loaded and ready.

Then I dug through my closet. Nick was on his way, and I needed something to wear.

I'd taken quite a few self-defense classes over the years. The former Marine who ran one course said that if you came in contact with an assailant who had a gun, run away. If they were too close and you couldn't run, then you should run toward them to try to remove the weapon. At that point he taught us several techniques for disabling the attacker.

I wondered if Jenny ran toward her attacker or away from him.

I'd spent my life running away.

When I finally figured out who this Muñoz was, I'd run toward him.

It took some effort for me to focus, but I finally cobbled together a wedding outfit. Complete with a birdcage veil. I'd bought the white silk suit and pumps to attend a new client meeting last spring.

I'd found the vintage floral lace veil when Levi and I popped into a small antique store on E. Liberty Street a couple of months ago. The saleslady in the antique store kept calling the veil a hat. A bridal hat. When I couldn't bite my tongue any longer, I had to tell her it wasn't a hat.

The antique lace fit close across my forehead, tulle burst low on the side in the form of a carnation-type flower. Authentic boho, 1920s. Levi had tried it on first as a joke and it was oddly stunning. His face was downright pretty. Like Rob Lowe-back-in-the-eighties kind of pretty.

When we left the store he surprised me and handed it to me as a gift. He said the veil didn't really go with his five o'clock shadow.

"You'll wear it on your wedding day," he'd said.

I'm sure he didn't think I would wear it so soon. Perhaps he didn't think I would wear it with anyone but him.

Shoot, I didn't think I would even look at it again until I was an old lady in my big, empty house with six overweight cats circling my ankles. I imagined I would take it out of its round box, remember the fun day with Levi, then put it in the donate pile.

I admired my wedding outfit in the reflection of the antique full-length mirror that had once been my maternal grandmother's. Until something deep inside, something frightened and vulnerable said this was all folly. That, like Jenny with her best-laid plans for the future, I could die soon.

Because what if my sister was saying: *Time's up*?

I pushed the thought away and lowered the veil over my face. Like a child who clung to all things incredulous, who clung to the purity of a dream, I needed to pretend that this dream could come true. I needed to pretend that I could actually live the life that Catherine wanted.

For her. For my mother.

The doorbell rang and I startled. I looked out the front window. Nick stood on the front porch, finger combing his hair, then brushing at the front of his shirt. He held a small bouquet of flowers.

I could have dashed upstairs, changed clothes quickly and made it back down before he had to wait too long. I could have told him the truth, that because I was in danger, he was, too. That we should take our time to get to know one another. Because once he got to know me he might not like what he saw. Instead, I walked toward the door like I was in a trance.

Nick's eyes fixed on the veil. Concern was written all over his face—like he wondered if I had had the veil on tap while I waited for a proposal, any proposal, to come through.

"A friend gave this to me several months ago," I said in response to the unasked question. I touched the veil. "Kind of a joke, I guess. But today seemed like the right day to bring it out."

A slow but brilliant smile broadened on his tanned face, something between relief and elation. Like he was grateful I wasn't the kind of woman who had her wedding outfit selected long before she knew the groom.

"It's gorgeous," he said, his voice deep and smooth. "You're gorgeous." He kissed me. Softly, beautifully. When he leaned away, his mouth widened into an illuminating smile that turned my insides warm.

I had expected some measure of awkwardness because his proposal of marriage had come out of the blue. Literally. Before his almost-crash, we hadn't at all been speeding in the direction of happily ever after. In fact, and at my insistence, we were taking it all rather slow.

"Ready?" he asked.

I opened my mouth to tell him that I needed to wait, that I needed a little more time. But he took my hand, kissed my knuckles and that sharp, jagged worry inside of me dissolved into hope and trust.

"Yes," I said.

I turned to set the alarm.

Magnolia perched motionless on the bottom step of the spiral staircase. Her stare was intense and condemning, like marrying someone I didn't know that well and spur-of-the-moment was the stupidest thing she'd ever seen.

"Shut up," I muttered then closed and locked the door.

16

———

Nick was dressed much more casually than I was—jeans and a navy button-down with the sleeves rolled to his elbows. I thought it might have been the same outfit he had been wearing when the plane made its emergency landing, except it didn't reek of smoke.

Maybe he stopped somewhere along the way to change, maybe he purchased new clothes at the last minute to look his best for me. He always went out of his way to be good to me—sent me roses each week, paid attention to my interests and favorite restaurants and catered to them.

He reserved a hotel room for me when I visited, never any pressure. He even overlooked my significant scars and their murky history. Not because I'd asked him to, but because he paid more attention to who I was on the inside than how I looked on the outside.

Guilt inched its way through my gut because I was repaying his kindness with dishonesty. We drove to Tybee Island. I should have, at the very least, told him that I had some broken pieces inside that might never heal. But I just wasn't ready for him to see those parts of me. Against all reason, I was holding out hope that this new beginning would, by default, make all of my problems go away.

Stupid.

Selfish.

"How about St. Thomas for our honeymoon?"

I drew in a deep breath, smiled like I'd never been happier, like I didn't have a care in the world. "I've never been."

"Good. It will be you and me, miles of vacant beaches and room service." He held my hand. "I have a flight later in the day, a business trip to the west coast. But I'll be back in New York in 48 hours and we'll leave from there. Or you can wait for me at my condo in New York, if you like."

I made an apologetic face. "I have a meeting tomorrow that I can't miss."

"In two days, then." He talked about his plans for our future. How happy we would be together.

I rode along on this adventure, living this dream, and it made me feel as if there was nothing to fear. It made me feel happy.

I wasn't sure that those feelings would last, but I soaked up as much as they had to offer. Because I hadn't truly felt either for a very long time.

Unexpectedly, Nick swerved off the main highway and turned onto a desolate road. "I have a little surprise for you."

"Another surprise?" I asked and found Nick staring at me with an intensity that made my chest clench.

He blinked like he'd seen my reaction and quickly drew his lips into a smile so brilliant that I immediately questioned what I'd seen.

He dragged his knuckles along my cheek. "Yes, another one."

While we drove, the echo of his earlier expression lingered. I was intimately familiar with that particular look. Not because I'd seen it on his face before, but because I'd often seen it in the mirror. The hatred of the Muñoz family that I carried deep in my own heart could often be found on my face.

That fierce kind of anger, that hunger for justice that knew no bounds, was borne from a wound that resided deep in the soul. The only satisfaction it sought was the sweet revenge of firing a bullet into the chest of the one who caused the pain.

So I wondered where his anger came from, what secrets he held close to his vest, and if his secrets were as bad as mine.

Or worse.

I'd checked Nick's background before we worked together. He didn't maintain any social media profiles, but a two-part series on him and his business had been published by an art blogger. It said that Nick had been born in Charleston with nothing. Less than nothing. Single parent home. Dad left early. He hadn't excelled at sports. But he'd had a weird talent for spotting genuine antiques. He found his first one in his grandmother's attic when he was sixteen. A 19th-century American sugar chest. He asked her if he could restore it and sell it, and she said yes. He made ten grand off that chest and hadn't stopped since.

I stole several glances at Nick, realizing that no background check or grassroots research effort would reveal everything. There would be, quite simply, things about him I didn't know. Secrets about him that had not yet been revealed. But we had spent several weeks together and he had treated me well, so I restrained myself from falling into any paranoid delusions.

I didn't know who had left that note for me, but I knew it wasn't Nick.

He caught me watching him and said, "I know what you're worried about." His dark eyes had become warm and soft again, and against my usual instinct to put up defenses, I calmed and softened.

"You do?" I asked, even though I knew he couldn't possibly.

"You have friends and family who won't understand what we're doing today. So, we'll keep our marriage quiet for now. We can have a ceremony with family later on, if you like. Or just a reception. Either one."

Nick pulled into a gravel parking lot surrounded by low-end storefronts, many of which bore signs that advertised "Wholesale", "Open to the Public," or "To the Trade Only."

He parked in front of a small, green warehouse with no windows, no sign and no handle on the only door. "Wait here," he said and got out of the car.

He banged on the door and after a moment a dark-haired man who could have been Nick's brother, except he approximated the size of a professional wrestler, opened the door. He greeted Nick with hugs and back-slapping. Then the man caught sight of me in the passenger seat. After he ushered Nick inside, he poked his head out the door again and gave me a hard stare.

When Nick didn't return, I got out of the car. The door to the warehouse hadn't shut completely and I pried it open enough to peek inside. The vacuous area was filled with racks and boxes, none of them labeled.

"What are your plans for the princess in the carriage out there?" I heard the large man ask from somewhere off to the side.

"I'm marrying her," Nick said.

"What?" the muscle man laughed. "Because it worked out so well the last time?"

"I have a plan," Nick said. "Do you have the ring I ordered last week?" Nick asked.

"Yeah, here. Cash only, dude."

I let go of the door and slipped back into Nick's rental car. Last week. Did he say he ordered the ring last week? My head spun.

We parked at the beach, across the street from a small chapel with a sign out front that read: Tybee Island Wedding Chapel—Wedding Capital of the South.

Sand poured into my pumps as we walked, leaving grit rubbing against my feet. I tried to ignore what I'd overheard at the warehouse. Maybe Nick had been thinking last week about proposing and wanted to go ahead and order the ring? What did he mean about a plan?

We reached the line where the white water crashed against the beach and Nick turned to me. He knelt on one knee and pulled a black ring box from his pocket. Inside was an oval cut pink sapphire shouldered by three princess cut diamonds on each side and mounted on a simple white gold band. It was breathtakingly stunning.

"Marry me, Harper," he said simply. "I love you more than life itself."

The morning sun reflected off the ocean and bathed us in its warmth, like our union was specially blessed.

"I love you, too," I said, and I did. I really did.

Nick slipped the ring onto my finger, and I felt as I did when we first met. Like we were made for one another. Like I'd found the missing piece of myself. The piece I'd lost when Catherine was declared dead.

I knew I hadn't found myself in him.

But he saw me. Really saw that sacred, authentic me that I'd thought was gone forever. He shined a light on that place within, that part of me I needed in order to feel alive, in order to feel whole again.

Nick stood, his thumb caressed the top of my hand, and for a moment I was able to blot out the obvious flaws in my choices for the day. I thought of one good thing.

I'd managed to avoid a primary pitfall our father preached to my sister and me from a very early age: that our wealth had its privileges but it also put us at risk. "If you're not careful," he said. "Someone will try to be your friend just because you have access to money. When you're older, they might try to marry you for the same reason. You'll have to be extra careful."

Hand in hand, we trudged through the deep sand in the direction of the tiny white wedding chapel across the street. Nick turned and flashed a broad smile and instantly my mouth turned as dry as dust.

My heart fluttered like a wild bird in my chest, like it knew something I didn't, like it warned me of impending danger.

I thought of my mother, how disappointed she would feel that she had missed my wedding. I also thought of my father and how angry he would be over the extremely short engagement and the fact that I'd married someone I hadn't known for that long. He would see the wedding as an impulsive move, something to hold against me, a violation of the terms of our agreement. But that wasn't what bothered me.

"Nick." I released his hand.

He turned toward me, his smile still broad. "Yes?"

My response stuck in my throat and I nearly choked. I pulled the ring off my finger and handed it to him.

"I can't," I said. "I'm sorry."

I kicked off my heels and ran.

I finally realized why his smile had made me panic.

It was the same smile I'd seen on the face of the man who had left the note in my window.

17

Back in my own house, I changed clothes immediately, downgrading from the finery of the silk wedding suit to faded jeans and an old black T-shirt. I left the suit crumpled on the corner of the bed and vowed never to wear it again.

I'd convinced the minister's wife from the chapel to drive me home, since I wasn't about to get into the car with Nick.

"It's ohh-kay," she said on the way home with a pat to my leg and a motherly tone. "Better to know these things in advance."

When I came down the steps, I saw Nick standing on the pre-Civil War bricks of my back driveway. His hands were stuffed in his front pockets, and the engagement ring he'd given me sparkled on the tip of his thumb.

We stared at one another through the window for a long moment. Then I went to my office and swallowed two more doses of every anti-anxiety supplement I had. I looked at myself in the full-length mirror. "You did say you were through with running."

Hands shaking, I opened the kitchen door and paused at

the threshold. I wasn't prepared for Nick's brown eyes to appear so warm, nor did I expect his expression to be so soft. There was no sign of the momentary rage I'd seen earlier in the day or any hint of that terrifying smile. In the face of his silence, I didn't know what to say.

Finally, he shrugged. "I'm not sure what happened. But...I'm sorry. I didn't mean to make you feel pressured. I'd only hoped you would feel loved and cherished." His expression shifted between sadness, disappointment and glimmers of hope.

A warm breeze played gently on my face.

Then, like the final passing of a storm, the frighteningly strong conviction that had possessed me, that had catapulted me away from the wedding chapel and out of my veil, disappeared. In its peaceful absence, a familiar insight so rational, so logical, so clear, laid itself at my feet in the form of a question: If it had been Nick who left the note, if he were the same man who had killed Jenny, why hadn't he killed me already? He'd had ample time and opportunity. And yet, he hadn't.

The intelligence kicked the worry right out of me, left me feeling like I'd made a huge mistake. I squeezed my eyes shut. Instantly, and with extreme embarrassment, I knew. I knew I hadn't seen that crazed smile on Nick's face at all.

Between the note, that man's knowing smile, Jenny's death, and reconnecting with Agent Hernandez, my lens had clouded. Actually, it became completely corrupted. Add to it that I'd stopped the meds cold turkey, and, well—it all added up to one of the bigger freak-outs of my life.

Nick rubbed his hand across his forehead. "This is all my fault. I shouldn't have rushed it."

I shook my head, in part because I wholeheartedly disagreed, but also because his kindness and patience were so evident. His smile was filled with humility and sweetness, I could see that clearly now. Like the gentle unfolding of a rose, the love I felt for him opened my heart and soul.

Nick came to me on the steps and when I didn't fight him, he drew me close. "I love you, Harper." He gently stroked my cheek with the back of his knuckles and told me once again that we should not consider how little we knew about one another. "Our love is pure. Our love is real. Nothing can change that."

NICK MADE coffee and we sat in the living room and talked for a long time. I told him there had been an attempted break-in (even though I knew it wasn't that) and I told him about the man's bizarre smile. "I didn't realize the effect that experience had on me. Until today."

He leaned in with such care and concern and under-standing that I found myself wanting to open up fully about everything: the kidnapping, the Muñoz family who still chased me, the required medications I'd quit, and the agree-ment with my parents that governed my choices.

But Nick checked his watch and said, "I hate to do this, but if I don't leave now, I'll miss that flight. I'll come back. If you'll have me."

I pressed my hand to my heart. "Of course. I'm sorry this morning was so...dramatic."

"Don't worry about it." He gave me a slow kiss. "We'll try again. Someplace else this time?"

I drew in a deep breath, searching for the right words that wouldn't sound like rejection. "As much as I love you, as much as I love us, I think I need to take us at a slower pace."

I didn't particularly trust my own observations as of late,

but I thought I saw his calm expression slip and give way to tension, maybe even anger. And I wondered for the second time today what he might be hiding.

So I said, "When I marry you, when I get to our wedding day, I want to know that there aren't any secrets between us. Right now I think there are things you aren't telling me. Things we need to know about one another."

Nick nodded. Quietly and reluctantly he said, "Okay." He knelt in front of me and returned the engagement ring to my finger.

I looked at the ring and at him, and instinctively knew that something was wrong. There was too much unsaid between us, and the engagement ring would come with expectations. Pressure. It wouldn't lend itself to openness, disclosure, discovery. Least of all, time.

But then he gathered me into his arms. "We'll work it all out."

I prayed that we would.

We walked outside, he handed me his keys, and drank another long gulp of coffee. "Thanks for letting me leave the car here. I'm sorry that I have to leave so soon. I should have planned this better." He took my face in his hands and gave me a long kiss goodbye.

The driver who waited on the street in his black Chevy Tahoe goosed the accelerator and the engine roared.

"I think that was a hint," I said, my lips still touching his.

"I'm not ready yet."

"Me either." I slipped my arms around his neck.

"Where are you going again?" I asked when we parted.

"Ah...L.A.," he said like he struggled to remember. "Then you'll meet me in New York, right?"

"In two days."

"It will be two days too long." His tone was low, soft,

secretive. His smile was half-sweet, half-wicked. He kissed my finger that wore his engagement ring, then he turned and hopped into the Tahoe.

When the truck drove away, I brought the neckline of my T-shirt to my nose, inhaled the citrusy, woodsy scent of Nick's cologne. I'd assured him that I would trust what we had found with one another. But the fact that I knew precious little about him never left my mind.

I looked across the brick street and found Gary, my neighbor and the owner of The Military Museum. He wore his black top hat and was removing the mannequin dressed in a WWII uniform, the one who kept his front door propped open during the day. He grinned his showman's smile. "Hey, Harper."

"Hey, Gary." I raised Nick's white coffee cup in a toast.

"New beau?" He waggled his eyebrows, Groucho Marx style, and thumbed toward the Tahoe that turned left at Columbia Square.

"Something like that," I said.

"Haven't I seen him around before?"

I laughed at Gary's fishing expedition. "No, I doubt it."

Once inside I put the coffee mug in the dishwasher, dumped what was left from the pot and made a cup of green tea. Much as I wanted coffee, I felt a slight burn from an old ulcer and decided I wouldn't drink coffee today.

I clung to the wall while I climbed the half spiral staircase. My presentation at Tatnall Antique Appraisals was scheduled for tomorrow and I needed to get everything organized.

At the second turn I glanced down to the living room. I'd restored the house to the authentic style of the late 1770s. But my furnishings in this room were an exercise in modern comfort with the gray L-shaped couch and an oversized square ottoman.

The style suited my way of living, but strangely I couldn't envision Nick living in my home. His style was more formal, and his business was not in Savannah. In fact I couldn't imagine him opening a Savannah office. The area didn't seem to suit him.

I found it odd that we were engaged and we hadn't even discussed something as important as living arrangements. My father's favorite accusation from years ago reverberated in my head, "What were you thinking?!!"

My stomach dropped and I sat on the steps.

When my father found out I was engaged to someone I hadn't been seeing for very long, he'd have questions about Nick and his background that I wouldn't be able to answer. I'd have to keep the engagement a secret until l knew more.

The doorbell rang. Through the side window I could see that it was Tim Mulvaney, the lead contractor I'd hired to do the renovations, and his brother Leo. I wondered if they were stopping by to check on the window they'd replaced on the first level.

I caught my breath, then carefully made my way down to the first floor again. I should have taken him up on his offer when he recommended installing a small elevator, even though it would have eliminated much-needed closet space.

"Hello, Ms. Brown," Tim said when I opened the door. He tipped his frayed white painter's cap and revealed a mop of sweaty brown hair that mostly stuck to his forehead.

"No accident," Leo said to no one in particular. His head was cocked to the side and it shook slightly, like he had palsy. One eye was permanently half-closed, and he leaned on a cane.

From his first visit Tim had told me that Leo might not speak to me. "Just know that it's not personal. We have cousins he won't even speak to."

Tim placed his hand on his younger brother's shoulder and squeezed. "I know. It's okay."

Leo was three or four inches taller than Tim, easily fifty pounds heavier. Under all of his mental and physical difficulties, Leo seemed smart, aware, kind.

"Leo is concerned that there might be an accident if we don't get that railing up soon," Tim said.

Leo shook his head like he disagreed.

"Thank you, Leo. I've had that concern myself lately."

"I know you weren't expecting us this week," Tim said. "But we were doing some work at Ms. Bunny's house and I thought since we were in the neighborhood we might double-check those measurements again." He pointed to the stairs. "I want to make sure they get the railing right this time."

I ushered them inside, happy for the distraction of their company.

Leo appeared aimless until Tim gave his brother instructions on how to help him with the measuring tape. Tim wrote the final numbers in a pocket-sized spiral notebook, then stuffed it into his back pocket.

"Oh, by the way," Tim pointed toward the kitchen. "When we were painting here the other day, a guy stopped by with an envelope. I put it in that first drawer for you."

"Oh?" I went to the kitchen and opened the drawer. A white 9x12 envelope was stuffed awkwardly inside and I pulled it out.

"I forgot to leave you a note," Tim said sheepishly. "I'd stepped out to get Leo and when I came back he was in the living room. The guy just walked in."

I must have turned three shades of pale because Tim put his hands up. "Now we always keep things locked up like you want. But we'd just painted the front door so it was open a little bit and that was when he came in. I don't think he touched anything."

"Who was it?" I opened the envelope and found several reports on pre-Civil War collections recently appraised by Tatnall Antiques.

"He didn't give a name. Just said you might be inter-viewing with them soon and he thought you might, uh, benefit from those papers, I think he said." Tim's brother handed him the tape measure. "Good job, Leo."

"Restroom?" Leo asked slowly.

I gestured to the half bath just beyond the main living room.

When Leo walked away, Tim said, "Thank you for your patience with Leo."

I shook my head and shrugged, as if to say I didn't need to be thanked. "It's great that he can work with you."

"Oh yeah. He was always very bright. Still is on certain days. The old Leo is still in there. Somewhere."

We were quiet for a moment. Tim shifted his weight from left to right, then he took off his cap, scratched his head, replaced the cap. He sighed hard and a heaviness weighted his features.

I recognized the signs. He carried an old story that had been revisited too often, repeated too frequently, and it didn't have a happy ending.

So I asked. Not to be nosy, but to give him a soft place to land. "He had an accident?"

Tim's jaw set firm and his lips formed an angry thin line. "We don't think it was an accident." He shook his head. "No."

Tim stared at the floor for a moment, and I understood Levi's approach with me all the more. When you saw someone carrying a heavy load, and if you were a kind person, you wanted to help. You wanted to see them lay it down, make peace, move on.

"He and I were doing a partial renovation job a while back. Someone knocked Leo off his ladder and he fell. He hit his head on a marble floor. Blood all over that black and white tile."

"On purpose?" I put my hand to my throat.

Tim shook his head and looked out the window like he was angry. Like he knew better than to respond to my question. "I can't prove it but he and I both know his fall wasn't an accident."

I wondered if that's what Leo meant when he'd said "No accident."

Leo limped around the corner, wringing his hands. He stopped and stared at the spiral staircase. Tim followed his line of sight, then walked toward him.

"Leo—" he warned.

"Not an accident. Forced per...spec...tive." He pronounced each syllable with exaggeration, like he wanted to be sure he got it right. "Things are not what they seem."

I offered Leo a warm smile and figured that Tim must have explained the odd measurements of the railing to him.

"We saw it before," he said. "And at Disney."

"A lot of buildings in those theme parks have forced perspective. Taller structure on the first story, shorter structure on the second story. It makes the buildings appear much taller than they are," I said.

Leo gestured to my railless stairway. "Dangerous."

Tim took Leo by the arm and guided him out the front door. "Alright, buddy. Time to go."

I searched the outside area, looking for anyone who might be watching my house. Tim wrapped his arm around Leo's waist to help him down the stairs. I heard Tim say in a low voice, "We agreed you wouldn't say anything about the railing."

18

Mariana Lopez pedaled her bike along Mission Beach, occasionally stopping to watch surfers ride the two-story waves. She inhaled the cool salty air, let it fill her lungs, soothe her spirit. At this early hour, and on a Monday no less, San Diego beaches were blissfully uncrowded. It gave the illusion that the world was a safe and beautiful place.

She coasted to a stop, closed her eyes, and listened to the waves crash on the sand. She wished for a life where she could live every hour of the day as free and unguarded as she was in this moment.

As she did before.

Before she had been kidnapped and kept in a cage for three weeks. Before the she gave her deposition against members of the Muñoz crime family. Before the death threats had rolled in.

A chill crept over her arms, leaving gooseflesh in its wake. She opened her eyes, looked over her shoulder and scanned the area.

Just as she'd often done over the last twenty years. At least since she had received the We Will letter.

No one there.

Just empty beach.

Her daughter would be up soon. She needed to get back and take her to school. She turned her bike around, pedaled fast. Not because she was late but because she felt watched.

She wished she had paid attention to her gut twenty years ago. When she was standing at the window in the pet store watching six adorable puppies tumble over one another in a play fight. Her mother was one aisle over picking up cat litter.

A woman tapped her on the shoulder. "Would you help us, please? I've found a puppy out front. I think he's hurt." Her accent was strong. "Please?"

She pointed toward the storefront window where a man held a sad-looking beagle puppy. A white bandage stained with blood was wrapped around his front paw.

An ill-at-ease feeling tickled Mariana's gut that day, but she ignored it. Because the puppy...and he was hurt.

When she got to the sidewalk the man with the puppy was gone. A blue van pulled up, two men jumped out, one of them jabbed something into her side, and electricity jolted through her body such that she couldn't breathe, couldn't move.

They dropped her into the back of the van, blindfolded her, bound her wrists with duct tape, drove until her butt went numb. No one spoke. When they arrived at the destination, they took her down two flights of stairs where they threw her into a cage. She lived in that cage with several other girls nearby for three weeks.

Occasionally one of the girls left. They never came back. After the police rescued her, they asked if she would testify.

She never hesitated. Four weeks after the trial in which she and several other girls helped convict members of the Muñoz crime family, the first death threat arrived. There had been two more. That's when she and her parents changed their last names and moved to California. It was as far away from Miami as they could get.

Mariana pedaled faster. Cursed herself for having a routine as of late. She'd always been good about mixing it up in the mornings. Never rode the same beach twice, at least not at the same time of day. But she had rolled her right ankle a few weeks ago, spent two weeks on crutches, and the darn thing still bothered her. She didn't feel comfortable driving long distances, and cycling to a faraway beach was out of the question. Mission Beach was closest to her house.

There was that feeling again. A nudge in the pit of her stomach that something was wrong. She looked around. Didn't see anyone following her. But if someone from the Muñoz family was following her—she wouldn't see anyone. They weren't amateurs.

She stopped at the light, took out her phone and texted her daughter. No response. She called her. Still no response.

Last night her daughter Lily had found a torn piece of notebook paper in the mailbox. There were numbers and fractions written out that neither of them understood. Mariana tried not to think anything of it. But once a person had been kidnapped and held for ransom, once they had received death threats, it was hard not to read into every little thing.

She texted her neighbor, Susan. Asked her to peek in on her daughter, to make sure she was okay. They lived in the same duplex, Mariana on one side with Lily and Susan on the other side with her teenage son, Aidan. They helped one another.

Susan responded: Sure!

Mariana exhaled relief. Her mother had offered her money so she and Lily could live in a higher-end neighborhood, one with gates and a security guard at the front entrance. But Mariana refused her parents' offer. She wanted the independence that came from living within her own means. She also didn't want the trouble that came with wealth. People noticed you when you had money; these days it could make you a target for the unstable.

She thought she could be more invisible this way. Waitressing while Lily was at school, some corporate design work on the side for extra money. She was just one nondescript person of many, one of the crowd, one that no one would pay attention to. Life was freer that way.

Lily was twelve. Old enough to set her morning alarm, put frozen waffles in the toaster and get ready for school on her own. She was also good about keeping doors and windows locked.

But experience had taught Mariana to be overprotective. So when she had that funny feeling, she acted on it.

She stood and pedaled the last few feet up the driveway, dropped her bike at the top. Lights were on in both sides of the duplex. Good sign. There was a rush of movement behind the front curtains. Susan might have been watching out the front for her since she had texted. Lily was probably behind schedule.

Then it hit her. She stopped on the front stoop, an eerie cold chill slipped into her gut. The first line of numbers from the notebook paper could have been a Bible verse. Maybe the same Bible verse that the Muñoz clan used? She wasn't sure, she hadn't seen it in twenty years.

She took the keys from her front pocket, unlocked both locks, stepped inside. The solemn quiet caused her stomach to hit the floor. Lily wasn't playing her music. No sound of shower water running. No scent of waffles cooking.

She forced a swallow. "Lily?"

No answer.

Her side of the duplex was small. Nine hundred and seventy-four square feet. When someone called out, everyone heard them. It was impossible not to.

"Are you ready for school?"

A soft whimper.

Mariana closed her eyes. They had her.

She pulled out her phone and dialed 911. Stepped outside, gave the operator the address. She told them someone was in her house and that they had her daughter. The operator confirmed that police were on their way and told Mariana to wait outside.

She wouldn't.

"Lily?" she called out from the foyer.

Another whimper.

She took two cautious steps inside. "Lily, sweetheart. You're going to be late." She tried to sound normal, singsongy. Nonchalant.

Something from the alcove on her left caught her attention. A pair of shoes with the soles facing out.

Another step. She could just see around the corner now. Blood on the carpet, beneath the shoes.

Another step.

Duct tape around the ankles. More blood beneath them. Bloody hands taped together, light blue fingernail polish and a silver ring with a blue topaz stone. That was Susan's ring. Susan's bloody hands.

Mariana searched the area without moving her head,

she listened for movement. Another whimper from the back bedroom. Lily's, she knew.

She kept a loaded handgun on the top of the slim china cabinet her mother gave her. But that was a good fifteen feet ahead of her and to the left. If she could get to it, she would blast the guy who held her daughter captive. The guy she knew was there to kill her.

She took a chance, leaned forward and looked into the alcove to see Susan. Her neighbor's mouth was taped. Her wide green eyes looked left, and left again, like she was telling her where the intruder was. Three rooms were to Susan's left. The utility slash laundry room, a bathroom and Lily's room.

Sirens blared in the distance. Cops were coming.

She debated what to do. The cops would want her outside so they could handle this. But her daughter was here and captive and she wouldn't abandon her.

Mariana squatted next to Susan, pulled the sticky tape from her mouth. Susan whispered, "He tied up Lily. He's in the back somewhere."

Mariana nodded, took the keys from her pocket, used the jagged edge from one key to rip holes in the wide tape around her wrists and ankles.

They worked to get the tape off. Bloody gashes lined her arms and hands. She must have fought.

"Go," Mariana mouthed and pointed to the front door that was still open.

Susan obeyed.

Mariana knew Susan needed to get to her son. She knew she needed to get him away from this situation.

She tiptoed four feet to the china cabinet, reached to the top for the gun.

Pain hit her from the right side. Deep pain. A quick jab

from behind that stopped her breath. He must have come from the kitchen. She fell against the wall, looked down. A dark wet spot widened across her shirt.

The man in front of her wore a ski mask and held a large knife. Blood covered the silver blade. Her blood. He leaned down until he was eye to eye with her. He removed the mask. Tanned skin and dark hair so thick it didn't look real. Deep brown eyes that were tainted with evil. She'd never seen him before, but she thought there was some resemblance to the Muñoz family members she'd known once before. The cheekbones, the jawline, his facial structure echoed the men she'd testified against.

She took in every possible detail because when she got out of this she would give Agent Hernandez a perfect description of the guy.

She studied his black shirt, black pants, white tennis shoes. Blue disposable gloves on his hands.

When she met his eyes again she whispered, "What do you want?"

His smile spread slow and wide, like he was glad she'd asked.

He leaned close to her ear and she smelled his cologne—a woodsy vetiver, citrusy lemon. He'd known he would try to kill her today, and still he put on cologne.

"Justice," he said softly.

Her heart seized so hard that her chest hurt.

"You took my father away from me," he whispered close to her ear. "You took his life. So now I take yours." He stabbed her again, as if the knife gave punctuation to his words.

Unable to breathe, she slid the rest of the way to the floor. Wetness poured down her back. The knife must have gone straight through.

He dropped the knife, pulled off the disposable gloves and shoved them deep into his front pocket.

Darkness encircled her vision, surrounded her, dragged her in.

He looked at his arms and shirt as if he searched for blood spatter. Then he casually walked down the hallway, and soon, muffled screams came from Lily's bedroom.

"Hey," Manny said when he arrived in the doorway of his partner's office.

"Hey," Stanford pulled a stack of papers from his briefcase and placed it on his desk.

"Everything alright?"

"Yeah. Had a meeting with Alice this morning. Actually, her attorney had a meeting with my attorney. Alice and I didn't speak."

Manny thought of his own divorce settlement. He had let his first wife take everything she wanted, just so he could avoid such a fight. He hadn't wanted to see all their once-perfect dreams debased into an argument over who got the china cabinet.

He was the one who had screwed up that marriage, so he didn't contest any of her demands. In the end he walked away with his ten-year-old car, his clothes and a small amount of his dignity. "Y'all reach an agreement?"

Stanford clicked his tongue against the roof of his mouth and gestured to the papers. "She wants the house, our savings, and most of our retirement fund. My attorney said she's probably going to get it."

Considering Stanford's drinking, his infidelity and his temper, Manny wasn't surprised. "Sorry, man. I know that's rough."

Stanford lowered himself into his chair slowly, deliberately and began to organize his desk. "You're right. It is."

Manny waited to see if Stanford had anything else to say. When he didn't, Manny said, "Didn't hear back from you this weekend."

"Yeah, I was busy getting ready for this morning's meeting."

"It was about the Muñoz case."

"I figured. There is no Muñoz case, Manny. That's the second reason why I didn't call you back." Stanford shot him a look that said he didn't want to talk about it. "I warned you not to go down this rabbit hole."

Manny felt the anger rise in his gut, but he ignored the bait.

Several things were odd about his partner today.

Whenever Stanford's divorce settlement came up in conversation, he typically threw something—coffee cup, book, bottle, whatever happened to be within reach. At the very least he slammed his fist or hit something. Also he hadn't referred to his soon-to-be-ex by her given name in quite a while. He usually referred to her as a common thief who tried to steal everything he'd ever worked for. Today he used her name and he boasted a strange confidence that Manny didn't like.

"Jenny Hansen was murdered," Manny said.

Stanford stopped shuffling the papers on his desk.

He became very still. "How did you know about her death?"

"Bruce called me," Manny lied. "He asked for our help." He told Stanford about the verse on the pamphlet and the minister who wasn't really a minister. "When you consider the note I received last week, it justifies our involvement."

"I've read the report. She was running in a closed-off park, after a heavy rain and in a muddy area. She was where she shouldn't have been and she fell. She wasn't the first one to fall off that cliff."

Manny shook his head. "Don't you think that's rather convenient? You remember how they stage their murders."

"I've warned you, Manny. This is a fish hook in your cheek. Let it go."

They stared at one another for a long moment.

Then Manny said, "Call the women and their parents and let them know about Jenny's death. Tell them about the guy's visit and the verse she received ahead of time. Tell them about the note I received beforehand. Give them the chance to protect themselves."

"People who write notes rarely follow through on their threats," Stanford said in a preaching tone. "The last time you reached out to the girls' parents, we all lost our ability to communicate with them. Did you forget?"

Manny shoved his hands into his pockets, clenched his teeth, attempted to steer clear of the emotional tar pit of his past. Several days after four girls were rescued out of the twelve who had been kidnapped, Manny called some of the victims' parents and told them he was to blame for their girls' deaths because he didn't investigate every lead. He didn't remember making the calls since he'd drunk enough vodka to put himself into a coma.

The Department covered for him. They also paid a hefty settlement to a few of the families, legally requiring their silence. "That was a long time ago, and I was the only one restricted from contacting them. Not you."

Stanford shook his head. "I don't think I could reach out to them without getting called in over it, not after everything that's happened. I'd have to check with the Chief first."

Manny felt a familiar and frustrating swirl of confusion.

"Did they make any demands?" Stanford asked.

"No," Manny said.

"That's not really the typical Muñoz style. Everything they've ever done they did for money. Jenny probably told the wrong person about her past and they sent the note to mess with her. Or maybe her husband wanted to get rid of her and he used the note as a coverup."

"There's a video of the guy with the pamphlet and you're forgetting that I received a note as well. I don't think she would have given someone my name and address. This isn't about money. This is one of Ricardo's sons following through on the We Will letters. They're fulfilling their promise to kill for revenge."

Stanford said, "If it was the husband, he could have sent you the note, he could have hired the guy to show up with the pamphlet."

Manny thought about bringing up the note that Harper received. But Stanford's blatant disconnect made him think better of it.

"Keep yourself out of trouble, leave it alone," Stanford said.

Manny walked back to his office, obsessively combing through the one thousand pieces of information he had just observed, trying desperately to make connections, to make sense.

Stanford was stupid about a lot of things, but he wasn't

an idiot. He had a keen sense to spot lies and corruption and places where things didn't add up. Today, he didn't.

Manny's pulse beat into his head because he knew he wouldn't leave it alone.

He had a feeling that Stanford wouldn't either.

20

———

Jagged lightning lit up the dark sky, and rain drummed loud against the metal roof of the cab. I glanced at my puny umbrella. I was not sufficiently armed against the downpour.

Max and I were supposed to meet earlier in the morning. But he changed the time of the interview saying he was delayed in returning from his trip. So I'd spent the entire day corralled in my home, wearing one of my Sig Sauer 9 millimeters at my waist. Unless a Muñoz was going to saw a hole in the roof or blow up one of my doors, no one was getting into my home without my personal invitation. Still, wearing the weapon made me prepared. I was going to be safe, not sorry.

Under normal conditions I would have rescheduled. But I had to have employment in short order. Otherwise I was in violation of the agreement with my father.

I searched the area to make sure I hadn't been followed, then I ran toward the front door of Tatnall Antique Appraisals. By the time I was under cover, the umbrella had been beaten into submission by the driving rain and I felt like a drowned rat.

"Very brave of you to come out in this weather." The receptionist greeted me with a dry towel and a sympathetic smile. "I'm Ginger. The power's out, again. Unfortunately."

Tatnall Antique Appraisals resided in a grand old house, prominently positioned in the heart of Savannah's National Historic Landmark District. Its interior was fully furnished in period antiques, and without electricity it appeared as I thought it had well over 150 years ago.

At this time of night, there were no employees roaming the halls, no client chatter in the reception area. Three silver candelabras on bombe chests illuminated the long, dark hallway in front of me.

When I had dried myself, Ginger took the towel from me and disappeared from view. The house was as still as a cemetery at midnight.

She reappeared with an ivory candle in a silver candle holder. "Tea? It was freshly made."

"I'd love to but I have several allergies, so I can't, unfortunately."

She gestured for me to follow her up the grand staircase. "Construction began on the house in the early 1860s by Charles Lancaster for his wife Edith. Of course when war was declared in 1861 construction was halted."

Ginger continued reciting the history of the house as she probably did for every new guest. But my thoughts were held hostage by Agent Hernandez's warning that I shouldn't accept a blind request for an interview or employment. Also how Max's invitation to interview followed the arrival of the note.

I'd emailed Agent Hernandez a photograph of the note

just so he would have it. He'd suggested I leave town for a while, to be safe. I'd also sent the same photo to my parents. I hadn't wanted to tell them, but after some thought I decided it would be a bigger problem if I didn't.

Why would you keep something like that from us? they would ask.

I'd mentioned that I felt concerned. But discussing anything with them meant walking a fine line. I had to balance the risk of telling them what I really thought and felt versus what a normal human would think and feel.

They called right away, asking about the near break-in, asking if I'd called the police, asking if I'd had the alarm system in place—essentially making sure that I had handled the experience like a mature, well-balanced adult.

When I told them about Jenny's death and the note she'd received beforehand—I don't know why I thought this —I did think they would see that my note was a threat too.

But instead my father said, "Let's not overreact or jump to conclusions."

It's what he always said in the face of my concerns, and it made me want to chew steel. I could tell him there was a bear crawling through the window and he'd say, are you sure? Let's not jump to conclusions.

But I got it. I'd lost my credibility and trustworthiness because of all the many emotional problems they'd seen firsthand prior to the kidnapping. Including the fact I'd stabbed my father. And I'd killed Catherine. If I were in their shoes, if my lone surviving daughter had killed her twin, I'm not sure I'd behave any differently. I'd be overprotective and untrusting.

"Do you need to talk with someone?" my mother asked.

"The nurse says you've been good about taking all your

meds," my father said. "But do we need to make any adjustments? An upsetting experience like this would cause stress for anyone. We can speak with the doctor if you feel the anxiety is too much."

I was relieved to hear the good report. That meant the nurse hadn't picked up on the fact that I didn't swallow the pills anymore. I told him I didn't think it was necessary, that the regimen I was following was sufficient. Although, given his questions, I knew I needed to remind them that Agent Hernandez was the one who had reached out and told me about Jenny's death. That *he* thought it was suspicious and that *he* was worried.

There was a long pause and then they said, almost in unison, "We'll call him."

Before they could hang up, I told them that Nick had proposed and that I had accepted. I told them we didn't have a date as of yet, but that we were in love and excited to plan our new life together.

They were speechless. I knew they would be.

Then my father said, "One of the terms of our guardianship is that you can't marry without our permission."

My heart sank all the way to the floor. I didn't remember that restriction in our agreement. I might have overlooked it because until recently I hadn't thought marriage was even a possibility. "I know," I lied. "I'll introduce you to him. You'll love him."

"Does he know about your past?" he asked.

"Not yet," I said.

My father cleared his throat and sighed heavily. "Then maybe you two aren't ready for marriage."

"We'll take it one step at a time," I said.

We hung up.

I screamed until my throat burned. I threw a vase

against the wall. I was now more motivated than ever to meet the terms of his agreement so I could get my freedom and my identity back. I had to get this job.

My text alarm buzzed and I peeked at my phone screen. It was Nick:

Successful trip, coming back early. Meet me in NYC tonight? Will arrange for private dinner on the terrace.

I REPLIED:

At my meeting, will call later

"HERE WE ARE," the receptionist said and gestured to the closed door. "This is the Florence Martus conference room, and this is a young Florence Martus." She pointed to a large print on the wall to the right of the door, where a young girl waved a handkerchief at a passing ship. A small dog was at her side.

"For 44 years she lived on Elba Island with her brother, the lighthouse keeper, and was known as 'the waving girl,' the unofficial greeter of all the ships that entered the Port of Savannah between 1887 and 1931," she said proudly. "Some say they still see her out there. Waving. Savannah has a special relationship with its dead, you know."

"I've heard," I said and thought of my sister. I touched the gilded frame. "Bring me luck, Florence."

Max stood with two other people near a round conference table in the center of the room. When he shook my hand, one of the prongs from his garnet ring dug into my hand and I forced myself not to wince.

He introduced the two other partners as Neal Sutherland and Joyce Walters, both appraisers who had been with the firm for years.

"Prosecco? Cheese or cookies?" Max gestured to a side table with sparkling wine and various snacks.

"I'm fine, thank you."

"Ginger makes these cookies herself. They're quite good!"

I ran into this situation a lot in the South because hosts often associated food and drink with hospitality. I found the easiest response was to be honest. "I'd love to but I have a peanut allergy and I have to be careful." I showed him my rose gold and pearl medic alert bracelet that was crafted to look like jewelry.

"Of course," he said. "My apologies."

When we were all seated, Neal explained that Max's appearances on the regional appraisal show continued to bring in significant business. They needed someone to take on a fairly large book of their clients for approximately a year. My expertise was a perfect fit.

While I presented my qualifications, I flashed my best PR smile. It wasn't my most natural one. But it was my infectious movie star-type smile and it made everyone smile in response.

Max reclined in the black, high-back executive chair and flipped through my portfolio of projects.

When I finished a review of my clients and projects for the last two years, the email alert on my phone buzzed. I ignored it.

Then everyone else's phones buzzed.

Joyce picked up her phone, tapped the screen. Her eyes narrowed with concern. She elbowed Neal who sat next to her, showed him something on her phone. His eyebrows perked up.

Heat climbed up the back of my neck, flushing my face.

"I have a good network in the industry. My contacts are wide and varied."

No one listened. No one paid me any attention.

I looked at Max.

He shrugged. "What's got everyone's attention?"

No one responded. Joyce rose from her chair, took her phone to Max. She showed him something and whispered in his ear.

Max took her phone and escorted me to the hallway.

"Seems we have a situation." Max pointed to Joyce's phone screen. "We each received this email and the, uh, photos."

The subject line of the email read: Want to lose your husband? Let him work with Harper Brown. My heart screeched to a painful stop.

The photos in the body of the email must have been taken with a telephoto lens from a neighboring building. Because the photographer captured what I had thought was a private moment between Nick and me several weeks earlier.

I remembered the night. I had been working late with him in his New York office. No one else was around and, I rationalized, no one would ever know. In the photos I sat on the edge of the desk, my legs crossed to the side, light reflected off my black patent heels. Nick leaned toward me, our lips pressed together in a passionate kiss.

"Harper?" Max asked. "Is that you?"

The blood drained from my head.

He enlarged one of the photos with two fingers and pointed to a Chamberlain Antiques sign that hung in the background.

"And is that...your client?"

21

———

Max escorted me down a long hallway to his large office and asked that I wait for him. He managed to avoid all direct eye contact.

I stood next to his wall-to-wall bookcase, not quite sure what to do with myself. Hands shaking, I pulled up the email everyone had received in the meeting and tapped on the sender's name: Sophie Taylor. The address read: Sophie Taylor at tempmail dot com.

Tempmail dot com was a disposable email company.

Thunder cracked overhead and I flinched.

I typed her name into an internet search box. Before I could click go, another email from Sophie Taylor came in. This one read:

You have no idea what you've gotten into.

THERE WAS a link at the end of the email that led to an article from the Savannah Morning News. I waited for the article to load. Sweat prickled beneath my shirt and my breath came so fast that a spaced-out feeling filled my head.

Nick had only briefly discussed his ex-wife and not by name. He said they'd married for the wrong reasons, didn't want the same things in life and the breakup had been messy.

I took his lack of discussion of her as a healthy sign, that he wasn't obsessed with his past. Besides, Nick's last name wasn't Taylor. It was Chamberlain. Although Taylor could have been her maiden name.

If this Sophie Taylor was his ex-wife, why wouldn't she just use her regular email? Why go through the trouble of setting up a temporary email address? I suspected that whoever took and sent the photos wasn't really Sophie Taylor.

The page took forever to load. Only one bar of cell signal in Max's office.

Max's bookcase was professionally arranged with framed diplomas, hardback books and numerous photos of him posing on the set of Hidden Treasures. There were also pictures of him and his family. Using my phone's flashlight in the dark room, I looked closely at a faded photo of him and his wife holding their newborn daughter. They looked incredibly young. They also looked as ill-matched then as they did today.

The photo next to that one was his daughter Annabelle. She was wrapped like a burrito in a hospital baby blanket and lying in a plastic hospital bassinet. The large index card taped at the end of the bed had a pre-printed pink teddy bear on it along with the handwritten words in fat black marker: Annabelle Tatnall Crandall, December 16th, 8:12 p.m., 7lbs, 6oz.

There was another photo of what looked like a large school group in front of the Eiffel Tower. Max had been short then, too. I thought I recognized someone else and leaned in for a closer look.

Max walked in holding a lit candelabra. He appeared smooth, confident, accomplished in his navy blue suit. Not at all nonplussed as I thought he might have been. He placed the candelabra on his desk, closed the door and dropped into his high-back executive chair. He adjusted the more-than-a-century-old garnet ring on his thumb, the same one I'd seen in his wife's social media video.

When I didn't move, he gestured to one of the two black leather chairs across from his desk and I took a seat. I searched Max's face for the glow of approval I'd seen on the first day we'd met, but that warmth had chilled.

"I don't know who took these photos or why they sent them to the firm, but Nick is divorced. And our relationship never interfered with my work."

Max didn't nod, he didn't smile. His steeled expression didn't give me any clues as to what he was thinking. He pulled his cell phone from his jacket pocket and thumb tapped something on the screen.

"At first I didn't recognize his face—his hair is different and he shaved his beard. But—"

"My consulting engagement with his firm was completed before we became involved."

Max spread his fingers along the phone screen like he was enlarging an image. He clicked his tongue against the roof of his mouth like I'd missed the point. "Honestly, my bigger concern would be this."

He handed me his phone, and a different version of

Nick's face stared at me from a magazine article. His hair was longer and he had a beard, but it was Nick. The headline sent a chill straight to the center of my bones: Husband Charged with Attempted Murder of Socialite Wife.

Nick Smith. I read and re-read this last name. I searched the photo of Nick's face hoping to find some feature that looked unfamiliar, but the face was definitely his.

Nick Smith, a transplant from Miami, married Sophie Taylor two years before her tragic fall down the stairs that landed her in a coma. Today the Chatham County Police Chief released a statement: "We have interviewed Nick Smith with regard to Sophie Taylor's fall. We have also interviewed numerous witnesses and believe that Sophie's injuries were not the result of an accident. We believe her fall is the result of premeditation and deliberate intent. Therefore the District Attorney's office has charged Nick Smith with first-degree attempted murder."

Smith? Miami? The heat of fury and shame crawled up my neck, warmed my cheeks. I scanned the rest of the article hoping to find a happy ending to the story but there wasn't one. There were, however, photos of Nick and Sophie from high school. Apparently, they had been sweethearts from years ago. One photo from a trip to Paris showed them arm in arm in front of the Eiffel Tower. I glanced at Max's bookcase. He had the same photo. They must have been friends.

My father's scorched-earth voice was loud in my head now, and just as condemning as it ever was. *"What were you thinking!?!"*

I snapped a photo of the image with my phone, and handed Max his phone.

I walked to the window, my head bursting with plenty of

you-should-haves: You should have thought this through, you should have researched him better, you should have taken the meds! A scream built in strength, climbed into my throat, and I covered my mouth with my hand.

I did check Nick's background. I didn't account for the fact that he might have legally changed his name. Those identifying details weren't evident in background checks. Just like my true identity couldn't have been found anywhere on the web.

Max stood next to me, his hand pressed against my upper back. "I'm sorry. But I thought you should know."

"No—I, I'm glad you did. Is his wife dead?" I asked, stepping away from his touch.

He shook his head, shrugged. "Last I heard, Sophie was in a coma. It was a big story for a while, dominated the front page of every newspaper for months. But her parents put her in a private facility and no one has heard much about it since."

"She must not be in a coma if she sent the emails." My head spun and I had to sit down again. This had to have been an accident. Some huge misunderstanding. The Nick I knew wouldn't hurt anyone, least of all a woman.

"I don't know. But if it isn't her, then you must have someone out there who really doesn't like you. Someone who doesn't want you to have this job."

On instinct I searched Max's tanned features for specific resemblances to the Muñoz family. They were there, of course—in the shape of his nose, the angle of his jaw. I could find those incriminating features in just about anyone. I wondered, as I had from the first time I met him, if he was a son of Ricardo Muñoz, if he released the photos and left the note, just to mess up my life. This could have been a part of the payback they promised. Perhaps he wanted to destroy my life before he ended it altogether, just so he could watch me suffer.

"I don't know who that would be," I said.

Max grabbed two bottles of water from the small black fridge across the room and handed one to me. He pulled a chair over and sat next to me.

From the expression on Max's face I thought he was about to let me down easy, tell me they couldn't hire me. I knew of a few appraisal firms across the river in Beaufort, S.C. that might offer some sporadic work. But it wouldn't be enough. Thanks to all the on-air appraisals Max did, the Tatnall firm had garnered most of the business in the southeast.

"I apologize that my personal life—" I shook my head, not at all sure how to finish that sentence. "I'm a competent appraiser, my qualifications would be a strong asset for the firm and to your clients."

Max leaned in, too close, in fact, and put his hand on mine.

Confusion hit my brain in waves. His firm was smaller than most firms I'd worked with. And Savannah was smaller than most towns, but he had to know he was crossing a line.

Max's office door opened abruptly and Charlotte, his wife, stood in the doorway.

When Max saw her, he released my hand and stood upright.

I stood as well.

No part of Charlotte was petite but she had feminine appeal with her aquiline nose and thick blond hair styled into gentle waves. A single strand of pearls at her neck accented her pale yellow suit. Her bright smile fell until her lips pressed together in a straight line.

She didn't ask what was going on, and her expression

didn't even show surprise. Rather, her closed lips pulled thin in old, familiar disgust.

Max walked toward her, nervously straightening his perfectly straight tie and smoothing the front of his crisp, white button-down shirt. When he stood next to her, she towered over him by at least a foot. "I'm just finishing an interview. We can leave in about ten minutes," he said.

I must not have looked like a threat to her or her marriage. Because she said, "I'll wait outside." She leaned down and Max obediently kissed her cheek.

Max closed the door again. "I'll see what I can work out with the other partners. I know Nick. We went to school together ages ago. I know how he can fool people. Especially women. In the meantime, you might want to check out The Savannah Morning News' coverage of the trial. Amanda Cummings' column was good. That series got her syndicated."

Max put his hands into his pockets. His voice was calm and professional, but the glint in his eyes told me he wasn't disappointed that the information was out in the open.

"When Nick's trial ended and he was acquitted, she wrote a final piece about the overriding perceptions that everyone took from the trial. It got national coverage.

"First, she said that Nick was a very good storyteller. Extremely good. Very convincing. Second, she said his good looks made an impression on the women of the jury. And third, she said that because he wasn't convicted, he would try it again."

I turned the door handle. "Try what again?"

"Seduce a wealthy woman, convince her to marry him, then kill her for her money."

22

───────

I ran smack into Charlotte who stood just outside his door. She had been listening. I apologized but she didn't smile or nod or say anything. She just stood there like a statue, like an immovable guard. The message was clear: Stay away from my husband.

Once on the street I glanced up and saw Max peering out one of the second story windows. I felt like a target.

I walked until I was out of his sight and then I broke into a run. I didn't slow down again until I was at my beloved Columbia Square.

Blisters burned my feet from running in heels and my throat ached from holding back the emotion.

The streets were dark, the air was thick and humid, and a light fog hovered in the square.

I was breathless and sweating and I felt everything.

The betrayal of Nick's lies and secrets, the threats on my life, and the fact that Nick was the bridge connecting the two.

I felt sick.

I bent and grabbed my knees. I expected sobs or vomit to pour as usual.

But what burst from my heart was rage.

Burning, shrieking rage.

I curled my fists tight.

All the safe decisions. All the rule following. All the hiding.

For what.

For what?!

For naught.

I pushed myself upright and tried to think.

I still couldn't catch my breath. My arms and hands shook with fury.

Who would take photos of Nick and me and why? To destroy my chances of working with Tatnall? Obviously. But how would they even know to send them to Tatnall? I knew I hadn't told anyone about the specifics of the interview.

Which made me think all the more that it wasn't an accident when Max bumped into me that day in Beaufort. The job offer must have been a set-up, now he was toying with me, and he'd been in my house.

Nick and Max knew one another. Nick was from Miami like the Muñoz family.

Unimaginable.

I studied my home and wondered if Nick was inside. I had given him his own code when I thought we were getting married.

I checked the house alarm app on my phone and there were no alarms, no alerts. Still, I couldn't bring myself to go inside. Not alone.

Across the green I saw Levi pedaling his stationary bike in the front room of his home. If I asked him, he would go into my house ahead of me and look for trouble.

I slipped off my heels and walked toward Levi's. The sidewalk was warm and wet beneath my feet. The fog was cool against my skin.

I reached the fountain.

I was still angry enough to kill Nick. Literally.

I pulled out my phone and clicked the link in the email. It was a newspaper article from The Savannah Morning News. The masthead read: Light of the Coastal Empire and Low Country. The photo they featured was the same one on Max's bookshelf, the same one from the other paper he'd shown me. High School Sweetheart Gone Bad, this caption read.

I enlarged the photo and studied all the faces.

My fingertips tingled. Outrage coursed through every nerve.

My reaction was ancient, reptilian, hard-wired.

Like shoving the black-toothed man into the lagoon to be eaten by alligators.

Or the night my father was stabbed.

I understood this rage now. From a whole new perspective.

I pulled up Nick's number.

But I remembered the last time my rage was unleashed, a very long time ago.

"You worthless drunk, you killed my sister! My only sister!" I'd screamed at Agent Hernandez.

He didn't flinch. He just stood there. He took it.

Without explanation, I knew. I knew he'd stopped drinking.

After a long moment I said, "You gave it up."

He nodded.

"Why?"

"Because sometimes you just have to learn."

I let the phone fall to my side.

Bunny was in her front room. Her hair was untwisted, cascading long in a torrent of gray and black. She wore the same white nightgown and lit the same ivory candles as she had the other night.

I stood there staring. Gas lamps hissed and water spilled into the fountain like fat drops of rain.

As if someone whispered to her that she should, Bunny looked at me directly. She waved, slowly, like her movement was choreographed.

One thing was clear.

No matter the rage, the lies, the secrets, I had to do something.

I didn't know what.

I wouldn't lock myself inside my house and sit there, waiting to die.

Before I arrived at her porch she opened the front door and extended her arm. When I reached the threshold she wrapped me in a tight hug and wordlessly welcomed me inside like I'd been expected.

"Have a seat in the parlor and I'll make us some tea." She patted me on the back and gestured to the first room on the left.

She was not wearing her social persona. She wasn't talkative or decorated in expensive gold jewelry. Her voice was quiet, her eyes were soft, her touch was tender.

"I have a lovely rooibos I've been saving for us," she said from somewhere down the darkened hallway.

Bunny's house was built in 1850, the youngest home on the square. The interior was a trip back in time, with swan's neck pediment, shuttered windows with splayed lintels, and hand-painted murals adorning the walls and ceilings. The house, full of history, full of memories, was empty and quiet.

I walked into the dimly-lit parlor. The warmth and scent of vanilla candles nearly knocked me over. I sat on a yellow-print cushioned chair that matched the dog bed. A large cannonball was firmly implanted into the hardwoods.

Eudora joined me, tiny jingle bells tinkling from the edges of her purple tutu. She sniffed at my bare and blistered toes, then she jumped onto her yellow-print dog bed and watched me.

I studied the many photos that covered the tables and the walls. Most of the pictures were taken in faraway locations from around the world. They featured a much younger Bunny and a man who was, I assumed, her husband. Lots of young people surrounded them.

Bunny returned with two cups of tea and placed them on the antique cherry coffee table. Her hair was newly captured in a long, loose braid. She'd wrapped a thin black shawl around her shoulders.

She gave me a slow wink and a gentle smile.

She pointed to the cannonball. Before I could ask what it was, she said, "Isn't that something? Union soldier shot it right through the front window and every owner of the house since then has kept it right there. I keep it to remind people that it's important to preserve history. If we don't, we forget." She sat on the matching couch across from me. "Then history repeats. A few horrible people take advantage of the masses all over again."

I smiled, covering the full distress and the live rage that jangled on the inside.

Bunny seemed to sense how I felt, so she chit-chatted about the beauty of the night and the earlier storm. She seemed to be waiting. Waiting for me to begin.

I drank the tea quickly and placed the empty teacup on the coffee table and she reached for it.

The candles flickered.

I watched while she stared into the bottom of my teacup, examining the leaf remnants.

"You have a broken heart." She turned the cup. "And you lost someone very dear to you at an early age. Oh, my, such a heavy burden. You lost yourself along the way, but also—" She frowned at the tea leaves, recoiled slightly as if she didn't like what she saw. Then she returned the cup to the saucer, stood and gestured for me to follow her.

In the kitchen there was only candlelight. No electric lights were turned on. She rinsed out the cup, then put a new tablespoon of loose leaf tea into a strainer, and tapped a few of the leaves into the bottom of my cup. She poured the water.

"When Tucker and I moved in I found this packed away in the attic." She reached into one of the kitchen cabinets and pulled down an old brown and tattered book with the word "Tasseography" engraved in gold on the cover.

I flipped through the pages of hand-drawn images and their meanings. The copyright page cited the author as A Highland Seer and the publishing date was 1881.

She nodded toward the tea. "Drink up."

We returned to the parlor and I decided it was time to show Bunny my phone with the photo of Nick and Sophie and the other thing I'd seen.

"Is this you?" I pointed to a younger version of her likeness who stood behind Nick.

She opened her mouth slightly, closed her eyes and nodded long and slow. Like a mystery finally made sense. She sighed and said, "Aha."

Based on her expression it seemed unnecessary to say, but I did anyway. "I've been seeing Nick, and I've been trying to figure out—"

She pointed to one of the photos behind me. "Have I ever shown you a picture of my Tucker?" Her tone held an ethereal quality, like she was a bit lost in her own world. But I didn't think she was.

"We had such a wonderful time traveling with Maribelle—she's one of my granddaughters. That's her right here." Bunny pointed to a teenaged brunette with alabaster skin and a stunning ultra-white-toothed smile.

She pointed to a family Christmas photo. "My boys are over there, Colton and Davis." A large decorated Christmas tree was in front of the parlor's bay window. Bunny stood front and center, a grown son on either side, each with an arm around her. One son with his other arm around a beautiful blonde. Three young grandchildren in front.

"Colton writes novels, like his daddy did. Here's his wife Suzanne, their daughter Presley and their son Jackson. They moved to Tennessee back when my Tucker was still alive.

"This is Davis, he's in film production, travels all over the place. Maribelle is his daughter." Bunny picked up a photo of a chubby-cheeked little girl touching the petal of a pink rose.

"Gosh, I remember that day. I took that photo in the backyard. Her mama was holding her. That's her hand there, with the gold wedding ring." Bunny lowered the photo, and her head, like she'd stumbled on a painful memory. "Her mama died when Maribelle was little. Drunk driver crossed the median and hit her head-on." Bunny returned the photo to the table. "So, Tucker and I helped Davis to raise Maribelle.

"We helped pay for her to go to good Christian private schools. Every year, from sixth to twelfth grade, the school took them on some special trip. That's where most of these photos came from.

"Davis needed to stay home and earn, so Tuck and I went." She smiled and the skin around her light blue eyes crinkled.

Bunny pointed to the framed photos on the antique black secretary. "That was Spain, when she was in ninth grade. This was London. This here was a day trip to Hampton Court Palace." She walked to the other side of the room and picked up a framed photo.

"But the photo you're asking me about is this one, from Paris." She handed me the photo and returned to her seat.

The image was the same one from the newspaper: Nick and Sophie arm-in-arm. Only this photo showed everyone, no one cropped out. Just like on Max's bookshelf.

"You know Nick," I confirmed.

"I've known Nick since he was a little boy. Haven't spoken with him in the last few years. But he and Maribelle used to be quite close." She leaned forward. "I guess you found out he was charged with trying to murder his wife?"

I swallowed against my tight throat. "I was interviewing with Max Crandall at Tatnall Antique Appraisals. He told me."

"How did *that* come up in an interview?" she asked. "Typical Max."

I didn't want to tell her what had happened. But I needed to know the truth. She was the only one I knew who also knew both Max and Nick.

I showed her the emails and the photos.

"My word." She stood, opened a drawer in the secretary and put on a pair of reading glasses. Then she began digging through one of the deep, lower drawers that were stuffed full of loose photos.

"Nothing happened," I said about the photos stupidly. Because that really wasn't the point.

"Well, of course not. Did Max take those?" she asked.

"I don't know who took them."

"I ask because Max was always taking pictures, and this seems like something he would do. He always had a, um— shadowy side about him, I guess you might say. And he and Nick were always at each other's throats. If Nick had something—anything good at all—Max would do everything to destroy it. To be fair, Nick did the same thing in return."

A gust of wind rattled the window panes.

She nodded at my ring. "You're in love with him."

"Yes," I said. Although I didn't know what I was at the moment.

She closed her eyes. Her gracious and perfect bearing slipped away. Left in its wake was something vulnerable, conflicted, alone.

"I have questions. As you might imagine." I didn't tell her what my questions were. That would have taken too long.

"My Tucker was the love of my life." She opened her eyes and kept digging. "But he kept things from me. To this day I still wonder how much I ever really knew him. I wouldn't wish that sort of relationship on anyone."

She pulled a handful of photos from the back left corner of the drawer and returned to the couch. She patted the cushion to her right.

I sat next to her.

"I used to tell him—if you'll just be open with me, I could find a way to accept or forgive. But keeping something from me—that's a betrayal. The wondering, the what-ifs, those eat the soul alive. But we love who we love."

She sighed and spread the stack of photos onto the antique coffee table.

She tapped a group photo that had been taken at the

beach. "I'll just tell you up front. I don't know if Nick is innocent or guilty of trying to kill Sophie. But I can tell you a few things about him that most people probably don't know. This is him, right here."

She pointed to a teenage Nick. He was thin, his hair was long and his expression was far more carefree than I'd ever known him to be.

"This is Maribelle next to him. She's almost a year younger than him, but they were in the same grade. They dated for a while."

Bunny pointed to the kids one by one. "This is Max, the one you interviewed with earlier today. Sophie, Nick, Charlotte, Piper, Maribelle, Nick C., Gunner."

I picked up the photo and looked closely at the faces.

"They were inseparable throughout junior high and high school."

"Most everyone came from Savannah families whose relatives have lived in town for generations. What you might refer to as a blue blood. Except for Max and Nick. They arrived when everyone was already in elementary school. Fifth grade, I think.

I rubbed at my chest, where my heart thrummed. Their coloring, the timing, the reference to Florida. One or both of them could be a Muñoz son.

"I remember because Savannahians are particular about who's local and who's not. You could have lived here for 35 years, but if you weren't born here, you're always from somewhere else. Still, they joined the crew, and they all became very tight.

"Nick C. is also from Savannah proper. His parents live across the square from Charlotte's parents. Both of those families are old blue-bloods. We started calling him Nick C. when our other Nick came along so we could identify them properly on school trips. It turned into a nickname—Nicksey—that stuck. God bless him, he died just after high school. Terrible hazing incident at the University of Georgia. Too much alcohol. Drowned in a pool. Horrible way to go."

"Nick C.?"

"Chamberlain," she answered.

Another bolus of adrenaline surged through my veins and I thought I might be sick. *Chamberlain.*

"Growing up, the two Nicks were inseparable. Very different, though. Nick Chamberlain came from a well-to-do family. Loads of polish. Nick Smith lived with his mother on the poorer side of town. I think they even lived in a trailer at one point." She leaned back. "Anyway. The other kids were worried initially about bringing Nick and Max into the group. They all came from money. Max and Nick didn't.

"Never seemed to be a problem, though. Nick and Max fit right in, oddly. Like they were accustomed to having money. Or at least being around it.

"I'll tell you, Maribelle loved that boy. Your Nick, I mean. All the girls fell in love with him at one point or another. Through the years they all dated each other. They were all still close until..." Bunny stopped and cleared her throat. "Maribelle and Gunner are married now. She's pregnant, expecting a boy." She nodded to another framed photo. A wedding photo of Gunner and Maribelle standing at the altar in a candlelight ceremony in St. John the Baptist Cathedral just a few blocks away.

"Until?" I asked.

Bunny stared at a candle flame. She seemed lost in a memory.

When she didn't respond I asked, "Did you ever meet Nick's mother?"

Bunny came to. "I'm sure I did." She shuffled through

the photos. She went to the top drawer of the china cabinet and pulled out another stack of photos and brought them to the coffee table.

Acne, braces and awkward hairstyles were a theme in these photos and I guessed we were looking at the junior high school era. I picked up a photo of the two Nicks together. My Nick wore metal braces and a hairstyle with an unfortunate part down the middle of his head. Still, the seeds of his handsome good looks were evident.

The other Nick, Nick Chamberlain, wore nicer, more tailored clothes with expensive logos. He was taller by three or four inches, more broad and he threw his arm around my Nick. The two smiled wide and held carrots out to the side like they were cigars.

"Here she is."

Bunny pointed to a slender, attractive brunette woman who wore a blue and white gingham check waitress uniform. She stood against the wall of what looked like a school hallway, arms crossed, behind all the other parents who posed for a group photo.

"She was a waitress?" I took a photo of her with my phone. "How did she afford private school tuition for him on a waitress's salary?"

Bunny gave a long shrug. "We never did figure that one out. Most of the families around here send their kids to the public elementary school. Then they switch them to private for middle and high school, because that's when the public school environments can get difficult.

"When Max and Nick came in during the fifth grade, we all thought they would stay in the public school system. But first day of sixth grade, both of them showed up at Savannah Country Day.

"I think one of the other families must have set up

private scholarships for them. Or I guess it's possible Nick's mother saved and scrimped to prioritize her son's education. She might have gotten a discounted tuition. Although if I had to put money on it, I'd bet it was Charlotte's father. That girl got whatever she wanted from her father. Never had to ask twice.

"Tuck and I always said he set a bad precedent by giving her so much. That ultimately she'd drive some boy nuts by trying to get him to cater to her the same way. Excellent school, by the way. Hundred percent matriculation to some of our best universities."

Bunny continued to dig through the stack of photos. "Here. This is what I wanted to show you."

She held up another photo with the entire group standing in front of the ocean. They all wore shorts and T-shirts with several out-of-place accouterments. Two of the boys wore formal black jackets with tails, Piper held a yellow parasol, Maribelle held a white parasol, and Charlotte wore a wide gold band around her head with an orange flower on the side.

"This is from their senior trip to Cumberland Island. I don't know if you've ever been. The island is very undeveloped, wild horses run the beach. It's beautiful. It's dangerous, if you're not careful. Here's Nick, Gunner, Max, Piper, Nicksey, Charlotte, Sophie and Maribelle. It wasn't a school-sponsored trip. It was a senior skip day. Did you ever do those?"

I smiled and nodded, even though I never did them.

"It was Charlotte's idea that everyone should wear something that celebrated their family's Southern heritage. Nick was dating Piper then. She was a beautiful girl."

Bunny handed me the photo and pointed to Piper.

She was skinny with shoulder-length dark hair and big

brown eyes. She and Sophie and Maribelle could have been sisters. It wasn't lost on me that the four of us shared a similar look.

Charlotte was blond and pretty in the way wealthy girls could be, with expensive jewelry and artfully applied makeup. But she wasn't a natural beauty. She was what my mother would have called a big-boned girl. She towered over all the other girls and though she wasn't necessarily overweight, there wasn't anything petite about her, either.

"Let's see if I get this right—This was right before gradu-ation, so Max was seeing Charlotte. Finally. She'd had her eye on him for years, but he was always busy with some other girl.

"Piper had broken up with Max a few weeks earlier, to be with Nick. Max was furious. He couldn't stand to lose anyone to Nick. But especially not Piper.

"Or Sophie. She and Max were very serious for a bit.

"Of course Nick and Sophie were, too.

"But Sophie had it bad for Max. She'd been seeing Max at the beginning of their senior year. I saw her notebook one afternoon when she came home with Maribelle and she had written Mrs. Max Crandall all over the front in cursive." Bunny shook her head. "Then she dated Nick, then Max again—

"So, as the story goes, things got heated between Nick and Max that night at Cumberland Island. Things got heated between Max and Nick an awful lot back then. Both handsome young men, both usually in competition for the same girl. Anyway, Piper was dating Nick and apparently she announced to the group at some point that she still had feelings for Max."

Bunny placed a hand on my knee like she braced me for

bad news. "Piper died that night, honey. She was strangled to death."

"Died?" The fury I'd been holding on to hardened my heart.

Bunny nodded.

In the silence I heard what she was saying, even though she wasn't saying it. She believed it was Nick who killed Piper.

"The police said that anyone could have been out on Cumberland Island that night and gotten to her. Back then all sorts of people went out there for camping and whatnot, it was largely uninhabited. No cars, no traffic, no police. She shouldn't have walked off on her own." Bunny glanced out the front window to the green, her lips pressed slightly together.

"But you don't think that it was just anyone."

Bunny smoothed the front of her gown. "Well, I did until—"

"Until Sophie went down the stairs," I interjected.

She walked to the bookshelf, removed a thick hardback book and handed it to me.

The title was *Midnight Murder, The Mysteries of Cumberland Island*. The author was her husband.

"Tucker couldn't get the story out of his head so he wrote it. I think he was haunted by the fact that it could have been Maribelle who died that night. That and the fact that they never solved Piper's murder.

"He wrote it as a novel to protect the kids' identities, but he took the details directly from police reports and Maribelle's early account of what happened. You might read it and see what you think. Make your own decision about who did it."

Bunny handed me the book and walked to the secretary, wrote something on a post-it note.

"How does the story end? I mean, who did he think killed Piper?"

"He makes it clear that he thought it was Nick. Tuck always said if it walks like a duck, quacks like a duck... I thought it could have been Max. Well, that's not entirely true. I thought it was Max. He had this insecure side. So desperate to belong, to fit in. He needed that external approval more than anyone I'd ever known. So I thought strangling Piper might have been his way of repaying her for the public humiliation of leaving him.

"Tucker thought it was just the opposite. He said Nick was the one who had been humiliated, and therefore the one who had the strongest motive. But I don't know. There was always something about Max I just didn't trust."

Bunny handed me the post-it note. Maribelle's name and address were written in a lovely script on the paper, along with her phone number.

"One thing is for sure. No one believes that it was some vagrant who murdered Piper. No one. I don't know if Maribelle would talk with you about that night. None of them have spoken about it since it happened. But try. She lives on Skidaway Island, not that far from here."

She took my teacup and studied the remaining leaves inside. "It's there again." She pointed to the side of the cup closest to me. "See the dagger?"

I peered inside expecting to see nothing of the sort. But there on the side was a tiny dagger I hadn't noticed earlier. And if I had been holding the cup to my lips, it would have been aimed at my mouth.

"It represents danger and it's close to you." She scanned the dimly lit green outside the parlor windows. "Very close."

Bunny opened the front door for me and stared into Columbia Square, which was still, quiet, mysterious. Her eyes glazed over like she had been transported to a different place and time. "I always wanted to run into Piper's ghost. You know, have her tell me who killed her. Because I know it was one of those boys. And anyone who kills at an early age like that kills again. And again."

"Have you ever seen a ghost around here?" I asked gently. I didn't want to put her on the spot by mentioning how I'd seen her at three in the morning talking to someone I couldn't see.

"This is Savannah, sweetheart. Most haunted city in America. Everyone sees ghosts here."

She turned in the direction that the fog had rolled in and squinted slightly. "You know, sometimes I miss my Tucker so much I think I won't make it through the day. Isn't that somethin'? He's been gone for so long, and still I remember how it felt to be loved by him. He saw me in a way that no one else ever did. Saw the very essence of who I was. And loved me at first sight.

"Why, I'd do just about anything if I thought I could have him back. Even for just a moment."

She turned back to me and studied my face.

"Be. Careful," she said firmly. "I think that whoever killed Piper is the same person who tried to kill Sophie."

23

S tanding in the dark outside my front door, I checked the alarm app on my phone one more time. With no alerts on the app, I turned and waved to Bunny, who stood on her front porch to make sure I got inside safely.

I closed the front door behind me and drew and cocked my gun. Could Nick have been the type to kill a woman? Was he the type to marry and kill for money?

I searched every room, every closet and darkened space. Except for the basement. I wouldn't go down there. I didn't have to. There was a locked door at the top of the basement stairs.

A dark green BMW pulled in front of my house and I watched carefully while it idled. To my surprise, Max Crandall got out and walked toward my front door.

I met him on the front porch.

He held up my zippered portfolio. "You left this in my office. I thought I'd drop it by in case you needed it."

"Oh," I said.

"Your business card is on the inside cover, with your address. I hope this is okay? I was just going to prop it next to your front door." His smile was friendly, like he was attempting to do something nice. Perhaps in response to what happened earlier in the day.

"May I?" He gestured with my portfolio, asking permission to hand it to me. He held his left hand awkwardly at his side.

"Thanks." I walked down the stairs, not wanting him anywhere near my house.

He handed me the portfolio and I noticed his left hand was bloody.

He saw me staring.

He turned it to the side, revealing a gash. "I dropped a mineral water bottle on the bricks, and I cut myself picking up the pieces. Could I trouble you for some paper towels?"

"Sure," I said and closed the door behind me.

I gathered a few paper towels from the pantry. I came back to the foyer and found the front door open. Max was no longer at the bottom of the steps.

I looked outside, his car was still parked on the street. "Max?" I called.

There was no answer, the house was quiet. I closed the front door and locked it. I grabbed my gun from my purse. "Max?" I called again, quieter this time.

With my gun drawn, I searched behind furniture and inside closets. I searched the study, including the underside of my desk. Then I made my way along the hallway, toward the dining room.

Subtle, yellowish light emanated from the small butler's pantry, the result of a tiny lamp I kept on the counter. Someone moved into the light and cast a shadow into the dimly lit hall. Blood and pressure thumped against the inside of my skull.

With my arms extended, my hands shaking and a bullet

in the chamber, I eased around the corner. Max stood with his hand over the small sink. He startled and backed away.

I tilted the gun toward the ceiling. "Sorry."

I wanted to keep my aim on him and to throw him out. But I had to think of my reputation. He was in the industry. He could talk.

He nodded toward his hand. "There was quite a bit of blood and I remembered a sink in the butler's pantry."

I handed him the paper towels and tucked the gun into the back of my waistband. "You've been in this house?"

"The realtor had an open house when it was on the market and Charlotte and I stopped in."

A blood spot formed on the paper towels Max held to his hand.

"Do you always walk around your house with a gun?" he asked.

"Someone tried to break into my house a few days ago. So, lately, yes." I watched his face for any reaction.

But he only clicked his tongue against the roof of his mouth and winced as if to say—bad luck. "Did they get anything?"

"No, they didn't make it all the way inside. Plus, I'm always armed," I said for good measure.

"Guns make me nervous," he said. "Would you mind putting it on a table or something?"

"Sure." I gestured that he ought to go ahead of me down the hallway. When we reached the main room I put the gun on the table against the wall.

He adjusted the paper towels on his hand. "Have you had a chance to talk with Nick?"

I shook my head. "He's traveling."

A glimmer of alpha-dog cruelty in his eye told me he hoped he'd ruined things for Nick.

He scanned the area and complimented me on the restorations, saying that he remembered what the house looked like before.

I watched him carefully. There was something spider-like about him. Something patient and grotesque. Like if I inadvertently fell into his web, he would feed on me. For days.

He walked around the room, examining the moldings. When he stopped, he was decidedly closer to me.

"I reviewed your portfolio after you left. Your experience really is a perfect fit for us, and we do need the help. There might be a way for you to work with us."

He turned toward me.

I took a half-step away.

"I could talk to the officer group, help them to under-stand that this is just a misunderstanding. A setup, perhaps, from someone who's jealous of your success." He gestured to the room around us. "Or even someone who doesn't like your political views." He looked at the cocktail cart.

He turned toward me again.

His smile widened inch by slow inch.

Something deep inside of me began to shake.

Lightning fast, he grabbed my wrist, then the other one.

He knocked one of my legs out from under me and I fell to the floor. He levered his leg atop my own until I was pinned. He put both of my wrists in one of his hands.

Max hovered over me, his face too close to mine, his breath stale and rank.

I wrestled against him but my wrists were frail in his grasp.

He ran his left hand along my neck, smiling with cruelty and appetite. I knew that smile. It was the same expression the black-toothed man gave when he looked at young girls.

I listened for the metallic sound of Max unfastening his belt buckle, and I struggled harder, trying to free one of my legs. But in spite of his size, he was stronger than I was. And my gun was across the room.

His squeezed my neck, his smile grew. "Don't fight it," he whispered.

I thought of Piper, how she was strangled to death, and I fought harder. His strength was like American steel.

The dark edges of my vision closed in, my ability to fight grew weaker, and his smile grew wider still.

Then it was black as pitch and I couldn't feel. Anything.

Dark, weightless, nearly lifeless. A deep nothingness. Nowhere. Nothing to breathe. Nothing to see.

Until a pinpoint of light appeared dead center. I leaned toward it.

I had the sensation I was moving forward. Drawn toward it like a magnet.

"Breathe!" I heard.

I tried and I couldn't. There was no air.

The pinpoint brightened, broadened, and I saw another smile I recognized. It was my own, but not quite. Slightly different if someone knew where to look.

"Breathe," she said, her loving smile holding firm.

It was my sister, and I felt her with me like she'd never left. Like time had never passed.

"Harper!" She pointed her finger at me disapprovingly. "Breathe!"

I awoke with a start, coughing, gasping, wheezing. My windpipe had shrunk to the width of a pen. I rolled over, gagged and retched until finally a rush of air made it through to my lungs.

I rubbed the tears from my eyes and spied my gun on

the table. Scrambling, I grabbed the gun, falling back to the floor in the process.

Max leaned against the wall, swirling a glass of brandy. His mouth lifted in a cockeyed smile of amusement.

"That was more enjoyable than I expected." He sipped the brandy. "And I've been looking forward to that for a while now."

I pointed the gun at his face, my hands shaking like they fought the wind. "Get out!" I tried to say, but my voice only squeaked.

He laughed and walked toward me. "You fight what you can't win."

I scooted backward until my back hit the front of the armchair. The air still wheezed through my throat. I brought my left hand under my right and tried to steady my aim.

He squatted in front of me, unafraid.

"I'm sure you know that our industry is a small, closely-knit group. In this digital age, compromising photos travel quickly. When that happens, I could make it known to every firm in our incestuous world that you handled your relationship with Nick with the utmost integrity. I could say that these photos are nothing but the folly of some vituperative co-worker.

"Or I could say that these photos prove how you compromised the integrity of your appraisals. How you didn't have any respect for our most basic tenet of professionalism—objectivity. Therefore you shouldn't be trusted. That will not only bring your reputation into question, but Chamberlain's work as well."

He leaned closer. "Your choice. I can elevate you in the midst of this mess or I can eliminate your career forever. All I ask in return for your protection is a little time with you. A relationship." He stood, finished his drink, placed the glass on the beverage cart.

I stumbled to my feet, my head pounding, aching. "Get out!" I forced the words out that time.

Max turned slowly, smirked when he saw the gun pointed at him. "You won't shoot me."

He stepped toward me and, to my horror, I backed away. "I will shoot you!" I coughed.

"I'm a respected member of the local community. A revered and trusted expert. No one would believe that you had a valid reason to shoot me. No one who would turn me in, anyway. Besides, if there's one thing I am it's an excellent judge of character." He spoke with such credibility that even I believed him. "And I know that you won't shoot me." He straightened his tie and smoothed his navy blue jacket and I knew he was right.

He was respected.

I was a nutcase nobody with a diagnosis, parents who still had guardianship over me and a cabinet full of meds. If I shot him all I'd do was seal my fate and lose everything I'd worked so hard for.

I lowered the gun.

I rubbed my neck.

"Just as I thought." He pulled the paper towel from the side of his hand. He examined the cut and tossed it onto the floor. "Call me if a relationship interests you and we'll get you set up with work."

He left the way he came in.

He didn't bother closing the front door.

24

———

Stanford tapped on Manny's door twice and entered without waiting for an invitation. "No go from Director Hall on investigating the Jenny Hansen death. Chief of Police in Crescent City said they have the matter well in hand. It's been ruled an accident, they don't want our help."

"Do they know there's a history with the verse that the alleged minister dropped off?"

"They do. They dusted for fingerprints and there weren't any matches in the system."

"That doesn't mean anything. The guy delivering the pamphlet could have been one of the missing sons."

"Or a copycat," Stanford said. "Or her husband."

"In which case he should still be investigated and all evidence should be compared against what we have in our Muñoz files."

"The cops have the Hansens' security footage of the guy. They're looking for him."

"They don't have a clear shot of his face. Not that it matters. The killer didn't stick around in Crescent City. He's moved on to kill the next girl who testified against Ricardo Muñoz."

"Maybe you should take some time off," Stanford said. "Regroup."

Manny ignored Stanford's jab. "Just contact the other girls and their parents, let them know about Jenny's death and the Bible verse note we received. They have a right to know. And we have a responsibility to pass that information on to them. "

Stanford lowered his head, nodding slowly. Finally, he said, "Okay. You're right. I'll take care of it."

Manny and his partner had made a pact a long time ago, and for years it worked beautifully. Effortlessly. They'd agreed that, while they didn't have to be of one mind on all things, they did have to know that each of them would do the right thing. No matter what. That way they could depend on one another.

They had never wavered in their commitment to one another in that pact.

Until now.

Manny knew Stanford wasn't going to make those calls.

He went back to his office, grabbed his keys and left the office. He drove a good ten miles away and called Bruce, Jenny Hansen's father, using the call signal he would recognize.

"Manny," Bruce's tone was terse and frustrated. "I just hung up with the Crescent City police. They said the FBI is refusing to look into Jenny's case?"

Manny was not surprised.

It wasn't just Stanford's lack of curiosity that clued him in, or his partner's unusual lack of interest in the things that didn't add up. It was his strange mix of fear and confidence.

Like Stanford knew he was doing something wrong and also that he was going to get away with it.

"I don't know," Manny said. "There's something rotten at the higher levels over here. I'm going to have to figure out a way to solve this myself."

I STOOD at the butler's pantry, talking to Nick on my phone and making coffee for Levi and me. "I'm fine. Just a sore throat is all."

"Are you sure?" he asked. "You don't sound like yourself."

"Hang on. A neighbor friend just stopped by and we're about to have a cup of coffee." I stepped outside and paced next to the pool.

Images in my mind flipped between the Nick I fell in love with and the Nick who was accused of murder. The Nick who was from Miami. The Nick who could have been a Muñoz.

I remained angry enough to scream at him. But between the load of anti-anxiety supplements I'd taken in the morning, and no sleep the night before, I couldn't. I was a zombie.

"It's just a throat thing. I'll call you later. I just wanted to let you know I won't be there today."

"Okay," he said quietly. "I love you."

My heart ached. I said goodbye and hung up.

I went back inside. When I reached the main room, I handed Levi his mug of coffee.

He took a sip. "Mmmm. Hints of chocolate."

I inhaled the rich scent and my stomach cringed. I'd lain sleepless in my bed all night, my gun and my cat and

Bunny's book at my side. My stomach was jumpy, raw, irritated and not yet ready for anything heavy and dark.

Levi's visit was unexpected. But when I saw him on my front porch, I knew it was a gift. I took the opportunity to tell him about Nick's and my engagement.

Levi was surprised but he was a professional. If he did feel any disappointment, he didn't show it.

"I'm happy for you," he said with a practiced smile. Then we chatted about everything but relationships while he finished his coffee.

When he said he needed to leave, I followed him to the door, adjusting my scarf around my neck. I wore it not just to hide my scars, but to hide the thumbprint bruises Max left on the side of my neck. I did not want to have to explain those.

The scarf also, inexplicably, made me feel more protected.

"By the way," I said before we reached the front door. "I need a favor."

His smile became warm, friendly, optimistic. "Anything."

I told him that someone had sent me an article about Nick's background and the trial. That the information was a surprise to me.

His smile fell inch by inch until it disappeared altogether.

"Do you happen to know Nick?" I asked.

"Now that you've told me who he is, I've read about him in the papers. You know he was charged with attempted murder, right?"

"Yes," I said.

He looked at the floor, nodding politely. Hesitantly. After

a moment he said, "It's not my place to say this, but I'm going to anyway. I think you need to be careful."

"Thanks."

I knew Nick could have killed Piper. Although after last night my bet was on Max. I knew he could have been a Muñoz. I knew he could have tried to kill his ex-wife.

I also knew that the justice system was so screwed up that justice wasn't only absent, it wasn't even the goal. How they could take your testimony in exchange for a deal and end up taking your life. How the powers that be could move on to the next case, while you're left trying to forge a life with a target on your back.

I didn't tell him that I had wondered if Nick had been wrongly charged, because that would have made me sound stupid and naive. Instead, I just said, "I know. That's why I need a favor from you."

Levi copped a ready, wide stance, crossed his arms and squared off with me.

"I did some reading last night." I nodded toward my laptop and the copy of *Midnight Murder* that Bunny had given me. I told him about Piper's murder, and how I wanted to know more about Sophie. "I think the two might be related."

He nodded thoughtfully.

"Because whoever tried to strangle Sophie throttled Piper, too?" he asked.

The blood drained from my head and my legs felt like two hollow noodles. I'd read where Sophie had fallen or been pushed down the stairs. But I hadn't known someone tried to strangle her.

"Yes," I managed. "It's possible she's still in a private facility in town. I think she was in a coma when they admitted her. But I'm wondering if she's awake now and if it might be possible to have a conversation with her. I'm wondering if you can find her for me."

Levi stared at me with such dead seriousness that I wondered if I had just inadvertently asked him to break the law or his Hippocratic oath or something.

"I want to know the full truth about Nick. I think talking with Sophie could fill in some missing pieces of the puzzle."

I don't know what convinced him to help but he finally said, "Okay."

Levi waved before crossing the square, his smile dampened by concern.

I never mentioned the emails from Sophie.

I never mentioned Max. Neither did I mention that because Piper had been strangled to death, and that because Sophie had almost been strangled to death and that because Max had choked me unconscious the night before, that I wondered if there was evidence of Max's guilt.

I LOCKED the front door and set the alarm. I made a cup of soothing throat tea, and settled into the couch with my laptop. It was time to research Nick Smith and Sophie Taylor.

I discovered that Sophie Taylor Smith was the only child of billionaire Evan Taylor, a man who made his money developing medical instruments. He was also a philanthropist, raising millions for charities. I found several photos of Evan and his pretty wife at fundraisers for a charity called The Sophie Taylor Institute for Battered and Abused Women.

Queasiness spread through my gut and I put the mug of tea on the table.

Sophie had been raised in Savannah, educated at Swarthmore. After college she returned to Savannah and began designing her own line of purses. Each bag held her Sophie T signature on a central gold bar. Her designs were so successful she branched into shoes, wallets, day planners.

The gossip blogs were filled with posts of how Sophie Taylor married up-and-coming art and antiques appraiser, Nick Smith, a local boy from Savannah, her high school love.

Local boy. He wasn't a local boy.

I clicked around and ended up on another gossip blog entitled Just Justice. A local blogger had charted the rise and fall of Sophie's marriage in salacious detail, complete with photos and interviews with the ever-dubious "unnamed, but reliable sources." I read several posts.

Sophie and Nick's union was, by all accounts, difficult. Public arguments weren't uncommon. Two years into the marriage, Nick filed for divorce, then filed a motion with the court to dismiss. Main conflict was apparently that she wanted children. He did not.

A few weeks after the dismissal, Sophie Taylor announced on her blog that she was pregnant. A few days later, she took a tragic fall down the front staircase of their home.

In spite of what Max had done to me, his warning that Nick would do it again—seduce a wealthy woman, kill her for her money—haunted me.

I clicked over to the Amanda Cummings articles that Max had mentioned. I could see why her column became syndicated. She had a flair for the dramatic. Everyone loved drama when it wasn't their own.

One of the most interesting videos was a news station's post-trial interview with two jurors, taped several months after Nick had been acquitted. I took note it had been filmed during a sweeps month—one of the four months out of the year when media research outlets measured and compiled their ratings data. News stations tended to save their most sensational coverage for those months. Their timing of the supposed exposé cut at their arguable journalistic integrity.

The news anchor began her half-hour special by emphasizing that every juror found Nick's testimony believable enough to acquit him of all charges. Then, the special aired a one-on-one interview with juror number eight, whose face was kept in the shadows. He said, "There just wasn't enough evidence to prove what happened one way or the other. Maybe he pushed her or maybe she just fell. There wasn't enough evidence. Not for me. Only Sophie knows for sure what really happened. And she's not talking."

The news anchor asked juror number eight what his personal opinion was and he said, "He might have done it. I mean, it's possible. He didn't want children, he didn't want to be married to her, and he stood to make a lot of money if she died."

Juror number three, an older female said, "He just didn't look like someone who would do that to another human being."

I remembered Max's implication that Nick got off because of his good looks and I lowered my head to my hands. I didn't know what to think.

The few times I'd acted on instinct, either I got myself into trouble or someone died.

I'd learned the hard way that the funny thing about not being able to trust yourself was that you couldn't trust anyone else, either.

The doorbell rang and on my small front porch I found six roses arranged in a vase with greenery. The card visible at the front said: Love, Nick. The number of roses wasn't lost on me. One rose for each week we'd dated.

A bee buzzed about the greenery. I looked more closely at the arrangement and saw that some of the green leaves in the middle were coated in a white substance that looked like sugar. Several small bees emerged and crawled on the white coating.

Suddenly I couldn't catch my breath and I grabbed the wall.

Nick knew I was allergic to bees. He knew that sugar, as well as most blooms left outside, attracted bees. In fact, when I'd told him that we had been sitting on his terrace. I'd shared how bees had been found at heights as high as 20,000 feet. They didn't typically fly that high because they didn't need to. But they could. Especially if they thought they had a reason.

I squinted and got the name of the florist from the card.

I called the florist and asked if she could tell me who placed the order that was delivered to my home. "The card got wet and I can't make out the note," I lied.

"Just a moment, let me check," she said.

I expected the young woman to say that it had been an anonymous call, at which point I was going to ask how they paid. Instead she came back on the line and said, "Oh, yeah, I remember him. He came into the store and bought six roses. He paid cash and wrote the card himself. Unfortunately, we don't have a copy of it, though. How wonderful that you have a secret admirer!"

"Yeah, right?" I said, controlling my breath and forcing outright glee into my voice. "So, here's the thing. I've been casually dating a couple of guys and I'd really love to know which one sent the flowers. You know what I mean?"

"Oh, for sure. You need to know."

I figured this approach would work better than telling her I thought someone was trying to kill me. People didn't want to get involved if there was danger. But a love story? Everyone loved a love story.

A wave of tiredness came over me and I caught sight of my full coffee cup on the table.

"Do you remember what he looked like?" I asked.

"He had dark hair and tanned skin. He was, um, good-looking, I think. But he wore a cap and he never took off his sunglasses so I don't know much more than that."

"I know this is a lot to ask, but do you have security footage of him by chance?"

"Ah, yeah, but that would have to come from the owner and I don't know how she would feel about sharing that kind of thing. She's very vocal about how people are entitled to their privacy."

"That's okay. Thanks."

I hung up. I threw the phone and it clattered on the hardwoods.

I ran upstairs and checked my own security footage. A dark-haired man wearing a dark cap and sunglasses put the flowers on the front porch. He moved quickly. He kept his head down.

It could have been Nick. It could have been Max. It could have been anyone.

If Max were a Muñoz, he could have followed me to Beaufort that day with the intent to tee up the interview. He would have already had the photos by then. Ruining my career might have been a bonus. But the real point of the photos was to expose Nick.

Then there would be an accident, as was typical for the Muñoz family. Something tragic to end my life. Max knew that Nick would be targeted as the main suspect. Because of what happened with Sophie. Because of what happened with Piper.

I went downstairs and looked out the front door again.

More bees swarmed around the sugared petals. My gut clenched.

It was one thing to know that someone wanted to kill you. It was another thing to see that intent in a three-dimensional form on the front steps.

Then I wondered. How did Max know that I was allergic to bee stings?

I didn't think I had mentioned it to him. I had commented on allergies. Did I say food allergies? I couldn't remember.

I turned my jeweled medic alert bracelet over. There were four lines of information. My name was across the top. Then:

Algys: Peanut, Bees

Give Epi/Call 911

My mother's phone number was listed as the ICE contact.

Had Max seen that information on my bracelet at the interview? Or had he seen it in Beaufort? The engraved plate was a couple of inches long and an inch and a half wide.

Wouldn't have been impossible for him to read it if he had good eyesight, but it was pretty dim in the Tatnall offices.

Nick was well aware of my bee sting allergy.

He knew it could be fatal for me.

But he was still out of town, wasn't he? He couldn't have ordered and delivered them himself.

I felt sick.

I went back to the sofa and closed the bookmarked

pages on my laptop browser. An alert slid across the page. It suggested I might want to read one of Amanda's earliest articles in the series, dated one day after Nick's arrest. Somehow I had missed that post. The photo at the top caught my eye. It was the exact staircase Sophie had fallen down, and it was a half-spiral, wide and gracious like the one I'd installed just off of my main hallway.

I sipped the cold coffee and choked.

"The railing has a unique design called forced perspective," Amanda wrote. "That means there is a lower railing at the top of the stairs to elongate the visual appeal and make the stairway look taller."

I choked again.

Nick had recommended the forced perspective railing to me. I'd known about this design trick but hadn't thought of it for the space until he mentioned it.

I kept reading.

"To be fair, her fall could have been accidental. With a low railing like that, Sophie could have easily lost her balance and fallen over the railing at the top of the stairs. But her fall could have been the result of a push."

How had I missed this article?

I opened another browser and searched for the article title by name. Nothing came up.

The newspaper had hidden this particular article. Their readership probably didn't blossom under articles that posed doubt in response to Nick's assumed guilt.

The phone rang and the caller ID said it was Nick.

He knew something was up.

I declined the call. I wasn't ready to have a conversation with him and I definitely didn't want to confront him over the phone.

I curled into the couch and drank large gulps of cold

coffee. My stomach rumbled. Nerves. Or maybe this much coffee on an empty stomach was a bad idea. I hoped it wasn't a virus. I headed to the kitchen pantry and chewed several papaya tablets to settle my stomach. That's when I noticed.

My lips swelled.

My throat tightened.

Not a coffee problem.

Not nerves.

I recognized the signs.

Anaphylactic reaction.

I looked at my coffee cup on the counter. Coffee was the only thing I'd ingested this morning. Coffee that I prepared in my own home.

No time to figure it out.

I yanked open the kitchen cabinet and reached to the right side where I kept the boxes of EpiPens.

But they weren't there.

I struggled for air—my breath was raspy, wheezing, restricted.

Contractors had been in the kitchen. Someone could have knocked the box out of place. I stretched onto tiptoe and shoved dinner plates and saucers onto the floor in a crash. I climbed onto the countertop and searched on the third shelf and other cabinets. Nothing.

I ran to my purse and searched for the emergency EpiPen I kept in the side pocket.

It was gone.

25

———

Agent Manny Hernandez sat hunched in his home office, held his cell phone to his ear, and listened to Harper's parents talk. At Blair's request he'd taken the rest of the day off since his in-laws were in town. But having a cell phone meant work could intervene at any time.

Out the side window he saw Blair's mom playing with Reagan in the pool, saw her dad fussing with burgers and hotdogs on the grill and saw Blair taking pictures of everyone.

"Engaged?" Manny asked, trying to keep the surprise out of his voice. Why hadn't Harper told him directly?

"Yes," Harper's mother and father said in unison.

"And still not employed, even though she's had more than enough time to get a job," her father said with a disdain for Harper's poor choices that Manny had heard many times before. Benjamin Brown—formerly Silveria—had been a prominent neurosurgeon in Miami before the kidnapping. He reluctantly retired after they relocated to the Midwest but he'd never lost the in-charge tone to his voice.

"Ben—" Lara, Harper's mother, cautioned softly, like she was hesitant to address his temper.

"Maybe the engagement is good news. Maybe she found someone she really cares about," Manny suggested. He hoped he was right.

"It's more than that. I'll text you the image she sent to us." Ben put the call on speaker. "And look, if she had gone about this in a reasonable manner—dating the guy for a year or even six months and then got engaged? Maybe. But she's getting engaged after only knowing him for a few weeks? That's nothing but more of the same careless behavior we've seen in her all along. We can't let her wreck someone else's life."

Manny blamed himself for Catherine's death. Harper did, too. But Ben blamed Harper. Manny had been there when Harper was pulled from the water, and he'd been at the hospital when Ben and Lara arrived.

They had gathered Harper into their arms like any good parent would. But when Harper sobbed repeated apologies, saying that it was her fault her sister had died because she had been driving too fast ("She told me to slow down and I didn't!"), and she hadn't remembered the jetty, Ben did the unthinkable. In his unimaginable grief, he blamed his daughter. "What were you thinking?!" he'd screamed at her. Lara fell to the ground sobbing.

Manny remembered the horrified look in Harper's eyes, like she'd taken a knife to the gut, like she'd sucked every one of Ben's razor-edged words into her delicate soul. Like she would have changed places with Catherine in a red hot minute, if only she could have.

From then on Ben did everything in his power to get

Harper medicated "before she kills us all!" Manny had heard Ben tell Lara on more than one occasion. Once when Harper had been within earshot.

Manny didn't know who Harper was engaged to, but given her history with her father, he knew it would require a miracle for her to have chosen someone who would honor her and love her. It was more likely that she had chosen someone who was just like Ben.

His text alert dinged. Ben's photo showed the note that Harper had sent. It was the same image Harper had sent him, an identical replica of the number sequences Manny had received at the office.

"She said she'd found it stuffed in a broken basement window. And we hate to even think it, but we're worried that she's written the note herself. She's complained a lot over the last year that you didn't perform the background checks she wanted. Just like she used to when she was a teen. Now we're wondering if she isn't just up to old tricks again? Making it look like she needs FBI protection when she really doesn't."

"I don't...think so," Manny said. "I received a note as well and—"

Harper's father sighed. "So, she sent you one, too?"

"No, I'm not suggesting that the note came from her. They dusted for fingerprints and hers weren't there."

"She's a smart girl, she knows how to avoid proof. She could have worn gloves when she wrote the letter. Look, Hernandez, I get how you would want to protect her. But you don't know her history like we do. All the old signs are there, unfortunately. She got engaged to this Nick fella who she hardly knows. No prenup, and there's a substantial inheritance at stake. She told us she had several interviews, but she's still not employed. I don't think she is employable. Now these notes."

No one called Manny by his last name and Ben's air of superiority made Manny want to reach through the phone and land his fist against the good doctor's nose. Given their history, Manny kept his frustrations to himself. "Didn't she have a successful consulting practice before she moved to Savannah?"

"Successful is a relevant term," Ben said. "She did build a base of reputable clients but she didn't make enough money to support herself. Her niche is too narrow. If she hadn't lived at home, she would have starved to death."

"That's not even remotely true," Lara said.

"The point is we've given her the opportunity to prove herself and she can't," Ben said.

"We just don't know what she's gotten herself into with this Nick person." Harper's mother's words were a little slurred. Manny guessed that her five-year medallion for sobriety had lost its meaning.

"When she mentioned Nick to us a few weeks back, we hired a P.I., paid him over seven grand, but he wasn't able to find much on the guy. I could have done a better job myself, frankly."

"You need to help us—" Lara began.

"We're going to have to help her out of this mess, you understand," Ben interrupted. "She's an adult, but we have the guardianship in place for a reason. Don't misunderstand me, she's our daughter and we love her. We just have to do for her what she can't do for herself. That's the way it's going to be for the rest of our days. After that, Lord only knows. I'd guess this guy has seen that showpiece she moved into and has figured her as his meal ticket."

"You don't know that that's what he sees in her," Lara said.

"We have to be honest here, she has the physical scars, the emotional scars, the anxiety, not to mention her history. No man would want to take that on for free—"

"You need to help us," Lara began again softly. "We need more information on this man."

He heard the tone of "should" in Lara's voice, like he should help them. Which didn't matter, because he agreed with the should.

"If you want to send me the reports the P.I. gave you, I can look at them," he said. "But the agency won't let me dedicate any resources to this."

Ben sighed with a heaviness that sounded like disgust.

"I wish I could do more," Manny said. He didn't know if it would alleviate their fears or contribute to them, but he told them about Jenny's death, how she had received a similar note.

When Harper's father suggested that Harper had sent Jenny the note, too, Manny discouraged Ben from pursuing that path. Ben refused and they hung up. Manny rubbed his hands over his face. Fatigue, disappointment and frustrations were simmering.

He thought about the life Harper could have had if only he had followed up on that lead. Catherine and several other girls would still be alive. Ben and Lara might have been happy. But he had had so many leads that week. The alcohol made him lazy, careless, stupid.

He looked out the window, noticed that everyone had gone inside. Missing out on family time was one thing he'd promised Reagan and Blair that he wouldn't do.

He opened his inbox and found Ben's email with the P.I.'s documents. Nick Chamberlain was the guy's name.

There were lots of photos, some crumpled up unpaid bills that had been gathered from Nick's trash. Mostly assessments for common area maintenance.

Age-old demons within taunted him like sirens from the shore, begging him to jump in, to try to fix things that couldn't be fixed.

That kicked off a powerful craving for whiskey. To numb the pain.

He squeezed his hands into fists and clung to the advice they'd given him in AA: You can't fix the past, you can only forgive and make amends as best you can. He paced around his office.

He had three choices—drink, which would cost him his family. Investigate, which would cost him his job and career. Do nothing, which would cost him his soul.

He glanced outside at the abandoned grill, pool toys, and beach towels. That was life, wasn't it? A series of moments. Here today, gone forever. No way to go back. No do-overs on the important stuff. Only one opportunity at a time to do the best one could with what one had.

He opened a private browser, turned on his VPN, then logged on to the system using Stanford's login credentials to check the Muñoz file. Notifications showed one document had been added the day before.

The newest document was a homicide report. He cursed in a whisper when he saw the name.

"Mariana."

A familiar sick feeling roiled in his gut. A reminder that a chunk of his soul was haunted and fully chained to the ghosts of his past.

The report stated there had been a break-in, forced entry through the back window. Home invasion. Mariana had been stabbed twice in the narrow hallway outside the kitchen. Her daughter was found alive and unharmed in her bedroom, her feet and wrists bound with duct tape. Next-door neighbor told how the intruder was already inside the house when she arrived.

Manny cursed again, louder this time, and he clicked over to the photos.

Unlucky for Mariana to survive the cruelty of the Muñoz family just to be taken out by a home invasion. Sad. Tragic. Unfair.

Manny downloaded the rest of the reports from the portal, reviewed them and saved them to folders on his laptop. He was tempted to think this was the work of the Muñoz family. But there was no mention of a note with numbers. He didn't want to read too much into Mariana's death and he didn't want to give the Muñoz family more credit than they deserved. Home invasions happened. Far too often.

He packed up and left his office. Halfway down the stairs he stopped, turned around, walked back to his office. He reviewed the reports again, wrote down the two details that bothered him.

First, it was possible that Mariana interrupted a home invasion in process. But her daughter and the neighbor had been bound with duct tape and allowed to live. And the intruder didn't steal anything. All of which was unusual for a home invasion.

It was more likely that the killer tied up the daughter because they were waiting for Mariana to come home. When she did, he killed her. Only her.

Not a home invasion. Too targeted. Too well planned. This was premeditated murder.

He studied the photos, including one of the kitchen. Waffles on the counter, next to the open box. A pile of school books with a calculator on top. A woman's purse, open.

He clicked on the photo of the purse and zoomed in. Inside the open purse was a torn piece of notebook paper with two lines of numbers written on it. The first two numbers on each line were identical to the ones he and Harper and Jenny had received.

Would Harper craft a mysterious message and send it to him so he would help her more than he had been? Maybe. Would she send it to herself for the same purpose? Possibly.

But he didn't think she would send it to the other girls. He didn't think she even knew how to get in touch with them. He didn't think she would hire someone to pose as a minister.

Harper was a lot of things, but for whatever reason he didn't think she would do that.

He dug through the closet and pulled out an oversized bulletin board, and hung it on a single nail on the back wall. He removed its outer covering, an old white bedsheet, and stared at the 5x7 photos.

A photo of Catherine's headless, armless torso was in the upper left-hand corner, next to photos of all the other girls who didn't make it out of the compound alive.

Their deaths marked the beginning of the nightmare that wouldn't let him go.

The Muñoz family patriarchs were next, then various pics of the old compound that the government confiscated and resold: The one large residence and the basement where the girls had been kept in cages, then several smaller homes that were bigger than Manny's. The pool, boathouse, gymnasium and a chapel with altars and stained glass windows.

Next were newspaper articles that told encapsulated

versions of Harper's and Catherine's harrowing escape. There were photos of other kidnapped girls' body parts that had washed up on shore: a detached leg and arm, a foot that was still in its blood-stained shoe.

He printed out several photos from the portal, including the notepaper sticking out of what appeared to be Mariana's purse. He clicked over to Jenny's file and printed out photos of her body on the rocks at the bottom of the cliff, as well as the pamphlet she received. He printed the photos of the notes he and Harper received and he added them all to the bulletin board.

Then he stood back, studied them, and worked to connect the dots.

Memories flashed like fireworks. Without any effort he could still see the divers clearing the wreckage from the boat crash in Miami, could still hear twelve-year-old Harper's uncontrollable screams.

"Daddy?"

Agent Manny Hernandez spun with a jerk. His sweet little girl in her pink and white nightgown stood in the doorway, her blue eyes wide with horror and fixed on photos of body parts behind him.

He moved fast, grabbed the old sheet from the floor and threw it over the board so that the crime photos were out of sight.

"Mommy says...Mommy says it's time...it's dinner," she whispered. Her face crumpled into tears and she ran down the hall wailing.

"Reagan!" He ran after her but she was down the steps and out the bottom door before he could reach her. He watched her fall into the arms of her mother, who scooped her up and held her close.

He waved to Blair, giving her the signal that he'd be right

back. Then he went upstairs to return the bulletin board to the closet.

Moments later, when quick footsteps bounded up the stairs, he heard them this time. He also knew who it was before she appeared.

"She okay?" he asked when his wife turned the corner.

"She's hysterical." Her tone scolded him and she put her hand on her hip in disapproval. Her long blond ponytail was mussed and pulled to the side, a sign that Reagan had clung to her in a fierce and panicked hug.

"I'm sorry. I didn't hear her come up. Where is she? I'll talk with her."

"My mom has her. The bigger question is what are you doing up here that has your daughter so upset?"

He nodded toward the sheet-covered bulletin board.

"Is it a new case?" she asked.

He shook his head. "Old case. Old files. Old story."

Slowly she pulled the sheet from the bulletin board. From her expression he knew she recognized the case. "Oh, Manny. Why?!"

"Two of the girls who testified have died in the past week. Their deaths are made to look tragic and accidental but they both received cryptic notes ahead of time. Harper has also received a note. She's still alive and I'd like to see her stay that way. So I'm doing what I can to help." He sighed, knowing Blair was calculating the consequences of what he'd told her.

"Harper's parents called me. That's who I was talking to earlier. Harper got engaged to some guy spur of the moment and they asked if I would look into it. See if I can find anything on the guy. I said I would because I'm wondering if the other girls' deaths and the guy she's engaged to are related."

She waved at the bulletin board. "None of this is your fault or your responsibility."

Seeing the concern on her face, he went to her and caressed her cheek. She leaned against the palm of his hand and something came loose inside of him.

"I appreciate how you protect me. How you protect us. But it *was* my fault. And if I want to do the right thing, it *is* my responsibility to help them," he said.

She shook her head, slowly at first, then more quickly. "Don't do this."

Manny stepped away and lowered himself to the edge of his old, secondhand desk and looked at his wife. The mother of his daughter. The woman he wished he'd met sooner in life. Although it seemed now that there wasn't a time when he didn't know her.

"I know the Bureau didn't put you on this case."

"No. They didn't."

She pushed her hands through her hair, stared at the ceiling and sighed.

He knew that as a former agent she understood what it was like when a case had a grip on you.

"What aren't you telling me?" she asked.

"What do you mean?"

"I have a not-so-funny feeling you aren't telling me everything about this."

He cracked a half smile that she didn't return. "Probably because I'm not."

She walked to the other side of the room, leaned against the wall and crossed her arms. "Tell me."

Manny grabbed his phone, pulled up the photo of the note he'd received and showed it to her. "It came in the mail last Friday, just before the first girl died—Jenny."

Blair took the photo to the bulletin board and compared it to the other notes. "So they're coming for you, too?"

"I don't think so. I can't prove that. But the timing of my note against the other girls' deaths—it's more like the killer wanted to alert me to what was about to happen."

"So he's taunting you," she said and began to pace.

"Yeah. That's what I think."

"That means he must think you can't do anything to stop him," she said.

Manny watched her pace, watched her think.

"Because he's confident he's hidden himself well enough that you won't find him? Or he knows he'll get the job done before you can get an investigation going?" she asked.

"I think both. Whoever is killing these girls has a contact on the inside," he said. "Because very few people know that I was banned from the case and why. Very, very few people would know that getting an investigation going would be delayed. Or that it might not happen at all, if I were the one who had to start the process." It was the first time he'd voiced his theory aloud and hearing it sent a bucket of ice over his gut.

"That's why this layout isn't at the office." She gestured to the bulletin board.

He nodded.

"All the more reason why you can't do this. Reach out to Miami P.D. Or talk to the Chief directly. Or someone else in your office. Please."

"Who would I talk with exactly?"

"I don't know. There's bound to be someone more objective, more able to get an investigation going. You need to remember what happened to you the last time you got involved in this case. It could ruin you again."

"It won't," he said softly. "I'm stronger now. I can handle it."

"You don't know that. And if they find out you're working on a restricted case, they'll fire you. Then where will we be? I haven't worked in years, Manny. I can't just wake up tomorrow and start working again."

"Then you tell me what I'm supposed to do. Because someone is killing these women, and the Bureau isn't doing anything to protect them. Harper lost her sister, and Ben and Lara lost their daughter because of me. All three of them plus Jenny's father have asked for my help. Do you really think I should ignore them?"

She paced again. "How about Stanford calls the survivors and their parents to let them know that something suspicious is going on? They could leave town for a while or get their own protection."

"I've tried that."

"And?"

"He said he would."

"So, that's that. You don't have to do this."

He looked at the floor then raised his eyes at her.

Her body slouched in increments, like a slowly deflating balloon. "What?"

Manny shrugged. "That's the other thing I wasn't telling you. Stanford said that when the Director of our office called Crescent City police to offer his help on Jenny Hansen's murder, that they said they didn't want our help. He said that while the Crescent City police had been informed by Bruce about Jenny's history with the Muñoz family, they had ruled her death an accident and they didn't want FBI involvement.

"But when I spoke with Bruce, Jenny's father, he said the Crescent City police had asked our FBI office for help, but had been told by someone in our office that we wouldn't. We apparently told them that we didn't see any connections that warranted an investigation."

After a moment she gave the tiniest smile of frustrated resignation, which seemed to say she knew how little control she had over him. "So there really is someone on the inside that's allowing or abetting these killings and you think Stanford is in on it?"

He nodded.

She went to him, wrapped her arms around him and asked, "Any chance you're wrong?"

He shrugged. "Sure."

She kissed him and he felt the sweet stir of love and desire.

After a moment, she headed toward the stairs and said, "You need to let someone else handle this. I know you want to help, but you have a family to protect, and we can't be without your job right now. Dinner's ready."

"I'll put the bulletin board away and I'll be down."

When he heard the door close and he knew Blair was gone, he went through his files once again, trying to find Natalie Pyne's phone number. He didn't have it.

Natalie and Harper were the last two surviving girls of the last Muñoz kidnapping, and Natalie hadn't been made aware of the notes and Jenny's and Mariana's deaths. Her parents were dead and Natalie must not have shared her most recent phone number with him. The FBI portal didn't have current contact information on her either.

He pulled the white sheet from the bulletin board and examined the photo of the chapel. He held a magnifying glass over the image of the frame affixed to the front door, and he could just make out the verse.

The incongruity of Ricardo Muñoz's religious beliefs

against his crimes reminded Manny of his own upbringing. His father spent Sunday mornings in his recliner with a beer in his hand and an old western on the TV. He insisted, however, that Manny go with his mother to the local church for Sunday School and services.

Manny opened his laptop and examined the reports that Harper's parents sent over. Then he picked up the phone, dialed the number of a colleague.

"Amaya Chang," the agent said when she answered the call.

"It's Manny. I need a couple of favors if you have time—a phone number and an extensive background check?"

"Yeah I can do it on Monday—"

"Today, right now if you would. Guy's name is Nick Chamberlain. I'm emailing you some documents that a P.I. pulled together, not bad for a running start but I need more. A lot more. And a phone number for a Natalie Pyne. P-y-n-e. Last known location Aiken, South Carolina. Married, but I don't remember the husband's first name."

"Okay. What's the case number?" she asked.

Manny knew she had to input the case number to get access to the resources she needed.

"I don't have one," he said.

Amaya didn't respond.

26

"And you made the coffee yourself?" Dr. Callahan asked, his tone gentle, his green eyes sharp and probing. I'd seen this particular E.R. doctor once before, just after I'd moved to Savannah. I'd been stung by a bee in the backyard and went into anaphylactic shock then, too. He remembered me, remembered how deathly allergic I was to bee stings and anything peanut-related.

I sat up, rubbed the inside of my arm where the nurse had removed the needle. A bag of fluid and a hefty dose of epinephrine and I was halfway to good again.

"Yes," I said. "I don't think anyone else has ever made coffee in my house other than me. Actually, I guess a contractor could have when I wasn't around." I remembered Max had been in my home when I wasn't around. Nick too.

"Smart that you carry an EpiPen in your purse," Dr. Callaghan said.

"I found one in the bottom of an old purse I hadn't carried in a while. It was on the shelf in my closet. I keep one in every purse, so I'll never be without." I was glad I'd never told anyone that.

Dr. Callahan crossed his arms and held my file close to his chest. "Do you know of anyone who might intentionally want to hurt you? Because it wouldn't take but a drop to cause you an allergic reaction. They could rub cold-pressed peanut oil in your coffee mug, or the inside of your coffee maker. Crude peanut oil doesn't have a scent. So they could have deposited the oil or the tiniest bit of crushed peanuts into the bag of coffee beans. The coffee would have masked the scent. Or do you put anything else in your coffee? Milk or cream or sweetener? Could have been in there, too."

"Milk," I said. My heart racing from the epinephrine, I pressed my hand against my chest. "I've been renovating so all sorts of people have been in and out of my house for months now."

"But this would have been recent, right?"

"Right," I said.

"When is the last time you had coffee, prior to today, and who would have had access to your refrigerator or coffee or coffee maker during that time?"

It had been a while since I'd had coffee. "Uh, I think Nick was the last one to use the coffee maker—"

"Nick? Who's Nick?" He opened the folder and scanned the front sheet.

"My fiancé."

"Your registration sheet says you're single."

"The engagement is a recent thing."

"I see. Everything okay there?"

I shrugged. "I think so."

He made a note in my file. "Because most murders are committed by someone we know. Someone we're in a relationship with."

"I wasn't murdered."

He nodded like he realized I wasn't ready to go there. "Okay. Who else?"

"Levi, my neighbor. Max, a business owner I interviewed with the other day. My contractor and his brother. Their workers. Painters often leave the door open when they're going in and out."

"Who knows about your allergies?"

"Everyone I just mentioned, really," I said. "Probably a few more. I'm pretty open about it, and I always wear my medic alert bracelet."

"So anyone who took a close look at your bracelet could also know."

"I guess so."

"I can call the police for you so you can file a report. Might be a good idea to let them investigate."

The nurse must have seen me go pale because she said, "When I had my living room and kitchen repainted last month, I came home early and found my painter in front of the open refrigerator drinking my Coke straight from the two-liter bottle. Just drank straight from the bottle, like it was his own home. Maybe a contractor had peanuts in his mouth while he drank from your milk carton?"

"Maybe." I thought about how Leo and Tim and their helpers often ate lunch while sitting on the living room floor. It wasn't impossible that someone could have drunk from the milk carton. "But would they also steal my supply of EpiPens?"

"There is a black market for EpiPens," she said. "It's illegal, because EpiPens require a prescription. But they do it and they can get up to $150 each. Sometimes more. I'm not saying you shouldn't be careful. But, maybe the EpiPens went missing for another reason."

I relaxed a little. Could have been a perfect storm of

unrelated incidents. I drew in a deep breath and heard every voice of counsel from my father to the countless therapists to Agent Hernandez telling me not to read too much into things, not to overreact, not to become a victim of circumstance.

But the timing of this incident—after receiving the note, after Jenny's tragic death, the bees on the roses. Nick's history, his wife's near death on the stairway of forced perspective, Max's threats. I thought I was setting myself up to be a victim if I didn't read meaning into this event.

"I'm not trying to make anyone out to be the bad guy here. I just want to make sure that you're safe in your own home," Dr. Callaghan said.

Doctors had to say that. After some law had been passed years ago, that do-you-feel-safe question began appearing on forms and in perfunctory physician discussions all over the country.

I shrugged again.

Dr. Callaghan left and returned with several small boxes.

"This is a fairly new product." He opened two of the boxes, held up a tiny strip and a small black device of some sort.

"You coat one of these indicator strips with whatever food or beverage you're about to ingest, then insert the strip into this reader. If any hazardous proteins are present, the device will flash and buzz. No more guesswork. No more trusting. No more wondering."

He showed me a small rectangular carrying case that I could wear inconspicuously as a necklace, bracelet, or put them on the back of my cell phone cover.

I told him I'd take two units.

Dr. Callaghan and the nurse left the room so I could get dressed.

Images of Nick passed through my mind—strangling Piper, strangling Sophie, dropping peanut oil in my coffee. In the empty, sterile room a wail rose up from within. There was no stopping it. I grabbed the pillow, buried my face in it and sobbed.

If Nick was trying to kill me, I needed to know.

I'd have to stop him.

27

Natalie Pyne parked in front of The Daily Perk Coffee Shop, checked her hair in her rearview mirror and brushed her bangs to the side. She missed her last hair appointment because Charles, her six-year-old son, had come down with a chest cold. He'd caught it from her.

Although she had had a bad case of bronchitis, after two prescriptions along with some over-the-counter cough medicine, she was finally right as rain.

Truth be known, Charles hadn't really been sick enough to stay out of school. He didn't have a fever and his cough wasn't all that bad.

But those little opportunities to snuggle and spoil were rapidly slipping away. She'd seen it with her twin girls. One day they were happy to crawl into bed with you and read bedtime stories. The next, they told you they could tuck themselves in. That independence was what every good parent wanted to see in their child. But it broke a mother's heart all the same.

She got out of her car and locked the door. A white Ford

Taurus paused in the road, the driver waved for her to cross. Friendliness wasn't the main reason why she and Trey lived in a small town, but it sure made life easier.

Once inside, she stood in line, ordered her tall cappuccino with soy milk. While she waited for her order she called the salon and made her hair appointment for the next Saturday.

When she was back in the car her phone rang.

"Hey, sweetheart," her husband said.

"Hey, darlin'." She had been raised in Miami and Natalie didn't have a Southern accent. But she'd been pretending to have one for so long, the slight drawl had become second nature.

"Just want to let you know that I've called a practice for after school today. So, I'll be home late," he said.

"No problem. Oh, shoot!"

"What's the matter?" her husband asked.

She looked at the blue lights flashing in her rearview mirror, and her heart thumped hard against her chest. "I'm getting pulled over!"

"You okay? Where are you?"

"I just got on State Road 19 about two miles ago, on my way to work. I might have been a little over the speed limit." Although she didn't think she was. Normally she did everything in her power to stay off of everyone's radar.

"Do you want me to come to you?"

She thought for a moment, decided she didn't want her husband involved. Didn't want to put him at risk. "No, I'll call you back in a minute."

"Okay, love you."

"Love you more."

She hung up the call and dialed Sheriff Ben Parkins from her favorites list. Not because she called him a lot but because if she needed him she didn't want to waste time looking for his number. Voicemail.

"Dang it."

She slowed the car and pulled to the side of the desolate road. Nothing but farmland on both sides of the two-lane highway. She thought about flooring it because the white car didn't have any police identification on the doors. there was only a blue light on the driver's side of the roof.

But it was eight miles to her teaching job at the school, and nothing between here and there but one gas station. Which she knew wasn't even open at this early hour. If the car that was pulling her over wasn't a cop, he could edge her off the road before she reached safety. Or worse. If it was a cop, she would draw too much attention to herself by getting arrested.

When the man in the white Ford got out of the car, she breathed a little easier. He was wearing a tan police uniform, just like Sheriff Parkins and the other cops on his force.

Sheriff Parkins's voicemail greeting finished and the beep sounded.

"Hey, Sheriff, this is Natalie Pyne. We spoke a few months ago? Um. I'm getting pulled over by a cop on State Road 19, right near old man Smith's farm. The cop is wearing a uniform but isn't driving an Aiken County cop car, it's just a white Ford of some kind. Anyway, if you could check on this please? And call me back? Thanks."

The cop stood outside her door and motioned for her to roll the window down. She looked at the man's face and couldn't decide if he was the same man that had been following her several weeks back. This man had a beard and mustache. The man that had been following her, the one she told Sheriff Parkins about, was clean-shaven.

Something didn't feel right. She dialed 911, just in case, tucked her phone out of sight and lowered her window.

"Yes?" Natalie asked.

"Natalie Pyne?" the man asked.

"Yes—how do you know my name?" she asked.

"It's Natalie Marrs though, isn't it?"

Natalie felt her jaw fall open.

Felt her mouth dry.

Felt the adrenaline shoot through her veins.

Twenty years of hiding. Twenty years of imagining how she would attack if they ever found her. Now all she could do was think of her kids and her husband.

She couldn't move.

The man who obviously wasn't a cop reached to the back of his waistband and pulled out a gun.

"911, what's your emergency?" The woman's nasal voice boomed through the car's speakers.

She floored the gas pedal. "I'm on State Road 19! A man dressed—"

Several loud pops shot off like fireworks. She lost control of the car, and slammed nose-first into a ditch. She hopped out of the driver's side door and started running.

She looked over her shoulder.

The cop, who wasn't really a cop, ran toward her.

28

Skidaway Island was only twenty minutes from Columbia Square. The Landings, where Maribelle lived, was the largest community on the island. Actually it was the largest community in the country—so the sign said at the entryway.

While I waited in line at the guard gate, I got a text from Hernandez saying he'd spoken to my parents. He didn't think they believed me on the note.

I wasn't surprised. I was disappointed.

I searched for sale listings in The Landings and scanned realtors' names. When it was my turn and the guard asked who I was there to see, I told him I was meeting realtor Bill Whalen for an open house. I wasn't, but he was the listing agent for several properties in The Landings.

The guard raised the gate.

Several golfers, wearing variations of pink and yellow and blue plaid, drove golf carts along curved sidewalks that wound along fairways. Every home in The Landings was loaded with low country charm. Like wraparound porches and white columns and gracious front lawns.

My throat still ached from Max's grip, my body ached from the allergic reaction and my head ached from the epinephrine and lack of sleep. But I was determined to know who was trying to kill me. That meant I had to know the truth about Nick and Max.

My phone rang with Nick's picture popping onto the screen.

I stared at his name and thought of the floral arrangement with the sugar and the bees.

I'd thought the flowers were a feeble attempt to kill me, especially when comparing it against the peanut fragments in my coffee. But when I considered they'd taken my EpiPens as well, I realized both attempts were more of a one-two punch. If one hadn't worked, the other most likely would have.

I declined the call.

My phone rang again. It was Tim this time.

"Hey Harper, Leo and I are here to install your custom railing. The door's locked and no one answered when I knocked. Just want to make sure it's okay if I use my key and go in? I don't want the alarm to go off."

"I set a unique entry code just for you and just for today," I said. "It's in your text, did you get it?"

"Let me check. Oh. Yeah, okay, it's here."

"Just remember to lock the door behind you. I'm not expecting anyone else, so don't let anyone in."

"Yep, got it. We'll handle the install today, then we'll be back to recheck everything. After we leave today it should be fine to use."

"Thanks. Also, Tim?"

"Yeah?"

"I don't know if I mentioned this before. But if you would make sure that no one from your group brings any nuts or nut butters into the house? I've got a peanut allergy and have to be careful."

"Oh sure, yeah. No problem. I've told everyone that. But I'll tell them again."

Maribelle's estate home was near the back of the community and backed up to the water. When I pulled up she was walking along her circular drive wearing a sleeveless, pale pink maternity dress and white tennis shoes. Excepting the extra fullness, she still closely resembled her high school photos.

"You must be Bunny's neighbor." Maribelle extended both hands and a well-practiced smile.

I hadn't expected Bunny to give Maribelle a heads up that I might come for a visit, but I wasn't upset that she had. "Yes, I'm Harper."

"Come and sit. I was just coming back from my morning walk." Her tone was singsongy. She squeezed my hands and released them, gestured to the front porch.

"Bunny sent a text the other day saying she thought you might stop by sometime soon." Maribelle led me to the far corner of the porch, where a pitcher of lemonade and two glasses sat on a table in front of a wicker swing and two matching chairs. "She said y'all are neighbors and that you're a friend."

"I live just across the green from her. We share a handyman."

"She mentioned that to me." She poured each of us a glass of lemonade, turned the ceiling fan on, then took a seat in one of the chairs. "Any friend of Bunny's is a friend of mine. Take the swing, please. If I sit in it I might not be able to get back up." She smiled and patted her large, pregnant belly.

An unexpected wave of longing rolled through me. A

telling sign that I'd ignored my own dream of a family for too long. I thought of Catherine again, and how I'd declared that I would live for her.

"When are you due?" I asked.

"Two weeks. And I think I'm finally organized." She crossed her fingers in the air to show she hoped she was right.

"That's good. That's great." My head pounded hard enough that I had to press two fingers over my right eye for a moment.

"You're not here to check on me or little Tucker, though, are you?" She rubbed her belly again.

"Did Bunny tell you why I might come by?"

"She said that you're fairly new to the area. Looking to have the inside track on a few things."

Maribelle launched into what she knew about local schools, social clubs and tennis teams. She talked about the fact that my home was on the National Historical Register and how much that meant to the city and certain restoration groups. She told me she was on the Savannah Historical Society board for the Christmas Home Tour and asked if I'd be interested in opening up a level of my home for the tour.

I took the request as an offer of quid pro quo and said, "I'd be happy to."

"Oh. Such good news!" She clasped her hands at her chest.

I put my glass on the white wicker side table. "I was telling Bunny about someone I met recently, and she thought you might be able to tell me more about him."

"Well, I do know just about everyone in Chatham County," she said with pride.

"His name is Nick Smith," I said. "Bunny said y'all went to school together."

Her smile faded by half. She looked down, wiped a drop of condensation from her glass. "How do you know Nick?"

"We've been seeing one another," I said. "And, uh, seems there's a little more to his past than what he shared with me initially. I'd like to know what you know about him. As I said to your grandmother, I care about him. I just want to know the truth. As you might imagine, I'm trying to make a good decision."

My honesty seemed to take her by surprise. "I would guess you're referring to what happened to Sophie, and I don't know anything more about that than what they've written in the papers."

I shook my head. "I want to know what happened the night that Piper died."

Maribelle's mouth drifted open.

Cicadas chirped loudly in the summer heat.

A black Mercedes G-class pulled in behind my car. Maribelle slammed her mouth shut and stood.

A gray-suited man who had the swagger of John Wayne and the stature of an NFL quarterback exited the Mercedes with his briefcase and bounded up the front steps.

"Hello, ladies!" He extended his large hand to me for a friendly shake. "I'm Gunner."

I would have recognized him even without the introduction. He, too, appeared remarkably similar to his high school photos.

"This is Harper. One of Bunny's friends," Maribelle said sweetly.

"Yes, we're neighbors," I said.

"Well, it's wonderful to meet you. Certainly any friend of Bunny's is a friend of ours."

Gunner kissed his wife and wrapped his arm around her possessively.

"What are you doing home so early?" she asked.

"I'm gonna grab nine with Judge Tatnall."

Maribelle gave me the one minute sign and stepped inside with Gunner. They whispered with one another and through the open door I caught sight of the inside of their home. The interior bore a striking similarity to Bunny's, albeit with a more modern sensibility.

Gunner shook his head at Maribelle, glanced at me, then shook his head again. She nodded, seemingly in agreement with whatever his concerns were.

Gunner went upstairs.

Maribelle stepped outside again and closed the door gently behind her. "Why don't we take a walk?" She pointed away from the house. "I think I'd like to get in a few more steps before the sun sets."

I had the sense that whatever she was about to tell me, she wanted to say it privately.

She grabbed her tan wide-brimmed hat from a side table, and we walked along the worn and shaded path that wound into the backyard. It angled past the rectangular pool and ended at the deepwater dock behind the house.

We walked underneath the covered boat dock where she stopped to glance at the house, then turned away and faced the deepwater inlet. She deliberately positioned her back to the house and she said in a low voice, "I haven't spoken about that night since it happened. Not since we had to talk with the police." She brushed a few wild strands of hair out of her face.

"None of us have. Reporters and investigators contacted Bunny when Sophie fell—because of my grandfather's book, you must know about the book."

I nodded.

"But she never put any of them in touch with me. She

must really like you." Maribelle's bright and easy countenance that had greeted me earlier was long gone, replaced by a solemn and careful guardedness.

I kept my mouth shut, afraid that if I said anything it might discourage her from sharing.

"Why we decided to go to Cumberland that day, I don't know. We should have gone to Tybee like we always did. It was a mistake. Too much empty space. Too much opportunity for people to let loose.

"Nicksey brought beer, Sophie brought two joints from her mom's secret stash. We were all sitting around that campfire drinking and smoking. We couldn't have gotten away with that on Tybee, but on Cumberland, you know." She shrugged. "For a while it was all good and fun. We were laughing hysterically at God knows what. Next thing I knew, Piper got weepy. Too much pot. She pulled me aside and said that she was conflicted about being with Nick. Except that, cheerleader that she was, she really didn't have an inside voice.

"What am I going to do?" Maribelle imitated a whine and a sophomoric sob. "I still love Max!"

"Everyone heard. Including Nick. Who was about three sheets to the wind like the rest of us.

"Poor Charlotte, she was all curled into Max when Piper overshared. Then Max's chest puffed up like a proud animal and Charlotte's face just fell. She knew what was about to happen. We all knew. Max wasn't that hard to figure out back then.

"Piper was a beautiful girl. Not that Charlotte was unattractive, but Piper's beauty just made everyone else pale in comparison. So, Max and Charlotte started arguing.

"Nick was utterly humiliated. I mean, the male ego is already fragile, but at that age it has the strength of an empty eggshell. So he yelled a few uncomplimentary things at Piper and stormed down the beach.

"That's when Piper realized she'd made a complete mess of things. She ran after Nick, saying that she was sorry. She caught up with him but he was so angry, he shoved her. She fell backward, lay there in the sand until Max went to her.

"Piper let Max hold her for a while, and that's when Charlotte really fell apart. I went to Piper. Piper left and seemed to go after Nick. She said she had to apologize. After a while, Max went in that direction, too. We guessed to go after Piper.

"Charlotte said she was going to tell Max it was over, which seemed like a moot point but no one stopped her. A little while later, Nicksey went after Nick because he thought Nick might kill Max if they got into it. Nick's temper was legendary back then.

"After an hour or so, Gunner and I sobered up enough to realize we needed to search for them. I found Charlotte crying on the beach, not far from the camp. But Nick was the one who found Piper. Gunner and I found him kneeling next to her, sobbing. Nicksey wasn't far behind. It was a horrible sight. She was face up on the sand, by one of the dunes. Eyes open, mouth open—just, gone. Nothing left but the shell. I remember, Nick couldn't stop staring at her. Such a gruesome sight.

"Sophie and Charlotte and Max showed up next. Much later, when the police came, Nicksey said that Nick had been with him and Sophie. That they'd found him not long after he'd left the bonfire, and that they'd just been sitting on the beach talking. Sophie agreed. Charlotte said Max had been with her."

"Who did it?" I asked.

Maribelle kept her eyes on the deep water. "We were

good kids. None of us were ever in trouble. Not serious trouble, anyway. So when the police came out, they immediately began searching for someone other than us who could have done it.

"The Greyfield Inn, which is the only hotel on the island, was closed for renovations then. The police found some empty beer cans and a bunch of smoked cigarettes behind one of the trees near our campsite, and the vagrant theory was born. None of us fought it." She shrugged. "But none of us believed it.

"After I'd found Piper, after Max and Charlotte made it back to the bonfire, Max looked so contrite. Like he'd done something he felt really bad about. I'd never seen him look that way before. He was disheveled, like there had been a struggle. He was never quite the same after that. So, I always thought it was him—" Her words hung in the air, unfinished.

Maribelle looked at me for the first time since she began her story. Her big brown eyes shimmered with something distant, something that haunted her. "It was right before we all went off to college. Bunny threw a graduation party at her house. Nick and I had just started seeing one another. Then Nicksey—" She licked her bottom lip, stared hypnotically at the deep water again.

"Nicksey cornered me, told me to keep my distance from Nick. That the night Piper died, when he told the police that he and Sophie had been with him the whole time—that wasn't true. He said he had lied to protect his friend Nick, who he had believed was innocent. Then later, when they didn't find the killer, he said he wasn't so sure he'd done the right thing."

My stomach dropped. Hard. "Why?"

She shrugged. "He didn't say. He died not long after that,

so there's no way to know. It could have been Nick who killed Piper. It could have been Max. In my heart of hearts, I'd always believed it was Max. But then Sophie went down the stairs, and Nick was charged. And it all just fit, you know?"

Anxiety shot through my arms and legs. "What fit?"

Maribelle spread her left hand in front of her, then curled it into a fist. "I had lunch with Sophie two days before she ended up in a coma. She told me she was having an affair, that she was pregnant, and that Nick wasn't the father. After I got the news of Sophie's accident, that image of Nick shoving Piper to the ground kept playing in my head—"

My breath picked up its pace. "Did she say who the father was?"

Maribelle shook her head. "She was very tight-lipped, which was not like her. All she said was that Nick knew the baby wasn't his and that she wasn't giving up her baby."

My throat closed around something—a gasp, a scream, the word no. I swallowed it down.

"Someone must have known who Sophie was having an affair with," I managed.

"If she was going to confide in anyone, it would have been me, and I didn't know who the guy was. The only other person who might have known—was Nick."

"What happened to the baby?"

She pressed her hands against her swollen belly and closed her eyes briefly. "He didn't survive the fall."

He. Sophie must have been far enough along in her pregnancy for them to know the baby had been a boy. We walked along the narrow dock and when we reached the grass again I asked, "Where is Sophie now?"

"After she left the hospital, her parents put her in some private facility. I asked but they never would say which one.

They said they didn't want Nick to find out where she was. There are only a few in the area. I could probably narrow it down. But they aren't allowing any visitors, so it wouldn't matter."

We reached the front yard again.

"Thanks for talking with me," I said. "I appreciate it."

"Bunny is the only mother I've ever known, there isn't anything I wouldn't do for her. But Nick and Max have been out of my life for a long time now and that's the way I want to keep it.

"I don't know what you plan to do with this information, but if anyone asks me to validate what I told you today, you should know that I'll deny I ever told you anything. And for the record? I'm an excellent liar." To prove her point she smiled instantly, beautifully and with no sign of conflict or deceit.

"I understand," I said and walked toward my car. "Oh, um—Bunny said that Nick and Max relocated to Savannah from somewhere in Florida. Do you remember what city they moved from, by chance?"

"Miami." Maribelle went into her house, then shut and locked the door.

29

Manny sat in his office, logged in with Stanford's credentials, and searched for any new intel on Jenny's and Mariana's cases.

The image of an hourglass popped up, showing that it would be a minute before the system gave him access. He checked his phone while he waited.

On a hunch he texted Harper:

Did you get a call or email from FBI re Jenny Hansen's death? Maybe from guy named Stanford?

SHE RESPONDED IMMEDIATELY:

No. No calls or emails from anyone

NOW HE KNEW FOR SURE.

The hourglass disappeared and the dashboard popped up. He clicked to the Muñoz family files and found that a deceased label had been placed over Natalie Pyne's photo.

He exhaled like someone punched a hole in his lung with a penknife.

Natalie had taken a hint from Harper's way of living. She changed her last name to Pyne, cut and dyed her hair. She wore contacts that changed her eye color, and she moved to the middle of Nowheresville, South Carolina.

Several years later, she married Terry Hansen, history teacher and football coach at the local middle school. They had twin daughters Hannah and Leah, a boy named Damon, and they lived a low profile life. How had she been found?

"Manny?"

He looked up to see Director Hall standing in his doorway. His eyes were narrow, his jaw was set. Without another word he motioned for Manny to follow him.

Manny quickly downloaded the report on Natalie's death, then followed Director Hall to his office where he found his partner waiting for them.

Stanford nodded and shifted in his chair.

Director Hall gestured for Manny to sit and closed the door.

"Anything you would like to tell us?" Director Hall asked.

Manny gave a slight shrug. "About what?"

Director Hall held up a piece of paper with columns of numbers on it. "IT department says that there have been numerous logins into the Muñoz Crime Family files from your computer. That true?"

Manny thought about denying the accusation, or asking

for a closer look at the document, then decided it wouldn't matter. He'd been caught. And he didn't think Stanford was there for support.

"I received a piece of correspondence from someone who was familiar with the Muñoz case. It highlighted a verse they used to justify their crimes. Stanford showed me a portal so I could see if there had been any recent developments."

Stanford brushed imaginary lint from his pants.

"After which you took Stanford's credentials and logged in to the portal multiple times on your own?"

"That's right," Manny said.

Director Hall fixed his dark brown eyes on Manny and drew in a slow inhale. "So, you stole his login credentials and, posing as him, accessed restricted files."

The truth hit Manny like a fastball between the eyes.

He thought he'd been so clever to lift Stanford's passcode. Now he realized that wasn't the case.

Manny didn't blink. He didn't swallow. He didn't flinch.

"To understand if any of the Muñoz clan was active again. That was all."

Director Hall leaned toward the report and dragged his finger over each line. "You logged in quite a few times over the last several days. How often did you think you needed to check?"

The question was a test—would he admit that he knew Stanford and apparently Director Hall, too, had failed Jenny and Mariana and now Natalie on purpose? Most likely for a substantial payout?

If he did, he'd be fired. Maybe even killed to ensure his silence.

If he shrugged his shoulders and kept quiet, he'd keep

his job. But they'd always hold it over his head. Because they knew, he knew.

Still, even if he stayed silent, they might kill him anyway.

It took him less than a second to make his decision.

"After Jenny Hansen died, I was contacted by her father. We discovered that she had received a note, similar in content to what I received, before she died. Her father, husband and I found that commonality suspicious."

Director Hall leaned back in his chair and pressed his fingertips together.

"I asked Stanford to notify the surviving women and their families about Jenny Hansen's death and the notes, so they could protect themselves. He said he would, but he didn't. After that, I checked the portal again and learned that Mariana Lopez had been killed and that she too had received an almost identical note ahead of time. I checked the portal several times after that, looking for additional clues. I felt I owed it to the families to help them. Especially after learning that the Crescent City Police requested help from the Bureau, but their request was refused.

"I have all of this documented in a memo, in case you need a copy? I don't have it with me, of course. It's on a thumb drive. In a safe location. But I could make a call in case you need a copy sent to you right away."

The Director's eyes narrowed for a flash of a moment. "If you're implying that anyone in the department has done something wrong, you're even further off base than I realized. What happened to those girls is tragic but we have police and coroner's reports to verify the facts. So you can keep your memo." He walked to the front of his desk and towered over Manny.

"You were expressly prohibited from accessing these case files, for your own protection as well as for the protection of others. Considering your history, and in light of your blatant disregard for regulation, I'm placing you on administrative leave, effective immediately. We will use this time to review your case for the prospect of termination."

Manny glanced at Stanford, who stared at Director Hall's desk.

Manny went to the mail room, found a box, then cleaned out his desk like he was never coming back. Because he knew he wasn't.

Stanford rounded the corner and hovered in the doorway. "I'm sorry, man. I really am."

Manny didn't look up. "Sorry for what?"

"I'm sorry it had to go down this way. But maybe it's for the best."

"Best for whom?"

"Well, you were heading down a bad path." Stanford shifted his weight like he always did when he evaded the truth.

Manny stopped piling items into the box. "How'd you know that I was logging into the portal under your credentials?"

"I didn't. Not until I.T. confirmed it."

"Confirmed it. Interesting word choice. Confirmed would imply that you had suspicions it was happening in the first place. Confirmed would imply that you—or someone you'd spoken to—went to I.T. and asked them to check."

Stanford's lips parted slightly.

"You've always been careless like that," Manny said.

He looked at the framed picture he'd just taken from the corner of his desk. It was his wedding photo with Stanford at his side, his best man, his best friend. He dropped it into the metal trashcan with a loud clang.

30

I parked in my driveway, and Nick stepped out of my back door unexpectedly.

I drew in a sharp breath.

He wore his custom black suit and the gold initialed cufflinks I'd given him on his birthday. His light blue eyes highlighted his innocent-good-guy appeal, and for the first time in our short-lived relationship, I didn't want to trust them.

In fact, everything about him struck me now as calculated. Designed to manipulate. A song from the eighties about "the devil inside" danced in my head.

I slipped my hand into my purse and gripped the gun handle. "What are you doing here?"

His eyes narrowed like that wasn't even the right question. He walked up to my car and opened the door.

I sat there, studying that beautiful face I'd fallen in love with just a few short weeks ago. There had to be some mannerism or facial expression that revealed his true identity as a murderer. An attempted murderer. A Muñoz.

"I've been calling and couldn't get ahold of you. I was worried something was wrong."

"My ringer must be off," I said.

I worked harder to find some glimmer of deception, some physical evidence of all the things I'd learned about him in the last 48 hours. But those meds must have damaged my brain because stupidly, all I could see was the man I loved.

He offered a gentlemanly hand to help me out of the car and I released the gun. "You're sure everything's okay?"

"I'm fine." I drew in a deep breath, my lungs ached. I never felt right after a bolus of epinephrine plowed its way through my system. It would take several days before I felt truly clean and clear again.

He exhaled and closed his eyes for a moment in apparent relief. Then he surprised me by lifting me into a hug such that my feet left the ground.

With his heart next to mine, my suspicion fell away. The feeling that I'd come to know as his love for me filled my chest, and poured throughout the rest of my body.

He put me down. I stepped away. I felt more vulnerable and uncertain than I thought possible.

"Let's go inside," he said and extended his hand again.

I hesitated.

For as much as my home was a fortress to an intruder, it could also be a prison if I were trapped on the inside with the wrong person.

He raised his eyebrows in question, a comforting smile spread across his face.

I accepted his hand and followed him inside.

We walked up the stairs and I quickly planned a list of questions in my mind. Clear. Logical. Evidence-based.

But when we got to the kitchen I pointed to the cabinet

where my EpiPens should have been. "Are you trying to kill me?"

He stepped back. Laughed nervously.

"And are you married?" I asked.

He slipped his hands into his pockets. "What's this about?"

I grabbed my phone and showed him the emails from Sophie.

"This one came in during my interview. It not only went to me, but to Max Crandall and the other officers as well."

He stared at the photos and the emails without blinking, his wolf-blue eyes steady. "I was married before, I've shared that. We are divorced now. She might be crazy enough to send something like this, but I don't think she sent these."

"Why is that?" I asked.

"Because she's in a coma."

WE SAT in the living room. It was an architecturally formal room and offered some semblance of structure and order.

Nick made himself a vodka martini at the beverage cart in the corner. Twice he glanced at the forced perspective railing that Leo and Tim had installed on the spiral staircase.

He sat across from me and asked, "Who would have taken those photos?"

I didn't think that was the right first question, but I decided we could begin there. "The sender didn't say, but they came in when I was interviewing at Tatnall."

Nick's jaw clenched and his tanned skin flushed. "You don't want to work for Max."

I didn't disagree. But I assumed Nick said that because he knew his secret was out. One of them, anyway.

I opened a browser on my phone and showed him several pages of the media coverage from his trial. "Before I left Tatnall, Max gave me some good reading material. I also spoke with some folks from your high school era. Mr. Smith."

Nick exhaled heavily, like my words shot a hole in his lungs. He pressed his lips together and stared at the floor for a long moment. "When you kept putting off your trip to New York, I figured you'd found something."

"Why didn't you tell me?" I asked.

He inhaled long and slow and adjusted the wide band on his watch. "When we first met, and since you lived in Savannah, I assumed you already knew about my past. When you didn't—" He shook his head. "I took it as a gift." He took off his jacket, removed his cufflinks, and rolled up his sleeves.

"I had an unexpected clean slate with you. You looked at me without judgment. I took it as a rare chance for us to get to know one another without my past getting in the way. Selfishly, I didn't want to give that up."

I hadn't thought any explanation could be good enough. But this made sense.

It had been what I'd wanted. To be seen and loved for who I was. Without all the filters of my past—past experiences, past mistakes, past abuse. There was something fragile in the way he looked at me. I didn't think it was contrived. It tugged at my heart.

It also tugged at my integrity. I was grilling him over keeping his past from me. While I'd kept my past from him.

For good reason.

But I wondered if I blamed him unfairly.

I'd killed two people before I even had a driver's license. I refused to take prescribed meds. I had hallucinations of my dead sister. I was being chased by a drug cartel who wanted to murder me. Who might kill Nick, too. I hadn't even given Nick my real name.

Still I said, "You were accused of attempted murder."

That spark of anger turned his eyes electric. It was the same spark I'd seen when we were on our way to the chapel. He stood. My fight or flight instinct kicked in and I stood, too.

"I guess you also read that I was found innocent? Cleared of all charges?" His voice was loud and forceful. He paced like a lion in a cage.

"I also saw the interviews where the jurors said you got off with your good looks and your charm." I had to say it. I had to push.

"I never. Hurt her." He pointed at me.

"Just like you never hurt Piper?"

He stopped abruptly. Like he'd been shot.

He scoffed, shook his head, and looked away.

He threw his glass against the wall, where it shattered. "I didn't kill her!" His face flushed a deeper shade of fury.

Horrible, debilitating anxiety shook me on the inside. It begged me to back down or leave. I refused.

We stared at one another for a moment.

He looked away, splayed his fingers, pressed his palms down, like he told himself to calm.

"These are pretty big secrets. I guess you thought hiding your past wouldn't hurt, but—" I waved my phone to reference Sophie's email. "You should have told me."

My hand shook and I quickly tucked it under my arm.

He turned and stared at the mullioned window.

He looked shocked. Like a man whose plan had fallen out from under him.

He pushed a hand through his hair. "You're right. I'm sorry. I should have trusted you with the whole picture."

I didn't know if he genuinely humbled himself or just regrouped. I thought I saw traces of something dark in his expression.

"You had to know I would find out eventually." It was like I scolded both of us.

He shrugged slightly. Not like he didn't care, but like he didn't have a good answer. "I knew that. I wanted to tell you. A million times I tried to find the words to tell you everything. The longer I waited the more I tied myself in knots.

"But I was enjoying...you. I was falling in love with you."

He knelt in front of me. He held my hands and kissed them. "Please. Harper. You are one of the only people who knows the real me. Don't trust the papers. You know they write for profit, to push a narrative. Not for truth."

I sat down. I remembered how the media reported on my own experience. They worked very hard to make my story about vengeance. One rag suggested we kidnapped the little boy intentionally. Another hack newspaper ran a series on sororicide and printed Catherine's and my photos on the front page.

I knew he wasn't wrong. I nodded.

I had an idea. "By the way, thank you for the flowers."

He flinched. Like I flicked water at his face.

"What flowers?"

I couldn't tell if he was caught off guard because I'd called him out, or because the comment had seemingly come out of left field.

"The florist left flowers on my front porch. I assumed they were from you."

He shook his head slowly, deliberately.

"Maybe the florist made a mistake." I rubbed my forehead and sighed hard. "I don't know who you are."

"You do know me. You saw the real me from the first time we met. I meant everything I said to you on the night I proposed. Please. Think about what we've found with one another."

I did, constantly. Now I also thought about how someone laced my coffee with peanuts and lured bees to my front step. Someone who knew me. Someone who had been in my house.

"Maybe we need a clean slate. Tell each other everything, then see where things go." I was a hypocrite because I wasn't going to tell him everything.

He said, "I've never lied to you."

The trial and the stories about Piper and Sophie and Miami soared across my mind like fighter pilots. "A lie of omission is still a lie."

"Have you told me everything that's hidden away in *your* past?"

His comment stopped me cold.

"Have you?" His tone was insistent, like a man unjustly accused. Like a man who knew the truth.

I squeezed my eyes tight. "No."

"I should have told you about the trial. I should have. But I did not push my ex-wife down those stairs."

"What about Piper?"

He looked at me, slack-jawed.

"I didn't hurt Piper," he said finally.

"You pushed her that night. She fell."

He leaned back on his heels. "Where are you getting this information?"

I didn't answer and he dropped his head. When he lifted

it again he said, "I was a teenager, I was drunk, and I was stupid. I shouldn't have pushed her."

My only job in that moment was to decide if he was telling the truth. I had thought that face-to-face, I could see whatever it was I'd missed before. But I didn't see anything that looked like a lie. A manipulation. A deceit. Which only caused me to distrust myself even more.

His dark eyes pleaded with a sadness that reached the far corners of my heart. He was either a world-class actor, or he was telling the truth.

"I didn't kill Piper. I don't know who did. I had an alibi."

"From the *real* Nick Chamberlain?" I blurted. "Who gave you a fake alibi?"

He stared at me, like he wondered what else I knew. "Because he knew I was innocent!"

The anger flared in his eyes again and I readied myself for him to charge me.

Would I freeze like I had with Max?

"The case against me for Sophie's fall was circumstantial. There wasn't any proof that I was guilty. I was just a target for the D.A. to make a name for herself." He got to his feet, looked out the window, shaking his head. "Even though I was found innocent, it ruined my reputation. There was no place I could work. No one would hire me. People around here believed what they read in the papers, so I lost most of my friends. I had to create a new identity. Nick Chamberlain had been my best friend. So when I decided to change my name, I took his.

"The truth is—you and I haven't known each other for all that long and there are bound to be things in our histories that are...surprising. But we've had the chance to get to know each other privately, without the media's filters, without our pasts getting in the way. That's everything right there." His voice had the kindness to it I'd always known it to have.

More questions ran around in my mind, chased by the answers he'd provided. I tried to pick just the right question to ask.

"Do you love me?" he asked.

"That's not the problem," I said.

"How much do you love me?" he asked.

"What do you mean?"

"Because I love you like I've never loved anyone. And I think you feel the same way about me. I don't need to know what's in your past to know that we're better together than we are apart. I know we need to talk and there are some things I need to share. There are things I need to explain. But if you love me half as much as I love you, then what we have is worth saving."

Slowly, he pressed a palm to the side of my cheek. The emotion between us built and expanded like an aura, until it filled the room. He leaned in and kissed me gently.

He had kissed me hundreds of times and yet the feel of our bodies coming together shocked me, made me want to draw closer to him.

The danger thrilled and frightened me.

Still, I couldn't stop loving him.

He pulled away.

"I'll answer any question, I'll tell you whatever you want to know. After that, if you still want to leave, then I won't stand in your way. All I ask is that you keep an open mind."

The offer sounded fair.

But I knew he could concoct and twist and throw a lens over his version of the story, and I'd have no way of knowing where his rendition varied from the truth.

I scanned the titles on the bookshelf beside me, wishing

some bit of classic wisdom could advise me. Mary Stewart's *Nine Coaches Waiting* caught my eye, and unfortunately the line that jumped to mind wasn't comforting: "I was very ready to meet any gesture, however slight, with the response of affection."

I knew that a woman's loneliness and vulnerability shone brightly on the radar of every ne'er-do-well man, and I wondered if Nick had homed in on my weakest spot.

If he were a gold-digger, an opportunist who had found the secret longing in my heart, then dropping his hooks into my soft, quiet desperation would have been as easy as showing me a little attention.

If he were a Muñoz, then his love and attention would easily have removed my discernment, such that I wouldn't have seen him for who he really was.

If he were a Muñoz, even if he had fallen in love with me, I knew that wouldn't supersede the loyalty he would feel toward his own family and their vendetta.

If he were a Muñoz, that need for revenge would be in his blood.

31

Manny walked into his garage, went straight up the stairs and slammed the box of his office items onto his desk. He reached into his pocket to retrieve his badge out of habit, then remembered he'd been forced to surrender it before he left the office.

He reread the report he'd printed out about Natalie Pyne. She had died in a car explosion. Accelerant had been detected at the scene, a typed, unsigned note had been found nailed to a tree nearby that said simply, "I'm sorry. I can't anymore."

Harper was now the final surviving girl who had testified against Ricardo Muñoz. Manny kicked the wastepaper basket across the room.

The downstairs door opened and closed, and a moment later Blair came to the top of the stairs. "What are you doing home so early?" Her hair was pulled into a messy ponytail at the nape of her neck.

Manny stood silent with his hands on his hips, papers from the trashcan scattered about his feet.

Her entire body slumped. "You've been fired, haven't you?"

He sighed. Nodded. "On paid leave."

She ran her hands over her face, leaned against the nearest wall and slid to the floor. Her eyes filled with fat tears. "What are we going to do?"

They'd had dreams of putting Reagan in the best schools, then retiring by the time their daughter went to college. They'd planned on traveling the world and gathering experiences they could tell their grandchildren. "I can open up a private investigative firm."

She scoffed. "And what? Film cheating husbands at low-rate motels? You've never wanted your own firm." Her stare became hard as granite, strong enough to waste anyone who went against it.

"It was a set-up," he finally said and hoped she would hear him. He told her about Stanford's login credentials and the I.T. surveillance. "He was the only one who knew I'd received the note. He was the only one I'd asked about the Muñoz family activity. He was the only one who made his login credentials available to me. I.T. doesn't routinely monitor who's looking at what. Neither would Stanford have had the authority to direct them to investigate me."

"Stanford..." Blair's unyielding countenance lost an ounce of strength.

"I think Stanford was offered a chunk of money in exchange for the girls' identities and locations. Alice is about to take him for everything he's got, so—"

"He was an easy target."

"Something like that," Manny said. "I think he thought this would all go down without my knowing anything until after the fact. But then the note arrived. He hadn't planned on the killer wanting to brag in advance."

"I guess Stanford is on leave, too?"

Manny sat in a metal folding chair and it groaned beneath his weight. He shook his head.

"What?! How?!" Her voice pitched high and thin.

"Because three of the four girls who testified against Ricardo Muñoz have died within two weeks of one another and Director Hall says there's nothing related, nothing suspicious.

"Crescent City P.D. requested the FBI look into Jenny's death and Hall refused. No investigation gets refused, delayed or shut down without his approval. I think the bribe started with Hall, then he cut Stanford in.

"He knew that once the news of the girls' deaths was out, I was the one wild card in the department. He knew I'd raise my voice and demand an investigation. So he needed someone close to me to keep me in line. Or at the very least, give me the opportunity to incriminate myself."

"So the note gets delivered to you, which no one expected," Blair said. "But Stanford and Director Hall have already thought about how to handle you when you learn about the girls' deaths."

"Director Hall knew I'd go to Stanford with any news first. He's my partner, I trusted him. Plus, he wasn't restricted from the case files. So, I get the note, I show it to Stanford. It's not what he expected but he knows what to do. He leads me right to his office where he types in his login credentials nice and slow and in plain view. Then he leaves the room."

"They played you," Blair said.

"Like a banjo." Manny pushed the heels of his hands against his eyes.

"Since Stanford or Hall gave this guy the girls' identities and location information from in the portal, couldn't Harper just move again? Change her name again? You could get word to her, her parents and relatives not to give anyone her new location information. Then she'd be safe. In the near term anyway," Blair said.

Manny thought about the portal. One by one the different screens flashed across his mind. He fell against the back of his chair like he'd been pushed.

"What?" Blair asked.

"The girls' current address info. None of that detail was in the portal. Neither were their current last names."

"Are you sure?"

"Yeah," he said. "I am."

I DROVE to the pharmacy to pick up my prescription for six new EpiPens, while Nick stayed at the house to make breakfast for dinner. I chose not to supervise his efforts and I didn't allow him to bring new food into the house because I wanted to use the kits I'd purchased from Dr. Callaghan. I wanted to know all the places where someone had put traces of peanuts, thinking that might help me narrow my list of suspects.

My phone rang. It was Agent Hernandez.

"I have news," he said. "Are you someplace where you can talk?"

My entire body tensed. "Yeah, I'm in my car."

"Alone?"

"Alone."

"Natalie Marrs is dead."

This news hit me like a bullet to the chest. I couldn't move. I couldn't breathe.

"Harper?"

Vivid memories of sweet Natalie being beaten ripped

through me with their usual savagery. She had learned early on how to play dead when the drubbings were prolonged. Pretending to be unconscious was the only thing that made them stop.

Someone that smart, someone that strong, I couldn't imagine how they'd found her.

"How?" I whispered.

He shared a disturbing yet unsurprising story of a death that looked like a suicide.

"Now you're the final survivor of the original ten girls who were kidnapped. You're the last survivor of the four who testified against Ricardo Muñoz. Which means you're their next target."

So he was sure now.

For as long as I could remember, I'd wanted official confirmation that the Muñoz family was hunting me, I'd wanted proof that I wasn't paranoid like my parents believed.

Now that I had it, it was no comfort.

I told him about the sugared flowers and the bees and that peanuts got in my coffee, that someone took my EpiPens and I ended up in the ER in anaphylactic shock. I told him that based on my research, either Nick or Max was a child of Ricardo Muñoz.

"You have to leave town. Immediately. Alone. Maybe your parents' house. Don't tell anyone where you're going."

I told him about Nick's trial, Sophie's fall down the stairs and Max.

When I finished the story in its entirety, he said, "He choked you?"

Then he sighed, so heavy and hard it sounded like a growl. "Give me as much information as you can on both of them and I'll try to get the local police on this. I'd bet that one of them is our guy. The other one is a sick bastard."

"What about you? Why aren't you taking care of it?" My tone was panicked.

"I've been put on leave for looking into Jenny's and Mariana's deaths without departmental approval."

Something inside of me, something old and rotting started to ache. It reminded me how alone I was. "You're kidding."

"I wish I was. I don't have any FBI resources behind me anymore. I'm going to do my best to get local attention on this, but in the meantime, get out of town, away from those men."

We hung up and I drove away from the pharmacy knowing that I had a decision to make.

I could go straight to the airport, fly to my parents' house as Hernandez wanted. Or I could fly to parts unknown to hide out for a while or even to begin a new life under a new name.

Or I could go home to Nick and try to find out what really happened with Sophie. I could try to find out who he really was.

I drove slowly over the unevenly bricked road, turning left, then after a few blocks, right. I arrived at the juncture where I would either turn toward the airport or toward home. I looked both ways, hoping one path might illuminate itself as the better way.

But there were no signs.

I gripped the steering wheel and prayed for one. A sign. An answer.

Nothing came.

Until, like a force from an underwater volcano, a quote from Mary Shelley's *Frankenstein* erupted from within: "I have love in me the likes of which you can scarcely imagine and rage the likes of which you would not believe. If I cannot satisfy the one, I will indulge the other."

And it all became clear.

If the Muñoz who stalked me knew where I lived, then he probably knew where my parents lived. Plus, I'd rather live in a cardboard box than live in the same house with my father. Either way, going home wouldn't work.

If I left town and started fresh somewhere else, that wouldn't sync with my father's idea of a wise and healthy choice. Then I'd never get my life back, I'd never get my freedom.

And I was determined to have both.

It was time.

I opened my purse and took out the small manicure kit I kept in the side zippered pocket. With the cuticle scissors, I made a cut in the lining of my purse at the bottom. Then I took one of the EpiPens and hid it inside, where no one would see it. I took some tape that I'd picked up at the pharmacy and affixed another EpiPen to the underside of my car seat. I saved the other four to secretly hide around the house.

Then I turned toward home.

I was driven by two things: my love for Nick and my hate of the Muñoz family. If I could not satisfy one, I would indulge the other.

32

I arrived at home to find Nick standing at the stove, flipping eggs and turning bacon.

"Take the first serving," he said and handed me a plate of bacon, eggs and toast. "Go ahead and eat while it's hot. The rest will be ready in a minute and I'll join you."

I snuck into the butler's pantry with the plate. One by one, I used the test strips that Dr. Callaghan had given me on the food, the coffee and the milk.

No peanuts in the eggs.

No peanuts in the bacon.

No peanuts in the coffee.

When I tested the small carton of milk that I kept in the butler's pantry fridge, the lights flashed and the monitor buzzed. The test strip showed significant traces of peanuts in the milk. A fact that didn't help me identify any one person in particular.

Still I breathed a sigh of relief. It might not have been Nick. It could have been an accident, just as the nurse had said. A contractor with a mouthful of peanuts could have taken a swig of milk.

I threw out the milk. But not my conviction that someone put the peanuts into the carton intentionally.

Nick and I situated ourselves in the den with coffee and our breakfast for dinner. I sat at one end of the couch with my knees drawn up. "You're originally from Miami?" I asked.

He stopped chewing, didn't move. The question startled him, because Miami wasn't the answer he'd given me before. He swallowed with some effort.

"Yes," he finally admitted. "My mother and I moved here when I was twelve."

"Brothers? Sisters?" He'd told me once that he was an only child. I was curious to see if this answer would change as well.

"No siblings," he said.

I thought of all the Muñoz brothers and sisters.

"Why did y'all move to Savannah?"

He stared at the floor for a long moment then told me that they left Miami because his mother no longer thought the city was a safe place to raise a child. That his maternal grandmother lived here, that his mother wanted family nearby since his father was out of the picture.

I couldn't help but think he was hiding something. "What happened to your father?"

He shrugged. "He's been gone for a long time."

I made a mental note to ask Agent Hernandez to help me check out his history.

He glanced over my head and I turned. The forced perspective railing was behind me.

"Just installed," I said. "According to your specifications."

His lips parted like he was about to say something.

"I need to know what happened the day that Sophie fell down the stairs. I need to know everything," I said.

Nick put his plate on the side table. "I'll start at the beginning." He clasped his hands together.

"I didn't usually get home until seven or seven-thirty. But I was home early that day, right at 4:45. I sat in my car in the driveway to wrap up a call. At about 5:00 I pulled into the garage next to Sophie's car.

"I washed my hands in the kitchen, made a drink. I stood at the kitchen counter eating prosciutto and crackers for about ten minutes or so. I thought she might have been outside or up in her room.

"It wasn't until I decided to go upstairs and change that I found Sophie at the bottom of the staircase. There was a lot of blood on the floor. She was unconscious. I called 911. It took the ambulance fifteen minutes to arrive. I didn't see anyone coming or going during that time. To my knowledge, she never regained consciousness."

Nick's story sounded like it had been rehearsed. Like he was giving testimony. I guessed this was probably what he'd said on the stand.

"What made them charge you?" I asked, unable to keep the suspicion out of my voice.

"The police, everyone, thought Sophie's fall was an accident."

"Because of the railing?" I pointed to the railing behind me.

"Yes, but I never thought it was an accident. I'll get to that. Everything changed when a reporter got ahold of Sophie's blog posts. She discovered that Sophie was wealthy, pregnant, and that I hadn't wanted the baby. She wrote a series of articles in the paper that sparked public interest, then popularity. Then the D.A.'s office filed charges.

"We had security video that showed someone entering the house through the back door about the same time I pulled into the driveway." Nick took his phone from his pocket and showed me a still shot.

"This was taken from the security camera on the back patio on the day when Sophie went down the stairs."

The high angle of the camera, the dark glasses, and the dark cap made it impossible to see anything truly identifying about the person. This person resembled the one from my own security feed.

He swiped the screen and played the video from the beginning. The man ran up the side of the yard, pausing once when he was at the back door to punch in the access code, then walked inside.

"Prosecution said I parked my car in the driveway, then cut through the woods on foot to come up the back lawn. They said that that's me on the video, with my identity deliberately camouflaged. So that I could say an intruder attacked Sophie."

I took Nick's phone and played the video again. The man could have been him. I understood the jurors' comments now—that Nick could have done it. But there really wasn't any proof either way.

"Was it true that you didn't want the baby?" I handed him his phone.

He stared at me. His face appeared exactly like the photos from the newspaper: Eyes darkly serious and focused straight ahead, every hair in place like he'd prepared for his close-up.

"That was true," he answered reluctantly.

A coldness settled into my gut.

"Because I think that man coming in the back door is her lover. I think the baby she carried was his. I think she wanted to keep it and he didn't. I think if it got out that she had his baby, it would have ruined his marriage, his standing. So he killed her.

"Her parents and the D.A. believed that the baby was mine, that I didn't want it and that that's why I pushed her. That synced with Sophie's earlier blog posts that said she wanted children and I didn't.

"My attorney said we shouldn't drive the affair theory or my claim that the baby wasn't mine. She said if we proved that Sophie had an affair, that would only give me additional motive in the jury's mind. She said it was better to focus on the fact that the prosecution didn't have any proof. Evidently that was the right approach because we won. But the fact that we didn't address her affair meant that the public never seriously entertained any suspect other than me."

He stared at the still shot on his phone and I found myself longing for hard proof of his innocence. A witness. A security cam shot of him in his car at that time. Something. Anything.

"I think that's Max Crandall." He pointed to his screen.

I took his phone and watched the thirty-second video again. And again. Trying to find the resemblance.

The man moved like Max, smooth and elegant. Didn't lumber like most men. I couldn't estimate height because the camera's angle was too high. I couldn't see his hands because he wore slim-fitting leather gloves. But it could have been Max.

Nick leaned back and told me what Maribelle already had. That Sophie had been in love with either him or Max all through high school. It was Nick's theory that Sophie only married him because Max had already married Charlotte.

"After Max and Charlotte had their daughter, Sophie

took a gift to their home. Later she told me that there was no way their baby was born prematurely. That she was a healthy full-term baby. She suggested that Max had married Charlotte out of necessity. Not out of love.

"She was visibly excited when she told me her theory. Gleaming. Almost giddy. I think because she realized Max had just done the honorable thing by marrying Charlotte. That and Max wasn't really in love with Charlotte.

"I think Sophie took that as a sign that the door was still open with him. Not long after we were married, there were signs that Sophie was having an affair. She disappeared for several hours around midday, she became distant, she had a dreamy look in her eye—like she'd fallen in love." There was nothing angry in his tone, but there was nothing wistful, either.

"The prosecution really hammered us by making my side of the story sound utterly coincidental and unbelievable: Mystery man enters and potentially leaves through the back door. Even though husband's cell phone records prove he was home at the time."

He exhaled hard, seemingly spent from the retelling.

As I'd feared, there wasn't any irrefutable proof of his innocence.

He scooted closer to me. When he was finally just a breath away, I realized I'd forgotten to feel afraid.

"I would never hurt you. I would never have hurt Piper or Sophie. It's not in me to do something like that." There was a softness in the way he looked at me, the same surprising gentleness I'd seen in one of our first conversations together. A vulnerability, perhaps, the result of our unexpected connection.

"Do you believe me?" he asked.

Something clenched in my chest, like a small fist.

Because only he and Sophie and Piper knew the truth, and Piper and Sophie weren't talking.

"Yes," I said.

He wrapped his arms around me, whispering, "Thank you. Thank you for trusting me."

The chemistry between us was as electric as always. Our connection was nothing less than mystical, unexplainable. The kind that said there was something eternal between us, that what we had couldn't be destroyed.

Even so, my stomach quivered.

I knew Nick could have pushed Sophie.

I knew he could have killed Piper.

I knew I saw him through a colored lens.

The fist in my chest got tighter and I excused myself to the study and checked the list the N.D. had given me. Then I took double doses of everything.

When the edge came off, I made a tea of chamomile, holy basil and motherwort for good measure.

"I'm going to take a shower," I said as I carried the tea back to the den.

"Good idea. I need to make a call," Nick replied. He opened the back door to take his call by the pool, then asked, "Do you still swim?"

"I haven't lately. But I'll get back into it."

On my way upstairs, I ran my fingers along the classics on the bookshelf, stopping on a collection of letters and stories from Emily Dickenson. As usual, one line bubbled up from memory and spoke to my situation at hand: "When the Best is gone—I know that other things are not of conse-quence—The Heart wants what it wants—or else it does not care—"

Emily had written that to a dear friend and I understood

her meaning now as I hadn't before. "The heart wants what it wants—or else it does not care."

I headed to the shower to wash off the stress of the day, stripping my clothes item by item once I hit my room. The water was hot enough that steam clouded the small room, and I breathed it deep into my lungs.

I got out and dressed in light sweats.

I opened the bathroom door and found Nick sitting in the white armchair in the corner of the room.

I drew in a sharp breath. His presence set me on my heels.

Nick had never been in my bedroom before.

"The railing turned out well on your half-spiral. Measurements are perfect. Ideal forced perspective."

I stood motionless.

He pointed to the computer equipment, security system and monitors in the corner of the room. "That's quite a setup."

"Security," I said.

"Are there cameras inside the house?"

I hesitated. "No," I said finally.

He moved to the bed and laid fully dressed on top of the comforter.

"Let me hold you. We'll figure out more tomorrow."

I took a breath to voice my objections.

But Emily Dickenson proved right, the heart wants what it wants. After a moment, I took the blanket from the corner of the bed, draped it over us and curled into him. I knew, as I always had, that the day would never come when I could stop loving him.

33

———

Manny sat at the round dining table where he studied images of the notes Mariana, Jenny and Natalie had received before they were murdered.

He was lost in a sea of questions without answers.

He was lost in the memories of Ricardo Muñoz.

He was lost.

Until he saw his wife walking toward him.

Blair's face was free of makeup. She clutched a storybook and a pink, plastic cup in one arm. She had a wet spot on the front of her shoulder—a telltale sign that she had given in and rocked Reagan until she conked out.

"She's asleep?" Manny asked, even though he already knew the answer.

"Yeah. Finally," she said.

A phantom chill, a shadowy silence fell between them.

He nodded to Reagan's book. "You gonna read that to me?"

She gave a half-smile, tossed the book on the couch and pointed to his computer screen. "What's this?"

"Photos of the notes that were sent to Mariana and Jenny and Natalie before they were killed. Different paper, same handwriting, same message."

She nodded but her expression didn't change.

"Of those who testified, Harper is the last survivor. Now she's received the same letter. So I'm searching for clues. Trying to figure out who this guy is."

"You told her to leave town, right?"

Manny nodded.

"Then she can contact local authorities wherever she is and get their help. Right?"

Manny didn't answer.

She walked into the kitchen. He heard her put Reagan's cup in the dishwasher and slam the door shut. He went to her.

"Do you want to talk about it?" he asked.

She faced the window. "Not really, no."

"Are you sure?" he pushed.

She turned to him and pressed her lips together slightly. It was an infinitesimal shift that no one else would have noticed, but Manny knew what it meant. She was mad and holding back the words. She didn't like hot words and hot tempers in her home. Not in the least since Reagan arrived.

He placed his hands on her arms. "I have to do this, and I'd rather we weren't at odds over it."

"You don't *have* to do it. You're *choosing* to do it."

"You're right. I am choosing. I'm choosing to do the right thing."

She leaned against the counter and crossed her arms. She stared at him, sighing loud and heavy, and he knew she still hadn't heard him.

"You're putting this case ahead of your family and ahead of your marriage. I don't want to sound heartless, but there are other law enforcement officials out there. Good ones. They can help Harper. You should be putting family before work. That's our agreement."

He nodded, slowly, then said, "I am honoring our agreement. I'm honoring you by doing this."

Her eyes grew fierce with accusation. "How?"

"Because if I didn't help Harper, I would be running again. Running from what I did—or from what I didn't do—all those years ago."

She shook her head, her mouth parted slightly, like she wondered if he would ever learn. "What's done is done, you can't change the past. I thought you'd accepted that."

"I have. I've also learned from it. Last time I was in this situation where these families needed my help, I was too consumed with drinking away the pain of my past to run the investigation properly. Consequently, those families lost their daughters forever. Helping Harper isn't about fixing the past. It's about doing the right thing now. That's who you married. You married a man who does the right thing, when the right thing needs to be done."

Every harsh, hard angle on her face softened, in recognition, he thought, of who he was.

After a long, quiet moment, she came to him and, without a word, wrapped her arms around him. Love was what he felt from her, and relief that they were still on the same team, still together as one. What he didn't feel from her was agreement.

She stepped away and looked at him with her signature intensity and said, "Why don't you put in for a transfer to a different department? So you could keep employment?"

He shrugged. "I know too much. They won't allow it."

"You can't lose your job."

"They need a fall guy to cover what they've done. So,

plan B might be my own agency. Or detective work on the local force."

She stood still. Chewed one side of her bottom lip. It's what she did when she mulled things over and didn't like her options. Like clouds gathering for a storm, it was a sign that her anger was accumulating.

Blair was bright and beautiful and bold. When they were on the same team, they were a powerful force.

He stepped toward her. "I could use your help. Codes and patterns were always your strong suit."

"Even if we figure out who's behind the murders, the Bureau won't do anything. They're too compromised at the top," she said.

"We can stop him ourselves." He said it like he had a plan. "Harper got that note days ago and she's still alive. He didn't pop into her world anonymously to stage a home invasion, an accidental fall or a suicide like he did the others. The killer has wormed his way into her life. He's made the effort to develop a relationship with her. For various reasons, she probably doesn't think she can walk away from him. So he continues to have access to her."

She chewed the side of her bottom lip again. "This is someone she cares about?"

"I'm pretty certain," Manny said.

A veil of steeliness slid over Blair's face. Since bringing Reagan into the world, Blair had an increasing awareness of all the many vulnerabilities that could beset a young woman. Being strong for oneself was easy. Figuring out how to instruct a daughter to be strong required deliberate thought and study. Most of all, it required an exploration of all the potential weak points.

She nodded slowly, confidently. Like she would want Reagan to have a protector if she needed it. If she had a blind spot. She grabbed two cans of ginger ale from the fridge and headed toward the breakfast area.

Blair turned on the nanny cam and brought the family whiteboard to the breakfast table where Manny had been sitting. She asked, "Where is Harper?" She didn't look at him. Instead she erased that week's grocery list and propped the board upright against the wall.

He popped open the ginger ale and took a swig in the way he used to drink Jack and Coke—with a long pull and a deep swallow. "I don't know."

"I thought you told her to leave town?"

"I did. But Harper doesn't always follow rules or direction. She's unpredictable at best. Incompetent or dangerous at worst if she's not on her meds. If she does leave town and if she's completely fooled by this guy, if she trusts him, she'll probably tell him her whereabouts." He told her about the anaphylactic shock and the flowers and the missing EpiPens.

"Why is he developing a relationship with her if he could have killed her by now?" Blair asked.

Manny pointed, acknowledging that was the right question. "I think he cares more about her suffering than he did the others. The others were about settling the score, fulfilling the promise of the We Will letter." Manny opened a green file folder, found the We Will letter and slid it in front of her. "The letter promised death. Simple straightforward revenge.

"But with Harper he's taken the time to gain her trust. No easy feat with her. But he's done it so well she's opened the door to him. Literally. He wants to hurt her in a way that he didn't hurt the others."

"Or he wants something from her," Blair said.

"Revenge, I think. He must suspect she drove the boat."

"Sweet revenge," Blair said. "He's taunting her. She's his final kill. So he could be drawing it out. That's classic sociopathic behavior. Killing isn't enough. He has to push the limits and prove he's intellectually superior."

"Could be," Manny said. "Regardless, since he's in a relationship with her, in the end he'll want her to know who he really is before she dies."

Across the top of the board she wrote: WHO? Then she drew a line down the middle. On the right-hand side she titled the column: Traits. Beneath it she wrote: sociopathic.

"What else do we know about this guy?" Blair asked.

Manny knew she was asking for clues, details. Instead of giving her what she asked for, he said, "I know this is one of Ricardo's sons. No one else really has the motive."

She wrote "Muñoz son" to the left and to the side she wrote: methodical. Not emotional. "Because each woman was well hidden. That took time, planning and investigation."

"Bribery," Manny said. "And patience. He has to be thirteen or so when Harper and the others testify. He hears the adults in the family talking about revenge. He either witnesses or knows about the We Will letter. He knows about the failed attempts on the girls' lives. Maybe he starts working his plan to find them when he becomes an adult. Then it's another ten years before he can act on it.

"Our two main suspects are Nick and Max. Harper also said she has a friend named Levi. So we'll look at him, too."

Blair put their names on the board and then wrote: How is he finding them?

"Underline that," Manny said. "Because if we can figure that out, we'll know who he is."

Manny pointed to the photo of the note he'd received. "The verse is definitely the same one the Muñoz family used a long time ago. But the fractions...I don't know. Some sort of message. A warning, maybe."

Blair stared alternately at the slip of paper with the handwritten numbers, Manny's Bible that was open to Deuteronomy 24:19-22, and the photos from the Muñoz chapel spread out in front of her.

She glanced at the small screen that showed Reagan asleep on her pink sheets imprinted with princesses, unicorns and castles. Then she wrote all four lines of the Bible verse onto the lower part of the whiteboard, including the numbers from the note.

24: 19-22

1/12 1/13 1/16 1/20 1/10 2/17 1/6

Manny drank several more swallows of his ginger ale, and he took note of his body's appetite for something stronger. Then, with a great deal of effort, he relaxed his grip on the craving, remembering that no drink or numbness would solve problems or fix pain. He leaned back and watched Blair's lips move silently. He knew she was deep in the numbers and the words, rearranging them in her mind to get them to make sense.

Together they checked the girls' former addresses, their new addresses, the order in which they'd been kidnapped, their ages, their parents' ages, the states where they'd relocated—everything they could think of to find a pattern or a code.

Nothing worked.

"It's not a pattern." Blair scribbled letters on a sheet of notebook paper, crossed out what she'd written and began again. "I saw a code years ago where a killer used the first number of a sequence to represent the first line of a passage.

Then the second number, the number after the slash, was a particular letter. Like the tenth letter or the forty-ninth letter and so on. The killer had spelled out the addresses where he'd buried the bodies. But applying that formula here doesn't spell anything." She narrowed her eyes at the verse. "Any chance that the fractions aren't from the same verse? Could it be a different one?"

There was a gentle knock on the back door. Manny and Blair exchanged a glance. No visitors ever came to their back door. Plus they didn't get visitors this late at night.

Manny opened the security app on his phone and saw Amaya Chang standing on the back step holding a stack of folders.

He showed the screen to Blair, then opened the door.

Amaya hurried inside, closed the door behind her. "Sorry not to call. I didn't want to run the risk that Big Brother might be tracking me."

Manny and Blair stared at her with eyes wide and mouths half-open.

"When you said you didn't have a case number, I figured something was up. Then I heard about your suspension." Amaya flashed a thin-lipped smile and waved the red folders. "If it had been anyone else I wouldn't have believed they were innocent. But since it's you, I knew you must have uncovered something you weren't supposed to."

Blair released an audible exhale.

Manny ushered her to the table.

Everything Amaya wore was soft pink—from her blouse to her slim-fitting skirt to her pumps. The delicate coloring was typical for her and also deceptive. Because she was a shark. If a suspect so much as hid the cost of a paperclip in their financials, she could find it.

"What did you find?" he asked.

"Unfortunately, I didn't find a number for Natalie Pyne. I found one for her husband, though." Amaya handed Manny the folder.

"Oh. Okay. Thanks." He quickly flipped through the pages. Blair looked over his shoulder.

"This isn't a complete report, I'll have more tomorrow. But I wanted to bring you what I had so far. We'll start with the first guy, Nick Chamberlain. This was a big story a while back. He was known as Nick Smith back then. Charged with attempted murder of his then-wife Sophie, but found innocent. Largely a circumstantial case. Public became outraged after one of Sophie's loyal followers began sharing Sophie's blog posts on social media. Sophie had written that her marriage was in distress because she was pregnant and her husband didn't want the child.

"Her posts suggested that the marriage might have been a mistake. That she had been taken in by his good looks and charm and now she thought she saw the real him: the temper, his insistence to have things his way. There were plenty of statements saying he'd only married her for her money.

"On that initial post there were 13,572 comments and most of them were telling her to leave him, that they were afraid her life was in danger. Another 52,489 comments on various platforms were posted after her fall. National feminist groups linked to the post, then 522,654 other social media shares did the same, and the D.A.'s office filed suit."

"What do you think?" Manny asked.

"Hard to say. On one hand, someone who writes publicly about private issues like that...she could be narcissistic, desperate for attention, desperate to be seen as a victim. Which means she has to demonize Nick to make that work.

"Her wealthy father, Evan Taylor, is a master at waging

public battles and legal campaigns against anyone who challenges him. Press writes largely favorable articles on him and his company. Likewise they write fairly damaging articles against his challengers. I should mention that he also owns a significant share of the local paper and several other media companies. So, the apple might not have fallen far from the tree."

"Meaning?" Blair asked.

"Assuming Nick was innocent, if Sophie wanted a divorce, and given there wasn't a prenup in place, her blog could have been her father's way of avoiding a major payout. Or Sophie could have been reaching out for help, making her circumstances known as a way to ensure her safety. Final theory is that she was having an affair and she has to make her husband look bad to cover her extramarital behavior."

"Any proof of that?" Blair asked.

Amaya shook her head. "If someone did have that kind of information on his daughter, mainstream reporters were probably too afraid to speak up for fear of being ruined.

"Plus the feminist groups and the social media mobs had taken up her cause. If anyone had spoken out against her, saying she might have been cheating, they would have been publicly accused of being a misogynist, of blaming the victim and so on. Truth is not necessarily something social media crowds are into."

Amaya picked at the corner of one of her pink nails, then flipped through the file she'd assembled on Nick. "Without a case number I wasn't able to get any current information on his bank accounts. But I did find this." She handed Manny a two-page document. "Just after the trial, there was a 10- million dollar divorce settlement filed with the courts."

"From?" Manny asked.

"Evan Taylor. Paid in crypto after the trial and when the divorce was final."

"So Nick got paid," Blair said.

"Looks like it," Amaya said.

"Why would Sophie's father pay him if he thought Nick tried to kill her?" Manny asked.

"Divorce papers show that Nick agreed to release all rights to heirs, property, jewelry, furnishings, cash, investments and—wait for it—claims to Sophie's right to life."

Manny leaned back in his chair. "He threatened to pull the plug unless Evan paid."

"That's what it looks like," Amaya said. "I mean, could have just been a standard divorce settlement. But as her husband, it would have been his say as to whether she stayed on life support or not."

"Any connections to the Muñoz crime family?"

"Born in Miami to Esme Smith. No father in the picture—"

"Smith." Manny remembered the chart that Stanford had shown him. "Several of the Muñoz wives selected Smith as their last name when they left the area."

"Mother and son left Miami right after Ricardo was arrested, came to Savannah to live with Esme's mother," Amaya said.

"Timing is right," Blair said, making more notes on the whiteboard.

"Nick legally changed his last name to Chamberlain after the trial, which is, interestingly, the same last name as a friend of his from high school—Nick Chamberlain. Or what looks like a friend, based on what I saw in the yearbooks," Amaya said. "The original Nick Chamberlain died in college from a hazing incident. Nick Smith was with his buddy Nick Chamberlain on the night he died."

"Any foul play suspected?"

Amaya shrugged. "Coroner ruled his death a result of alcohol poisoning. Could just be a weird coincidence. But the original Nick Chamberlain was Nick Smith's alibi in an investigation of a girl's death just a year or so earlier. A Piper Monroe. I'm wondering if the original Nick Chamberlain threatened to publicly pull his alibi and Nick Smith—now Nick Chamberlain—didn't like that. I'd like to dig further. I'd especially like to get into Nick's bank accounts to see if he still has that payout from his former father-in-law or if he blew it. But doing this research off the record is limiting."

Manny's phone rang. "Special Agent Hernandez."

"Yeah. Uh, this is Sheriff Ben Parkins."

The man's Southern accent was strong and classic, non-rhotic. Different from most of the accents in and around Charlotte.

"From Aiken, South Carolina."

A nauseating twist tightened Manny's gut. Aiken, South Carolina was where Natalie Marrs had moved after she left Miami.

"What can I do for you, Sheriff?"

"I don't know, specifically. But we have a victim down here, name is Natalie Hansen. Initially her death was called a suicide. But—uh, we have a 911 call. Well, we don't get many murders down here, Agent Hernandez. Even fewer suicides. But the ones we do get aren't difficult to solve. This one isn't what it seems.

"Her husband found your name and number hidden in her jewelry box, along with a note. It said if anything should happen to her, that he was to call you. He's too upset to talk, so I'm calling. Any of this mean something to you?" Sheriff Parkins asked.

"Unfortunately, it does." Manny clenched his free hand into a fist, forced his tone to stay even.

"Well, she called my cell phone and left a voicemail just before she died. She said there was a man following her, walking up to the car and something about his uniform didn't look right. We also have a 911 call."

"Send me those, if you would. Do you know if she received a piece of paper with two lines of numbers written on it? First line looks like a Bible verse and the second line looks like a set of fractions," Manny said.

"I'll check with her husband. We do have CCTV footage of the guy from outside a coffeeshop that Natalie visited before she died. I'll send that, too. For what it's worth, I don't know of anyone who buys a cup of coffee before they commit suicide."

"I'm with you on that." Manny gave him his personal email address.

"Agent Hernandez."

"Yeah?"

"Are we looking at an FBI investigation here?"

Manny's heart skipped over the pang in his conscience. "Not at this time. We're still gathering information. I'll let you know."

Manny shared what Sheriff Parkins had told him, then asked Amaya, "What were you about to say?"

"I have some information on the other two men you asked me to look at, Max Crandall and Levi Wright. Max was raised by a single mother, no father present early in life. He relocated to Savannah from Miami about the same time that Nick Smith did."

"Miami," Manny confirmed.

Amaya nodded. "Levi Wright, nothing much there. Raised by two parents in Virginia, undergrad at UT, grad school and med school at Emory. Stayed in Atlanta until he moved to Savannah for work.

"Nick and Max bear the closest resemblance to our target. Let's see what we can find on these two."

34

When the morning light peeked through the transom windows, I was still curled against Nick's chest. Distractedly, I measured the passing of time with the even cadence of his long, deep breaths.

The occasional old-house sounds from downstairs creaked and popped, unnerving me as usual. Magnolia stared at Nick from her gray, faux fur bed across the room. She had not accepted Nick's presence in this room.

My text notification buzzed from the bedside table.

It was Agent Hernandez:

CALL me when you get a chance.

I WAS ABOUT to head downstairs when my phone buzzed again.

This time it was Levi:

. . .

FOUND private facility where Sophie Taylor is kept.

You can't get in on your own. Don't know if she is conscious or not. But I could arrange a professional visit where you could come with me, as my assistant? Let me know what you'd like to do.

When?

Next week

Today?

IF I COULD TALK with Sophie, she might tell me who snuck through her back door that day. She might tell me who pushed her down the stairs. She might tell me who the father of her child was.

That truth could clear Nick's name. It could also implicate Max.

Neither of those things would give me insight into whether Nick or Max or both were related to the Muñoz family. At least I didn't think it would. But it was a step in the right direction.

I looked at Nick while I waited for Levi to respond.

Nick slept peacefully on my side of the bed. Tanned skin, shock of dark hair, arms stretched overhead. Hauntingly beautiful.

He had to be innocent.

He had to be.

The sound of Levi's reply shook me from my daze.

. . .

OKAY. Be here by 7 and I'll make it work.

I DRESSED QUICKLY AND QUIETLY. I applied the thick cover-up to the scars on my neck, and I noticed Max's thumbprint bruises were fading. In their place were several V-shaped marks from his ring.

I finished my makeup and made certain that I had two EpiPens hidden in my purse. Then I went downstairs, wrote Nick a note, and collected two things I'd almost forgotten about.

I WENT to my favorite coffee shop for a large coffee with an extra shot. I dutifully dipped the testing strip from my kit and inserted it into the small machine.

All clear.

Common wisdom said we all needed eight hours of sleep a night, or at least six, but I liked about five. The night before, however, I hadn't slept at all. I wasn't accustomed to having anyone else in my house at night, let alone in my bed. So I'd lain awake, thinking mostly how I didn't have proof of Nick's innocence.

I walked along the tree-shaded brick streets and was not concerned, at least for the moment, that a Muñoz would try to kill me. The Muñoz family made their murders look accidental. Savannah didn't have any crime in this area, let alone at this hour of the morning.

Columbia Square came into sight and I remembered seeing my sister standing there, pointing at her silver watch.

Time to act.

Time to live.

Time to catch a Muñoz.

I stopped just shy of my house and looked up at my bedroom window. Nick was in there, probably still sleeping. I sipped the scalding coffee and considered how risky my behavior had been. *The heart wants what it wants.*

All of my dreams, childhood and otherwise, rode on him. A terrible burden to put on anyone. A projection, even. And yet I wanted to—needed to—believe that his love for me was real. I needed to believe that he was who he said he was. After all I'd been through, and clinging to the little bit of myself that I had left, he was my final hope in humanity.

I remembered to call Agent Hernandez back, but I got his voicemail. I left a quick message.

I drank the rest of the coffee quickly, hoping to clear my mind.

But it didn't work. My head was full of Max and Nick and sugared flowers with bees and peanut-laced coffee. It was full of Nick dragging his knuckles along my cheek, holding me close, proposing marriage.

It was full of murdered Piper.

And nearly murdered Sophie.

My heart beat a little too fast.

By the time I reached Levi's condo, I felt like an overly-caffeinated zombie. Levi walked out the side door. He wore a gray suit and a white button-down shirt. No tie. A kind smile. He hugged me.

I drew in a deep breath and calmed. I wasn't alone. Levi was going to help me. "Thank you for doing this," I said.

"I'm always happy to help you. You know that." He winked and opened the car door for me. We fastened our red seatbelts and sped around the city squares in his Porsche 911.

"Sophie is at the Chatham Medical Center for Rehabilitative Care. It's about an hour and a half northwest of Savannah proper, which means it's basically in the middle of nowhere. Our appointment is with Beverly Adams, who's the Director of the Center. She thinks I'm coming in to interview them for a patient of mine. I told her the patient was in critical condition and that this was urgent. So she's going to give us the full tour. You'll pose as my new office manager.

"I'm saying office manager so no one will ask you any medical questions, and I'm saying new so if you don't know the answer to something we can easily explain that. I'm not exactly sure how we get you into a position to look for Sophie. We'll have to play that one by ear."

I drained the last drops of my coffee. "How did you figure out where she was?"

Levi accelerated onto the interstate, shifted into fifth gear and put on his sunglasses. "I did some research and read in the paper where Sophie was admitted to Savannah Mercy Hospital after her fall. I have privileges there, so I started poking around in the records and saw that she had been transferred to this particular facility."

Levi took my hand, squeezed it in a be-strong kind of way and shared his worried smile that reminded me of Catherine's.

35

When we arrived at the facility, Levi rang the bell. A stifling breeze meandered through the portico and I lifted my arms. I hoped the draft would pick up, hoped it would pass through my high-neck, ivory silk blouse and cool the nervous sweat that rolled down my torso.

Levi held his ID to the camera and the lady on the other end of the call box buzzed us in.

I was proud of myself for showing up this morning. Being here took confidence and bravery. I gave myself credit for that.

The plan for getting to Sophie, I decided, was to cozy up to the Executive Director who was giving us the guided tour. I'd learned how to be ingratiating from the best. My mother had a masterful talent in that area.

We stepped into the elegant lobby and an uneasy sense fell over me. A sinister feeling. Sophie Taylor was locked somewhere inside these walls and someone had tried to murder her. Someone who would do the same to me if he could. I tightened my ponytail, smoothed my hair.

"We have our process," the nurse behind the counter announced firmly. "Everyone *must* have a red visitation pass to enter that corridor, and to get *that* particular pass you must show me your ID." She delivered her words clearly and distinctly and with megaphone-level loudness.

The impatient family at the front desk was in a hurry to get their special passes so they could see their newly-admitted father. No one was pleased that the nurse was taking so long.

When it was our turn, Levi showed the nurse his physician credentials. She understood we weren't there to visit a patient. So she gave us white guest passes on a lanyard, which we hung around our necks. Then we sat in the small seating area and waited on Beverly.

The lobby was nicer than I would have expected of a rehabilitative facility—white marble floors, silk curtains, fake Persian rugs and fresh flowers on every table. But the sterile, medicinal scent of alcohol and ammonia wafted through the air, a constant reminder that first and foremost, this was a serious medical facility.

There was no public listing of patients' names on the welcome marquis, but there were signs with arrows posted next to the two side hallways. To the left were two red signs that said Critical Care, Restricted. A uniformed guard sat at the entrance to the hallway and checked that visitors' IDs matched their passes.

To the right was a hallway marked Memory Care, Aquatic Therapy, Administrative Offices, Physical Therapy, Meeting Rooms. To the back of the building were two-story panels of glass walls that overlooked a peaceful green space and a lake. Patients in wheelchairs enjoyed the sunshine. White-uniformed nurses stood close by. My guess was that

Sophie was somewhere to the left, in the wing that required the red passes.

Out of the Critical Care hallway appeared a couple I recognized immediately. The man was tall and broad, with dark hair, dark eyes and wearing an expensive dark suit. His wife was blond, petite and well-jeweled. Neither smiled and both carried an air of sadness that was nearly three-dimensional. They appeared exactly as they did in the photos from Amanda Cummings' column. They were Sophie's parents.

An all-too-familiar feeling of panic crept over me, and I almost turned and left the building. Sophie's father had been extremely outspoken in the media that Nick was the one who tried to kill their daughter. I found one courtroom video when the jury's verdict of innocent was read aloud. Sophie's father stood and pointed and screamed at the jury, "You've put women all over the world in grave danger! When the next woman dies because of Nick, her blood will be on your hands!"

Beverly, the Executive Director, was a half step behind the Taylors. She wore a purple suit and tan hose. I couldn't remember the last time I'd seen someone wear natural-colored hose. Distractedly, I wondered if they were L'eggs and if they still came in those egg-shaped containers.

At 5'3" she was almost as wide as she was tall, and from the way her feet were stuffed into her wide-heeled shoes, I guessed they were a half size too small.

I offered her my most pleasant smile, but Beverly pursed her red rosebud lips like she'd just sucked a sour prune, and I knew we weren't going to be fast friends.

"Tell me what you do in the practice, honey," she asked.

"She's our new office manager," Levi interjected. "I brought her with me this morning so she will be able to speak knowledgeably with patient families about your facility."

"Oh, so lovely. I wish more doctors would do that."

Levi pulled his phone from his pocket and declined a call. Beverly side-eyed me from top to bottom and back to the top again.

My plan for rapport and favor was a total bust.

We began the tour by walking down the hallway on the right. I turned and studied the uniformed employee who guarded the Critical Care hallway. The one where Sophie's parents had come from. She wore a gun at her waist and sat in a tall chair. With Beverly watching me too closely and the guard taking her post seriously, I didn't think I would be able to get down that hallway.

Beverly described the facility's extensive capabilities, their patient success stories and their intense security. "Many of our female patients have someone on the outside who put them here—an abusive husband or boyfriend. So, we are extremely careful in terms of access." She pointed to the security cameras and discussed the front desk system we'd witnessed firsthand.

"Patient families decide who gets access and who doesn't. They have complete control. We're more secure than most banks," Beverly said with a wink to Levi.

I elbowed Levi and he nodded like he understood the challenge. We entered the cafeteria that was surrounded by wide floor-to-ceiling windows. Beyond the windows I saw a garden, and the same lake I'd seen from the lobby. A sign was posted on the door leading to the outside: Restricted Access. A black sensor was situated on the wall next to the door.

Levi nudged me this time, nodded toward the outside, and I agreed with a quick nod.

I wasn't sure how I was going to get the door open.

Levi turned on the charm with his wide smile, and Beverly nearly swooned. "I'd like to know more about the menu options that you offer. Could I get a personal tour of the kitchen?"

Levi touched Beverly's arm and she seemed to forget all about me. So I hung back.

Several nurses and doctors and visitors came in and out the door. Each of them was careful to shut the door behind them. I stayed around the corner and out of sight, waiting for the right opportunity.

My phone buzzed.

Agent Hernandez.

I declined the call.

Ten minutes passed and I began to worry if I would find a way.

A heavy-set nurse in teal scrubs pushed a man in a wheelchair up the exterior sidewalk. Her hair was wound into a tight bun near the top of her head and she smiled warmly at her patient who leaned to the side of his wheelchair.

About halfway to the door she stopped, straightened the man's posture so that he sat upright. Then she used her fingers to smooth his hair. This was my opportunity.

She opened the door, I rounded the corner and held the door open for her. She smiled and thanked me and I slipped by her. She stopped me. She examined the guest pass around my neck and her warm smile faded into professional concern. "Are you a relative?"

"No, actually I'm looking for Sophie Taylor's room. Can you point me in the right direction?"

She left the man's wheelchair in the threshold to keep the door propped open. She looked left and right, then back to me. "All visitors have to check in at the front desk." She pointed toward the front lobby.

"I'm a friend of hers from high school. I just wanted to let her know that we were thinking about her. I've heard she doesn't get many visitors. We haven't been in touch for years, but I wanted her to know I'm here for her."

The nurse glanced at my guest pass again, considered my story, and seemingly looked for anything that might not fit. She leaned in close. "You're not a reporter, are you?"

"No, ma'am," I said with a gentle laugh. I clasped my hands together in front of me to appear compliant. "I'm here with my boss, he's a doctor. We think the facility would be a good fit for some of our patients."

She looked around cautiously and asked, "You were friends in high school?"

"Yes, ma'am. We traveled in the same small group together. We lost one friend years ago, Piper. Now this with Sophie." I waved to my left, knowing that's where she was. "I think there will always be something special about our school friends. Even though we don't see one another on a day-to-day basis anymore, I still love them. I still care about them. You know how it is."

The woman's expression softened. Her shoulders relaxed. Her guard began to waiver.

I was suddenly grateful for all the times my mother enforced manners. They'd become second nature and thankfully they could still open a few doors, they could still relax a few barriers. I was also glad I didn't wear much makeup today. I'd figured that anything that made me look underdoggish helped.

She sighed, glanced over my shoulder. "I would really like to help you. I think Miss Sophie could use the emotional support. But her parents have insisted on very tight security. I'm sorry. You have to have a specific type of visitor's badge to get into that sector of the facility." After a moment she tipped her chin toward the building behind me. I followed her line of sight.

There were about twenty individual sliding glass doors that extended all the way to the end of the building. Those had to be the rooms in the critical care section. The light blue curtains in the first room moved gently, like someone had just stepped away.

The woman's name tag read: Nurse Jeffers. She raised one eyebrow, lowered her chin in a you-didn't-hear-it-from-me kind of way. "I think Mr. Green here would like to go to the lake to look at the ducks again. I probably won't be back for about ten or fifteen minutes."

The man wearing blue pajamas and sitting in the wheelchair slowly raised his hand like he'd heard his name. Nurse Jeffers nodded again toward the room where the curtains had moved. With a pat on my arm she wheeled Mr. Greene toward the lake.

I turned toward the left side of the building and the curtains moved again. This time I was sure of it. All of the sliding glass doors were closed, so wind was not a consideration.

I walked toward the window I thought was Sophie's. Not directly toward it because I didn't want whoever had been watching to see me coming.

Doubt told me that when I got to Sophie's room I was going to see someone wearing a blue button-down cleaning uniform and they'd have a feather duster in their hand. Or maybe it was a nurse who brushed by the curtains. But I kept heading toward the room.

"Yes, Mr. Green," I heard Nurse Jeffers say. "We are going

down to the water to feed the ducks. But it's a quick visit and then we're back in time for breakfast, alright?"

The door was open about an inch. I took it as an invitation. Inside the room, a woman lay flat on her back on the hospital bed with her eyes closed. Asleep or unconscious I didn't know. She was thin and frail and her skin was nearly translucent.

It was Nick's first wife.

I recognized her from the photos in the newspaper.

A sizable indentation marked the left side of her forehead. That must have come from her fall down the stairs. A shiver ran up my spine.

There weren't many medical machines in the room. Only an IV bag attached to her arm and some other basic medical things. She was capable of breathing on her own.

A wide bowl of fragrant magnolia blossoms was on the desk.

The walls were painted robin's egg blue, the same color as the curtains. I remembered from the newspaper that this was the same color as Sophie's bridesmaids' dresses.

I stepped closer and studied the indent on her forehead. In my mind I saw Nick strangling Sophie at the top of the stairs, then easily shoving her over the railing. He watched her fall to the bottom.

Something on Sophie's neck caught my eye.

A small scar.

I leaned closer.

A V-shaped scar.

The exact shape and size of the mark on my neck after Max choked me.

The exact shape and size left by the sharp edges of his ring.

The images of Nick strangling and pushing Sophie over

the railing melted away, replaced by Max doing the same. Max was short but strong-looking. Pompous little grunt that he was, wearing that ring was going to be his downfall.

The pieces fell into place. My chest rose and fell with excitement.

If Max were a Muñoz, he would have grown up watching his father and uncles kidnap, rape and kill young girls.

When Max became a teenager, he followed in their footsteps. First, killing Piper as punishment for ever leaving him in the first place.

Then, having an affair with Sophie because...why not? To his mind that's what women were for. But when she became pregnant, that threatened his lifestyle. He tried to strangle her. His hands were around her neck long enough to leave the mark from his ring.

But something went wrong and she fell down the stairs. He's short. In younger photos she appeared fit and strong. Maybe they fought and she lost her balance.

"Sophie," I whispered.

She was deathly still. I stared at her in case she blinked. When she didn't respond, I wondered if she was even conscious.

I looked around the room for any evidence of day-to-day activities—coffee cups, pens, crossword puzzles, magazines. A newspaper was folded perfectly on a yellow armchair, like it hadn't yet been read for the day.

A remote sat on the bedside table, and a flat-screen TV hung on the opposite wall. Unconscious people didn't need televisions, but that could have been standard in every room. There was a stack of novels on the desk, as well as a phone and a thin laptop. I opened it and the first screen showed the name SophieT. above a password box.

The bed creaked, and I turned quickly.

Sophie lay still, her eyes closed. I kept my eyes glued to her. A minute or two went by and her breathing stayed even, her eyelids didn't flutter. I decided that the noise was just one of those sounds that couldn't be explained. The same kind that happened when I was alone in my house.

The longer I stood there, the more worried I became that I would get caught. Keeping my footsteps quiet, I returned to her bedside and placed my hand on her bare arm.

Her skin was warm, soft, and she didn't flinch at my touch.

I'd thought she would.

"Sophie?"

I gave her arm a pat, then a gentle shake.

Still nothing.

I leaned close to her ear and whispered her name again. The lavender scent of her dark hair caught me by surprise. It smelled expensive. Not at all hospital-like. Her face was freshly cleansed, exfoliated, moisturized, like she'd been to a spa.

Now I was more convinced than ever that she was awake.

So I did the unthinkable.

With my forefinger and thumb, I pinched the skin on her arm, hard enough, I hoped, to generate a reaction.

She didn't flinch.

She could have been medicated or maybe she'd never regained consciousness. Her mother was just at the facility. She could have personally tended to her daughter to keep her looking her best.

I grabbed my forehead. "What am I doing?!"

Pinching an unconscious woman like that. She wasn't my enemy. She was a fellow victim of the Muñoz family.

"Sorry," I said softly and rubbed the red spot my pinch left on her skin. "If you can hear me, Sophie, I really need to talk with you. My life is in danger and I need your help."

She didn't budge.

I left her room the way I came in.

Nurse Jeffers walked back from the lake, struggling to push Mr. Green uphill in his wheelchair.

I waved.

"Good visit?" she asked when we finally met. Her smile was full of secret joy, like she knew she'd done a seriously good deed to reunite two old friends in a time of need.

"Yes, I think so. I guess you never really know if they hear you. I tried, anyway." I shrugged. "I noticed she wasn't connected to any machines in her room. She's doing better, I guess?"

"Oh, better than that. Miss Sophie is doing extremely well. I think it's all the alternative therapies her mother has insisted on. They're taking her home soon, you know."

"Home?" I asked. I was just about to ask another question when the nurse nodded toward the building behind me.

"I think she did hear you."

I turned.

Sophie Taylor stood at the sliding glass door.

36

I walked toward Sophie, half-expecting her to disappear before my eyes, like my sister did in Columbia Square.

My heart thrummed in my chest. A whooshing white noise filled my ears. I thought I heard Nurse Jeffers yell something like, "Five minutes!" But I wasn't sure.

Sophie stared at me.

She slipped away from the door.

I walked faster. I felt a cold chill in spite of the heat.

The sliding glass door was still unlocked and I slipped inside. Sophie stood across the room with the IV connected to the crook of her arm. Her brown eyes were wide and wild with fear and she held her arm where I'd pinched her.

"I'm sorry about that." I nodded to her arm. "Really sorry."

She looked briefly at her arm, then crossed her arms and held her body tight. "I'm used to tests," she said softly.

"What tests?" I asked.

She didn't answer.

I wondered if these "tests" had something to do with other visitors.

Her eyes darted left and right. She was afraid, but I had the sense that she wasn't afraid of me. She could have rung for a nurse or run screaming into the hallway, but she didn't.

"You didn't want me to know that you were awake?"

She studied the door like she expected someone to walk through any moment. "I needed to make sure you were alone." Her voice was weak and timid. "You are here alone, aren't you?"

"At the moment, yes."

"But you're not here with Max." She picked at the sleeve of her dark blue hospital gown.

"No. You know who I am?" I asked.

Her eyes welled with tears. "You're with Nick. You work for Max."

"I interviewed with Max, but I wasn't hired. An email with some photos came in from you."

"I know you must be angry about that, but I had to do something." Her voice shook.

I lowered myself to the edge of the bed in an attempt to be nonthreatening. The woman was terrified.

I wasn't sure what she meant. "So you did send those photos?"

"Charlotte found the photos that Max took. She knows. She's mad."

"The photos of Nick and me?" I asked.

She nodded.

"How did you get them?"

"I knew you had no idea. No one ever does with him." She leaned forward and whispered, "Max and Charlotte left the room. He had a photo file with your name. I sent them to my email. Then I sent them to you and Max and the two other people who were on his calendar for that meeting. I didn't want you to be a victim like me."

"Max did this to you?" I asked.

"The pictures are the beginning—he finds a woman, he starts shooting. He starts a collection. Then he wants you all to himself." She stepped closer to me. Her eyes were wide and round like dinner plates. She was sharp. She was aware.

My mind flashed to the first time I met Max and the 35mm camera he had around his neck. Over coffee he'd shown me the photos he'd taken. At the time he'd said he was taking photos of the architecture and just happened to get me in the frame. I'd suspected that wasn't the case.

"I only sent the two with Nick. But he has a lot more. He watches you." She frowned. "What time is it?"

I looked at my watch. "Almost ten."

Sophie rubbed her wrist. "It's later than I thought, you have to go. I don't want them to find you."

"Who?" I asked.

"My mother, Charlotte or Max."

She shuffled to the sliding glass door and moved the curtains, peeked out. A young woman with an infant girl on her hip stood next to a young man in a wheelchair. The mother placed the baby on the man's lap. The father held the baby overhead, much to his daughter's delight.

Sophie was mesmerized and tears streamed down. She caught me staring, wiped her cheeks and sniffed. "I was pregnant. That's how this started." She ran her hand over the front of her neck absently. Just as I had after Max choked me.

Her nails were bitten down to the quick.

"Max was the father of your baby?"

She nodded. "I need you to tell my mother—not my

father. Tell her to get me out of here. I'm in danger now that Max knows I sent the photos—"

Female voices sounded outside the door. Sophie gasped and jerked her head toward the door, then back to me. She rubbed her wrist, like she was trying to remove a stain from her skin. I took her hands in mine, tried to console her, and she held on. The inside of her wrist was red. In the middle of the redness was a small, white, V-shaped scar, just like the one on my neck. On her neck.

"You're in danger. You have to leave!"

The door to Sophie's room flew open. Charlotte Tatnall Crandall walked in with a bouquet of pink peonies and a robin's egg blue ribbon tied around the stems. "Sophie, love! I have your favorite flow—" She stopped short. Her eyes darted from Sophie to me and back to Sophie again. "Are you okay, Soph?"

Sophie shook her head. Like she flipped a switch, tears fell down her cheeks. Her lips pulled back in a quiet sob, revealing several chipped teeth that looked like tiny white daggers.

Charlotte's lips pressed together tight and firm. She rushed to Sophie's side, hugged her and guided her and her IV stand toward the bed. "What are you doing here?" Her tone was as sharp as a knife and I felt the hatred coming off of her.

Charlotte helped Sophie into bed and carefully covered her up to her neck, like she was a sick child.

I tried to recall if Bunny had said that Charlotte and Sophie had been close but I didn't remember anything. Neither did I remember the two of them even standing together in any of the photos.

Sophie said that Charlotte knew about the photos Max

had taken of me. The look on Charlotte's face when she came into Max's office and I was there—familiar disgust.

She hadn't been angry. She just knew. She'd seen it happen before.

With Sophie.

Charlotte must have cared for Sophie because she knew what Max had done. He'd liked Sophie, had an affair, gotten her pregnant and tried to do away with her.

Now Charlotte tried to make up for the harm Max had caused.

I wondered why she didn't leave him. Her family had plenty of money.

Maybe she was afraid.

Maybe Max had threatened to kill her, too.

Suddenly everything was clear.

Around Charlotte, Sophie pretended to be incapacitated, child-like. Probably Max, too. Sophie didn't want Max to know that she remembered who pushed her.

I imagined Sophie lying here in a fake sleep while Charlotte spoke to Max about finding the photographs of me, grilling him as to what he planned to do with them. I imagined them stepping outside for a minute and Sophie bravely going through Max's phone to see if she could find anything she could use to expose him.

Sophie faced the other wall.

Charlotte turned toward me. "Why are you here?"

I walked up to her and whispered, "Everyone in this room knows that Max was the father of Sophie's baby. Tell that perverted husband of yours that if he comes near her or me again, I'll make sure that proof gets spread all over the internet."

Charlotte's eyes widened. She shook her head. But not like she disagreed.

"You know your husband. You know his history. You know about Piper."

Charlotte's eyes went from shock to focused. She stood taller. Something strengthened her. "My Max didn't have anything to do with Piper's death or Sophie's *incident*. But he did tell me that you and Nick are together," she said. "He also told me that you must have means. I guess that's what this is about.

"Love makes a person do strange things—makes them overlook faults and even signs of danger. You need to take a hard and honest look at Nick. Max and I aren't the only ones who believe that Nick was the one who pushed Sophie down those stairs. The District Attorney and most of Savannah think so, too."

"Nick didn't hurt Sophie," I said.

Charlotte clasped her hands in front of her, lowered her chin over the single strand of pearls high at her neck. "I understand why you need to think that," she said in a soft, maternal voice. "But I want you to think about something. Piper and Sophie both had complicated relationships with Nick, and he was the only one to find each of them?" She raised a well-arched eyebrow, shook her head slowly in a no-one-believes-him-innocent sort of way.

Fury burned in my chest like I'd swallowed a lit match. "Think about what you're doing, Charlotte. You're setting Max up to do this again."

Charlotte raised a quick hand to stop me. "Whatever Nick told you, you should remember he has a reputation to hide and an image to rebuild. Or if it was Sophie who accused Max, you want to remember that she took a very hard hit to the head when she fell down those stairs. Half the time she doesn't make sense anymore." Charlotte glanced at Sophie who still faced away from us.

"Bless her heart. She was beyond devastated when she woke up and learned that not only had she lost her baby, but that Nick had divorced her and moved on."

"I don't think—"

She raised her hand again. "She's always had a problem with jealousy. I would guess even you heard something about that by now. We didn't think she had enough wherewithal to act on it, but behind our backs she emailed that private investigator that her father had used over the years. That's where those photos came from, the ones she sent to the firm.

"I'm so *sorry* that this blindsided you! If I'd known what she was up to, *please* believe me, I would have stopped her immediately. But of course none of us knew and—Well, I want you to know that we've done what we could.

"Max and I immediately told Sophie's mother what happened and she restricted Sophie's access to her computer and phone. She also called the P.I. and told him in no uncertain terms that he was never to do work for Sophie again. That she wasn't competent."

With a hand to my back, Charlotte all but pushed me to exit through the sliding glass door.

I stopped.

"Please remember, she doesn't know what she's doing. Best thing you can do is just forget about her and look at the facts where Nick is concerned. And don't worry about what folks will think, they'll understand. He has fooled a *lot* of people over the years."

She pushed me even more firmly toward the sliding glass door.

I stepped aside.

"I would guess that you, like most women who have been married for a while, know your husband incredibly well. I would guess that you know about his wandering eye and his tendency toward a certain type of violence." I mimicked a choking action around my neck and Charlotte's eyes flared with hatred.

"You could put a stop to it."

She leaned close. "Max is *not* a murderer. If you choose to ignore Nick's involvement with all of this, that will be on you. Don't say I didn't warn you."

Like examining a stone for authenticity, I searched her expression for barely noticeable tics or twitches, signs that she might be lying. Signs that what she said was as manufactured as cubic zirconia.

But nothing moved. She was as strong as southern steel.

The idea that she might be telling the truth deflated me like a popped balloon.

My thoughts started racing again. Images of my sister pointing at her watch. Her worried expression. Levi's worried expression. Nick's angry expression.

My father and the doctors were right. I didn't make good decisions. I couldn't trust my instincts.

The meds. I should have taken them. Then I wouldn't be on this wild chase.

"I don't want to appear rude, but Sophie is very vulnerable and for that reason alone they are strict about who has access to her. Without the proper pass, I'm afraid I'll have to ask you again to leave." Charlotte pulled back one of the curtains and jerked on the door, which was stuck.

I cut my eyes at Sophie, who faced me now. She clung tightly to the blanket that Charlotte had tucked around her.

Help me, she mouthed.

I almost gasped.

Charlotte freed the door. She turned to me, and smiled in such an unfeeling way that my skin actually crawled.

She wasn't telling the truth. She was protecting her reputation, her husband, her way of life.

I dug my nails into my palms.

"Darling!" Sophie's mother walked in carrying a small basket of lotion and nail polish, as well as an outfit on a hanger over her arm. "I'm back!" She wore a warm smile that hadn't been there when I'd seen her in the lobby.

Sophie immediately sat up and reached for her. "Mother!" she cried.

I felt Charlotte startle.

I had a vision of Charlotte using her alone time with Sophie to threaten her to keep her mouth shut about her affair with Max. That she couldn't be responsible for what Max might do otherwise.

Sophie's mother stopped short when she saw me, the bright smile she'd put on, seemingly for Sophie's benefit, flatlined.

She glanced at the badge around my neck (which was obviously the wrong color for proper access), and finally, to my face.

"I think you should leave," she said.

"I need to speak with you. For just a second. You could walk me out," I pointed to the sliding glass door.

Sophie's mother glanced at her daughter who mouthed the word, "Please?"

"Pick your color and we'll do your nails as soon as I'm back. Thirty seconds." She placed the basket in her daughter's arms and touched her cheek.

Once outside, Mrs. Taylor stood across from me and folded her arms. "Is this about the pictures Sophie sent to the firm? Those came from a P.I. that my husband has used over the years. He's denied taking those photos, but he would. He's always had a soft spot for Sophie. Anyway, I've taken care of the problem. It won't happen again."

I shook my head. "It's not about—"

"Money, then? Max said you didn't get the job. So, I'm guessing you want payment for damages? I'll authorize my attorney to settle with you for one year's salary. You can move and find a new job if need be. I'll get you my attorney's contact information." She tapped on her phone screen.

"I don't want your money, Mrs. Taylor. Where is Sophie's baby?" I reached into my purse and felt around.

Mrs. Taylor cringed like I'd just asked her to dig up her dead grandson.

"The remains. Did the hospital dispose of them? Or did you create a grave and bury them?"

"My grandson has a grave in the family plot. What are you getting at?"

"You need to do a DNA test, because I don't think the baby was Nick's." I dug through my purse for the two items I'd collected before I left the house. "The person who pushed her down the stairs is the same person who was the baby's father."

"I guess you would think that." She tapped her phone screen again and said, "You realize that even if the baby wasn't Nick's, that gives Nick even more motive to hurt her?"

I kept pressing. "It also gives motive to the person who tried to kill her, the real father. Someone who might be married to a prominent Savannah family. Someone who stood to lose a lot if the pregnancy became public."

"Okay, and you think the real father is—?"

"Max Crandall," I said.

She rolled her eyes. "That relationship was over ages ago."

"No, it wasn't." I pulled the sandwich bag out of my

purse and held it in my open palm. Clearly visible were two crunched up paper towels with large spots of blood on them. "This is Max's blood."

She turned away and I grabbed her by the arm.

"Surely you realize that when he pushed Sophie down those stairs he didn't plan on her surviving. And surely you've noticed a difference in the way she acted before she sent the photos versus after? She knows she's in danger. She's terrified. She must have mentioned that to you."

The color drained from Mrs. Taylor's face.

"Has she told you who pushed her down the stairs?"

"Sophie says a lot of things since she fell down the stairs. Not all of which makes sense."

"Mrs. Taylor. I wasn't sure before today. I believe that Sophie's life is in danger, too. Max knows by now that Sophie was lucid enough to email those photos to me. Which means that he has to suspect that she remembers who strangled her, who pushed her and who the father of her baby was.

"Just do the DNA test. Restrict Max's visiting privileges. Regret and guilt make poor life companions. Once your loved ones are gone, nothing brings them back."

Sophie's mother stepped toward me.

"Painting Max as a murderer isn't going to make Nick innocent. I suggest you get your own house in order before you start telling me how to organize mine."

I pressed the sandwich bag into her hand. "You have nothing to lose by running the test."

Sophie's mother glared at me for a long moment, turned and walked toward her daughter's room.

"Now that Max thinks Sophie remembers," I called after her. "He'll try again. I don't think he'll fail a second time."

Mrs. Taylor stopped abruptly.

I hoped she would turn around, I hoped she would say something in response.

And she did, just not what I expected. "When I get inside I'm going to call security. You have until then to get off this property." She threw the bag on the ground, shut the door behind her.

I pressed against the glass and she locked the door.

I took off running to the other side of the property, followed a nurse inside the building and ran to the front lobby, where I found Levi smiling, laughing and flirting his hardest with Beverly. She looked at Levi like she'd just emerged from forty years in the desert and he was a tall glass of water.

I apologized and made my excuses, that I'd gone to the restroom and then couldn't find my way back. Beverly didn't seem to care. She was too high on Levi's attention.

When I passed the front desk, I noticed a plentiful collection of 5x7 photographs pinned to a bulletin board on the back wall, all of them men. Above them was a sign that read DO NOT GRANT ENTRY.

The photo in the center was of Nick.

37

Levi thanked Beverly for her time and for the tour. Said he'd be in touch with any questions. In response, she wrote her cell number on her business card and slipped it into Levi's hand with a coy, schoolgirl smile.

Over Beverly's shoulder I noticed Mrs. Taylor at the entrance of the restricted hallway pointing at me. She stood in discussion with four uniformed security guards and I elbowed Levi, nodded in their direction.

Once in the exterior portico, I kicked off my heels and broke into a run. Levi sprinted ahead, aiming his key fob at his car. The engine started at a distance. All four security guards ran after us, shouting at us to stop.

Levi's tires squealed when we sped out of the parking lot, and I checked the side mirror. Two of the security guards aimed their phones at the back of Levi's car.

"I think they're taking photos of your license plate!" I said breathlessly.

Levi checked the rearview mirror. He gripped the black steering wheel hard enough to turn his knuckles white.

"Is this going to get you into trouble?" I asked.

He kept his eyes on the road. "That was Sophie's mother with the guards?"

"Yes," I said.

"Depends how far she takes her complaint, I guess."

"I'm sorry," I said.

Levi took my hand and gave it a squeeze. He also gave me his worried smile. "I'll figure something out. No one's following us. Maybe I'll call Beverly and ask her to smooth things over. I'll offer to buy her a coffee or something." Her card was crushed in his fist and he held it up before putting it in the cupholder.

His phone rang. "It's the hospital. I need to take this."

I half-listened to his call that blasted over the speaker-phone—a consult with another doctor about a patient they shared. I half-stared out the window, reflecting on my visit with Sophie, her mother and Charlotte.

I couldn't shake the vision of Sophie standing in the corner, picking at her gown. I had expected she would either be unconscious or angry that I showed up. Possibly even afraid that I'd come to her in person. But I hadn't expected what I did find—a very frightened young woman who was terrified for my safety as well as her own.

When Levi hung up, he said somewhat sarcastically, "You found Sophie, I guess?"

I downloaded the major takeaways from the visit. Including the fact that Charlotte and Mrs. Taylor still blamed Nick.

"Did she *say* it was Max who tried to kill her?" he asked.

"Not specifically. But, basically."

Levi drew in a deep breath and exhaled hard. "Well, that's not conclusive. And Charlotte and Sophie's mother still insist it was Nick. Are you sure Sophie is telling the truth?"

"She mouthed the words 'help me' when no one else was looking."

"But she has that brain injury from the fall, doesn't she?" He touched his forehead. "That area of the brain is intelligence. Memory. She might have her facts wrong."

My heartbeat pulsed in the base of my throat and I thought I might be sick.

How I felt must have shown on my face because he asked, "You okay?"

"I don't know why she would tell me how dangerous Max was if Nick was the one who tried to kill her. It has to be Max."

Levi bowed his head slightly. An acknowledgment, or maybe a show of disappointment, that I wasn't ready to write Nick off just yet.

"Just be careful. Don't take any unnecessary chances right now. We'll keep digging. We'll find the truth," he said.

Levi parked on the street in front of his house and offered to escort me home. I thanked him and told him not to worry about it, that I would enjoy the walk.

Nick opened the front door for me before I could turn the knob and he drew me into a hug. After a moment he asked, "Where are your shoes?"

I looked at my feet. I'd been so bothered by Levi's comments that I'd forgotten them. "Um...well, I had to run —and, uh—" I exhaled hard. "Nick, I went to see Sophie this morning."

His normally prepossessing appearance faded and his pupils shrank into pinpoint dots. "Sophie? As in my ex-wife Sophie? She's awake?"

Nick stood in the open doorway, unmoving.

"She's awake."

We sat in the main living room.

Nick took his work and personal cell phones out of his pockets and put them next to him on the chair cushion. He leaned on his knees.

"I have a neighbor who's a doctor and he found where Sophie is staying. I went to her because I wanted to find whatever truth I could about that situation. I'm sure you understand."

His lips pressed together.

"Sophie admitted to the affair with Max. She said the baby was his. She said that Max took the photos of us. She found them in his phone."

Nick lowered his head slightly like the news delivered a punch.

"She was lucid, although completely terrified at times, and sort of childlike. The fall and the impact must have done some damage. But I believed her."

Nick drew in a quiet breath.

"She said that she and I were both in danger. Because Max would know now that she was awake and aware enough to have emailed those photos. Therefore probably aware enough to remember who pushed her and why."

I didn't tell Nick that the information I'd gathered didn't completely exonerate him. I didn't have to, because Nick was whip-smart. He gave a reluctant nod. Like a dog picking up a scent on the breeze. He knew.

"I guess it was a worthwhile trip, then. And I guess I can understand why you needed to go. I'm wondering why you didn't tell me before you went?" His dark eyes focused on me like sonar.

"When I got the text from my neighbor that he'd found Sophie and he could get me in, you were sleeping. Honestly,

I didn't want to offer the topic up for discussion. I just wanted to go and see her for myself and speak to her directly. I'm glad I did."

He stared and waited a minute. Like he had no idea what I might say next. Then he finally said, "I'm glad you did, too."

I chose that moment to go to my office and pick up the papers my father had sent me. While I was there, I took double doses of every anti-anxiety supplement.

"What's this?" he asked when I handed the papers to him.

"A prenup," I said.

MANNY FISTED a handful of his hair. Growled. Dialed Harper again. All those years of her pestering him. Now that he needed to get in touch with her, she wouldn't take his call.

After her voicemail greeting, he said, "I hate to leave this on voicemail, but I just got the security feed from the South Carolina coffee shop that Natalie went into just before she was killed. The guy who we think killed her looks an awful lot like your Nick. I need for you to check your calendar to see where Nick was on that day. I'll email you the dates and locations when Mariana and Jenny were killed. See where he was then, too.

"Chamberlain isn't his real last name, it's Smith. He and his mother, Esme, moved to Savannah from Miami right after we arrested Ricardo and his brothers. Nick is a Muñoz. You need to get away from him. Immediately. Call me. I'm going to send you a link to the footage, too. Oh, and Natalie did receive a note in her mailbox before she died. She never saw the note. Her husband picked up the mail and didn't think anything of it. But it has the Deuteronomy Bible verse and the fractions on it. Call me."

Manny hung up. Equal parts guilt and rage burned like liquid fire around his heart, reminding him that his failings had caused several families immeasurable, irreparable suffering.

He sent the email, then typed out a text to Harper, giving her a very abridged version of what he left on her voicemail. His finger hovered over the send icon.

Maybe Nick would see her text before she did.

He deleted the message.

He flipped open his laptop, lined up a plane ticket to Savannah. There was nothing available until the morning. That might be too late.

Manny looked up the driving distance to Savannah on his phone: Three hours and forty-two minutes. He checked his watch. He had to pick Reagan up from kindergarten in thirty minutes. Blair had taken her parents to Bald Head Island to look at a beach house they wanted to purchase. She wouldn't be home for another hour.

He grabbed the files on Nick and Max, called the babysitter and ran toward his car.

38

Nick didn't say anything when I handed him the prenup.

But his jaw and his eyes turned to steel. His skin flushed. With anger, I think.

I gave it to him, not just because my father said I had to. He said if he allowed me to marry, whomever he allowed me to marry—my father said it just like that, *allowed* me to marry—would have to sign a prenup. And that if Nick didn't sign it, then he probably didn't love me for who I was. So I gave Nick the prenup.

I also wanted to see how he would react. He never said he wouldn't sign it. But I could tell he was taken aback.

He said he had some calls to make, said that he preferred to make them from the car and so he would pick up sushi for dinner while he was out. I headed upstairs to change clothes. On the security monitors, I saw him walk past the pool toward the garage, where he'd parked his rental car.

Exhausted from lack of sleep, and more than a little drowsy from all the anti-anxiety supplements, I laid down and dozed off. I awoke forty-five minutes later to the sound of Nick opening the back door.

He came upstairs and I thought he would have our dinner. But he was empty-handed except for his phone. He sat next to me on the bed.

"Good news and bad news. Good news is that Mrs. Lowell decided to give us her father's estate to appraise and auction. Bad news is she wants a face-to-face first thing in the morning with her and her attorney to finalize the details." He stroked the side of my cheek. "I have to catch a flight to Naples tonight. I'll be back in twenty-four hours."

I wrinkled my nose. "Why does your hand smell like chlorine?"

He pulled his hand away. "I felt the temperature of the pool. Which reminds me. Hang on just a second."

He disappeared into my closet, returned with my black halter bathing suit and laid it on the corner of the bed. "You've always said that you loved swimming, that it relaxes you and makes you feel like a kid again. Why don't you take a swim? Water feels great. It would be rejuvenating."

He pulled me toward him and kissed me softly. Lovingly. Then he held my face in his hands, his gaze deep and focused, and he said, "I love you. Remember that. No matter what. Okay?"

I gave a tiny nod.

"I've put the prenup in my briefcase. I'll read it through." He kissed me again. "I'll miss you." There was something flat in his tone.

His phone buzzed and he studied the screen.

The usual spark of hope in his eyes was gone.

I wondered if the jig was up. Perhaps there was no longer a reason to pretend.

He waved, walked out the door, never once looking back.

FROM MY BEDROOM WINDOW, I watched Nick's black rental car turn left at Columbia Square and disappear around the corner. I had the strangest sense that I'd never see him again. My stomach dropped and lurched, like I was on a plane that hit a deep air pocket.

I wondered if, by going to see Sophie, I'd gotten too close to the truth for Nick's comfort. As Levi had pointed out, Sophie never said Max was the one who pushed her.

She had admitted that Max was the father of her baby. But was she only warning me not to get involved with Max? Was she saying that if I fell for Max—that Nick would retaliate? And that's how she ended up the way she was?

We'd been interrupted, so I hadn't gotten the full story.

I sat on the edge of my bed, pressed the heels of my hands against my eyes. Every time I thought I had the truth about Nick, it skittered into the shadows again.

I thought back to how Max created an opportunity with me, how he took control, how he grabbed and choked me. It made me think about Piper. It made me wonder if Max didn't give Sophie a choice. It made me wonder if he'd raped them both.

Adrenaline surged.

I wanted to run downstairs, grab my phone and call Nick.

I wanted to ask him what he was hiding from me—I squeezed my eyes and fists shut and willed my feet to stay put.

Because there was still the possibility that Nick was related to Ricardo Muñoz.

I dug my nails into my palms until the pain caused the adrenaline to ease.

If he were a Muñoz, the prenup might have caused him to lose patience with me. Or he could have just realized we'd reached the end of the game.

Maybe the relationship had all been sport to him. Maybe he was just using our relationship to toy with me like a cat with a mouse. Maybe he made me hope and love and dream on purpose, so he could dash those dreams in the end. A part of his revenge.

I'd caused more harm to that family than any of the other girls who testified against Ricardo. I'd killed Alejandro when I crashed the boat. So, it made sense that he saved his best efforts for last.

Anxiety ratcheted up from my gut and tightened the muscles in my chest. I opened my bedside table and downed multiple doses of anti-anxiety supplements. I remembered to call Agent Hernandez again. I needed to hear if he had learned anything else. Because I didn't have enough proof. Not one way or the other.

The anti-anxiety meds weren't working as well as I wanted and I eyed the bathing suit Nick had laid on the bed. Swimming did relax me. Strenuous laps could take away some of the nervous energy. I changed into the black bathing suit and threw a towel over my shoulder. A hundred laps or so would help. It would clear my head.

On the way to the kitchen to get my phone, I noticed the corner of Nick's phone—a bit of black sticking out from the side of the chair cushion. It must have wedged out of sight when he was sitting there earlier and he only picked up his work phone.

I stood over the phone.

He'd asked me to trust him. To trust what we'd found with one another.

I stared at the phone.

Wondered if I would choose trust.

I glanced out the window at Columbia Square, remembered my sister tapping her wrist. It's time.

Time to trust?

Time to know the truth.

Time's up.

I grabbed Nick's phone and tapped in the 6 digit access code I'd seen him use before. It was a word: sugar. And then the letter c. An abbreviated version of sugarchest.

I studied the app icons, figuring out where to begin. My stomach growled and I went to the kitchen and searched for the to-go bag of sushi. Strangely there wasn't one. I opened the fridge, but there wasn't any sushi in there either. Had Nick gotten stuck on the phone with his client and never made it to the restaurant? Seems like he would have said something.

I looked around for my purse and phone and couldn't find either. I mentally retraced my steps and realized I hadn't brought them into the house with me. I must have left them, along with my shoes, in Levi's car.

I sliced a few pieces of cheese from a block and decided it was just as well that I didn't have sushi. That would have been a lot of layers to test for allergens.

I ate the cheese and thought how, if Nick really wanted to kill me, he could. He could have injected a tiny amount of peanut oil into the sushi or the middle of the cheese. I didn't know—would my new allergen sensor pick up every drop within a certain proximity?

I swallowed the cheese.

And waited.

Nothing happened.

Fatigue sank through me like wet sand. I could no longer tell the difference between irrational and rational thought.

It was too exhausting to guard against every potential threat while endlessly hoping. I had to find the truth.

I headed out to the pool. Twenty minutes of a hard swim would center me before I reclaimed my phone and called Agent Hernandez. I glanced at the bookshelf and another Mary Shelley quote came to mind: "When falsehood can look so like the truth, who can assure themselves of certain happiness?"

Who, indeed.

The outside heat hit me like a wet army blanket, thick and nearly suffocating. I put the towel and Nick's phone on the ledge and dove into the water.

I swam several laps with the same intensity I had when my twin and I were on the local swim team. Then, at the deep end, I popped up, breathing hard.

Nick's phone seemed to glare at me and judge me for what I was about to do. I did the breaststroke toward the shallow end, keeping my eyes on the phone like I met its accusation.

I stood in the water at the shallow end, dried my wet fingers and tapped the access code again. I swiped through all the screens, deciding what to tap first.

I rationalized that I'd tell him I did it. And then I'd tell him why I'd done it. Because I needed to know for sure what I'd gotten myself into. He'd understand.

Wouldn't he?

No, probably not. He'd asked me to trust him.

To bide time, I opened a private browser and logged into my own email. Then I emailed Levi, told him I'd left my purse and phone and shoes in his car and asked if I could pop over to pick them up.

I quickly read an email from Agent Hernandez and I began to feel incredibly stupid. I began to hyperventilate.

With a shaking hand I checked Nick's calendar against the dates and locations Agent Hernandez had given me. Nick was in California and within driving distance of Mariana and Jenny when they were killed. My mouth turned dry.

I tapped over to his emails but found that they were full of nothing but business issues. One from his commercial landlord who said that his Common Area Maintenance charges were being increased to fifteen thousand for the year. They asked if he wanted to pay it monthly or all at once. He'd forwarded the email to his bookkeeper and told her not to pay it and not to renew the lease.

There were some emails between the two of us, nothing I hadn't seen before. I pulled up his SearchIt browser and tapped on history. I checked his history for today, yesterday, last week, last month.

Nothing unusual.

I clicked on a cloud application that held online folders and documents.

Some folders were research for Civil War era antiques and jewelry. Some of the specific items inside the folders were the items and appraisals I'd prepared for him.

I scrolled through the remaining folders. My eyes locked in on a folder entitled: Harper.

I tapped the icon. Up popped a document entitled: The Miami Herald. Both of my hands were shaking badly now, and my breath came fast. I thought I might be sick. I forced myself to tap again and was directed to an online page from The Miami Herald. The headline read: Twin Sisters Kidnapped from Home.

My legs gave out and I held onto the side of the pool.

Nick knew.

He knew who I was.

He knew about my family's wealth.

I thought about the roses on the front porch that swarmed with bees. The peanuts in the milk. The missing EpiPens. And I thought about what Max had said: that Nick would do it all again. Marry a wealthy woman and kill her for her money. No reason why Nick couldn't have been a Muñoz who had done all those things.

I emailed the link to the Miami Herald article to Agent Hernandez along with a one-sentence confirmation that Nick had traveled near Jenny, Mariana, and Natalie when they were killed.

Then I called him.

"Hernandez."

"It's me. Harper. Calling from Nick's phone. You were right. He was within traveling distance of the other three girls when they were killed." My breath came even faster and my head spun. "And I just found proof that he knows my real identity. I don't know how. But he knows who I am."

"Where are you? Are you someplace safe?"

"I'm at home."

"Is he there?"

"No. He went to the airport. He said he was going to see a client in Naples, Florida."

"I'm on my way to you, but you need to get out of there."

"Here? I don't have anywhere to go. I'm not going back to my parents. I'll change the code on all the locks—Ow!" Something hit my leg like lightning and I dropped Nick's phone.

The zap hit me again, and I screamed.

I shook my leg but it wouldn't leave me. I grabbed at it and yanked. It was slick and squishy and felt like I held a live wire in my palm. I flung it.

Nick's phone sank to the bottom of the pool.

I grabbed my legs and screamed.

I hoped Levi or Bunny heard me.

Lightning struck my other leg. I scrambled up the steps, screaming all the way. I detached a small jellyfish and threw it. It was about the size of my fist and its tentacles stretched at least four feet long.

I'd seen these pocket-sized jellyfish on the beach at Tybee. Sea wasp jellyfish—deadly. My legs and hand burned like they were engulfed in flames. My skin was covered in lines of red welts—swelling fast.

My thoughts, my heart, my breath—all racing.

Vinegar. Anything to stop the pain. I stopped halfway to the kitchen. A metallic taste in my mouth. My tongue swelled. Lips, too.

My hand and legs puffed like the Pillsbury Doughboy.

An anaphylactic reaction to the venom.

I ran to the kitchen for my purse to grab the EpiPen. "Five seconds, you'll have the medicine you need," I assured myself.

But my purse wasn't there.

I'd left it in Levi's car.

I screamed in frustration, in panic, but my voice came out like a squeak.

The upstairs hallway.

I'd taped an EpiPen underneath the marble base of the full-length mirror.

My eyes were so swollen I could hardly see.

Crying made the swelling in my throat worse. I tried not to. But my legs felt like they were stuck in electrified barbed wire. I didn't have much time before I wouldn't be able to breathe at all.

I limped upstairs, my swollen foot caught the edge of a stair and I fell and banged my forehead. I cried harder. I crawled my way up the rest of the stairs on all fours.

I felt underneath the marble base of the antique mirror and found the EpiPen I'd hidden. My hands shook so hard, I fumbled the cap and dropped the pen.

I bent to pick it up.

Two hands landed on my back and pushed with an unmistakable shove.

The forced perspective railing hit my legs thigh high, causing me to flip over and land hard on the stairs. Something in my body cracked.

I fell head over heels until I finally hit bottom. I could only lay still. The taste of blood on my lips. I felt liquid pool beneath my cheek.

I could no longer see, my eyelids were completely shut.

In the quiet I felt a presence. I was not alone. Did I hear something? I wanted to call out but couldn't. I didn't have the breath. I strained to hear but the only sound in the room was the laser thin stream of air squeezing in and out of my lungs.

"Help," I managed in a whisper.

No response.

No movement.

No noise.

"Nick?" I cried.

It was Nick.

I knew it was.

I'd been a fool.

I heard something. A shift in body position, maybe. A gentle friction of fabric or clothing. Then, steps. Heavy, slow, like a man's shoes against the hardwoods.

My world had gone dark, the pain in my broken body unbearable.

"Sshhhhh," the man said.

He dragged his knuckles along my cheek.

Just as Nick had done so many times before.

39

Manny didn't need to double check his notes to make sure he had Harper's correct address. Several police cars and an ambulance gathered in front of one house on the corner of Columbia Square. Blue and red lights flashed in the dark. A crowd stood nearby.

Manny ran to the back of the ambulance where the doors were open. Four paramedics hovered over Harper—one pumped her chest, one squeezed a manual resuscitator, one gave her an injection and one read the heart rate monitor and yelled, "We're losing her!"

Manny grabbed the top of his head, cursed the fact that he hadn't gotten there sooner.

Another paramedic slammed the back doors then jumped into the driver's seat. The ambulance sped away with the siren blaring.

Manny buckled over, like someone had taken a two-by-four to his gut. If she didn't make it, it would be the second time he'd failed Harper and her family.

Fury drove him upright. He might not be able to save

Harper, but he could still make sure that Nick was arrested for what he'd done. Manny searched the crowd. He'd have to be careful since he didn't have a badge.

Police officers poured in and out of Harper's residence like it was a vomitorium. He looked at their silver name tags, trying to find Officer Patterson. When his call with Harper was disconnected, he'd made a call to the Chatham County Police and asked for one of the local cops to go to Harper's house. He told them he'd had reason to suspect she was in immediate danger. Manny was told there was an Officer Patterson in the neighborhood and he would be instructed to visit the residence.

Local cops who were stuck on relatively safe neighborhood beats were usually older and ready to retire. Manny searched the dispersing crowd and found a uniformed cop with a slight paunch and white hair. He stood at the edge of Columbia Square, hovering over a youngish man who sat on the ground rocking back and forth. Seemingly to self-soothe. Another man, roughly the same age, squatted next to him and patted him on the back.

Manny approached them. "I'm Agent Hernandez," he said to the cop. "Are you Officer Patterson?"

The older cop stood tall and gave a small nod. His eyes narrowed slightly.

"I'm the one who called and asked for someone to check in on Harper Brown. Can you tell me what you found?"

Patterson nodded at the young man who rocked back and forth, as well as the guy standing beside him. "I found Leo and Tim here standing beside her. They're contractors who have been doing some work in her house, apparently. They let themselves in with a code to check on a railing installation and they found her at the bottom of the stairs.

She had fallen and was having a pretty bad allergic reaction."

"Dangerous! Dangerous!" the guy rocking yelled and banged the heel of his hand against his knee.

"Shhh, Leo," the other guy said.

Officer Patterson winced the way people did when they said they found the missing neighborhood cat, dead at the side of the road. It was a no-hope kind of expression. "I don't know if she's going to make it, frankly. But if she does live it'll be because of Leo, here. He was the first one to find her. He was also the one who found her EpiPen."

Manny lowered himself to Leo's level. "You know how to use an EpiPen, son?"

"I'm Tim, Leo's brother." The guy who was standing stuck out his hand for a shake. "Our mom has a shellfish allergy and we've known how to administer an EpiPen since we were kids. Leo found it across the room and it wasn't spent. Her face was really swollen and she wasn't getting any air. We figured she had been at the top of the stairs when she tried to jab herself, then fell before she could. Leo jabbed her in the thigh with it."

"Thank you, Leo. You did good, buddy." Manny turned to Officer Patterson. "I was on the phone with Harper when this all started. Did y'all find a phone?"

"Yeah, I think so. But, uh, lemme show you something first."

Manny followed Officer Patterson through the house. At the bottom of the stairs was a massive amount of blood.

Officer Patterson pointed to the blood. "Head injury."

When they reached the pool area, a uniformed cop was using a long handled net to scoop something out of the water. He deposited it into a large bucket with a plunk.

"What the heck is that?" Manny asked.

"Jellyfish."

"Jellyfish?"

"Cade," Officer Patterson called. "How many are you up to now?"

The uniformed officer looked into the bucket and counted with his pointer finger. "Nine so far. I see more, though."

"What about the phone?" Manny asked. "Did you find one?"

"Yeah, it was in the pool. I've got it over here in a bag."

Manny went to the kitchen pantry and found a bag of rice. Then he dumped it into the evidence bag with the phone over Cade's objections.

"This is her fiancé's phone and there's evidence on it. We need it dried out. That's what the rice is for." Manny handed his card to Officer Patterson who was on the phone. He also handed one to Cade. "Call me on my cell when forensics uncovers what's on that phone."

"Are you the one who called in the APB on Nick Chamberlain, the fiancé?"

"Yeah," Manny said.

"I just got word that he's at the station. They picked him up at the airport. Do you want to head over there to talk to him?"

Much as he wanted to, Manny knew he couldn't talk to Nick, not as a suspended FBI agent. He'd already stretched his luck by calling in the APB. "I need to check on Harper. Do you know where they took her?"

"Probably Savannah Mercy."

By the time Manny got to Savannah Mercy Hospital, Harper was in surgery. He sat in the waiting room like the nurse suggested, but he couldn't sit still. He went outside and called Blair, but she didn't answer the phone.

He went back inside and looked around for a coffee machine.

"Agent Hernandez?"

Manny turned to see a tall doctor with blond hair approaching him. Manny didn't think he'd introduced himself at the front desk by saying agent, but he might have out of habit.

"Yes?"

"I'm Dr. Levi Wright, Harper's friend and neighbor." He extended his hand and Manny shook it.

"The front desk said you called her parents and that you were waiting on an update?"

"That's right."

The doctor put his hands on his hips. "She went into cardiac arrest as a result of the anaphylaxis. She has a broken pelvis, one arm is broken in three places, one leg is broken in six places. Pretty bad concussion, severe bruising. Several fractured bones in her face. She won't be out of surgery for a while."

Manny rubbed his hand across his forehead. His jaw actually dropped. He wanted to ask if she was going to survive. But he couldn't. He was too afraid to hear the answer. His brain cycled through everything the doctor said...cardiac arrest, anaphylactic shock, broken pelvis, concussion...

"May I ask if you're investigating Nick Chamberlain in association with her fall?" Dr. Wright asked.

Manny knew that question wasn't his to answer. But if the good doctor knew Nick, Manny might find more information on Nick. And that would help Harper. "Local police just picked him up."

Dr. Wright exhaled deeply. "Good."

He told Manny about a visit he and Harper made to Sophie's rehab facility, how Sophie admitted to her that Max was her baby's father. "I know Harper wants to believe that Nick Smith or Chamberlain or whatever he's calling himself these days, is innocent. But I don't know.

"Right after we come back from talking with Sophie and Harper ends up in anaphylactic shock from jellyfish in her pool and nearly dead at the bottom of the stairs? That's too coincidental for me."

Manny took notes. "Dr. Wright, is there someplace around here where a person could buy sea wasp jellyfish?"

"Call me Levi, please. Not that I know of. Although summer is the jellyfish season, so our coast is flooded with them right now. I guess you might find some live ones without trying too hard. Right now we're treating hundreds of tourists for stings. Some are mild, others are life threatening like Harper's. But as far as a store that sells them? The sea wasp's venom is so potent, I don't think they would publicly advertise. Otherwise they'd run the risk of getting shut down. If a store like that exists, it's probably an underground thing. Like exotic pets or something like that."

"Could you tell me if any of the patients treated for sea wasp jellyfish stings weren't swimming in the ocean at the time?" Manny asked.

"Meaning, they were stung by a pet jellyfish in their aquarium?"

"Yes. Or maybe they were a handler at a store or some other location. That might help me home in on where the jellyfish were sourced," Manny said.

"Yeah, the hospital is connected to a national medical database. I could search by injury or illness."

"That would be great, thanks." Manny handed him his card. "My cell phone is the best place to reach me right now."

"Sure thing."

"Oh. And, uh, Harper." Manny's mouth went dry. "She's going to make it, right?"

"Most likely."

40

M anny tipped the rickety motel room chair onto its back two legs and the wooden joints groaned. He and Blair talked via a video call while they waited for Amaya to join them.

It was the first time he'd spoken with Blair face-to-face, sort of, since he'd left Charlotte. Seeing her was a relief. A joy. A simple act that brought him back to himself.

"So your parents aren't going to buy it?" Manny asked, referring to the house they'd seen on the coast.

"They're talking about getting something in Florida. No state income tax, warm winters, year-round sunshine," Blair said.

Manny smiled. He could see her parents enjoying all of those things.

"But they don't want to be that far from Reagan, so they're trying to convince us to move down there with them." Blair's expression was serious, not at all joking. It was another reminder for Manny that he was about to be formally released from the Bureau. He felt his smile wane.

"How much longer are you going to be there?" she asked.

"The Bureau?"

"No, Savannah."

"Oh—" He shrugged. "Long enough to make sure that either Nick or Max is charged. Long enough to make sure that neither one of them can get to Harper again."

Blair nodded slowly. Like she wasn't happy with his answer but she wasn't going to contest it. She looked down.

Manny said quickly, "I'm sorry I left town so suddenly."

His wife shared a small, conciliatory smile. "It's okay."

"I'm sure Reagan was upset."

"I had the sitter set up a video chat so I could let Reagan know I'd be there soon and she was fine. It all worked out," Blair said. "Look. Manny. Before Amaya gets on this call—"

Manny's chest tightened. "Yes?"

"I just—I want to say that I understand. I do. When all this began, I didn't want to accept that the system—your department—had become so compromised. So corrupt.

"But—it is. And knowing who you are, I get that you can't work with that. Not that they're giving you much of a choice. But, I just wanted to say that. Also that I love and appreciate that about you."

Her words went to Manny's heart like summer sun to an icicle. For the first time in a while, in spite of all that was going on around him, he felt that all was right in his world.

"Thanks," he said.

She placed the I love you sign over her heart.

Manny did the same.

The video conferencing screen divided from two squares into three and Amaya appeared onscreen. She was in her kitchen, her phone or tablet must have been propped on the counter. She poured coffee into a mug.

"Amaya, hey," he said.

She looked into the camera. Her eyes were narrowed. She sat on a stool and sipped her coffee. "Sorry I'm late. I was going to call from the car, then I got this. She held a typewritten letter in front of the camera.

"This is a department-wide memo that encourages everyone to report any co-worker suspected of accessing internal files without proper authorization."

Manny let out a hard exhale. "They know."

"Can they trace your work back to you?" Blair asked.

Amaya sipped her coffee again. She shook her head. "I doubt it. I was careful. They know someone was looking, though. I definitely hit a nerve. I don't think I should go any further."

"No. Don't," Manny said. "Were you able to find anything?"

"I only got as far as the Muñoz files. They weren't that hard to break into, honestly. The front of that application is password protected, like you said, Manny. But there are plenty of back doors. I was able to check the login files. Listen to this. Stanford logged in six months before you received your handwritten note with the Bible verse and the fractions. Six months. In fact, he logged in three times in one week."

"He wouldn't log in three times in one week just to check the status of a closed case," Manny said. "He must have been searching for something. Didn't find it. Went back a second and third time just to be sure."

"That's what I think," Amaya said. "None of the victims' addresses were listed in the electronic files, as you said. The only addresses listed were their old Miami addresses from decades ago."

Manny lowered the front chair legs to the floor and

crossed his arms. "So, Director Hall has Stanford search for identifying information to hand to the killer, but Stanford doesn't find it. He looks again and again. Then he has to try something else." Manny ran his hand across the stubble on his jaw. "Question is, what did he do next? And how did he find it?"

"Well, he didn't call the families. Because I also contacted each of them to see if anyone from the Bureau reached out to them in the last year or so about their daughters' whereabouts. Each of them said no. And all of them said their daughters would have alerted them if someone had gotten in touch with them directly. Especially if someone inquired about their address," Amaya said.

Based on what Manny knew about each of the families, he knew that was true.

"What about the original case files in Miami? Were the parents' new addresses recorded there?" Blair asked. "Because Stanford could have given the killer the parents' addresses, the killer could have broken into their mailbox and found correspondence from the daughter with a return address. Or he could have broken into the parents' homes and—"

Manny shook his head. "When the D.A. took witness protection off the table for each of the families, they all relocated on their own. No one knew where they went. After a while, I knew generally where they all ended up. But I didn't know their specific addresses. Not until Harper gave me her address recently. All I had were a few phone numbers and I certainly didn't share those."

Manny, Blair and Amaya stared at their screens.

No one said anything.

They'd run out of ideas.

After a while, Amaya said, "This Nick Smith—or Chamberlain—is still in custody, though, right?"

"For now. My Chatham County P.D. contact tells me there's enough similarity between Nick's ex-wife's fall down the stairs and Harper's that the D.A.'s office is interested. They don't have any hard evidence. But a teed-off D.A. who feels she got cheated out of a conviction from the first case could go a long way.

"They have security feed from the exterior of Harper's house that shows a hooded individual, probably male, sneaking into her house through her back door while she swam laps.

"Nick drove away, then Harper went outside a little while later. Then this hooded guy appears. So, Nick could have parked his car around the corner, then run back to Harper's house.

"Problem is, the D.A. isn't considering any suspects other than Nick, and the hooded character could have been someone else. Like Max. He could have been watching and timed his entrance perfectly. And if he knows that Harper is still alive, he'll try again. If he's a Muñoz, he won't stop until she's dead."

"And we don't have anything on Max?" Amaya asked.

Manny shook his head. "Nothing other than Harper saying that he choked her. Harper's statement on Max will be enough for Chatham County to talk to him. But it probably won't go any further. FBI could have dug up something. But when the D.A. reached out to them for information, the Bureau declined to participate. Hall said their review of the facts revealed nothing suspicious with regard to the victims' deaths."

Blair rolled her eyes.

Manny's stomach roiled at how far his beloved law

enforcement agency had fallen. "Three women, all of whom testified against Ricardo Muñoz, receive cryptic notes. Within a few days they're dead, the last one nearly-so, and the FBI's response is no proof, no connection."

"If that doesn't reek of cover-up and corruption, nothing does," Amaya said.

They hung up. Manny studied the four large poster-sized sheets of paper he'd taped to the wall. He'd filled out one sheet each for Mariana, Natalie, Jenny and Harper with all the details he and Blair and Amaya had gathered on the women's lives and their murders. He'd hoped to find some clue, some commonality that would highlight how the killer had found them. But the only connection between the four of them was the fact that they had all been kidnapped and tortured by the Muñoz family over twenty years ago.

MANNY STOOD at the top of Harper's half-spiral staircase with her parents and watched Dr. Levi Wright carry Harper upstairs to her bedroom. Harper closed her eyes, clung to him and whimpered occasionally.

"Sorry, sweetheart," Levi said softly. "Almost there."

He lowered her to the bed with such great care, Manny wondered if Levi felt more for her than just neighborly friendship.

Harper's mother and a neighbor named Bunny flitted around the bed, trying in vain to make Harper more comfortable.

Harper's father offered direction from the corner of the room with the sort of confident yet aimless sincerity often seen in politicians.

After everyone went downstairs, Manny lowered himself

slowly into a nearby armchair, unable to take his eyes off of Harper. Her face was swollen and bruised. A long line of stitches extended around the side of her head. She had two casts.

She didn't look quite as bad as she had after the boat crash. But it was close. Manny didn't know how much more of this life she could possibly take. "How're you doing?"

She scoffed and closed her eyes. When she opened them again, she asked, "How did Nick find me?"

Manny shrugged. "We still don't know. My source at the police department says that Nick denies being related to the Muñoz family. He said he did grow up in Miami. He said he saw your photo in the papers, on TV and online probably hundreds of times when he was a kid. When y'all met, he immediately recognized you." Manny pointed to his neck. "He saw the scars and that rang a bell for him. He looked up some old Miami Herald articles. Then he compared photos he had of you today against the post-kidnapping photos of you in the paper. He said he put two and two together."

"I don't believe him." Harper's voice shook.

"I don't know that I do either. And I haven't yet ruled out Max. But I think the Miami Herald article that you found in Nick's files does seem to point to him."

Her eyes shimmered with tears.

Manny's heart broke for her. It was nothing less than miraculous that she was still alive.

"You're a strong person and you probably don't need to hear this from me. But, I just want to say that none of this is your fault. He could have fooled anybody."

Harper turned her head and looked out the window. A wide swath of shaved, white scalp surrounded a contrasting black row of stitches. She swiped at tears that slid down her cheek.

"The police took your statement on Max, so they'll talk to him. But without proof to back up your story, it is going to be tough to make anything stick."

"Speak with Sophie Taylor." Harper's tone was firm. "Nick's first wife. She's got a story to tell. See if her mother changed her mind about doing the DNA test." Harper told nearly the same story that Dr. Wright had told him about visiting Sophie in the facility. Manny made a note regarding the bloody paper towels since that was new.

"Either Nick got jealous when he found out Sophie was pregnant with Max's baby. Or Max didn't want her to have the baby because that would wreck his marriage and his life," Harper said. "But I'm confident that the man who pushed her over her forced perspective railing was the same man who pushed me over mine."

Manny nodded. "And that man is a Muñoz."

41

———

Like he did when I was younger, like a thief in the night, my father entered my room.

He slithered in without a word, without a sound. He leaned next to the large mirror on the far wall.

I wouldn't have even noticed him had I not just put my book down.

I watched him.

He passively examined his fingernails. Admired them, maybe.

He was deliberately silent.

I knew what he was doing.

He was letting the memories of our past awaken.

Stir and build.

Memories of shame, guilt, regret. But most of all—memories of fear. He wanted them to take form again.

Like a snake, my father had an innate sense for knowing when to strike. He knew the exact moment when his victim's fear had reached its peak. When his intended had become paralytic and was no longer able to fight. When they would let him do whatever he wanted. In exchange for nothing more than the promise of escape.

He waited. He silently appraised me.

I had no idea what he was about to say or do. But I could almost hear the rattle at the end of his tail.

My father's evil was not the obvious sort.

He was fit and tanned and unlike most men his age, he still had all of his hair. His smile, when he used it, was wide and white and gracious, and it had the power to charm. He hadn't practiced medicine in years—a consequence of our changed identities and relocation. But his presence still emanated the authority of a well-respected surgeon.

He had stolen my childhood. He had stolen my innocence. Yet his perversion stayed hidden under the guise of intelligence and attractiveness and confidence.

He must have had a portrait in his attic that carried the true weight of his sins.

I thought of Lord Henry's quote from *The Picture of Dorian Gray*. "Every impulse that we strive to strangle broods in the mind, and poisons us...Resist it, and your soul grows sick with longing for the things it has forbidden to itself..."

My father denied himself nothing.

"I think it's time we moved you back home," he said.

Like fangs into my flesh, he'd struck.

"Despite the extended amount of time and freedom we've afforded you, you haven't fulfilled the terms of our agreement."

Hatred boiled in my gut.

"There have been extenuating circumstances," I said, trying to keep my tone low.

He stared at me with lifeless eyes. He lifted the short sleeve of his golf shirt and, with one finger, he delicately skimmed the scars from the knife wounds. Wounds given to him by his own child.

He was quietly reminding me of the evidence he held against me. He was saying: You attacked your own father with a knife. You are unstable. You have no credibility.

"A Muñoz family member tracked me down and tried to kill me." I raised my casted arm, in case he'd forgotten. "He did kill all the other women who testified against Ricardo. My challenges are not the result of an unstable mind."

"No, but they are the result of your inability to make good and reasonable life choices. They are the result of your poor discernment. You were in a relationship with him." He rolled his eyes. He walked toward me.

Beneath the covers, I grabbed a fistful of sheet.

He picked up a prescription bottle, emptied a pain pill into his palm and shoved it in front of me.

"I don't want one," I said.

"You should take it. You should stay ahead of the pain."

He was really saying that I would be easier to control if I were medicated.

I didn't care how much pain I was in. I would not, under any circumstance, be drugged around my father. I was no longer an attractive age to him, so I wasn't concerned that he would violate me. Again.

But his M.O. was abusing those who couldn't defend themselves. The painkillers dulled my senses. Being muddled around him was a bad idea. I thought I might wake up in the trunk of a car. Or worse.

I stared at the pill in my father's outstretched hand and shook my head. "No."

He gave me his dull-eyed, disapproving stare. His intimidating stare. The stare I'd often withered under.

My insides started to quiver.

But not with fear.

With anger.

A sudden reflected light in the large mirror across the room caught my attention. The gas flames from the lamps in Columbia Square were no longer subtle. They blazed like bonfires. They blazed with all the rage I felt toward my father.

Columbia Square echoed my feelings and my desires.

Columbia Square...understood me.

Which made sense to me now.

The space had been named for Columbia—the early female personification of the United States. WWI posters of Columbia quickly flashed across my mind. She wore an American flag gown and a soft, brimless cap of the same material, signifying freedom and the pursuit of liberty.

Freedom and liberty were what I wanted more than anything. More than breathing, even.

"Harper! Are you listening to me?"

I wasn't.

I was mesmerized by the fires.

And then, even though it was too early for her to visit, my sister emerged from the shadows. She stood next to the fountain and I raised onto my good elbow to see her more clearly. She stood there in her red dress with the soft crinoline, her expression no longer loving or worried.

She pointed an accusing finger at our father. Her jaw dropped and her mouth gaped wide in a scream.

Not with fear.

With rage.

Her scream shook something deep inside of me and I understood her as I never had before.

I knew.

Twins just knew.

She tore at the skirt of her dress.

Still screaming.

Crying.

Our father had done to her what he'd done to me.

I turned to our father.

He continued his tirade about how I needed drugs.

He did not hear.

He did not see.

"You hurt her. Like you hurt me," I said. "We just reacted in different ways."

He stopped. He stared at me.

"You stole her childhood. Like you stole mine. Did you take pictures, too? I bet you did. I bet you still look at them."

He stood stock-still. Mouth open like he'd been shot.

I looked out the window again.

My sister stopped screaming.

She pointed at the watch on her wrist. With Nick in custody, I now realized she intended a different meaning.

Time.

Time to flee.

Time to be free.

I suddenly realized that like all tyranny, my father's demands were a moving target, a finish line that extended each time I gave in. No matter how many of his demands I acquiesced to, nothing would ever be enough to gain my freedom. In fact, it was quite the opposite. Each time I did what he wanted, I moved further away from everything Columbia represented. I moved further into a prison of my own making.

My father's demands weren't about ensuring my safety or anyone else's. His demands were about achieving control. He was never going to give me my freedom.

"You're insane." He lifted his short sleeve and touched his scars. "You're a threat to society."

"The welfare of humanity has always been the alibi of tyrants," I said calmly.

"What?" His tone was sharp, his eyes turned as dark as oblivion.

"Albert Camus. French novelist."

Albert Camus had also said that the only way to deal with an unfree world was to become so absolutely free that your very existence was an act of rebellion. I knew then that was exactly what I'd do.

For me, yes. Also for my sister.

My father shoved the pill into my face again but I didn't look at it. I stared into his beetle-black eyes.

The pain in my body unbearable.

Broken bones, broken spirit, broken heart.

I'd handled it once before. I would handle it again.

"No," I said.

The hatred in his eyes bored holes into me.

He took the pill between his thumb and forefinger and tried to shove it into my mouth.

I snatched the pill with my good hand and threw it at him. It hit him in the eye and his face twitched with red hot fury.

His nostrils flared, his chest pumped up and down.

And then, like some evil whisperer gave him an even better plan to score, he calmed.

Eerily.

I preferred his rage on the surface where I could see it.

He walked toward the hallway and said, "Since you don't have any other beds up here, your mother is going to sleep on the couch downstairs. I'm checking into a hotel. I'll call my attorney in the morning to let them know the deal is off."

I lifted myself onto my good arm again to see if Catherine was still in Columbia Square. She wasn't.

My father stood in the hallway, looking around, examining the moldings. "We ought to get a good price for the place," he said aloud. "The funds from the sale should pay for the facility I have picked out for you."

His second strike.

A final blow.

Without a word and without looking at me, he just stood there.

My father was a tormenting bundle of horror who had returned to haunt me in person.

I couldn't find the words to respond.

I didn't even want to break the silence for fear he'd come back with something even worse.

When he knew he'd won, he walked away.

The front door slammed.

I'd had enough.

I wasn't sure how, but if it was the last thing I did, I was going to stop my father.

I was going to claim my freedom.

My life.

My eyes flew open to the dark. Awakened from a deep sleep.

There had been a loud noise, some sort of crash.

Wasn't there?

My body was rigid with fear, a hollow panic thrummed in my chest.

I didn't know where I was.

This wasn't the hospital.

No sterile scent of bleach and despair.

No light under the door.

No laughing from the nurses' station while those of us in beds clung to threads of life.

And the mattress was too soft.

Magnolia meowed somewhere in the pitch-dark.

I fastened myself to that noise.

That sound of home, my invisible north star.

She meowed again, longer this time, like she called to me. Jigsaw pieces of reality floated back together.

I was in my own room, home from the hospital. After my father left, I'd taken a bite of a pain pill. I must have fallen asleep.

The nightmare settled around me. The pain in my body throbbed and screamed.

I fixated on Nick.

The one man I'd fallen in love with—Ricardo Muñoz's son.

He had been at the compound with all the other kidnapped girls.

He tracked me and tried to kill me. He must have proposed just to get his hands on my money, and the house, just like Max had said. Maybe they were in on it together.

There was a sound in the dark, something subtle, and I strained to hear it. But the movement stilled and I wondered if I'd imagined it.

I drew in a quiet breath, watching the dark.

There was something. Perhaps the bulge of a head. A blurred shape roughly the size of a man.

Magnolia hissed.

I pushed back toward the headboard. "Mom?"

No response.

But a presence.

I felt around for the gun I kept in my bedside table. But the drawer was empty.

My phone wasn't on my bedside table where it had been.

I glanced at the security monitors, but they were black. "Paranoia is not a good compass," my father had said when he not only turned off all the security monitors but unplugged them, too. "I wish you would learn that."

I fumbled for the light switch and couldn't reach it.

"Dad," I whispered.

Flickers of panic ignited.

My body quaked.

A scream wedged itself in my throat.

I waited.

Waited.

The patchwork of dark shifted and I lost track of the form.

A floorboard squeaked in the hallway. Then another squeak, only further away. A few moments later I heard the front door open and close.

My body shook harder.

Tears slid down my face.

My house cast off shadows and it creaked and groaned, but doors did not open and close by themselves.

Nick no longer had the correct code; plus he was in custody. Leo and Tim had a code. But they wouldn't hurt me. They had saved me after I fell. After Nick pushed me.

It couldn't have been Max, he didn't have a code. It had to have been my father. Or would he have hired someone to do away with me altogether? Perhaps I was proving to be too much trouble for him.

I tried again to turn on the light and couldn't reach it.

I scooted to the edge of the bed.

My body was covered in sweat. The air conditioning blew against my wet skin and I shivered.

I turned on the light and quickly scanned the room.

No one.

My breath was shaky.

Next to my bed were two options—a walker and a wheelchair. The doctor had told me that I was lucky my pelvis only had one break on the pelvic ring and it wasn't displaced, which meant I didn't have to have pins or plates. I hadn't practiced with the walker yet and didn't want to fall. I didn't want pins or plates. So I hoisted myself into the wheelchair. Pain shot through my body like fireworks.

I wheeled across the room, shut my bedroom door and locked it with the skeleton key that was still in the lock.

I held onto the key.

My mother was probably downstairs, sleeping like the dead as she did. She would have awakened to my phone call, but whoever had entered my room took my phone.

Why?

So I wouldn't call for help.

He must have already planted his trap.

I wheeled to my bedside table for a closer look at my pain pills, antibiotics and anti-inflammatories.

I no longer trusted them. Whoever was here might have switched them out for something toxic. I flushed them all and made a mental note to ask Levi to pick up refills on everything.

Outside the window the gas lamps blazed again. I wheeled closer to the window and saw my sister standing at the very edge of Columbia Square.

Just a few feet from my house.

She was surrounded by fog and her eyes fixed on me with piercing intensity.

She tapped the silver watch on her wrist, slowly but dramatically this time. The gesture was purposeful, exaggerated. Like she begged me to understand.

"Not time to be free?" I whispered.

She focused on me with even more ferocity and she tapped her watch again, theatrically.

"I don't understand."

The fog began to roll up from the far corner, and she pointed toward it.

"The fog?" I grabbed my forehead, forgetting about the stitches. Fierce pain reminded me. I jerked my hand away.

She shook her head no.

I banged my hand against the glass pane. "What are you telling me?!"

Catherine looked like she wanted to say more, but the fog reached her bare feet. Like she didn't have a choice, she turned and walked to the end of Columbia Square, and disappeared.

42

———

Manny mindlessly chewed another slice of cold pizza for lunch and tried to ignore how it landed in his stomach like a greasy brick.

His phone rang.

"They let him out," Officer Patterson said quickly.

"Nick?! When?"

"Early yesterday evening. Just found out. Nick's attorney submitted his cell phone records and the company's rental car tracking system details as an alibi. There's nothing that puts him at the scene of any of the women's deaths."

"He could have driven a different car. He could have left his cell phone in his hotel—"

"That's what the D.A. said, too. But the judge told them if they wanted to keep him locked up, they had to come up with something that put him at any of those women's houses, including Harper's house at the time of her fall."

Manny called Harper to warn her. She didn't answer. He left a voicemail. Then he called her father.

"She could have sent those notes," Dr. Silveria said. "She might have hurt those other women. I wouldn't even put it past her to throw herself down those stairs to cover her guilt, to make it look like she was being hunted, too. You don't know what she's capable of like we do."

Manny called Harper's mother. He warned her that Nick was out and that she should keep the doors locked and the alarm on.

She said she'd gone out to buy a lift recliner for Harper, but that she'd locked up the house before she'd left. She said she would call a neighbor to sit with Harper until she could get back.

Blair called.

"I think I figured out the code," she said breathlessly.

Manny spun toward the poster-sized pages he'd taped to the wall, ready to know the identity of the killer. "You did?"

"Pretty certain. Look at the verse and the fractions. We have:

24: 19-22

1/12 1/13 1/16 1/20 1/10 2/17 1/6

"The numbers that delineate the chapter and verse are the exact same numbers that the Muñoz family used to rationalize their crimes. That's Deuteronomy.

"Then the fractions aren't fractions at all, but a code. As I thought. The one references the first line of the passage and the number after the slash points to the letter. So, the twelfth letter of the passage and then the thirteenth letter, then the sixteenth letter and so on."

"But that formula doesn't work in this case." Manny looked at the scratch paper on the desk where he'd tried that formula.

"It works when you realize that 24: 19-22 isn't from

Deuteronomy, but rather from a different book in the Bible," Blair said.

"I don't follow," Manny said.

"When the killer wrote the note, he used 24:19-22 because, I believe, he wanted you and the other note recipients to know that he was a Muñoz.

"When I realized that the code didn't work for Deuteronomy, and considering Ricardo Muñoz's affinity for Old Testament, I went back to Genesis and read Chapter 24 verses 19 through 22.

"The text didn't seem relevant but I applied the formula anyway—the first line, twelfth letter—and so on. To see if it would yield a clue.

"It didn't.

"I moved on to Exodus and had the same result. But the next book was eye-opening. Chapter 24 verse 19 says: "Anyone who injures another person must be dealt with according to the injury inflicted—an eye for an eye, a tooth for a tooth. Whatever anyone does to injure another person must be paid back in kind.

"So, using my formula, number one refers to the first line of the passage. Then count over 12 letters, you get J. Take that approach all the way through the rest of the numbers and you get the word JUSTICE."

Blair's answer resonated through Manny like someone had rung a gong next to his head.

"The killer didn't use the code to tell us who he is? It only gives us his motivation?" Manny stood up in the stale motel room that reeked of dead ends. He had a twist in his stomach. An ache in his bones. Something wasn't right. Something was off.

"I went through all 39 books of the Old Testament, read each Chapter 24 verses 19 through 22. I applied the formula using the code from the note. None of the others worked. This was the only one," Blair said.

The twist tightened. The ache deepened.

"No," Manny said. "That's not right. A killer like this one, who lets his victims and law enforcement know ahead of time that he's about to kill? He thinks he's smarter than everyone else. He's got a history of getting away with murder. He thinks he can get away with it again. Somewhere in that note he's telling us who he is and he's betting that no one will figure it out."

"Usually," Blair said. "But maybe not this time."

"Okay," Manny said. "So he doesn't want us to know who he is. Then he sends the note—why?"

"Because he can," she said. "Because he's arrogant. Because maybe he wants you to spend time thinking that he sent you a viable clue. When he hasn't."

Manny sighed twice. His head throbbed. "So, by the time he sent the note, he knew I had a corrupt Director and a corrupt partner. He knew I'd make waves, that I'd get fired. Then all I'd have left was to sit around and focus on the note. Like it was a clue. Which means I don't have a clue."

"Then we go back to the beginning to find one," Blair said without missing a beat. "Before the killer wrote the notes, he got information from Stanford, most likely, that led him to his victims' true identities and locations. It wasn't addresses. It wasn't phone numbers. He didn't call any of the parents. What was it?"

Nothing moved in the motel room. Nothing on the poster-sized sheets gave any clues. Nothing connected the details. But Manny chased those details down dead-end streets anyway. "He had something that made the women stand out. Maybe we look for something they had in common," Manny said.

"They lived in different places, some had children, some didn't, some were married, some weren't. They all had different professions," Blair said. "I don't think they had a commonality."

"He found them because of something Stanford gave them. Hall wouldn't have been the one to hand it over. He's too political. He would have kept his hands clean. That's why he cut Stanford in. Because he knows Stanford is weak and greedy. Hall needed a patsy in case this all blew up."

"Think Stanford would tell you who this monster is if you asked?" Blair cut in.

Manny barked a humorless laugh. "And implicate himself? No way. But there's something. A connection. It's in each of their lives. Drawing his attention. It's how he found them," Manny said. "I can feel it. You feel it, don't you, Blair?"

"I feel it," she said softly.

But he didn't know if she did.

"Because Stanford didn't have their addresses," he said. "No one did. So it had to have been something else. Something—"

An appointment alarm dinged loud from Blair's phone.

"I have to go. Reagan's got an appointment."

The old craving screamed for a drink more desperately than it ever had. Because they weren't any closer to answers. And Manny knew if Harper died, the craving might win. Just for a moment. But that would be enough to do him in. "Now?" he asked. "Can it wait?"

"I need to dress, I need to get Reagan dressed, and I need to find those new insurance cards that came in the mail last week," Blair said. "I thought I put them in my wallet but they aren't there."

"I made copies. They're in our personal files," Manny said. "In the garaoffice."

"Oh. I didn't look there."

"I figured a paper copy was a better back up than calling the insurance company for a replacement card. Especially if there was an emergency. Insurance companies are such a pain."

"In the filing cabinet, I guess?" she asked.

"Yeah. In the drawer with our marriage and birth certificates and the uh—the..." Something sprung loose in Manny's chest.

The twist unraveled.

The ache disappeared.

Bullet pointed items he had written on the poster-sized pages enlarged and jumped out at him.

Dots connected.

Details slotted into place.

"Manny?" Blair asked.

"Social security cards," he said.

"Okay, I'll find them."

"That's it," he whispered.

"What's it?" Blair asked.

Manny looked around for his shoes. He found one under the desk. "Stanford could have gotten the survivors' social security numbers from the Miami office. We got 'em back then, because WITSEC was on the table. Those numbers are still there. On twenty-year-old paperwork, stuffed in a box and parked in an air-conditioned warehouse someplace." Manny tore around the room looking for his other shoe.

"One phone call, maybe two, to an admin in charge of record storage. Stanford would have flashed his badge, he would have said that he was updating case files and he would have clearance to go through those records. No one would have questioned him. No one."

"And then what, the killer calls a P.I. or uses one of those online services to locate them?" Blair asked.

He put the call on speaker, opened his laptop and did a quick search. The results on the first page gave him what he needed.

"Manny?"

"Hang on," he said. He clicked a few links and quickly scanned several articles.

After a couple of minutes, he said, "That's it."

He grabbed his phone. "Uh, no. I doubt it. P.I.s and online services are traceable. The killer isn't someone who really wants to be found. He's not like other serial killers. He has too much to lose, so he isn't going to involve another person in this. Other than Stanford and White. And they took blood money so they're not going to say anything."

Manny found his other shoe under the bed. He grabbed his keys and let the motel door slam behind him. "Look at what was going on in their lives before each of them got killed."

Manny ran down two flights of motel steps and jumped into his car. "Jenny was pregnant. Mariana had an ankle injury. Natalie was getting over some sort of upper respiratory thing. Harper had an allergic reaction to a bee sting just after she moved to Savannah.

"All insurance companies require social security numbers for coverage. All doctors' offices ask for social security numbers, and most patients blindly hand them over," he said.

Manny sped through a red light and floored it when he got to the ingress for the freeway. "When Harper was in surgery, I spoke with Dr. Levi Wright. He said he had access to a national medical database and that it was searchable.

"I just did a cursory search and found several exposés by The Wall Street Journal. Hospital networks and urgent care group facilities are willingly turning over hundreds of thousands of patient records to SearchIt's health and medical arm. No individual has given their permission for their info to be shared, so SearchIt is being panned for its violation of individual rights and medical privacy. I'm sure SearchIt says that they don't retain any personal identification information. But I bet they do. Tech giants and governments lie all the time about how much information they collect on us. And I'd bet personal information is available and searchable, especially if you knew where to look.

"What was the name of the book in the Bible where you found the eye for an eye verse?" Manny asked.

"Leviticus," she said.

The name sent such raw terror into his heart he felt he'd been electrocuted. "The killer does want me to know who he is. I'll call you back."

He hung up and dialed Harper.

43

———

Levi held the bowl of soup and raised a spoonful to my lips.

"I do have one good arm." I smiled at his kindness. It was obvious how he was accustomed to caring for children.

"But no tray." Levi took a large, thick book from my desk, put it on my lap and balanced the soup bowl on top of it.

"Thanks," I said. "For the soup. For coming over. My mom gave you her alarm code?"

"Yeah. Couple of days ago, actually. In case she wasn't around and you needed something. She asked me not to tell you." He winked.

Normally I would have been furious with her for giving out a security code like that. But with Nick locked up, it didn't matter.

"You didn't see my phone over there, did you? I've been looking for it."

"I think I saw it downstairs. Your mom said she was concerned that reporters might harass you because of Nick's arrest."

I gestured to my broken bones. "I would feel better if I had my phone with me."

"Sure. I'll bring it up before I leave." Levi seemed to study me, then he asked, "How are you doing with all the Nick stuff, by the way?"

I shrugged and let out a deep exhale. I really didn't want to talk about it. "Ah, well. I guess I chose the wrong guy, huh?"

Levi tore a piece of bread and dipped it into his soup. "He probably could have fooled anyone."

I thought of my sister tapping her watch. She had to have been warning me about Nick. "Maybe I—missed the clues somehow."

"Don't be hard on yourself. People do bad things. You'll feel better when he ends up in jail for what he did to you."

"I never took you for the vengeful type."

He winked at me. "How are your parents doing?"

"Well, right now, my dad is making arrangements to move me back home."

"Permanently?"

"If he has his way, yes. But—"

"He's overprotective. You're his last surviving daughter," Levi said.

I nodded, but I didn't agree that he was overprotective. He was going to do everything in his power to remove every last freedom I had.

"My mom was that way after my brother died. She held on very tightly to me."

"I didn't know you had a brother," I said.

"Long time ago. Kidnapped." He stared into the soup bowl, stirred it slowly, spoke as if he was talking to himself. "And murdered."

"Oh my gosh, Levi."

"After that, my mother was different."

"I understand," I said.

"Do you?" His stare flicked from his soup bowl to me and something cold and hard formed in my chest. His leftover hatred for whoever killed his brother was palpable.

I shared a sympathetic smile. "My mother was like that after my sister died. She was despondent." My phone rang downstairs, but Levi didn't move. He kept his eyes steady on me.

It wasn't the norm to have a friend who had also lost a sibling. This was a delicate topic and he probably wanted to discuss it further.

With Nick in custody and Hernandez confirming he was a Muñoz, I didn't see any reason to hide the truth anymore. It would all come out publicly soon enough, anyway.

"When my sister died—it wasn't a car accident that killed her. We had been kidnapped and we were escaping in a boat. We crashed. You were right. I was the one driving."

He drew in a deep breath. He looked down and pressed his lips together like he relived a painful memory.

"How did you deal with that?" he asked.

"Not well."

"I guess we have that in common, then." He took the spoon from my bowl and offered me a bite of soup. "Eat up. You need your strength."

For as much as he had pushed me to share my history, I expected him to want to talk about it more. Maybe my history was too close to his own.

I opened my mouth to receive the soup, but a bit of ink poking out from beneath his wide watchband caught my attention.

A tattoo on the top of his wrist. If I wasn't mistaken, it was the letter A. I pulled back.

"What's that?" I asked.

He lowered the spoon to the bowl. Saying nothing, he removed his watch and put his palm over the inked and cursive name.

The vision of my sister pointing to the top of her wrist burst to the forefront of my mind.

My throat turned dry.

My stomach turned sick.

Levi's eyes turned to hardened black onyx.

They locked with mine.

I understood it all.

I feared I understood it all too late.

"Same type of tattoo as yours." He nodded to Catherine's initials on my wrist.

I pressed my thumb against my tattooed initials, like they might send me strength. "What was his name?"

I knew—he knew.

My heart rate sped and I forced myself to breathe slowly. "Did he have a Biblical name like you?"

Time slowed. We stared at one another.

My phone continued to ring downstairs.

Levi made no attempt to get it for me.

We both knew that whoever was calling was trying to warn me.

Finally, he arched an eyebrow. "You know the Bible?"

"I used to know it quite well. After my sister died my parents turned to the church. I did VBS—Vacation Bible School—six years in a row." My face felt as stiff as a rock but I forced a smile.

"Let's see if it's still in here," I said, opening the bedside table with my fingertips. Although I knew full well that the Bible was there. What I hoped beyond reason was that my gun had been put back. It hadn't.

I held the Bible in my hands, turned the thin scritta pages. My right eye began to tic.

That was why I'd felt the silent nudges to read the Bible. That was why my mother had been prompted to think of me when she re-read Genesis. That was why my mother picked up the phone and called me when she read about God changing Abram's and Sarai's names.

Because the Bible was where the answers were.

A vital memory I hadn't thought of in years came to me with alarming strength and clarity: Sitting in the pew in Iowa with my parents. The minister spoke about the power of a name and how names in Biblical times meant much more than they did today. How, when they were changed, it gave the person a new identity, a new purpose. God changed Jacob's name, which meant deceiver, to Israel, which meant prince with God.

He changed Abram's name to Abraham, which meant father of many nations.

Saul to Paul.

Simon to Peter.

And there was another name change.

One I'd completely forgotten.

"No, he didn't have a Biblical name like me. Although I do have three half-brothers named Mark, Luke and John."

"And Matthew?"

Something changed in him when I said the name. Some insignificant difference in his expression. Some flicker of acknowledgment, like I'd hit the target dead on.

I lay there, bruised and broken, unable to move quickly.

Barely able to move at all.

Matthew Muñoz. Ricardo Muñoz's son.

The boy my sister had tripped on her way to the boat.

The boy who was trying to rescue his brother. The boy who sat in front of me, ready to take his revenge.

It hadn't been Nick who had snuck back into my house, pushed me down the stairs and left me to die.

It hadn't been Max.

Levi took my bowl of soup, placed it on the bedside table and stared at it.

My mother had made the soup from scratch and with Nick in custody, I hadn't thought to test it. I thought it was safe. My mother called Levi to sit with me while she went out. She gave him her door code.

With Levi in charge the soup was probably rich with peanut oil. Levi stared at it like he weighed his options. Like he was figuring out his Plan B. Like I'd figured things out too soon.

He turned to me. He smiled.

Greasy. Wide. Evil.

A thump to my gut.

Because I'd only ever seen that particular smile on my kidnappers' faces.

The urge to laugh challenged me. But I fought it off, for fear that my terrifying laugh would turn into a scream.

He'd hidden that smile from me on purpose. He knew I'd recognize it. He'd hidden the tattoo. He'd hidden his real hair color whenever a security camera was nearby. How could I have been so stupid? How could I not have seen?

"Yes, there is a Matthew. Well, there was a Matthew."

He took the Bible from me and flipped through the pages. "What gave it away?"

"What do you mean?" I asked. But the veneer was gone, there was no more charade.

He no longer smiled.

He handed me the Bible. It was open to Leviticus. "Chapter 24, verses 19-22."

Not Deuteronomy. Not the verse the Muñoz family used to justify their stealing, their drug dealing and their kidnapping. But the numbers were the same.

"Read it aloud," he said.

I cleared my throat and a tiny laugh slipped out. "Anyone who injures another person must be dealt with according to the injury inflicted—a fracture for a fracture, an eye for an eye, a tooth for a tooth. Whatever anyone does to injure another person must be paid back in kind. Whoever kills an animal must pay for it in full, but whoever kills another person must be put to death.

"It's Old Testament," I said quickly, hoping to dispel his flawed logic. "Jesus changed this—"

"Old Testament was my parents' favorite. And justice, as my mother always said, must be served. In fact, this whole thing was my mother's idea. She knew I would have done anything for her." His tone was emotionless, automatic.

"She'd named me Matthew, which means Gift of the Lord. But after Alejandro was murdered, she changed my name to Levi, which means 'to take.' The reverse, of course, of what Jesus had done with Levi's name. He changed Levi's name to Matthew when he became a disciple. One's purpose is reflected in one's name. She said that when I was old enough, when we finally found you, we would take from you what you took from us. You took my father's life, my uncles' lives, my brother's life, so it is only fair."

"Eye for an eye," I whispered.

"Eye for an eye," he echoed. "It's justice."

He took the wheelchair and moved it all the way to the other side of the room.

"How did you find me?" I asked.

"You all did quite a remarkable job of staying hidden. In fact, I almost gave up. I searched for a long time, many years. I hired private investigators, I used online services, but you all were nowhere to be found. But then, as luck would have it, a behemoth search engine corporation decided to get into the medical field.

"SearchIt sold hundreds of thousands of hospital groups, doctors' practices and urgent care facilities all over the country on how their system would allow doctors to diagnose their patients more quickly, more accurately by having immediate access to any patient's information. As well as other patients' information.

"All they had to do was pay a monthly fee and turn their records over, en masse, to SearchIt. Of course, they did. They are. In droves. I recommended the resource to each hospital I worked with. Because I knew all of you would end up in that data collection.

"I didn't have a way to get your new last names. So I decided I needed your social security numbers. It took several tries. As luck would have it, there's always some government employee who is willing to sell out for a few bucks. I found someone who needed money. For a total of two hundred and fifty grand, he gave me the social security number of each woman who testified against my father.

"I searched the system regularly. It took some time. Then, as I thought, each of you eventually visited a health-care institution that had shared your most confidential information with SearchIt. I decided not to make a move until I had all of your addresses, until I'd thoroughly studied your habits and your history." He walked across the room and fiddled with the walker that was folded against the wall.

"Imagine my surprise when I learned that you and I not only lived in the same town, but in the same neighborhood.

I decided that I wanted to know if it was you who had driven the boat. I wanted to know if it was you who had tripped me, trampled over me, kicked me. I wanted to know who stopped me from rescuing Alejandro, my baby brother.

"I figured you would only open up to me if you trusted me. So, I pursued you. When that didn't work, Nick appeared. Along with his history. I thought it would be an easy frame."

I shook my head.

Levi flexed his forearm with a fist, the name Alejandro tattooed in blue ink on the top of his wrist.

His mouth broadened into a ghastly grin. His eyes darkened into pools of liquid death.

I said nothing.

He pushed the walker toward the door and I realized what he was about to do.

"Why not just kill me when you killed the others?" I asked, trying to keep him talking as much as I could. To buy as much time as I could. In case my mother was on her way.

"I thought that you were going to tell me sooner as to whether you had driven the boat."

I didn't know what he was talking about. My breath came so fast my head spun. I forced my breathing down and tightened my stomach. I searched the room frantically and tried to figure how I would get out of this.

"The Mexican restaurant," he said to my unasked question. "I slipped peanut oil into your margarita. But then you said we'd talk and I thought I'd give you a chance."

He reached for my hand. "Now be careful getting out of bed. A broken pelvis makes one unsteady."

I scooted away from him. "You're the one who's been taking care of me today. Don't you think they'll pin this on you?"

"Oh that's right, you haven't had your phone. So you don't know. Nick Smith or Chamberlain or whatever his name is, was released from jail last night. I think he's going to be the one they suspect. You'll take a nasty fall over the railing just like his ex-wife did. I'll say I stepped out. That I wasn't here when it happened."

He hoisted me out of bed and I twisted away from him. He dropped me. Crippling pain shot through my hips. I screamed and swung my arm and smacked him in the head with my cast as hard as I could.

Levi cried out in pain and stumbled back.

I kicked my foot with the cast on it into his crotch. Levi fell to the floor.

I scrambled over the bed, landed on the floor on the other side and searched beneath the mattress. Taped to the metal frame was an EpiPen I'd hidden after they were stolen the first time.

By the time I got myself upright, Levi was mobile again and coming at me. Blood ran down his face where I'd clocked him in the forehead, and he was slightly doubled over. Even injured, he was stronger and faster than I was.

His arms were outstretched, His hands aimed for my neck.

My good arm down at my side, I flicked off the orange cap with my thumb and as soon as he was close enough I jammed the auto-injector into his hand.

Levi screamed, held his hand close.

I tried to get away. He grabbed me by the broken arm and threw me to the floor.

He towered over me, breathing hard, rubbing his hand. The area where I stabbed him turned white.

"Enough!" He reached down, seized my leg with his

good hand, his grip painfully strong. He dragged me toward the door.

I tried to scream but it came out garbled and stuttering. I snatched at everything in sight—table legs, bed legs, the carpet. Finally I got ahold of the leg of the armchair.

He pulled me into the hallway, the chair stuck in the doorway and he stomped on my wrist until finally I let go.

"Stop it!" I screamed.

He pulled me upright, twisted my good arm behind my back and positioned me at the top of the spiral staircase. The railing pressed against my thighs. I didn't know how I could survive another fall.

Levi shoved me headfirst over the railing.

Three loud pops sounded like fireworks.

44

It was a wee hour in the morning by the time my mother and I were home from the hospital and the last policeman left. My mother called Tim and Leo and they ripped up the blood-stained hardwoods where Levi had fallen and bled to death.

When Levi shoved me down the stairs, I'd managed to grab ahold of the railing and held on.

Agent Hernandez had gotten the entry code from my mother and arrived in time to fire three rounds into Levi's chest. Then he caught me just after I slipped from the railing.

I'd ripped my once-good shoulder from its socket. And I smashed my face against the railing, which gave me several new contusions and new fractures on my cheeks and forehead. I still didn't need pins or plates.

Thank God.

Agent Hernandez was there when we got home.

When we were settled in the living room, I asked, "Did you have any luck reaching Sophie's mother?" I still hoped to have solid proof to use against Max.

He shook his head. "I left a message on her voicemail and didn't hear back. I'll try again tomorrow. Or considering the time, later today, I guess."

"What about the guy who sold our social security numbers to Levi? Do you know who this man is?"

His features turned to iron, like he braced himself against darkness and hardship. "He was my partner. I'll make sure Chatham County police know who to talk to." He patted me gently on the shoulder. "But there is a lot of corruption in the Bureau. And I was the one who was fired. So the Director might say that my former partner defended the entire justice system by reporting me. The Director might even promote the guy."

The news made me sad. Although not hopeless. "Well, I don't want that."

Two weeks ago my instinct would have been to recoil from his touch or to remind him that because of him I'd lost my sister. But tonight I asked him for a hug. "Thank you," I whispered in his ear. "Thank you."

My father was still at his hotel. I told my mother not to alert him. She agreed and didn't ask why.

I always wondered how much she knew about who he really was.

She fell asleep in my bed after I said I didn't want to go up the half-staircase again. Or anytime soon.

Downstairs, alone on the couch, I expected to feel lonely or at least a little afraid, but I didn't. One very long and very torturous chapter of my life had closed forever.

Matthew was gone.

I felt relief. I felt an awful lot of physical pain, but mostly I felt relief.

I also felt sad, because in spite of all that was still unresolved, I missed Nick. I missed the sound of his voice, the comfort of his touch. I missed his presence that, inexplicably, made me feel like my true self.

It was late. I picked up the phone and called him anyway.

No answer.

Maybe he had his ringer off.

I sent a text: Can you talk?

No answer.

I wondered if he was angry with me.

I stared into Columbia Square with its moon glow and flickering gas lamps and bubbling fountain. From my angle on the couch, I suddenly realized something.

My sister pointing toward the back corner of the green... She wasn't pointing to where she came into the square or to where the fog rolled up.

She had pointed to Levi's home.

Tears burned in my eyes. My heart swelled with emotion.

And the watch.

She hadn't pointed to the watch. She referenced the tattoo beneath the watch.

Across the green, Bunny sat in her cannonball room reading a book next to a single lamp. She didn't sleep much. She'd been a very good friend and neighbor throughout the ordeal: checking on me, bringing food and talking with my mother.

I thought Bunny was right. Whoever tried to kill Sophie was the same person who killed Piper.

I felt a kinship to the two women. I could have ended up like either one. And very nearly did.

I wished I hadn't called or sent the text to Nick. I still didn't have proof of his innocence where Sophie and Piper were concerned.

I thought of my twin. How she'd come to me when I needed her most. I wasn't sure what I had left of the life I tried to make for myself, I didn't know if I would be able to stay in Savannah. Or if Nick and I had any future. But I knew I had her. As always, my sister was on my side.

I wanted a cup of tea to help me sleep. But I didn't want to deal with the pain that came from ambling across the house to get it. So I drank from the glass of water my mother had left on the folding tray next to the couch.

I picked up the book that Bunny's husband had written: *Midnight Murder, The Mysteries of Cumberland Island.*

It was a thick book. The story was based on actual events, so there were photographs of Cumberland Island and Piper's murder in the middle. There were also police reports.

All photo credits were attributed to newspapers and magazines. With the exception of one from the Chatham County Coroner's Office.

I stared at Piper in her final pose—lying in the wooded area where she had been killed. Her lifeless body lay in an unnatural position, arms and legs sprawled at bent angles.

Her head was twisted up and to the side, her mouth and eyes wide open, tongue swollen and protruding and strangulation marks visible around her neck where she had been choked to death.

Her ripped panties clung around her right ankle. Her breasts and her privates were covered by two black rectangles. The caption said there were traces of spermicide, and no evidence of sperm or a condom at the scene.

Police surmised that the murderer had worn a condom, perhaps one lubricated with spermicide, which eliminated identifiable DNA, and taken it with him. Also indicating that the encounter began as a romantic one. Because rapists didn't typically wear condoms. The police used this angle to point the finger at Nick, since he and Piper had been dating at the time.

The first few chapters went into great detail about the investigation, how it was largely nonexistent because all of the teenagers had alibis, and each of them told the same story. Piper had gone off by herself, upset that she was still in love with Max, while he had moved on with Charlotte. When the teenagers went to look for her, they did so in small groups. That was when the story of a vagrant or stranger, and a crime based on happenstance or opportunity, was born.

The next photo was a close and haunting shot of Piper's neck and face. The caption emphasized the absence of ligature marks. Red circles drawn on the photo pointed out thumb bruising at the neck and finger-sized bruises, indicating Piper had been throttled or manually strangled. I squinted at several tiny marks below the red imprints.

I hobbled into the kitchen on my crutch with the book tucked under my arm. I flipped on the under-the-cabinet lights. I took a large magnifying glass from the junk drawer and held it over the photo. The mark was unmistakable. At least to me, because I'd seen it before. On my own neck, and Sophie's.

I took my crutch and hobbled around the green toward Bunny's house. Navigating my way over the uneven bricks was horrifyingly treacherous. One fall would either displace my pelvis so that I would need pins and plates, or turn my facial fractures into full-blown breaks that would likely change the appearance of my face forever.

I didn't stop until I reached Bunny's front door and rang the bell.

She opened the door. "What on God's green earth—"

"I need to see all the photos you have from the night Piper was killed," I blurted before she could say anything else.

Bunny waved for me to come in and I doddered right past her and headed toward the cannonball room.

"I think I know who killed Piper, and who tried to kill Sophie," I said breathlessly. "But I need to see the photos from that night to be certain. All of them."

Bunny helped me to sit. Then she opened the bottom drawer of the secretary and sifted through the morass of photographs. When she didn't think she made progress fast enough, she dropped to her knees and yanked the entire drawer onto the floor.

"They're mostly in the back, I think. At the bottom. No one has looked at all of them in over twenty years." She pulled out a stack of ten photos or so. Then another stack that was roughly the same size. She handed them to me.

I studied them under the light of her singular lamp.

45

———————

Three days later I rang the front doorbell of Charlotte and Max's beautiful home on Montgomery Square, and waited.

I watched through the glass on the side of her front door. Charlotte finally came halfway down the front staircase. She stood there. Stared at me for a good thirty seconds. Then she came the rest of the way down the stairs and opened the front door.

"My, my. Looks like you've had a rough go of it lately." She gestured to my broken bones. "Is this Nick's doing? I won't get you in to see Sophie again if that's why you're here."

I waved a small manila envelope. "Mind if we speak for a moment?"

Her wise-ass smile fell until it rested in a flat line. "If this is a rehashing of your baseless accusations about my husband, you can—"

I reached into the envelope and pulled out the group photo of the gathering at Cumberland Island. "My accusations aren't baseless. And you might be interested in what I know."

After a moment she reluctantly stepped back and gestured that I should come inside.

Her front room was just as I'd seen it on her social media video. Formal. Elegant. Historic.

I sat on the edge of the couch to the right of the door. It was the first time I'd sat without elevating my broken leg and it throbbed.

"See this photo?" I asked Charlotte. "It's from the night that Piper was killed. And this one?"

I showed her the photo of all the girls standing arm in arm in front of the ocean. Piper held a sun-yellow parasol. Maribelle wore a vintage scarf.

Charlotte shrugged.

"It's from the same night. Everyone wore some item in a nod to their Southern heritage."

"We were teenagers. Looking for a reason to party. To be away from our parents for a night."

"No, I quite agree. Very nice. Good thing to show pride in your personal history." I tapped the photo. "What did you wear?"

She shrugged again. "I wasn't really into the whole costume thing. I just went because Max asked me to go."

I held up the next photo of the girls making a toast with their red plastic cups.

"What about this photo?"

Her eyes took on a steely shine. "What about it?"

"Everyone was drinking that night. Except for you. You just held a cup. Why is that?"

She nodded like she'd had enough. "Shouldn't you be out looking for a job?"

"I also read the police reports from that night. You were very keen to tell the detectives that you hadn't been drinking. You mentioned it several times. Because you wanted to be the one they listened to, isn't that right? You wanted to be the one who spoke for the group. Why was that?"

She rolled her eyes. "This is all ancient history."

"Why were you so insistent to take control and drive the narrative that night? Were you protecting someone?"

She crossed her arms, stood quiet, still.

"If we count backward from the date of your daughter's birth, we find that you were already pregnant that night on Cumberland Island."

"Our daughter was premature by two months."

"No. She wasn't. The photo of your daughter on Max's office bookshelf shows her wrapped in a hospital blanket on a hospital baby bed. 12/16 is written on the card that's stuck to the hospital crib, her birthdate. Along with her birth-weight: 7lbs 6oz."

Charlotte rolled her eyes again.

"7lbs, 6oz isn't a preemie birthweight. That's a full-term birthweight. Do you see where I'm going with this?"

Charlotte stood. At her six-foot height, I half expected her to grab me by the arm, throw me to the floor and stomp on my neck.

Instead, she sat in the nearest chair. A rocking chair.

Back and forth, back and forth.

Her face expressionless.

"I think you were already pregnant with your daughter on the night Piper was killed, and that's why you weren't drinking."

Charlotte didn't respond.

I shifted my weight on the couch, my leg and hip swelling and screaming in pain. "Somehow you and Max managed to get together. From what I've heard, you were heartsick for him for an awfully long time. But it took a while before he came around, didn't it? I'm guessing he didn't even seriously consider you until he was between relationships. Probably after Sophie and before he knew Piper was still interested.

"Knowing Max, I would guess he was a hard sell for you, wasn't he? You just weren't his type. He liked Maribelle, he liked Sophie, he liked Piper. He likes petite girls. Girls who are smaller than him. Someone who makes him feel big and tall. Which would be hard for you considering his height. Or the lack thereof.

"He has small hands, small feet. You probably intimidated him. You must have had to throw yourself at him in order to get him to sleep with you. I would guess you had to get him into a situation where he decided there wasn't a reason to say no.

"What I haven't quite figured out, though—not that it matters—is if you set him up. Did you time it just right so that you would get pregnant? You must have known that was what it would take to keep him. Or was the pregnancy unplanned?"

She said nothing, but the chair squeaked with each rocking motion.

"Did he know that night at Cumberland Island that you were already pregnant?"

She stopped rocking. "Yes."

"See, that's what I thought. And being the seventeen-year-old boy he was, that wasn't what Max wanted, was it? He wanted to go to college, make something of himself. But you changed all that.

"I think...when Piper announced to everyone that she still loved Max, you didn't think much of it. Not initially. And even when he followed her, I don't think you were worried. Because you were pregnant! And he knew you were pregnant!

"But as the clock ticked and they didn't come back, you had to wonder if you'd lost him. You had to know that if Piper threw herself at him, Max would take advantage of that opportunity.

"Because that's what he did with you. Right?

"That's the big drawback that comes from winning someone by cheating. You can never trust them. You went after them that night and you found them. Max and Piper. Together."

"Max didn't kill Piper," she said.

"No, I don't think he did. Max is a lot of things. He's weak. He's shallow. He's...sick. But deep down I don't know if he could actually kill someone. You, on the other hand—"

Charlotte laughed aloud and began rocking again. "Well, I certainly didn't kill Piper."

"I think you did, and I have proof. See this photo? And these?" I laid about seven photos on the coffee table. All of them featured Charlotte somewhere in the frame.

She leaned forward and looked at them. "So?"

"Look at your hand. The garnet ring. That's the Civil War item you wore that night. Your salute to your heritage. Which was just your style. I doubt your parents would have knowingly let you take the ring. But I guess you slipped it out of its display case without them knowing. No one would have noticed it missing for 24 hours.

"Here's the thing. Your hands are...large. Bigger than the average female hand. So, you wore the garnet ring on your middle finger. See?" I pointed to her hand in the photos.

"Max has smaller hands. He wears the garnet ring on his thumb. Always has. I looked at almost every episode of Hidden Treasures where Max was the resident expert, even the episodes from several years ago. He always wore that ring on his thumb."

"You're rambling."

"I'm guessing that you decided to look for Max and Piper in the woods because you knew. You knew that Piper still loved Max and that she was heartbroken over your engagement. You knew that Max didn't want to marry you and Max didn't want the baby. You knew how things would go if Max and Piper had time alone.

"And that's exactly what happened. That's why the coroner said there was evidence of spermicide and sexual intercourse.

"You must have caught them in the act. Knowing Max, he probably took off when you showed up. Left so fast he didn't even remove the condom."

Charlotte's mouth tipped on one side in a smirk. Like she remembered something that amused her. "Not entirely right."

She stood and extended her hand. "Give me your phone."

"What?"

"Give me your phone."

I took my phone out of my pocket and handed it to her.

"Unlock it," she said.

I tapped in the code and offered her the phone again.

She flipped through it, probably checking to make sure I wasn't recording our conversation. When she was satisfied, she turned it off and put it on the table.

A light sparkled in her eye. A flash of desire that said she relished this rare moment. Maybe she knew this was her only chance to brag to another soul about how brilliant she'd been to not get caught.

Charlotte eyed me for a long minute.

Weighing the risk, I supposed.

She walked to the window, her eyes scanning the area.

I said not a word.

When she turned to me, the polished, pearl-wearing persona she'd always put forth was gone. In its place was something plain and hard.

"I found them, like you said. Piper laughed when she saw me. She told me to go away. She said that she was the one Max wanted. I said that wasn't true. But then she said he'd told her about the pregnancy and that it didn't matter. She said he was going to tell me after that night."

"What happened to the condom?"

"When Max realized that I'd found them, he scrambled off of her then tucked her behind him. He gave her her dress and shielded her while he pulled on his pants. He told me to leave. That it was over between us."

"He protected her," I said, knowing that was something he would never have thought to do for Charlotte.

Charlotte's eyes hardened. "Max said he was sorry. That he would pay for an abortion. He said he wasn't going to marry me. He said he didn't love me.

"I told Max that if Piper was who he wanted, that I wasn't going to try and change his mind. I told him I wanted a moment alone with her. I told him I just wanted to talk. Then he turned to her, asked if that was okay.

"She kissed him, right in front of me. She stroked his face like I wasn't even there and she told him she'd be fine. Max said again that he was sorry, that in the long run I would be happier with someone else. After one last look at Piper, he walked away.

"Piper said that neither she nor Max meant to hurt me. That they didn't plan this, their feelings just were what they were. I listened, but I didn't look at her. I was watching Max walk away. About fifteen steps out I watched him stop, remove the condom and toss it into the woods.

"I strangled Piper, I found the condom. I carefully put it into my purse. When I got home I put it in a freezer bag and tucked it into the deep freezer that my mother kept in the garage. I buried it under all the venison and quail that my father brought home from his hunting trips, since I knew they weren't going to deplete that supply anytime soon.

"Later, after Max and I were married, I found a storage unit that allowed electricity. I bought my own small freezer and put the freezer bag with the condom, the one with Piper's and Max's DNA on it, inside the freezer. I even had an electrician install a small backup generator in case the power went out. It's still there—the freezer, the condom, the DNA. My little insurance policy.

"It might not be the hardcore proof it once was. But it's enough to remind Max of the penalty for cheating."

Max's expression when Charlotte walked in his office made more sense to me now. The fear. The pandering. It wasn't her money he was sucking up to, it was her. He knew what horrible things she was capable of.

"How did you figure this out?" Charlotte asked.

"That garnet ring has an unusual setting." I pulled my scarf aside and ran my finger over the front of my neck where Max had left a new scar on my neck. "And Max has an unusual interest."

Charlotte smiled a wan smile.

"When I met Sophie I saw that she had the exact same shape of scar, but on the side of her neck. I didn't think much of it until I saw the police photos of Piper. She had the same small scar in almost the exact same spot on the side of her neck. Then I saw the photo of you at Cumberland Island wearing the same Civil War ring on your third finger.

"Everyone who knew Nick kept suggesting to me that the person who throttled Piper was the same person who tried to kill Sophie. So I kept looking for clues, thinking I might find something that would connect Piper's murder with Sophie's attack.

"And I did." I dug into the small manila envelope and pulled out one last piece of paper. "Sophie was five months along when she lost her baby. So, even a year later, there was enough DNA in his bones to determine paternity."

I unfolded the paper, put it on the coffee table and pushed it toward her. I pointed to the bottom where there were two names: Baby boy Taylor was listed as the child. Maxwell B. Crandall was listed as the alleged father. The results stated: Probability of paternity: 99.999%

"Max is the father of Sophie's baby," I said. "They were having an affair and she got pregnant."

Charlotte's face reddened.

"That's one of the things I love most about studying history. It prepares you well for the future. That old adage about history repeating is true. The names change, the faces change, even the circumstances change. But it always repeats."

"Where did you get that?" Charlotte snatched the paper.

"Mrs. Taylor wanted to know if what I'd said was true. She wanted to know if Max was the father of her grandchild."

Charlotte shook her head. "No, she didn't believe you."

"Can you read?" I pointed to the paternity report. "She changed her mind when she'd had a little time to consider what I'd said. She must have wondered if I was telling the truth when I pointed out that whoever tried to kill Sophie would try again. I'm guessing you and Sophie weren't all that close before her fall. After my visit, Mrs. Taylor might have wondered if all the recent attention you've given Sophie was really about something else. Because try as you may, Charlotte, you don't really come off as the charitable type."

"What do you want?" she growled and threw the paper on the table. "Do you want money?"

"I want you to set the record straight. I want you to start by making sure that scumbag husband of yours stays away from me. I want you to make sure he destroys those photos that he took of Nick and me."

She scoffed. "The photos are digital, he's not the only one Sophie sent them to. They could be anywhere by now."

"Then he'd better be careful to tell the truth about me and my professional reputation should anyone ever ask him." I pointed toward the paternity report.

"Anything else?"

"I want you to set the record straight about Nick. I want you to clear his name once and for all. Which means you need to confess to the fact that you killed Piper and tried to kill Sophie."

Charlotte laughed. "Sure. No problem." She stared at my casts. She was sizing up my frailties.

I dangled the paternity report in the air. "This isn't my only copy."

Charlotte stood next to me, her height and size even more intimidating than they had been at Max's office. Today I could neither defend myself nor run.

"I am curious about one last thing," I said, feeling the need to buy time. "Did you set Max up by wearing the ring when you strangled Sophie? Or were you just careless?"

Charlotte stood.

"Sophie actually thought Max loved her. She thought if

she told me about the baby that I'd give him the divorce. It wasn't that difficult to impersonate Nick."

She clicked her tongue against the roof of her mouth.

"Now. What to do with you, you stupid girl?" Quicker than light, Charlotte grabbed my ankle and jerked me off of the couch and onto the floor. The pain was a lot more than I was prepared for, and as much as it hurt, no noise escaped my wide-open mouth.

She dragged me like a rag doll down the hallway, the burgundy hall runner bunching up beneath my back. "I hope you like the cold. Because I'm going to put you in the cold storage until I can figure out what to do with you. While you're in there you might want to think about—"

"Hernandez!!" I screamed.

"Why are you—?" Realization smoothed the angry lines on her face.

I scuttled away from her like a crippled crab, not creating nearly enough distance fast enough, because she grabbed ahold of my shirt with both hands and ripped it open. Plastic buttons clattered on the hardwoods.

"Hernandez!" I screamed again.

The microphone was fully visible. So was the fury in her eyes. Her head shook, almost imperceptibly like a tremor. Then it stopped. Calmness seemed to wash over her. A flood of terror came over me.

"Hurry!" I screamed and scrabbled and clawed my way to the front door.

She straightened, turned to the newel at the bottom of the stairs. She lifted the hexagon finial, the same one where she'd filmed the mortgage button.

She pulled out a gun, aimed at me and fired.

46

———

I sat just inside the open ambulance.

Three medics fussed over me. One dabbed at blood on the side of my head. One inspected my casts. One took my vitals.

I studied the beautiful and historic Tatnall-Crandall house and wondered what had made Charlotte the way she was. She was attractive and wealthy. At one time she'd had a bright future.

Maybe her father cheated on her mother. Maybe Charlotte's father withheld his affection from her. Maybe like my sister and me, she'd been abused.

Someone somewhere had not done their best by her.

I'd never know for sure.

Agent Hernandez walked up. He stood on the road and faced me. Arms crossed, thin smile.

"You were late," I said to him.

His eyebrows raised, his mouth fell open. A subtle tell of his. He didn't like it when I was upset with him.

He gestured across the front lawn where Max stood surrounded by several cops. Blood was spattered down the front of Max's shirt. His nose and mouth were bloody and quite swollen. It looked like Max was listening to the recording.

"He came home right as Charlotte yanked you onto the floor, right as we were crossing the lawn. He got in our way. So, I got in his way."

Hernandez crossed his arms. He exhaled fully. His lips pulled into a satisfied smile.

There was a confident aura about him. A settledness I'd never known him to have before.

"You did good," he said. "You did great. You okay?" He nodded to my casts.

"Yeah," I said and swiped at the medic who poked at the stitches on the side of my head.

Hernandez and I laughed.

Then we looked at one another for a long time.

No words.

Just lost in each other's gaze.

Time traveling.

Back to the beginning when we first met.

Through all the terror that followed.

I saw Hernandez standing in my parents' living room all those years ago. Examining the We Will letter, reading it aloud, declaring it for what it had been. A threat. A promise. Revenge.

Levi must have known about the We Will letter. His mother would have told him about it. Maybe his mother had been the one to fashion it out of all those cut-out letters. Maybe Levi's mother had orchestrated the pipe bomb left on my front porch, the one that exploded onto my lap. Maybe she had been the one to wrap it in birthday paper. Or to deliver it to my doorstep.

I would never know.

What I did know was that the nightmare which began over twenty years ago was finally over. There had been no shortcuts.

Hernandez and I time traveled further.

Until we reached today.

This moment.

In spite of the pain vibrating through my body, I felt it.

A change in atmosphere.

Everything was different. Everything looked different. I was different.

The anxiety that had plagued me since I was a child was gone.

Most of it left when I realized I had to kick my father out of my life. The rest of it left when Levi, otherwise known as Matthew, died at the foot of my stairs.

"Good," Hernandez said simply. Like he took my word for it. Like it was his wish for me. Like it was his blessing.

The police put Max into handcuffs and he objected loudly. He wrestled against the cop. They finally dropped him to the ground and one of the cops placed his boot in the middle of Max's back.

It was a very satisfying moment.

Charlotte walked out of the front door, also in handcuffs and with police escorts.

Hernandez took a photo of each of them. "Good chance they'll both serve time. Thanks to you."

I flashed back to Hernandez busting my front door down, shooting Levi, catching me before I hit the floor. "Thank you," I said, referring to so much more than the role he'd played in the arrests that day.

He nodded.

I thought his expression softened just a bit. I thought his eyes were about to tear up.

But he was too strong for that.

His phone buzzed and he looked at its screen. He put his hand on my good knee, gave it a squeeze, then disappeared around the side of the ambulance.

"We'll need to take you to the hospital for a few scans," one of the medics said.

"No," I said. "I'm going to turn radioactive if I have any more scans. Just get me that wheelchair from the police van so I can go home."

"I'll help you."

I turned and saw Nick walking up with Agent Hernandez.

"Nick," I whispered.

He appeared to me as he often had: strong, self-made, confident. I also saw what I was only beginning to understand: his vulnerabilities and his secrets.

Agent Hernandez gave me a wink, then walked away.

One of the medics brought the wheelchair over to me.

Nick helped me out of the ambulance and into the chair. He kneeled in front of me and asked me about my injuries.

"What are you doing here?" I asked.

"I guess I could ask you the same question." His dark brown eyes broke past every wall and saw right into the deepest parts of me. How his eyes had the power to touch me, to make me feel. Like he had some supernatural ability.

"How about we go for a walk? Or...a ride?" he asked.

He got behind the wheelchair and pushed me toward the middle of Monterey Square. The white Italian marble statue dedicated to General Pulaski stretched high to the treetops. A warm breeze meandered through the branches of the great oaks.

He turned the chair to face one of the gray wooden

benches. He sat directly across from me and leaned on his knees.

"Agent Hernandez called the hotel where I've been staying and let me know what happened."

"I called you," I said.

"The police still have my phone. And my computer. And a few other things. My attorney said she ought to get them today or tomorrow. But she said that yesterday, too."

We kept looking at one another. No one said anything.

I saw his pulse beating in his neck.

So many words wanting to be said. So many questions burning to be asked. So many things building up behind a dam, trying to find a way through.

Finally, he drew in a deep breath.

"That's quite a thing you did there." He gestured to Charlotte and Max's house. "Took a lot of bravery. And surviving all the attempts on your life...you've been through a lot."

"Yeah." I looked at my hands, then back at him. In this new life where there wasn't a Muñoz chasing me, all the inexplicable things in his background tugged at me.

"There were so many things pointing at you. Circumstantial, I know that now. I'm sorry I suspected you."

He shrugged. Grinned. "Story of my life."

We chuckled.

A squirrel scampered close and watched us.

"Someone tried to kill you. You had to suspect everyone."

"You are from Miami," I said.

"I lived there with my mom until I was about twelve."

"And your dad?" I asked.

He shrugged. "My mom was in love. She thought it was

forever. When she told him she was pregnant, he left. She never saw him again."

"What about the newspaper article in your files? How did you know who I was?" The dam was broken. The words were flowing now.

"I didn't, not with any certainty. You and the others who were kidnapped had your photos all over the front page of the paper for about a year or so. My mom, like everybody else in Miami, read everything she could get her hands on about that story.

"When you and your sister escaped, there was another front page article with this huge photo of you before the kidnapping, and next to it was a more recent photo of you with the scars." He stroked the side of his neck.

"The truth came out about the compound, the drugs and the kids in cages, and how the police had screwed up. They didn't follow up on viable leads and kids died. My mom sat me on the couch one night. She held the front page article in her hand, pointed at your photo and said, 'We have to leave, Nicky. We have to leave because Miami is not a safe place to raise a family anymore.'"

I tilted my head back. Sunlight poured through the branches of the water oaks. I'd always felt that he knew me. He did. In more ways than one.

"We moved to Savannah, the story died down. One day I asked what happened to you. My mom and grandmother said you and your family were probably in witness protection. Because drug families had long memories and lots of connections. I remember feeling sad that I would never see you again.

"Years later you and I met and, maybe it was because I'd spent so much time staring at that newspaper photo of the twelve-year-old you, but I thought I recognized you."

Something settled inside of me. Like puzzle pieces finally coming together.

"I wrote off that feeling. But there were little signs I couldn't ignore. Like the time you switched out your contacts at my office. You didn't know I was there, but I saw that you had blue eyes, not brown."

He lightly traced my jawline with his knuckle. "The shape of your face was familiar. You use a dark hair dye. Most women use contacts and hair dye to lighten their eyes and hair. Then I saw the scars along your neck. I knew you had to be the girl I'd seen in the paper all those years ago. I researched those old articles and downloaded one with both photos."

We looked at one another for the longest time.

No tears. No words. No fears.

Before I could forge another thought, he gently gathered me into his arms.

"I love you," he whispered.

"I love you, too."

Emily Bronte's line from *Wuthering Heights* floated up from my library within, "Whatever our souls are made of, his and mine are the same."

I HAD TOLD my mother that I didn't want my father anywhere near me or my house. But my father was there when Hernandez, Nick and I returned. I didn't blame her. I didn't own the deed to the house. I didn't own my life. My father still had guardianship.

He stood out front next to the moving van, next to the movers. He appeared in control, as usual.

While I was unloaded into my wheelchair from a police van, looking frail, as usual.

With Magnolia sitting at her feet, my mother stood in the threshold of my front door, her hands clasped together in front of her.

Hernandez helped to situate me in the wheelchair and I quietly asked him to share how I'd helped the police and got Charlotte to confess. I asked him to share what we'd learned about Nick.

I didn't know if he would. Historically he'd always deferred to my father.

To my surprise and before he answered, his features evened out with a calm strength. Like he recognized an opportunity to stand up for the underdog. To right a wrong. To impart justice.

He told my father the story in full, right there in front of Nick, my mother and the movers. "And Harper figured out who Piper's murderer was," Agent Hernandez said proudly. "Which also cleared Nick's name. Charlotte fired her weapon right at Harper, tried to kill her." Hernandez put a protective arm around me. "Harper deserves a medal for bravery."

My father smiled but his eyes were chilled and dark. He stepped toward me like it was expected of him and he kissed my cheek. His lips were cold and lifeless. He stepped back.

I asked for my crutch. Then I hobbled close to my father. I got right up to his face and whispered in a low tone, "I now have all of Chatham County Police to testify to my wisdom, insight and bravery. By tomorrow and for some time, I'll have reporters begging for my story. It will probably get international coverage.

"I'm hiring an attorney today. So you will sign over to me the deed to my house, the rest of my inheritance, and you will drop all claims to guardianship over me. If you don't, I'll sue you. I will make known, in a very, *very* public way, what you did to me—and my sister—when we were young.

"When I'm through telling my story, and I will tell it often, no one in their right mind, least of all a judge, will blame me for those scars on your arm. So don't even bother lifting your sleeve."

I backed away and watched with long-awaited satisfaction as my father's normally tan face blanched.

47

When I was on the couch again and in a way that I was finally comfortable, my mother sat next to me and held my hand the way she used to when I was little.

"I've asked the police to share the recording of Charlotte's confession with Sophie's parents," Hernandez said.

"I hope they don't sue me for making up that paternity report. I knew it was the only way I'd get Charlotte to confess," I said.

"The report was faked, but not the truth," Nick said.

"Once Mrs. Taylor and her husband hear that recording, I have a feeling that the newspaper they own will want to tell the story about who the real perpetrator is."

Agent Hernandez received a call from the District Attorney's office who asked for a meeting with him and Nick.

I was left in my home with my mother.

I was just about to tell her what my father had done years ago when she said, "I told him last night I was leaving him."

"What?"

She nodded. "It's been a hard road for a long time now. I decided there was no point in doing it anymore."

"I'm glad," I finally said. "If you are."

She nodded, her smile was a bit sad.

"Where will you live?" I asked.

"I wanted to talk with you about that. If you don't mind, I think I'd like to move to Savannah to be close to you. I don't have to live next door or anything. And I won't move here if you don't want me to. If my being here makes you feel like I've descended into your life with Nick, then I'll figure something else out. But Bunny and I have developed a nice friendship, and—Well, it just feels like a good fit."

"Of course I want you here," I said. I thought of the condo that Levi left behind and I wondered if we could buy it, gut it, remove all traces of him and make it new for her.

We held each other and cried. For the first time in many years, I felt we were rekindling the relationship we'd once had with one another.

When our tears dried, she grew quiet and I knew there was something else she wanted to say. She went to my bedroom where she'd been sleeping and returned with something clasped in her hands. She sat beside me on the couch. Her face was slightly ashen.

"When Agent Hernandez called to say that someone had pushed you down the stairs, when he said that someone had tried to kill you by putting jellyfish into your pool, that you'd gone into cardiac arrest, I thought it was the end." She opened her hands to show me two full dental molds, upper and lower of my sister's and my teeth.

"Oh my gosh, I thought you didn't keep these?"

"Neither did I." She laughed, kind of a helpless cry. "But I tell you. I hung up that call and I went right up to the attic. I didn't wonder where they were. I just thought, okay, I'm going to have to identify my daughter's body and this is what I have to do. Isn't that strange? I mean, all that time searching for them when you asked for them years ago, and I never could find them. Then one day, without even thinking about it, I just went to the box where they were and pulled them out. I found x-rays, too."

I turned the dental molds over in my hands, marveling at the lone enduring proof of Catherine's existence. It was proof I'd searched for, for an awfully long time. The word Harper was written on the upper and lower set of one mold. The name Catherine was written on the other, both in black sharpie.

"Of course I didn't need those molds to identify Catherine because—" She squeezed her eyes shut and I knew she was imagining my sister's headless, limbless body.

"Mom," I said.

She didn't answer. She just laid her hand on mine without saying a word, without opening her eyes.

I knew the memories were still too much to bear, I knew she still suffered.

She opened her eyes. They were watery and the look in them was far away.

"Mom," I said. "There's something I need to tell you."

And then I told my mother.

I didn't care about telling my father.

He'd find out soon enough anyway.

As luck would have it, every local, regional and national publication did want Nick's and my story. Nick and I were asked to do interviews. We agreed we would do one together. We agreed that we would charge an exorbitant amount of money for our story. We agreed that we would donate that money to a non-profit group that helped sexual abuse survivors.

The public interest in everything from the kidnapping to my escape, to my solving Piper's murder and everything in between, was so extraordinary that I had several offers from reputable publishing houses to write my story. After much deliberation, I decided to write a book about it all under my own name.

Then, in a blessed touch of fate, customers began to move their business away from Tatnall Antique Appraisals in droves. Nick and I decided to open Smith Appraisal House in the heart of Savannah's historic district.

Bunny said she knew the perfect location. That it wasn't a large space, but it was elegant. She owned the building and wanted to rent it to us.

My mother asked if she could work the front office and keep the books.

Nick and I agreed that he would appraise the furniture items and I would appraise the jewelry. We agreed to staff and oversee a restoration division.

THE GAS LAMPS came on at dusk in Columbia Square.

Nick waited for me across the green with a bottle of red wine and two glasses at his side.

The wedding coordinator signaled for Tim to flip the switch.

Hundreds, maybe thousands of tiny white lights illuminated the branches above.

It looked like magic.

Bunny gasped.

My mother pressed her hands to her chest, her breath officially taken away.

I gave the coordinator a bright smile and a nod and said, "Beautiful."

I walked barefoot toward Nick.

With the help of hyperbaric oxygen therapy, all of my breaks and fractures healed ahead of schedule. Despite the seriousness of the injuries, I didn't have a limp. My gait was normal.

I went back to my natural light brown hair color.

I threw away the brown contacts.

I looked like myself again.

I'd finally let go of those moments when I had to hide who I was, when I had to pretend to be someone else.

The ER doctors peeling away sheets of my charred skin. The open door they gave me when they asked my name. My father glaring from the corner, and the split-second decision to lie. To get out from under him.

But all of the careful phrasing, the smoke and mirrors, didn't protect me the way I expected. I still carried around this secret and wore my scars like a mask. Now, more broken than ever, I could get my life back.

I bent and pulled a dandelion. I made a wish and blew the seeds. The wind carried them to new destinations.

I wondered if my wish was the same as my sister's when she blew her dandelion.

I thought that it must have been.

Even though she and I had different personalities.

The joke in our family was that she resented being born second. That she was always coming up from behind, fighting her way forward like a half-crazed bull. Too feisty for her own good.

Nick poured the wine. He put the bottle on the ledge of

the fountain. He picked up the two glasses and watched me approach. His smile was different from what it used to be. It was happier. More easygoing. The shadows of anger were long gone.

He stood exactly where my sister had when she came to see me.

I almost thought I could still see her.

I'd thought that all scientific proof of Catherine's identity was long lost or trashed. Twenty years was a long span.

But then my mother found the dental molds and the x-rays.

We didn't know for certain if it would be enough. But my mother helped and together we learned that no two people have the exact same teeth.

Teeth are as unique as a fingerprint.

With the help of an attorney, and a judge who understood why I did what I did, we obtained all the proper legal documents.

I finally had what I wanted.

Nick handed me a glass of wine. "Are you ready for tomorrow? Is there anything you need?"

I placed my hand in his. "There is one thing."

"Anything. Ask away," he said.

"I want you to call me by my real name. Call me Catherine."

EPILOGUE

It was an evening wedding.

White fairy lights that looked like stars clung to tree branches.

Ivory candles in silver candelabras illuminated Columbia Square.

I wore my red crinoline dress while I stood next to my beautiful twin sister Catherine on her wedding day.

She wore delicate ivory silk with a long train and a beautiful veil anchored by a half-crown of small, white flowers. Catherine held fast to the arm of the man named Hernandez, since our father had lost the privilege of giving her away.

They waited for the four-piece chamber orchestra to give their musical cue, whereby they would proceed down the long red carpet. And Catherine would marry Nick, the man she loved with all her heart.

When we were young, I knew I would stand at her wedding. I knew I would stand beside her. I never dreamed it would be like this.

She'd never looked more beautiful, more peaceful, more radiant.

Hernandez's chest puffed proud.

She clung to his arm.

He placed his hand over hers.

His little girl went ahead of them and dropped white rose petals on the red carpet.

There would be no better time. Catherine was open in a way she had never been before. She would hear me now.

I drew close to her and whispered, "It wasn't your fault that we crashed. Neither one of us remembered the jetty, so it wouldn't have mattered who was steering the boat that day. The end result would have been the same.

"I've never been mad at you for taking on my life, or rather for trying to escape your own.

"We dealt with our father's abuse in different ways. You withdrew while I rebelled and attacked him. With a knife in the middle of the night, no less. If there is any silver lining, it's that you're free now. Maybe in a way you never would have been otherwise."

Catherine drew in a staccato breath. Then exhaled deeply.

She heard me.

I knew.

Twins knew.

"I love you, Catherine. I will always love you."

ALSO BY ALYSSA RICHARDS

THE FINE ART OF DECEPTION SERIES

THE FINE ART OF DECEPTION, UNDOING TIME

SOMEWHERE IN TIME

LOST IN TIME

THE FINE ART OF DECEPTION, BOXED SET

THE ALCOTT MANOR SERIES

THE HAUNTING AT ALCOTT MANOR

A MURDER AT ALCOTT MANOR

A STRANGER AT ALCOTT MANOR

THE CHASING SECRETS SERIES

CHASING SECRETS

FORCED PERSPECTIVE

Be the first to know about Alyssa Richards' next novel, sign up here: www.AlyssaRichards.com.

ABOUT THE AUTHOR

ALYSSA RICHARDS is the USA TODAY BESTSELLING AUTHOR of romantic suspense and mystery thriller novels. She loves living in the South with her husband and two children. She also loves good espresso, her rescue dogs, magnolias and gardenias, and, of course, reading a great book. She grew up running barefoot in the Blue Ridge Mountains of North Carolina, where her favorite weekly adventure was a trip to the library with her mom.

Sign up for Alyssa's newsletter at www.alyssarichards.com to receive special offers, and news about her latest releases.

For More information
www.AlyssaRichards.com
Contact Alyssa at:
authoralyssarichards@protonmail.com

instagram.com/alyssaauthor

amazon.com/Alyssa-Richards/e/B00S1IGJ9O

bookbub.com/authors/alyssa-richards

goodreads.com/alyssarichards

ACKNOWLEDGMENTS

A huge thank you to my husband for the endless support. It means more to me than you know.

A special shout-out to my sons, y'all are such beautiful gifts in my life and a true inspiration. Each of you has my whole heart.

Mega-thanks to Peter Senftleben, my editor. Your insight into my story ideas, and especially the early drafts, is nothing short of extraordinary. Thank you for your encouragement and creativity and expertise. This book would not be this book without you.

To Deb Atwood, an incredibly talented writer, thank you for your friendship, for brainstorming and for sharing your keen eye.

To Charity Chimni, my assistant/proofreader/everything extraordinaire, I could never thank you enough for all that you do. Still, thank you.

CHASING SECRETS CHAPTER ONE

"You're lying." Barbara narrowed her eyes at her husband.

David raised his glass of champagne and broadcast his perfectly white, nearly electric smile that could have won an election. "Everything's fine."

She raised an eyebrow to scold him; he was evading. "I didn't say things weren't fine. I said you were lying."

He cleared his throat and gestured with his glass. "To our second anniversary, to yet another clean health report, and to the baby we weren't supposed to conceive."

He placed his hand over his jacket pocket. It was an unconscious move. She knew that's where he kept a photo of himself at the age of eight, his head resting across his mother's chest, her head wrapped in a colorful scarf, her skin pale and drawn against the white sheets of the hospital bed.

Barbara survived the cancer, his mother hadn't.

She ran her hand through her hair, grateful to have hair again. Grateful that it came in twice as thick as she once had, grateful that it didn't come back gray as she had been told that it might.

The ring of their champagne toast sounded clear in the quiet outdoor restaurant. She took only a tiny sip. A few cars drove by slowly, their engines relatively soft. A man whizzed by, standing on an electric-powered scooter, which hummed like the motor of a sewing machine.

David kissed her hand.

She studied his assuring smile and his soft expression. He was full of love and secrets. She never could read him clearly when his lips were on her skin or when he smiled at her in that way. In fact, she couldn't read him well at all. Not in the way she read other people.

"I saw another stack of medical bills come in this week," she said.

He looked at her hand and gave it a squeeze. "I'm making all the money we'll ever need to overcome whatever life throws at us. Don't you worry."

"I don't know how you do it." She cast him her most scrutinizing stare, the one she planned to use when their child was a teenager.

"I can do anything, when it comes to you." David tucked his napkin in his lap, his smile widening like he was pleased with himself. "And as far as not being able to read me the way you want, you're just going to have to trust me instead."

"I'd rather be able to read you." She arched her eyebrow again.

She'd never been able to figure out that little glitch with her talent. With anyone else, she got a gut feeling and would know quite a bit about that person. It was a skill she really appreciated because, oddly enough, she didn't trust people all that much otherwise.

When she realized she couldn't read David, her first

instinct had been to stay away from him. But she fell in love with him. She couldn't help herself. He treated her like a queen, never gave her any reason not to trust him.

Problem was, the more she overrode her instincts so that she could trust her husband, the less she trusted herself.

"One day soon I'll tell you why," he said.

"*You know* why I can't read you?" she asked.

"I have a theory." David sipped his champagne, kept his eyes on hers, like he was prepared for her question. Knew what she was going to ask and when. Everything he did was deliberate and full of care.

"Then tell me, because this has been driving me nuts for years."

"I will," he said. "Soon."

"Now. Please."

David was a planner. He always had a plan A and a plan B. Sometimes a plan C. Always thinking ahead. "Soon enough."

"Fine. Then you should know that I've been hiding something, too."

"You're not capable of keeping secrets from me."

"Actually, I am."

"Are you feeling okay? Is the baby alright?"

She pressed her hand to her still-flat stomach. "We're fine. Perfectly fine."

He gave a little exhale. "You're carrying my heart, you know. Our heart, actually."

She smiled and nodded. "I know."

"I've been thinking about something..."

"Wait, David, what I have to say is really important." She heard a whine in her voice she hadn't expected. He had spoiled her over the years and now she whined. She would have to break herself of that.

"Just real quick. Then I want to hear your secret. Okay?"

She wanted his undivided attention later, so she cleared her throat to make sure the whine was gone. "Fine. Shoot."

"Does the name Elias mean anything to you?"

"Elias...Elias..." Barb repeated the name in her mind and felt a swell of guilt in her chest. She wasn't supposed to know their baby's gender, yet. But the nurse had slipped and told her during the last ultrasound. David would flip when he found out they were having a girl if he was already thinking of boys' names. "No, I don't think so. Why do you want to know?"

"He works with one of my customers. I think there's something off about him."

She and David often discussed their impressions of other people, especially when they didn't know them that well. People had tells, signs they unwittingly shared that gave insight into who they were. Barbara picked up on those little signs better than most. She had a bizarrely keen radar when it came to reading people. It was probably genetic, her dad was the same way.

That knack had always come in handy. In college she could tell which boys were genuine and which ones were looking for meaningless hookups. Within a few moments of meeting new sorority sisters she knew who would be a loyal friend, and who wouldn't be trustworthy.

David had good instincts about people, too, but hers were better.

She couldn't remember anyone named Elias. "Why would you think I know him? Did he ask about me?"

"No, but my customer warned me that he has a history of making moves on other men's wives. Friendly and non-threatening at first, then crossing the line from professional to inappropriate. Seems he might be a little...unbalanced. I got the sense he could be dangerous." Intensity flashed in David's eyes, just for a moment.

She recognized the sign. It was an unconscious thing he did when he wasn't comfortable with what he was saying. Some people rubbed their nose when they weren't telling the truth. Others spoke rapidly, blinked too much or even broke into a sweat. For David, his eyes flared. Just slightly.

Deliberately, she'd never told him that he did this, it was one of the very few tells he had.

She exhaled hard to help clear her mind and focused on the cars that drove by as a distraction. Barbara didn't believe David's story about Elias. But she knew David was warning her off of him for a reason. Probably something more serious than he wanted to share. He was always protecting her.

"Then you need to stay away from him as well," she said. "Keep him away from your business."

He raised his glass of champagne. "I will. Another toast. Then I want to hear your secret. To your continued good health. And a wish on this, our second anniversary: May our next fifty years of marriage be as wonderful as our first two."

"And a lot healthier."

"They will be." He pressed his hand against the breast pocket of his blazer again. "I'll make sure of it." Their glasses clinked in a toast. "Now that you're healthy, I want to reopen the conversation about shutting the business down for a while so we can travel. We need to see the world while we can, just like we always wanted."

"Oh, David." They had talked about traveling the world together almost from their first date. But now that her mother had passed and her father had had his second heart attack, things had changed. "I can't leave Pop alone for that long. You know he depends on me."

"Then we'll plan a long vacation, to celebrate your recovery. Just a few months. I'll explain it all to you once we're away, but it's important." His eyes were wide and intense. His hands were tucked into tight fists on the table, the skin stretched taut over his white knuckles.

"A few months, David, that's—does this have something to do with that Elias person you just told me about?"

The brown sedan that drove toward them slowed down enough to catch her attention. The driver wore a trucker's hat and aviator sunglasses, and he stared straight at them.

"David—" She pointed to the driver. At the last second, he raised his arm level and straight and pointed a gun at them.

David turned, then quickly stood to hover over her.

"I love you, Barb! Go to the—" David's words were cut short by several loud pops. Blood spattered across her face and covered her glasses. Her husband's body jerked violently, then fell to the ground.

"NO!" she screamed.

Restaurant guests shrieked, dishes crashed.

Searing pain ripped through her shoulder and knocked her to the floor. Barbara crawled beneath the table, yanked her husband's arm and tried to pull him to her.

But he was heavy, unmoving.

Blood poured from the back of his head, his eyes wide open and unseeing.